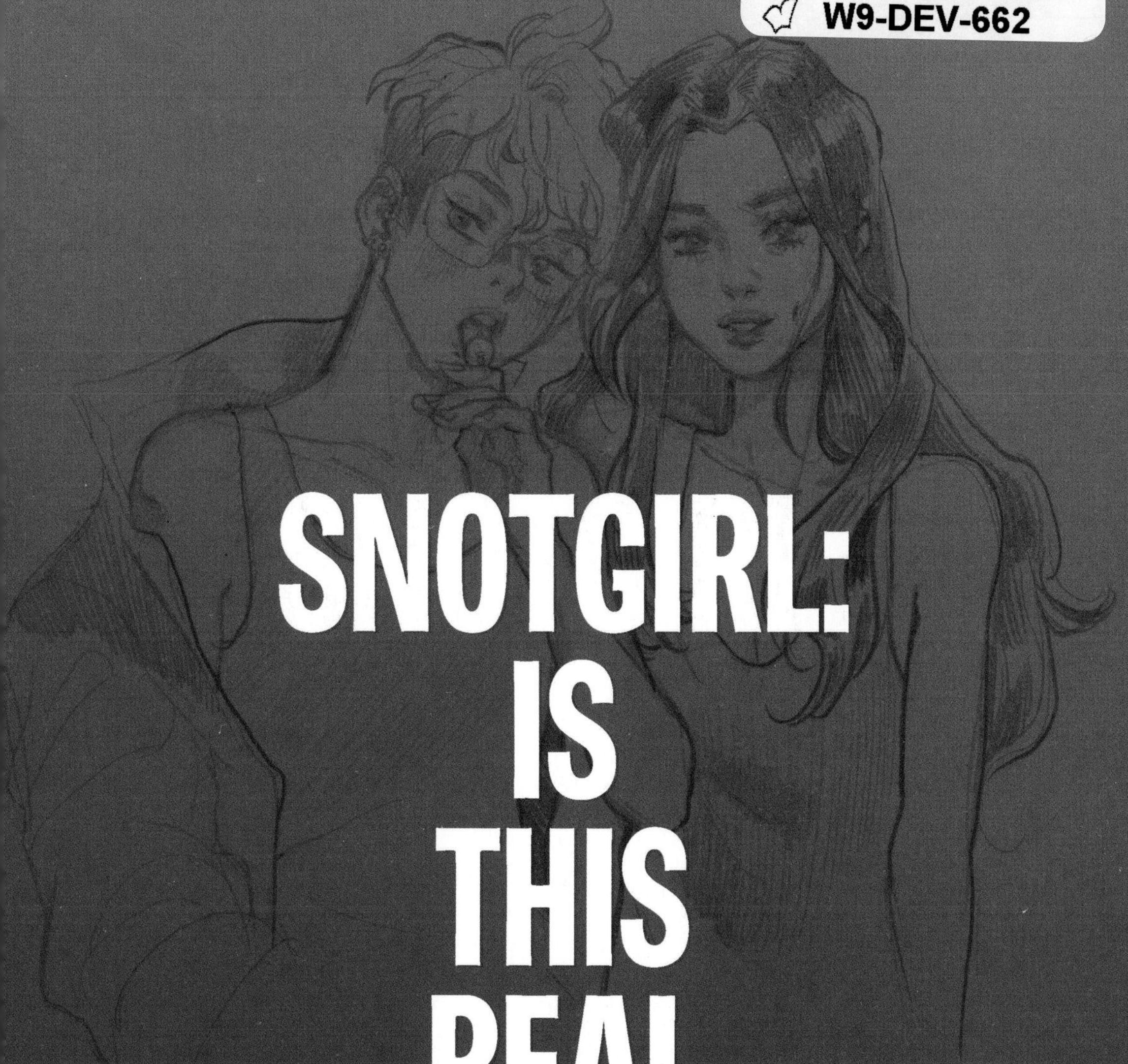

SNOTGIRL: IS THIS REAL LIFE?

Script: BRYAN LEE O'MALLEY
Art: LESLIE HUNG
Colors: RACHAEL COHEN
Lettering: MARÉ ODOMO

Created by
BRYAN LEE O'MALLEY & LESLIE HUNG

Originally serialized as SNOTGIRL #11-15.
Special thanks to STUDIO JFISH

IMAGE COMICS, INC. • **Robert Kirkman**: Chief Operating Officer • **Erik Larsen**: Chief Financial Officer • **Todd McFarlane**: President • **Marc Silvestri**: Chief Executive Officer • **Jim Valentino**: Vice President • **Eric Stephenson**: Publisher / Chief Creative Officer • **Jeff Boison**: Director of Publishing Planning & Book Trade Sales • **Chris Ross**: Director of Digital Services • **Jeff Stang**: Director of Direct Market Sales • **Kat Salazar**: Director of PR & Marketing • **Drew Gill**: Cover Editor • **Heather Doornink**: Production Director • **Nicole Lapalme**: Controller • **IMAGECOMICS.COM**

Standard ISBN: 978-1-5343-1238-8
Barnes & Noble Exclusive ISBN: 978-1-5343-1523-5

SNOTGIRL, VOL. 3: IS THIS REAL LIFE? First printing. April 2020. Contains material originally published in single magazine form as SNOTGIRL #11-15. Published by Image Comics, Inc. Office of publication: 2701 NW Vaughn St., Suite 780, Portland, OR 97210.

11. MY SECOND DATE

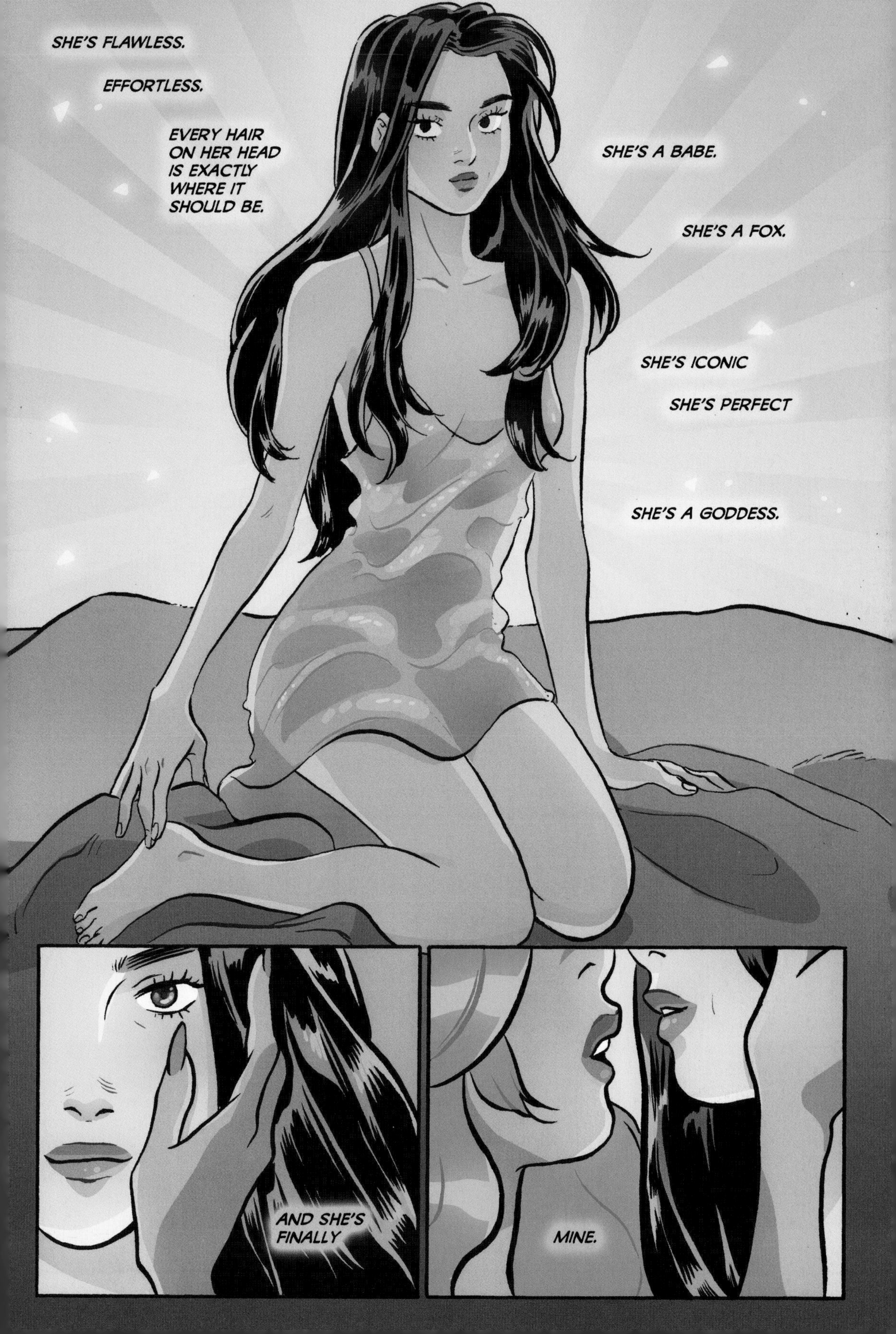
SHE'S FLAWLESS.
EFFORTLESS.
EVERY HAIR ON HER HEAD IS EXACTLY WHERE IT SHOULD BE.
SHE'S A BABE.
SHE'S A FOX.
SHE'S ICONIC
SHE'S PERFECT
SHE'S A GODDESS.
AND SHE'S FINALLY
MINE.

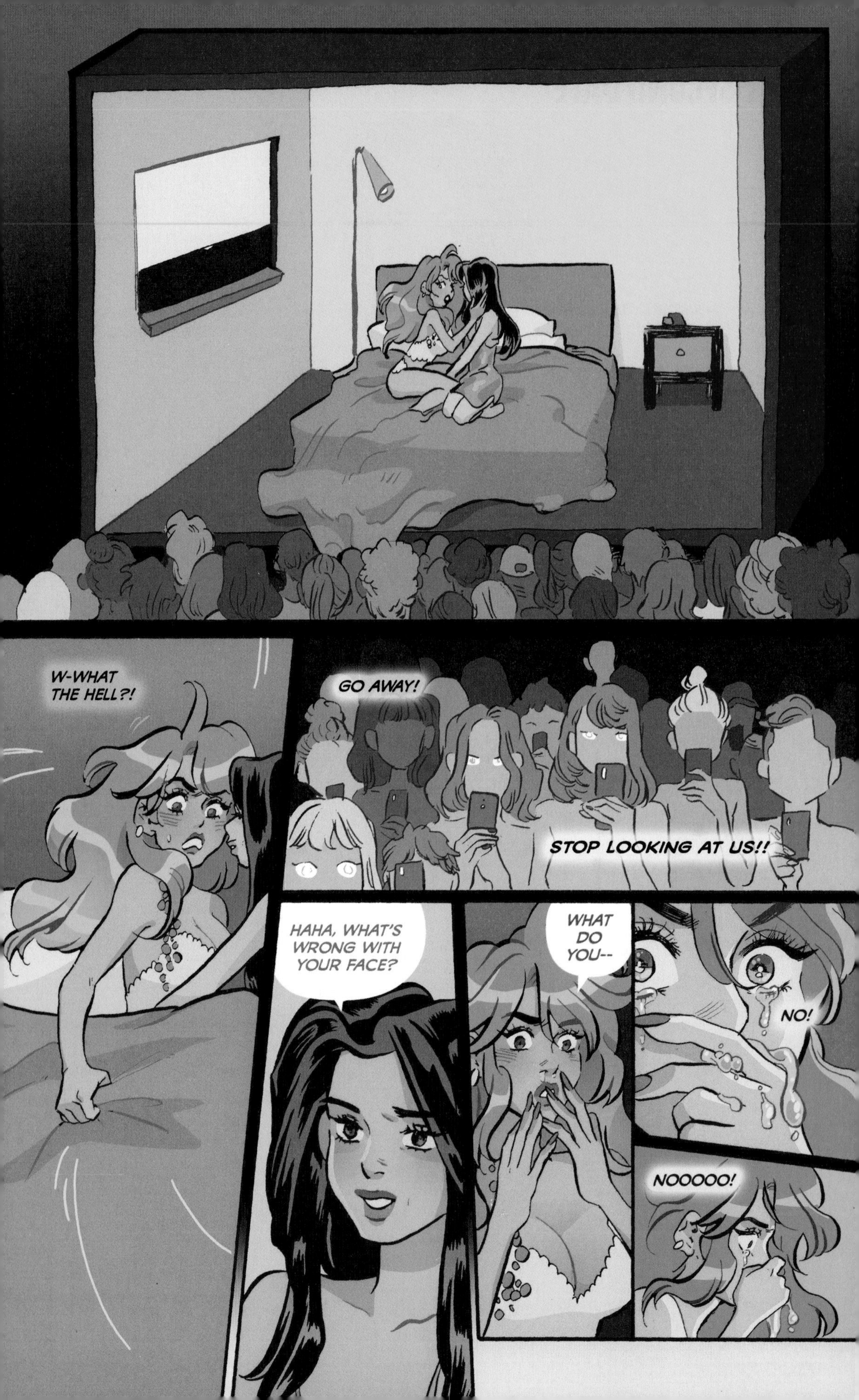
W-WHAT THE HELL?!
GO AWAY!
STOP LOOKING AT US!!
HAHA, WHAT'S WRONG WITH YOUR FACE?
WHAT DO YOU--
NO!
NOOOOO!

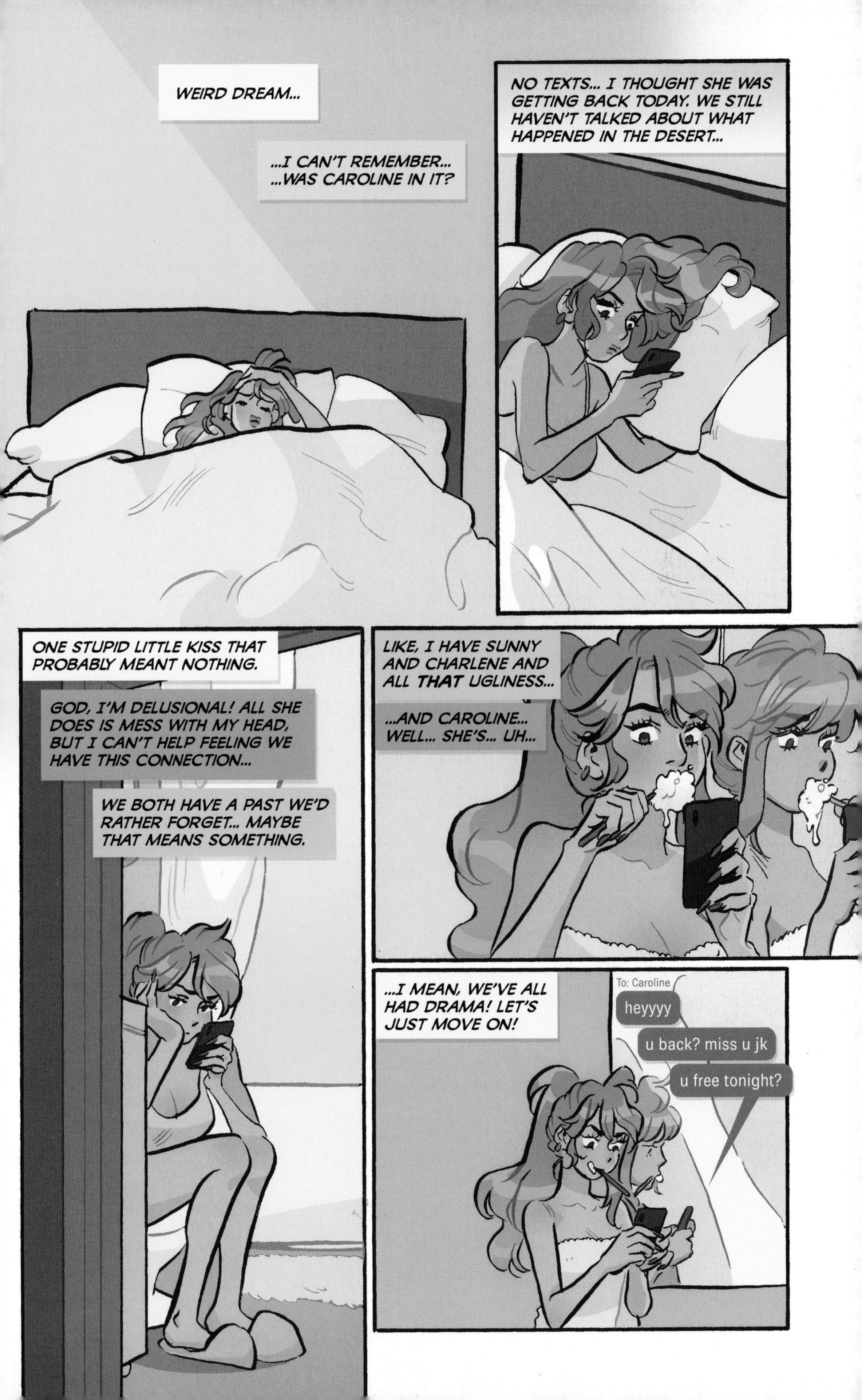
WEIRD DREAM...
...I CAN'T REMEMBER...
...WAS CAROLINE IN IT?
NO TEXTS... I THOUGHT SHE WAS GETTING BACK TODAY. WE STILL HAVEN'T TALKED ABOUT WHAT HAPPENED IN THE DESERT...
ONE STUPID LITTLE KISS THAT PROBABLY MEANT NOTHING.
GOD, I'M DELUSIONAL! ALL SHE DOES IS MESS WITH MY HEAD, BUT I CAN'T HELP FEELING WE HAVE THIS CONNECTION...
WE BOTH HAVE A PAST WE'D RATHER FORGET... MAYBE THAT MEANS SOMETHING.
LIKE, I HAVE SUNNY AND CHARLENE AND ALL THAT UGLINESS...
...AND CAROLINE... WELL... SHE'S... UH...
...I MEAN, WE'VE ALL HAD DRAMA! LET'S JUST MOVE ON!
To: Caroline
heyyyy
u back? miss u jk
u free tonight?

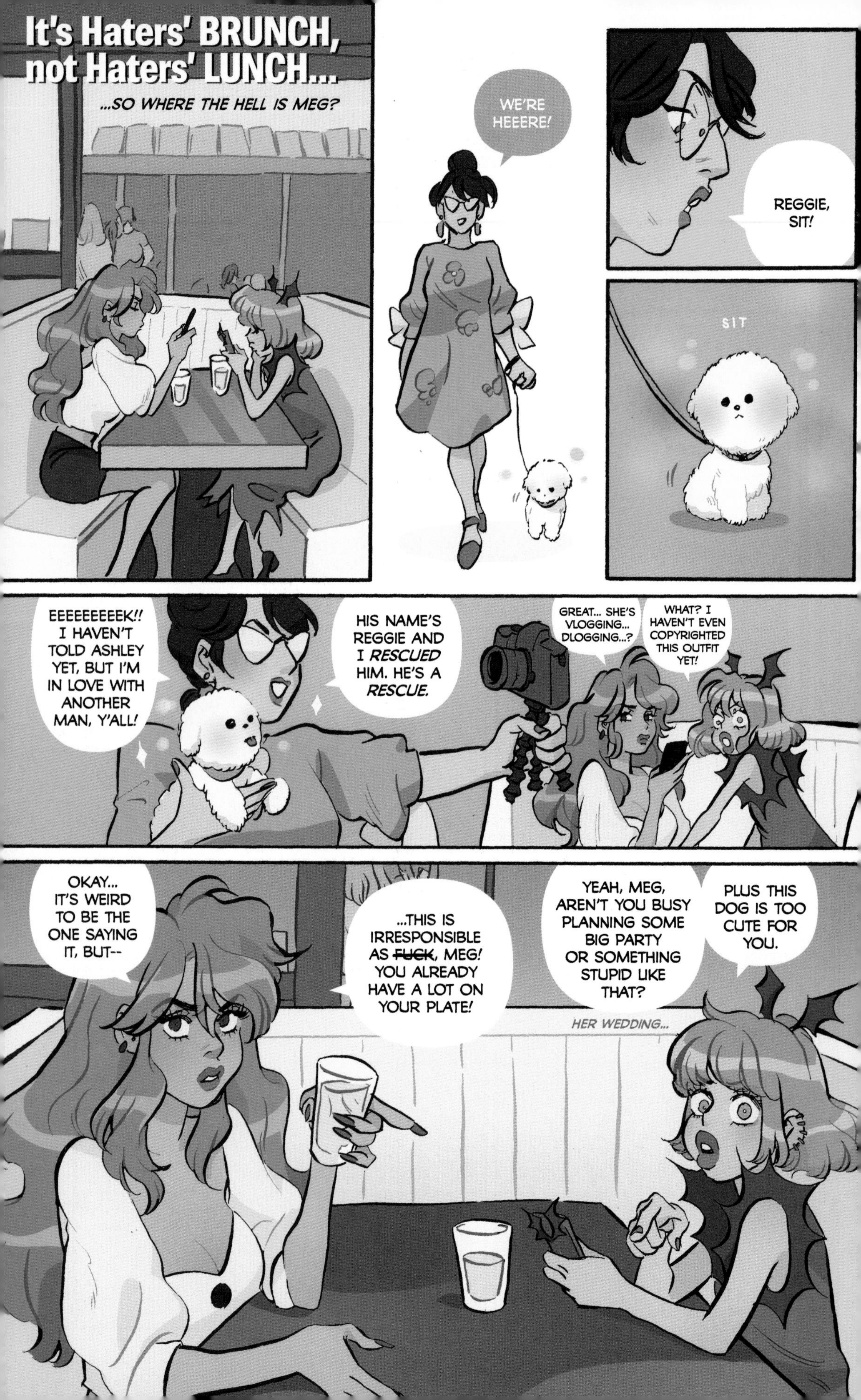

It's Haters' BRUNCH, not Haters' LUNCH...
...SO WHERE THE HELL IS MEG?
WE'RE HEEERE!
REGGIE, SIT!
SIT
EEEEEEEEEK!! I HAVEN'T TOLD ASHLEY YET, BUT I'M IN LOVE WITH ANOTHER MAN, Y'ALL!
HIS NAME'S REGGIE AND I *RESCUED* HIM. HE'S A *RESCUE.*
GREAT... SHE'S VLOGGING... DLOGGING...?
WHAT? I HAVEN'T EVEN COPYRIGHTED THIS OUTFIT YET!
OKAY... IT'S WEIRD TO BE THE ONE SAYING IT, BUT--
...THIS IS IRRESPONSIBLE AS ~~FUCK~~, MEG! YOU ALREADY HAVE A LOT ON YOUR PLATE!
YEAH, MEG, AREN'T YOU BUSY PLANNING SOME BIG PARTY OR SOMETHING STUPID LIKE THAT?
PLUS THIS DOG IS TOO CUTE FOR YOU.
HER WEDDING...

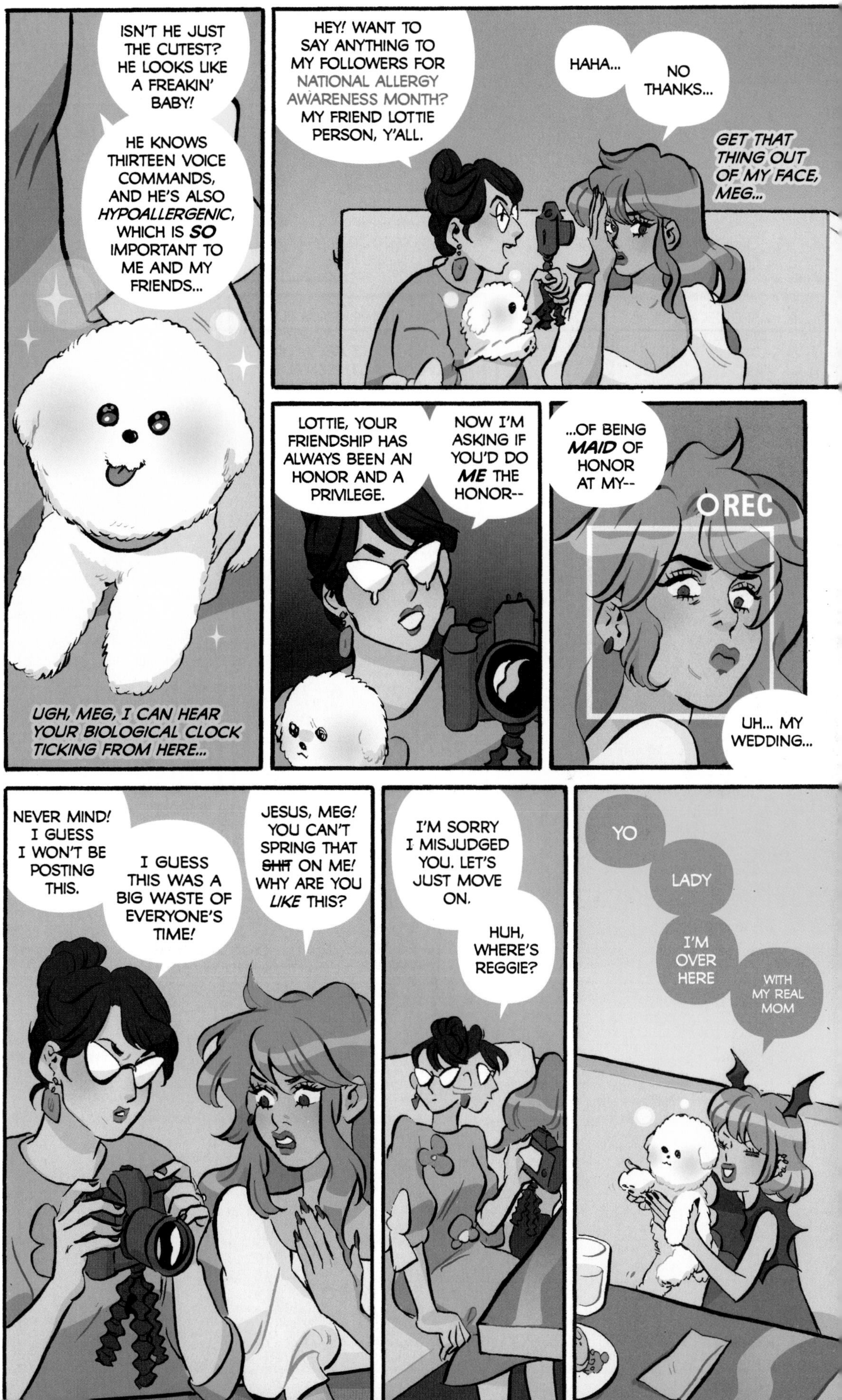
ISN'T HE JUST THE CUTEST? HE LOOKS LIKE A FREAKIN' BABY!
HE KNOWS THIRTEEN VOICE COMMANDS, AND HE'S ALSO HYPOALLERGENIC, WHICH IS SO IMPORTANT TO ME AND MY FRIENDS...
UGH, MEG, I CAN HEAR YOUR BIOLOGICAL CLOCK TICKING FROM HERE...
HEY! WANT TO SAY ANYTHING TO MY FOLLOWERS FOR NATIONAL ALLERGY AWARENESS MONTH? MY FRIEND LOTTIE PERSON, Y'ALL.
HAHA...
NO THANKS...
GET THAT THING OUT OF MY FACE, MEG...
LOTTIE, YOUR FRIENDSHIP HAS ALWAYS BEEN AN HONOR AND A PRIVILEGE.
NOW I'M ASKING IF YOU'D DO ME THE HONOR--
...OF BEING MAID OF HONOR AT MY--
REC
UH... MY WEDDING...
NEVER MIND! I GUESS I WON'T BE POSTING THIS.
I GUESS THIS WAS A BIG WASTE OF EVERYONE'S TIME!
JESUS, MEG! YOU CAN'T SPRING THAT SHIT ON ME! WHY ARE YOU LIKE THIS?
I'M SORRY I MISJUDGED YOU. LET'S JUST MOVE ON.
HUH, WHERE'S REGGIE?
YO
LADY
I'M OVER HERE
WITH MY REAL MOM

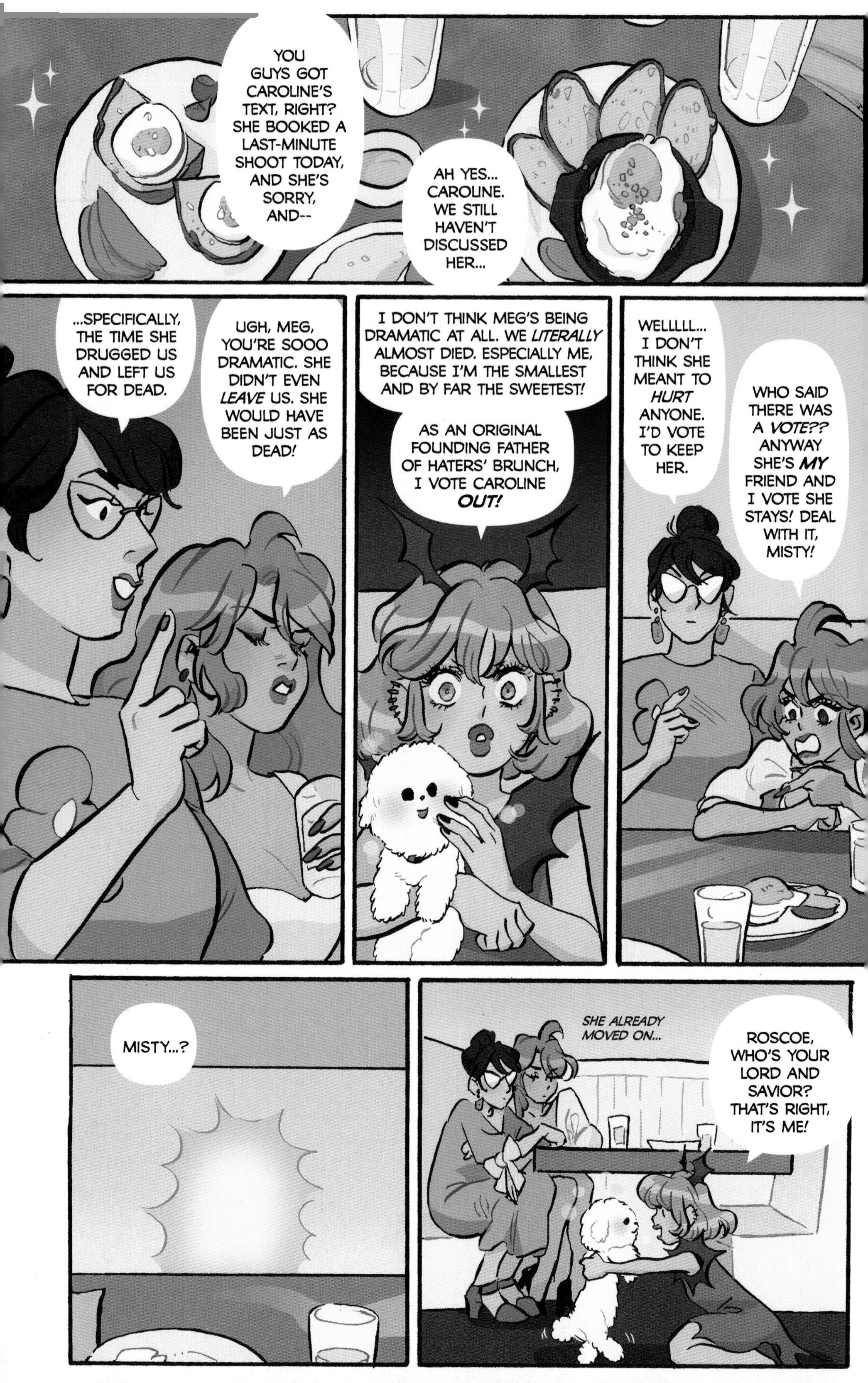
YOU GUYS GOT CAROLINE'S TEXT, RIGHT? SHE BOOKED A LAST-MINUTE SHOOT TODAY, AND SHE'S SORRY, AND--
AH YES... CAROLINE. WE STILL HAVEN'T DISCUSSED HER...
...SPECIFICALLY, THE TIME SHE DRUGGED US AND LEFT US FOR DEAD.
UGH, MEG, YOU'RE SOOO DRAMATIC. SHE DIDN'T EVEN *LEAVE* US. SHE WOULD HAVE BEEN JUST AS DEAD!
I DON'T THINK MEG'S BEING DRAMATIC AT ALL. WE *LITERALLY* ALMOST DIED. ESPECIALLY ME, BECAUSE I'M THE SMALLEST AND BY FAR THE SWEETEST!
AS AN ORIGINAL FOUNDING FATHER OF HATERS' BRUNCH, I VOTE CAROLINE ***OUT!***
WELLLLL... I DON'T THINK SHE MEANT TO *HURT* ANYONE. I'D VOTE TO KEEP HER.
WHO SAID THERE WAS A *VOTE??* ANYWAY SHE'S ***MY*** FRIEND AND I VOTE SHE STAYS! DEAL WITH IT, MISTY!
MISTY...?
SHE ALREADY MOVED ON...
ROSCOE, WHO'S YOUR LORD AND SAVIOR? THAT'S RIGHT, IT'S ME!

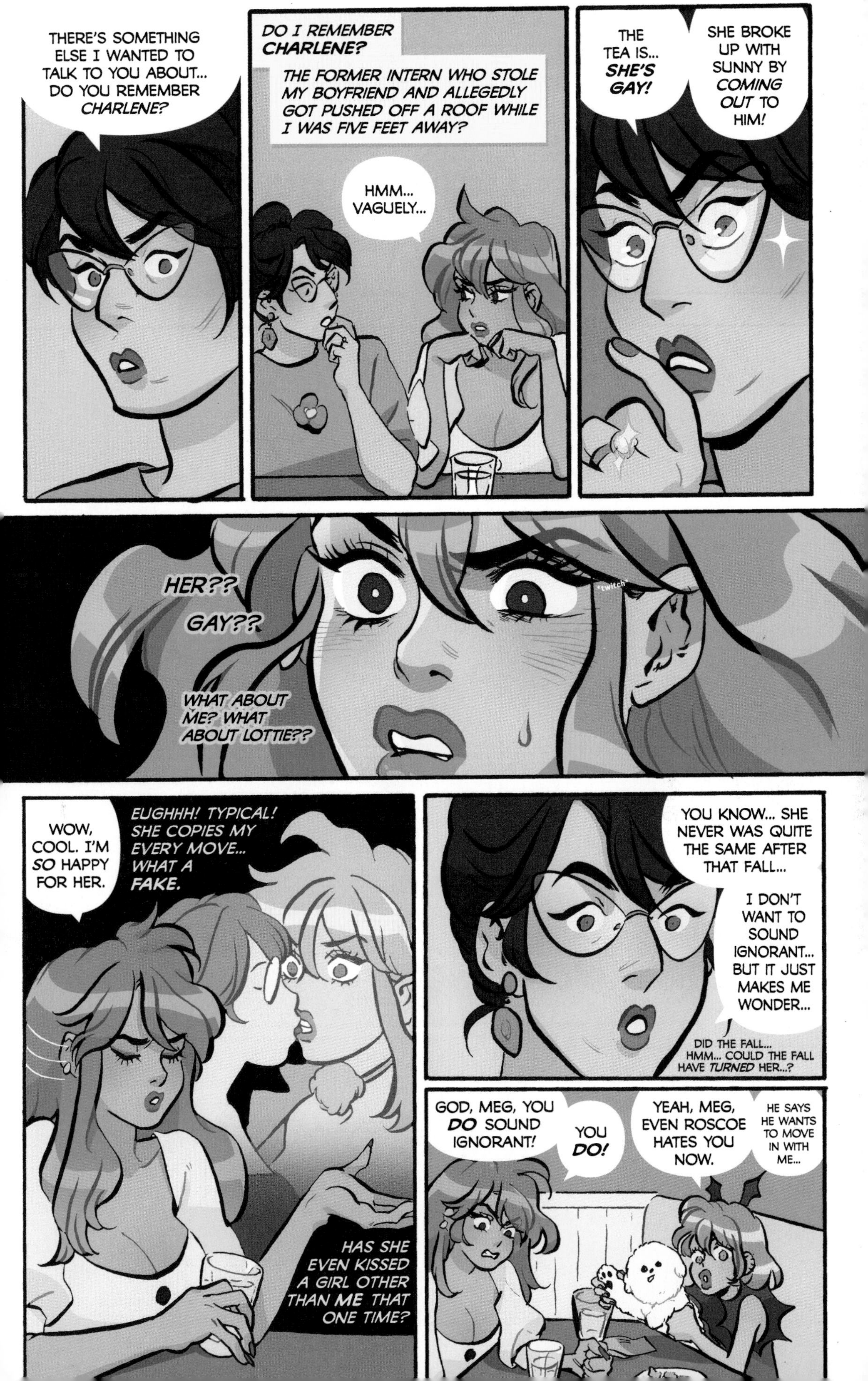
THERE'S SOMETHING ELSE I WANTED TO TALK TO YOU ABOUT... DO YOU REMEMBER *CHARLENE?*
DO I REMEMBER **CHARLENE?**
THE FORMER INTERN WHO STOLE MY BOYFRIEND AND ALLEGEDLY GOT PUSHED OFF A ROOF WHILE I WAS FIVE FEET AWAY?
HMM... VAGUELY...
THE TEA IS... ***SHE'S GAY!***
SHE BROKE UP WITH SUNNY BY *COMING OUT* TO HIM!
HER??
GAY??
twitch
WHAT ABOUT ME? WHAT ABOUT LOTTIE??
WOW, COOL. I'M *SO* HAPPY FOR HER.
EUGHHH! TYPICAL! SHE COPIES MY EVERY MOVE... WHAT A **FAKE.**
HAS SHE EVEN KISSED A GIRL OTHER THAN **ME** THAT ONE TIME?
YOU KNOW... SHE NEVER WAS QUITE THE SAME AFTER THAT FALL...
I DON'T WANT TO SOUND IGNORANT... BUT IT JUST MAKES ME WONDER...
DID THE FALL... HMM... COULD THE FALL HAVE *TURNED* HER...?
GOD, MEG, YOU ***DO*** SOUND IGNORANT!
YOU ***DO!***
YEAH, MEG, EVEN ROSCOE HATES YOU NOW.
HE SAYS HE WANTS TO MOVE IN WITH ME...

SUNNY & ASHLEY'S SECOND MAN-DATE

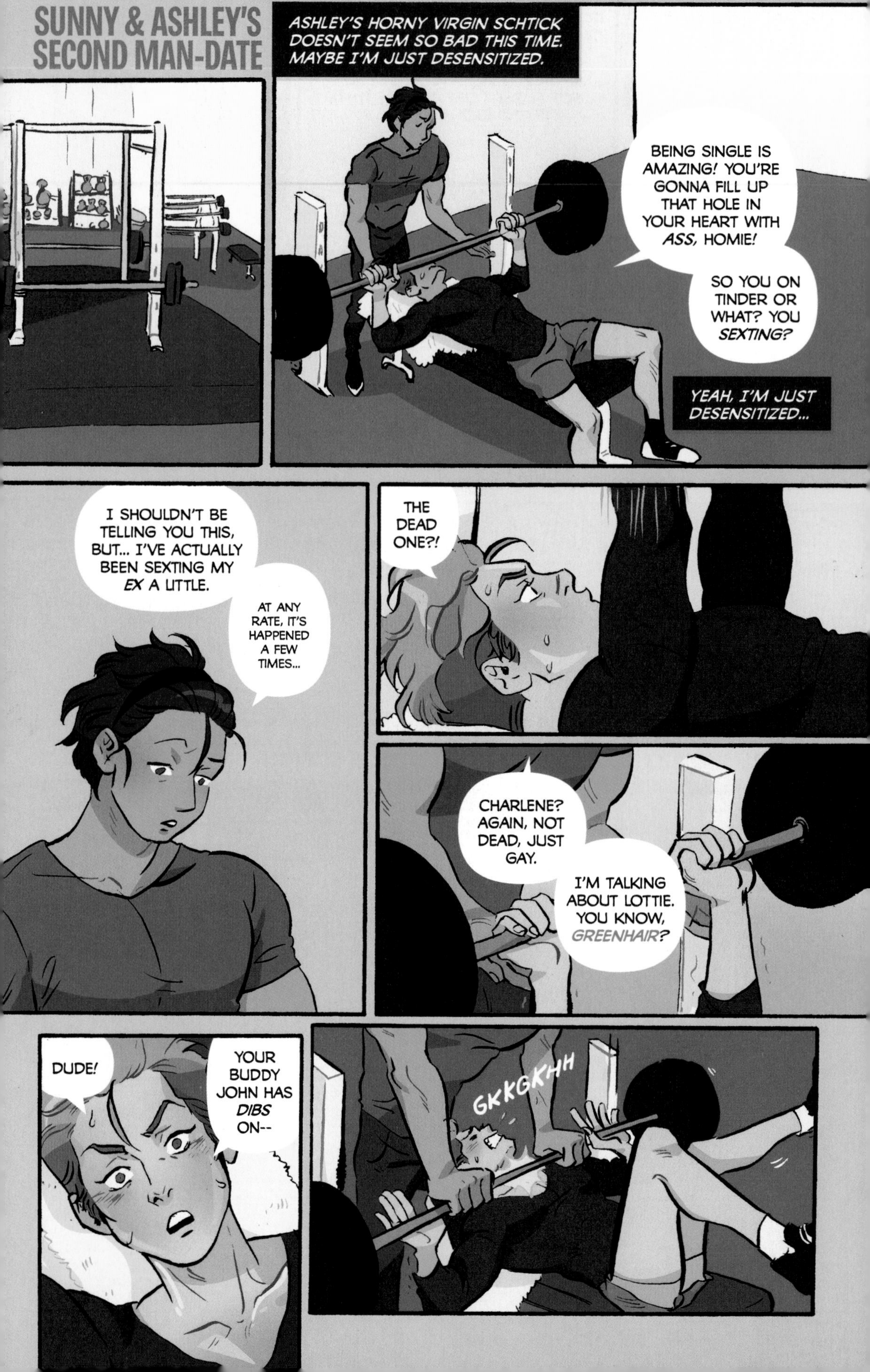

ASHLEY'S HORNY VIRGIN SCHTICK DOESN'T SEEM SO BAD THIS TIME. MAYBE I'M JUST DESENSITIZED.
BEING SINGLE IS AMAZING! YOU'RE GONNA FILL UP THAT HOLE IN YOUR HEART WITH *ASS,* HOMIE!
SO YOU ON TINDER OR WHAT? YOU *SEXTING?*
YEAH, I'M JUST DESENSITIZED...
I SHOULDN'T BE TELLING YOU THIS, BUT... I'VE ACTUALLY BEEN SEXTING MY *EX* A LITTLE.
AT ANY RATE, IT'S HAPPENED A FEW TIMES...
THE DEAD ONE?!
CHARLENE? AGAIN, NOT DEAD, JUST GAY.
I'M TALKING ABOUT LOTTIE. YOU KNOW, *GREENHAIR?*
DUDE!
YOUR BUDDY JOHN HAS *DIBS* ON--
GKKGKHH

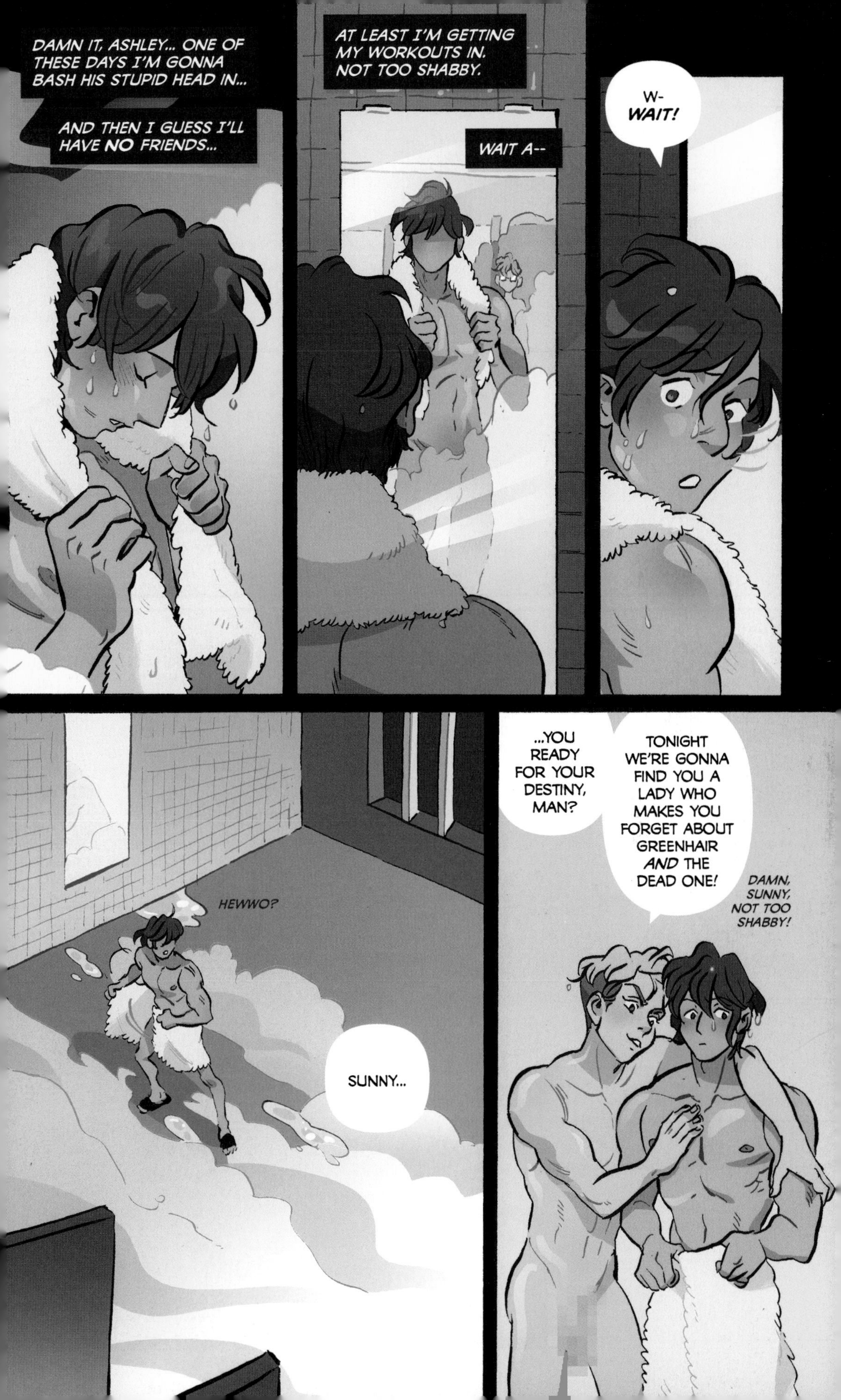
DAMN IT, ASHLEY... ONE OF THESE DAYS I'M GONNA BASH HIS STUPID HEAD IN...
AND THEN I GUESS I'LL HAVE NO FRIENDS...
AT LEAST I'M GETTING MY WORKOUTS IN. NOT TOO SHABBY.
WAIT A--
W- WAIT!
HEWWO?
SUNNY...
...YOU READY FOR YOUR DESTINY, MAN?
TONIGHT WE'RE GONNA FIND YOU A LADY WHO MAKES YOU FORGET ABOUT GREENHAIR AND THE DEAD ONE!
DAMN, SUNNY, NOT TOO SHABBY!

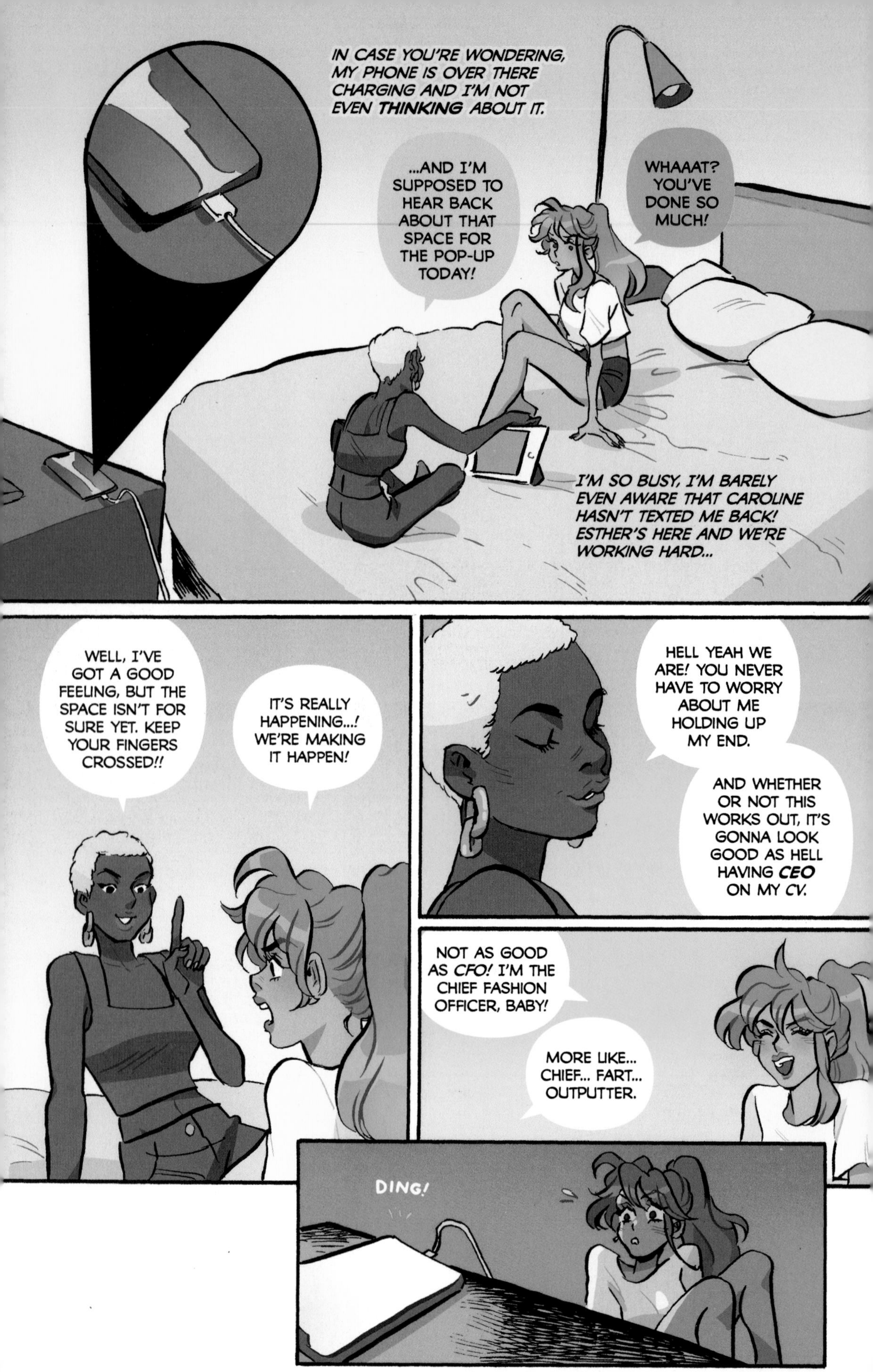
IN CASE YOU'RE WONDERING, MY PHONE IS OVER THERE CHARGING AND I'M NOT EVEN THINKING ABOUT IT.
...AND I'M SUPPOSED TO HEAR BACK ABOUT THAT SPACE FOR THE POP-UP TODAY!
WHAAAT? YOU'VE DONE SO MUCH!
I'M SO BUSY, I'M BARELY EVEN AWARE THAT CAROLINE HASN'T TEXTED ME BACK! ESTHER'S HERE AND WE'RE WORKING HARD...
WELL, I'VE GOT A GOOD FEELING, BUT THE SPACE ISN'T FOR SURE YET. KEEP YOUR FINGERS CROSSED!!
IT'S REALLY HAPPENING...! WE'RE MAKING IT HAPPEN!
HELL YEAH WE ARE! YOU NEVER HAVE TO WORRY ABOUT ME HOLDING UP MY END.
AND WHETHER OR NOT THIS WORKS OUT, IT'S GONNA LOOK GOOD AS HELL HAVING CEO ON MY CV.
NOT AS GOOD AS CFO! I'M THE CHIEF FASHION OFFICER, BABY!
MORE LIKE... CHIEF... FART... OUTPUTTER.
DING!

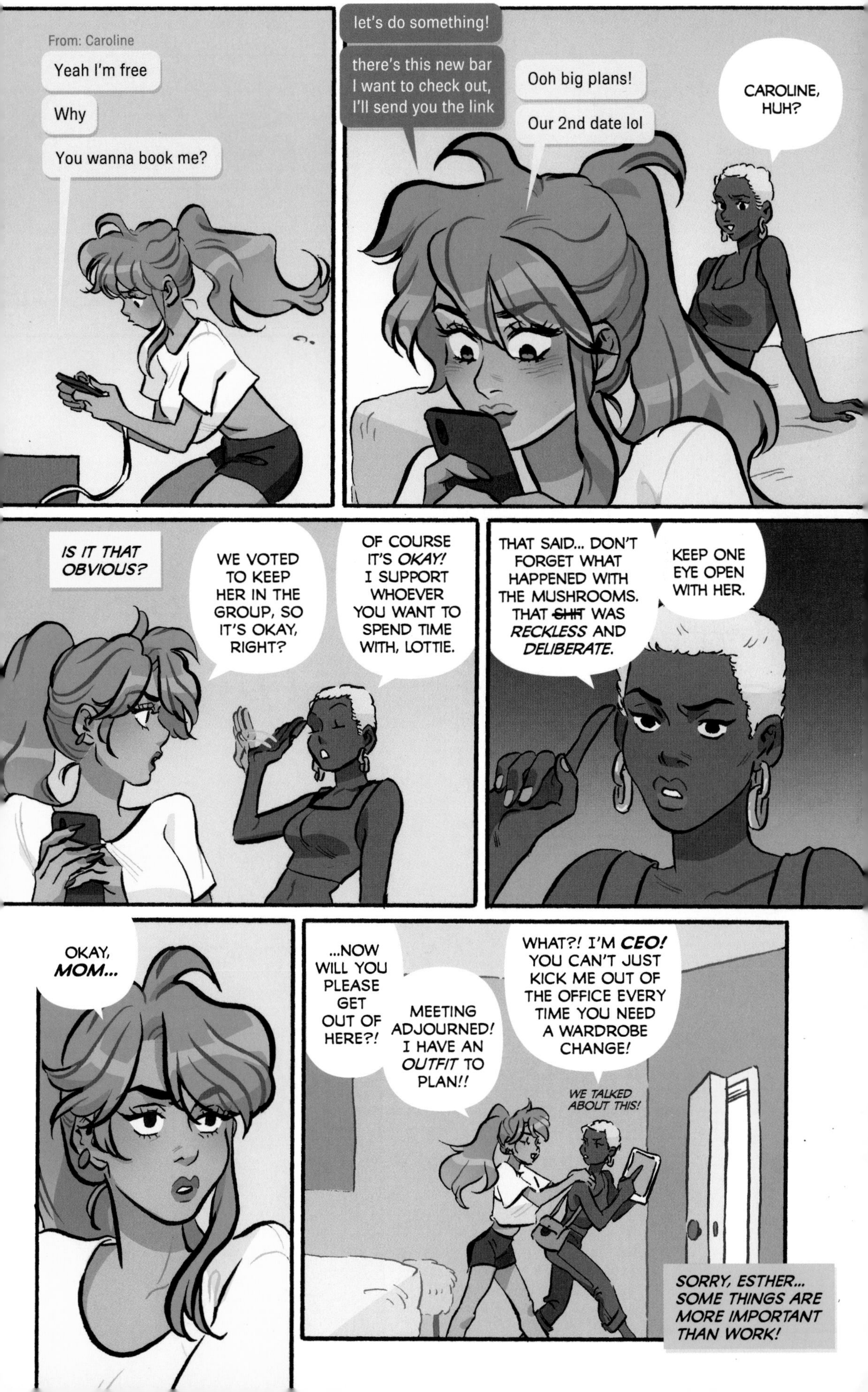

From: Caroline
Yeah I'm free
Why
You wanna book me?
let's do something!
there's this new bar I want to check out, I'll send you the link
Ooh big plans!
Our 2nd date lol
CAROLINE, HUH?
IS IT THAT OBVIOUS?
WE VOTED TO KEEP HER IN THE GROUP, SO IT'S OKAY, RIGHT?
OF COURSE IT'S OKAY! I SUPPORT WHOEVER YOU WANT TO SPEND TIME WITH, LOTTIE.
THAT SAID... DON'T FORGET WHAT HAPPENED WITH THE MUSHROOMS. THAT ~~SHIT~~ WAS RECKLESS AND DELIBERATE.
KEEP ONE EYE OPEN WITH HER.
OKAY, MOM...
...NOW WILL YOU PLEASE GET OUT OF HERE?!
MEETING ADJOURNED! I HAVE AN OUTFIT TO PLAN!!
WHAT?! I'M CEO! YOU CAN'T JUST KICK ME OUT OF THE OFFICE EVERY TIME YOU NEED A WARDROBE CHANGE!
WE TALKED ABOUT THIS!
SORRY, ESTHER... SOME THINGS ARE MORE IMPORTANT THAN WORK!

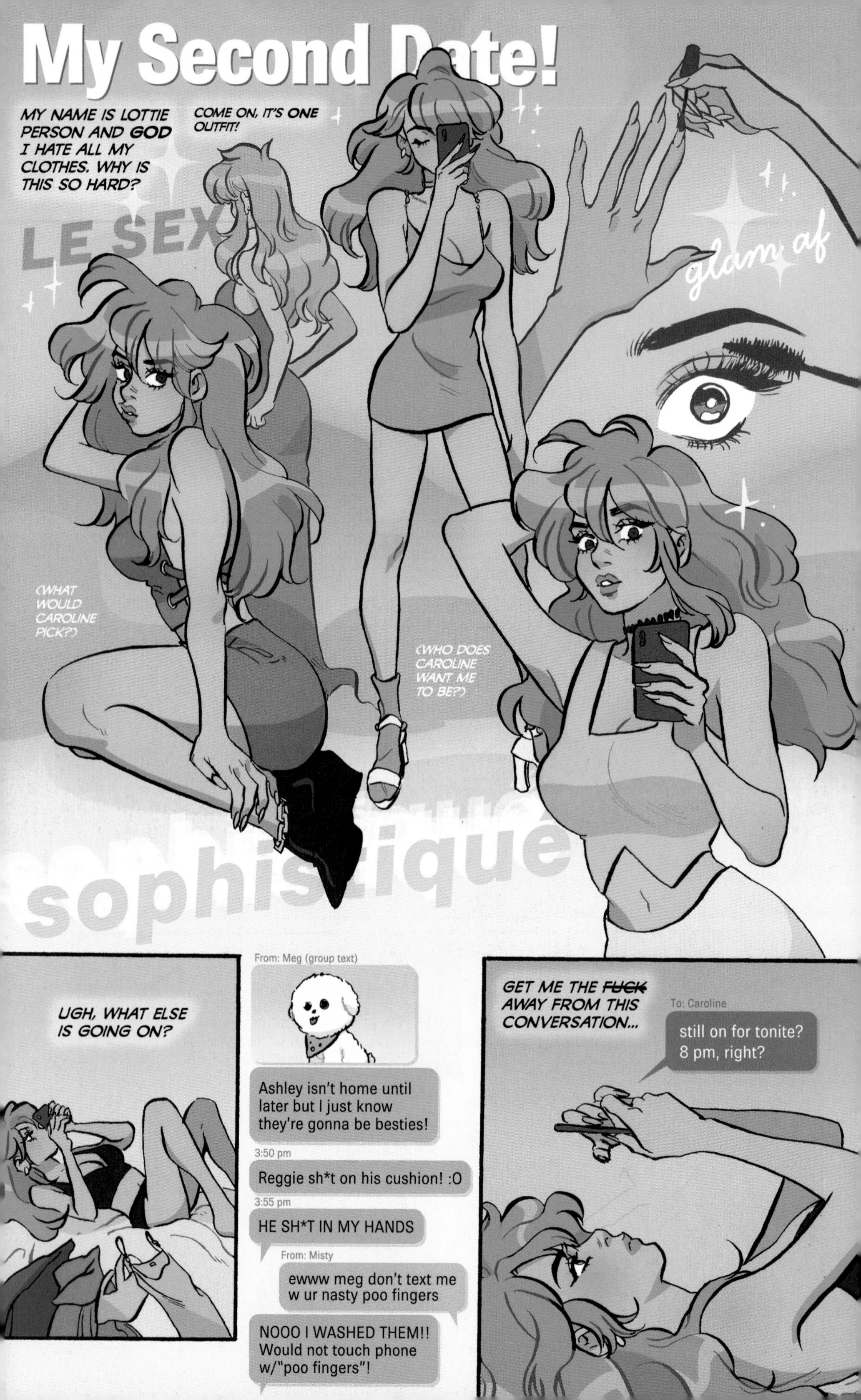
My Second Date!
MY NAME IS LOTTIE PERSON AND GOD I HATE ALL MY CLOTHES. WHY IS THIS SO HARD?
COME ON, IT'S ONE OUTFIT!
LE SEX
glam af
(WHAT WOULD CAROLINE PICK?)
(WHO DOES CAROLINE WANT ME TO BE?)
sophistiqué
UGH, WHAT ELSE IS GOING ON?
From: Meg (group text)
Ashley isn't home until later but I just know they're gonna be besties!
3:50 pm
Reggie sh*t on his cushion! :O
3:55 pm
HE SH*T IN MY HANDS
From: Misty
ewww meg don't text me w ur nasty poo fingers
NOOO I WASHED THEM!! Would not touch phone w/"poo fingers"!
GET ME THE ~~FUCK~~ AWAY FROM THIS CONVERSATION...
To: Caroline
still on for tonite? 8 pm, right?

5:00 PM

SHE STILL HASN'T REPLIED! I MADE IT AMBIGUOUS... I PLAYED MYSELF! UGH, WHY AM I *LIKE* THIS?

I SHOULD JUST STOP WORRYING. SUN'S STILL UP...

...I'VE GOT PLENTY OF TIME...

DING!

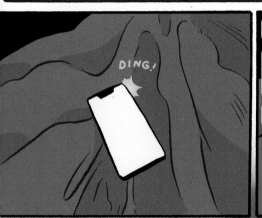

Almost therrrre

Oh sorry didn't see ur text earlier lol yea its on

See u in 5!

7:55 PM

running late LOL start without me!

la vitesse

screaming

don't think!

I FELL ASLEEP?!

DAMN! I DOUBLE-PLAYED MYSELF!!

HURRY

DAMN, DAMN, DAMN!!

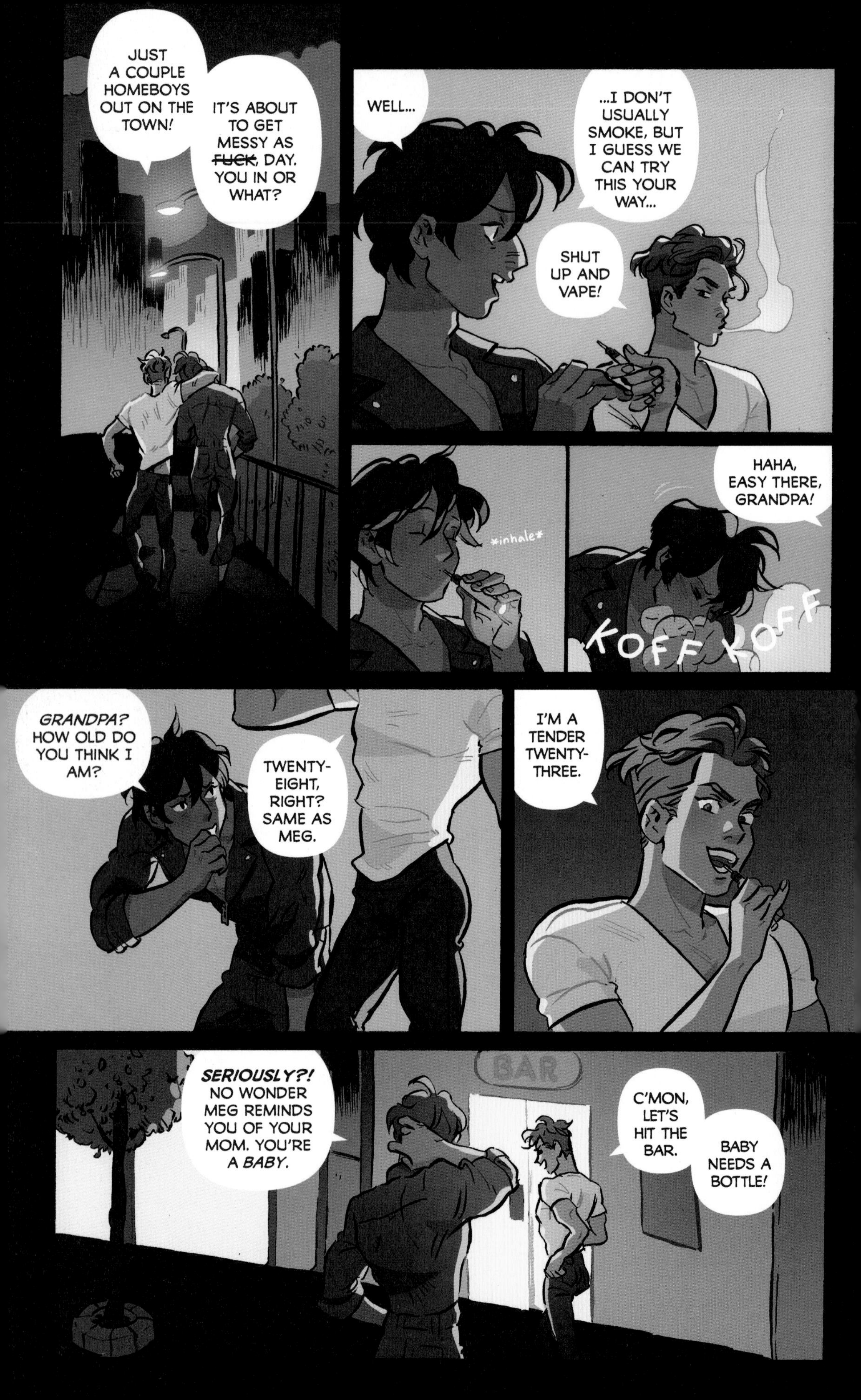
JUST A COUPLE HOMEBOYS OUT ON THE TOWN!
IT'S ABOUT TO GET MESSY AS FUCK, DAY. YOU IN OR WHAT?
WELL...
...I DON'T USUALLY SMOKE, BUT I GUESS WE CAN TRY THIS YOUR WAY...
SHUT UP AND VAPE!
inhale
HAHA, EASY THERE, GRANDPA!
KOFF KOFF
GRANDPA? HOW OLD DO YOU THINK I AM?
TWENTY-EIGHT, RIGHT? SAME AS MEG.
I'M A TENDER TWENTY-THREE.
BAR
SERIOUSLY?! NO WONDER MEG REMINDS YOU OF YOUR MOM. YOU'RE A BABY.
C'MON, LET'S HIT THE BAR.
BABY NEEDS A BOTTLE!

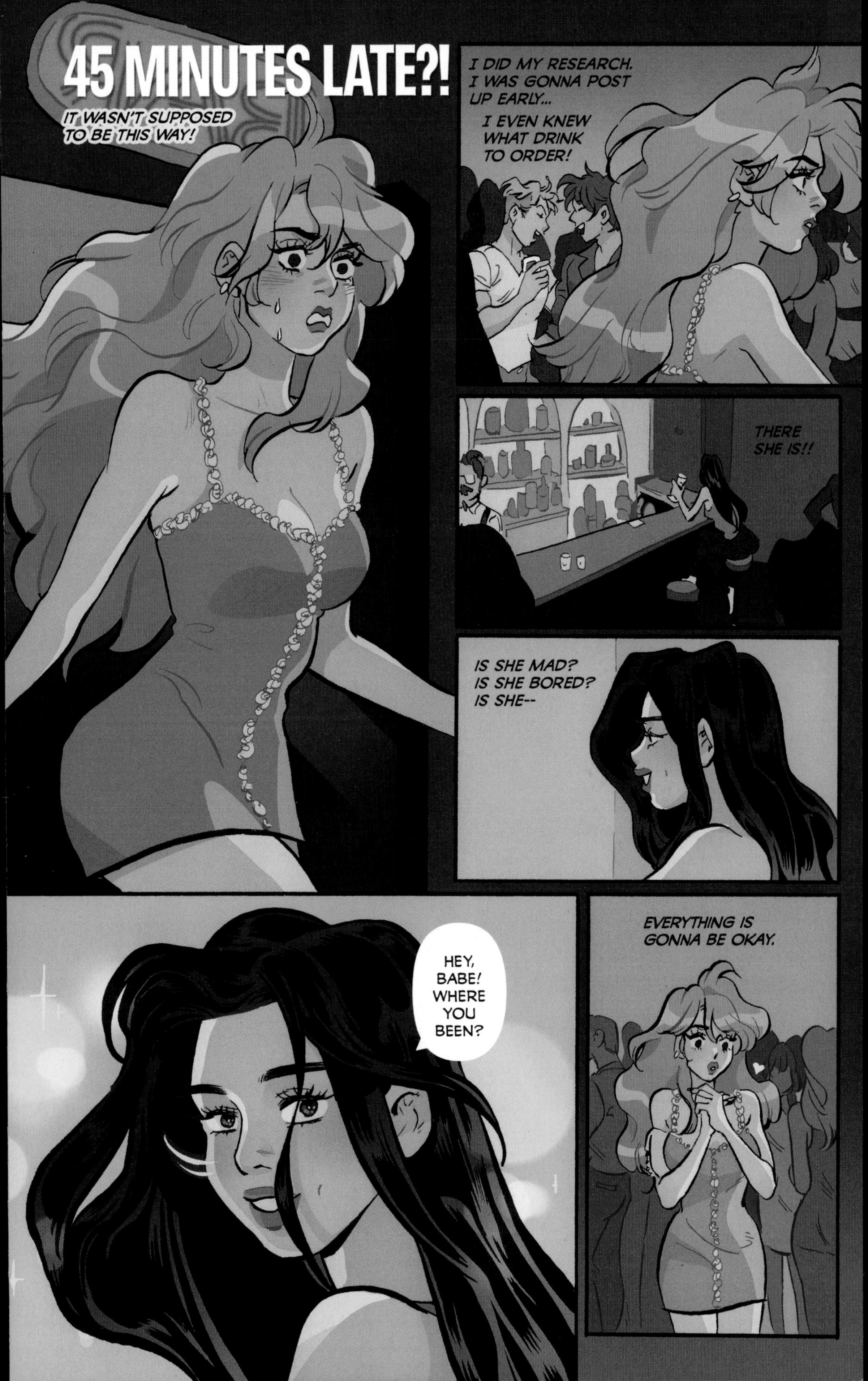
45 MINUTES LATE?!
IT WASN'T SUPPOSED TO BE THIS WAY!
I DID MY RESEARCH. I WAS GONNA POST UP EARLY...
I EVEN KNEW WHAT DRINK TO ORDER!
THERE SHE IS!!
IS SHE MAD? IS SHE BORED? IS SHE--
HEY, BABE! WHERE YOU BEEN?
EVERYTHING IS GONNA BE OKAY.

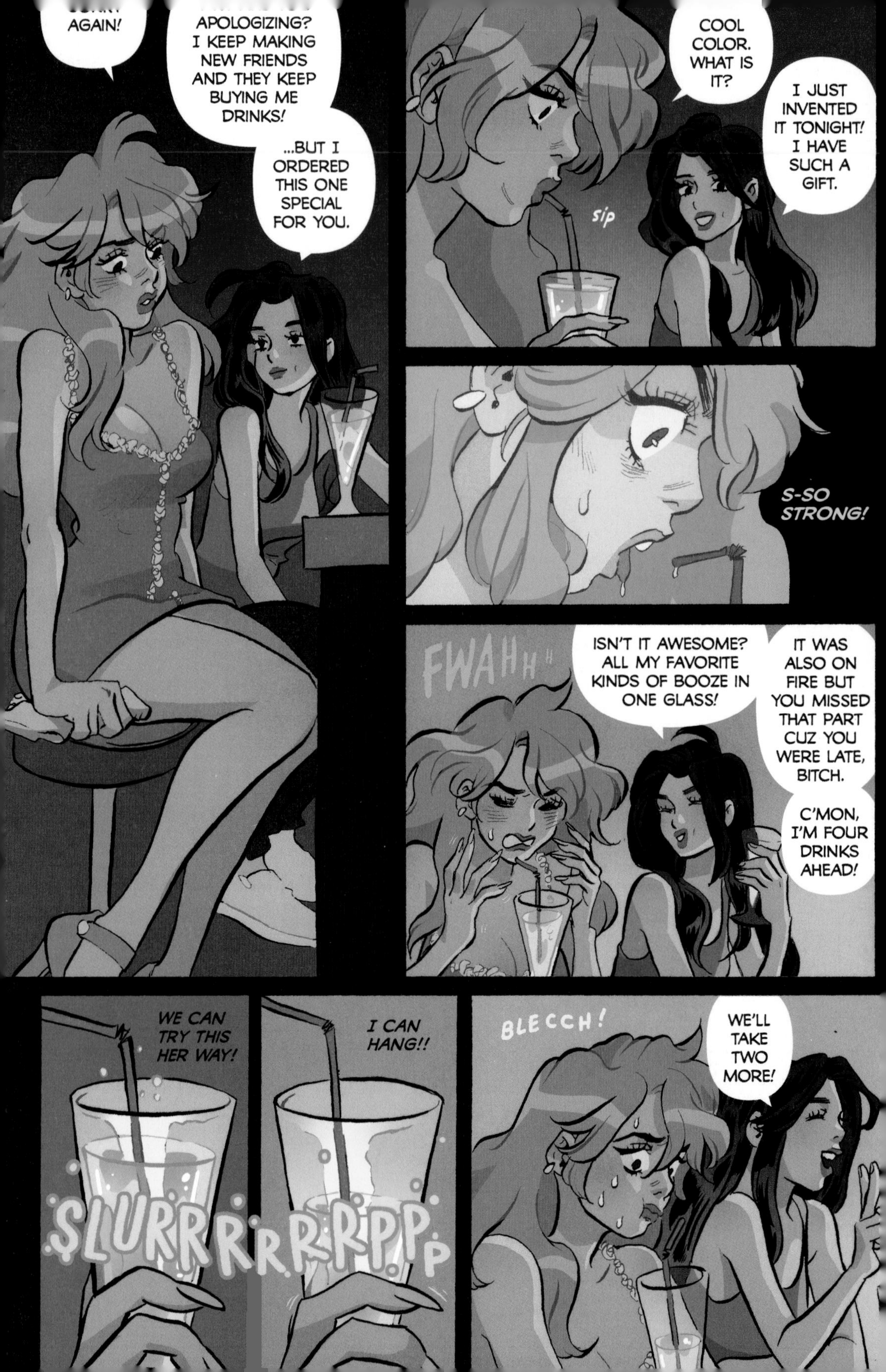

AGAIN!
APOLOGIZING? I KEEP MAKING NEW FRIENDS AND THEY KEEP BUYING ME DRINKS!
...BUT I ORDERED THIS ONE SPECIAL FOR YOU.
COOL COLOR. WHAT IS IT?
sip
I JUST INVENTED IT TONIGHT! I HAVE SUCH A GIFT.
S-SO STRONG!
FWAHHH
ISN'T IT AWESOME? ALL MY FAVORITE KINDS OF BOOZE IN ONE GLASS!
IT WAS ALSO ON FIRE BUT YOU MISSED THAT PART CUZ YOU WERE LATE, BITCH.
C'MON, I'M FOUR DRINKS AHEAD!
WE CAN TRY THIS HER WAY!
I CAN HANG!!
SLURRRRRRPPP
BLECCH!
WE'LL TAKE TWO MORE!

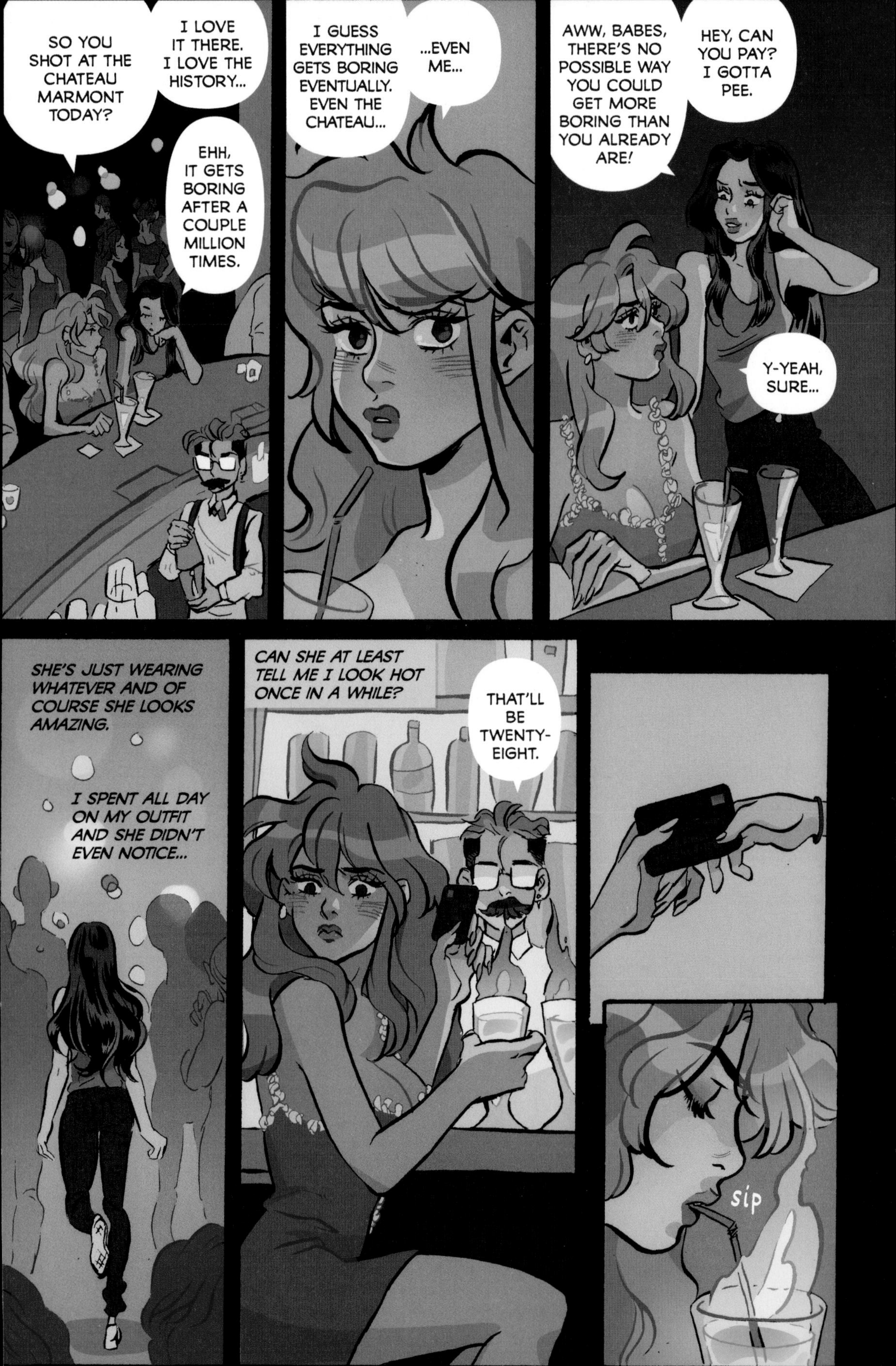

SO YOU SHOT AT THE CHATEAU MARMONT TODAY?
I LOVE IT THERE. I LOVE THE HISTORY...
EHH, IT GETS BORING AFTER A COUPLE MILLION TIMES.
I GUESS EVERYTHING GETS BORING EVENTUALLY. EVEN THE CHATEAU...
...EVEN ME...
AWW, BABES, THERE'S NO POSSIBLE WAY YOU COULD GET MORE BORING THAN YOU ALREADY ARE!
HEY, CAN YOU PAY? I GOTTA PEE.
Y-YEAH, SURE...
SHE'S JUST WEARING WHATEVER AND OF COURSE SHE LOOKS AMAZING.
I SPENT ALL DAY ON MY OUTFIT AND SHE DIDN'T EVEN NOTICE...
CAN SHE AT LEAST TELL ME I LOOK HOT ONCE IN A WHILE?
THAT'LL BE TWENTY-EIGHT.
sip

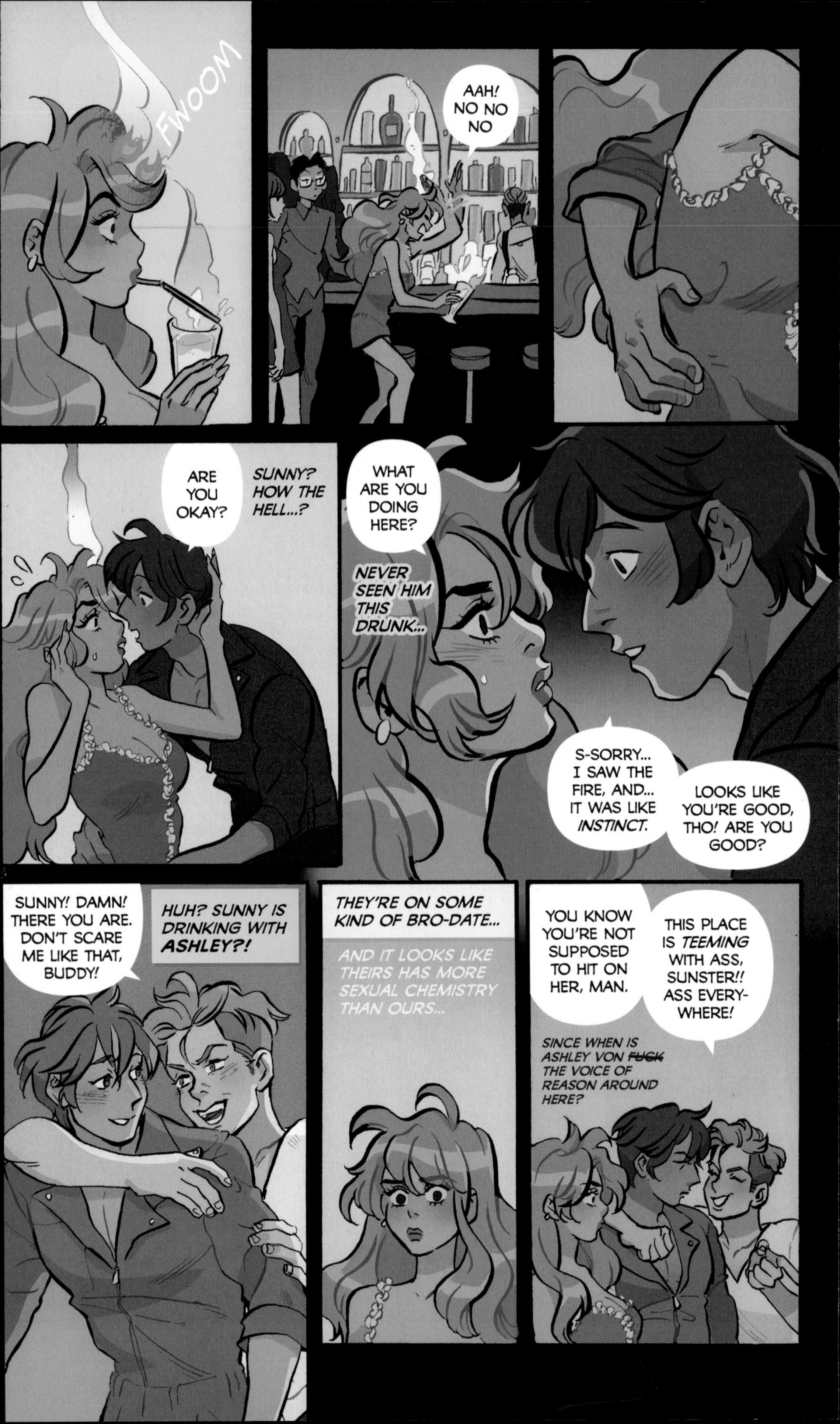
FWOOM
AAH! NO NO NO
ARE YOU OKAY?
SUNNY? HOW THE HELL...?
WHAT ARE YOU DOING HERE?
NEVER SEEN HIM THIS DRUNK...
S-SORRY... I SAW THE FIRE, AND... IT WAS LIKE INSTINCT.
LOOKS LIKE YOU'RE GOOD, THO! ARE YOU GOOD?
SUNNY! DAMN! THERE YOU ARE. DON'T SCARE ME LIKE THAT, BUDDY!
HUH? SUNNY IS DRINKING WITH ASHLEY?!
THEY'RE ON SOME KIND OF BRO-DATE...
AND IT LOOKS LIKE THEIRS HAS MORE SEXUAL CHEMISTRY THAN OURS...
YOU KNOW YOU'RE NOT SUPPOSED TO HIT ON HER, MAN.
THIS PLACE IS TEEMING WITH ASS, SUNSTER!! ASS EVERY-WHERE!
SINCE WHEN IS ASHLEY VON FUCK THE VOICE OF REASON AROUND HERE?

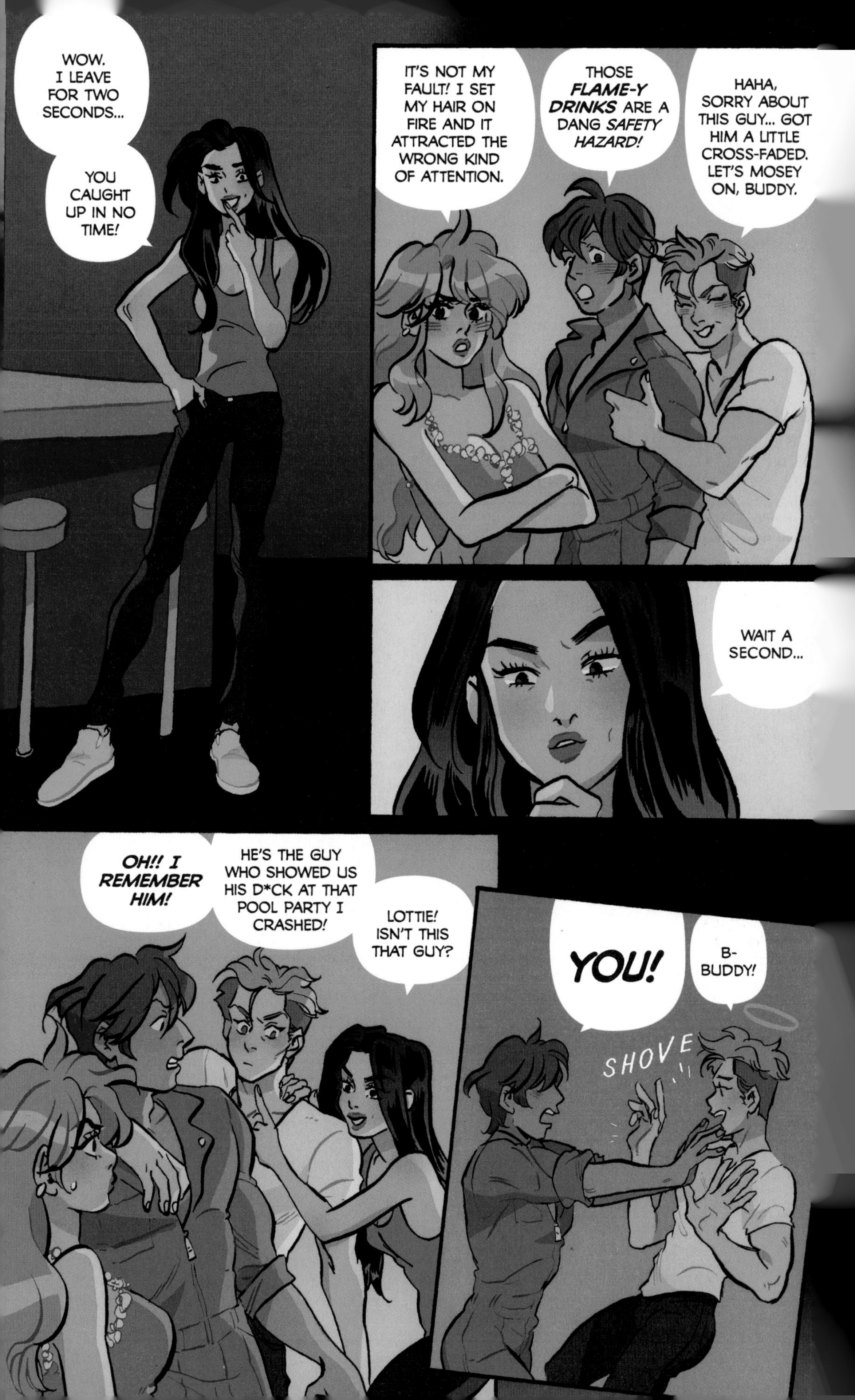
WOW. I LEAVE FOR TWO SECONDS...
YOU CAUGHT UP IN NO TIME!
IT'S NOT MY FAULT! I SET MY HAIR ON FIRE AND IT ATTRACTED THE WRONG KIND OF ATTENTION.
THOSE FLAME-Y DRINKS ARE A DANG SAFETY HAZARD!
HAHA, SORRY ABOUT THIS GUY... GOT HIM A LITTLE CROSS-FADED. LET'S MOSEY ON, BUDDY.
WAIT A SECOND...
OH!! I REMEMBER HIM!
HE'S THE GUY WHO SHOWED US HIS D*CK AT THAT POOL PARTY I CRASHED!
LOTTIE! ISN'T THIS THAT GUY?
YOU!
B- BUDDY!
SHOVE

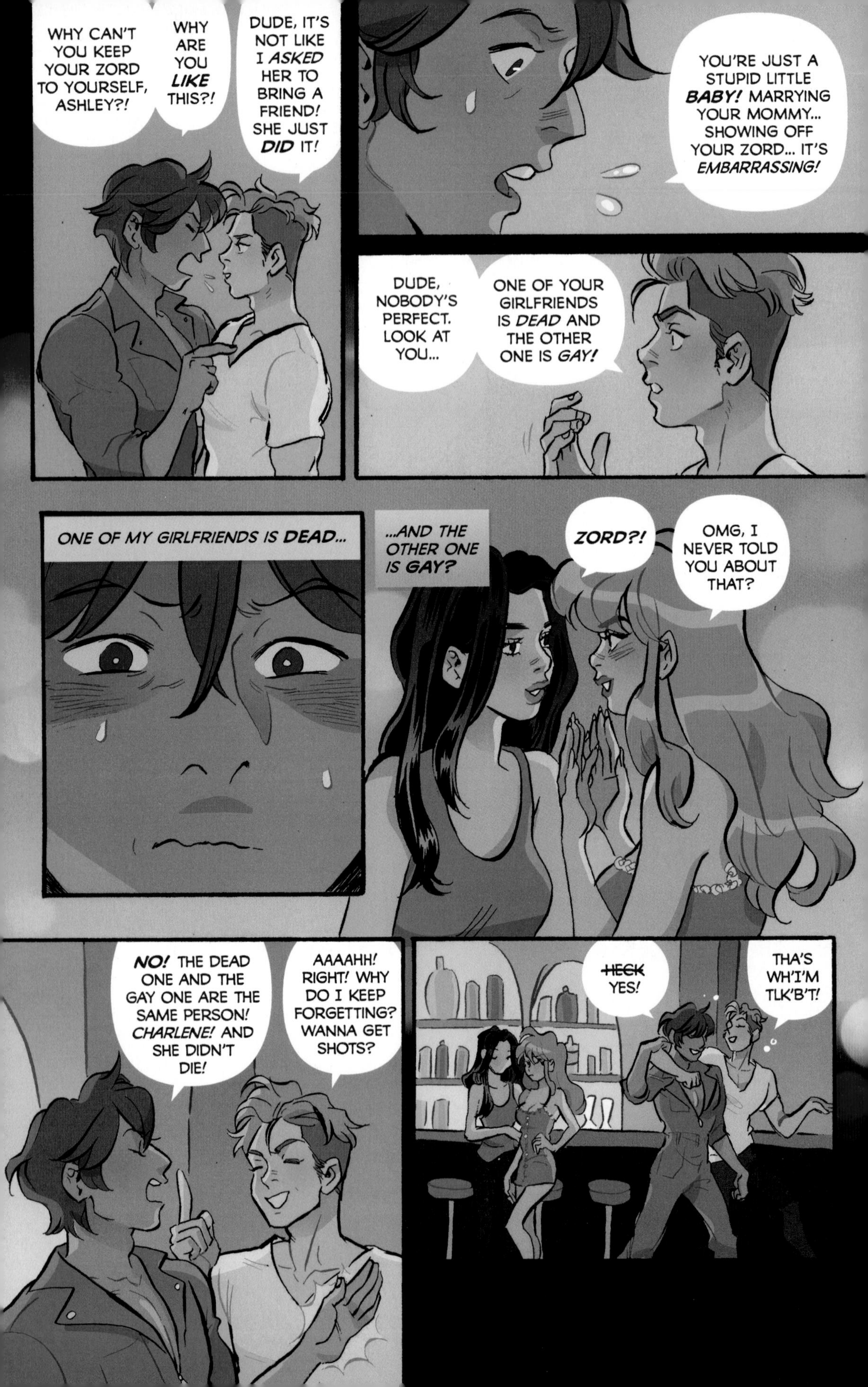
WHY CAN'T YOU KEEP YOUR ZORD TO YOURSELF, ASHLEY?!
WHY ARE YOU *LIKE* THIS?!
DUDE, IT'S NOT LIKE I *ASKED* HER TO BRING A FRIEND! SHE JUST ***DID*** IT!
YOU'RE JUST A STUPID LITTLE ***BABY!*** MARRYING YOUR MOMMY... SHOWING OFF YOUR ZORD... IT'S *EMBARRASSING!*
DUDE, NOBODY'S PERFECT. LOOK AT YOU...
ONE OF YOUR GIRLFRIENDS IS *DEAD* AND THE OTHER ONE IS *GAY!*
*ONE OF MY GIRLFRIENDS IS **DEAD**...*
*...AND THE OTHER ONE IS **GAY**?*
ZORD?!
OMG, I NEVER TOLD YOU ABOUT THAT?
NO! THE DEAD ONE AND THE GAY ONE ARE THE SAME PERSON! *CHARLENE!* AND SHE DIDN'T DIE!
AAAAHH! RIGHT! WHY DO I KEEP FORGETTING? WANNA GET SHOTS?
~~HECK~~ YES!
THA'S WH'I'M TLK'B'T!

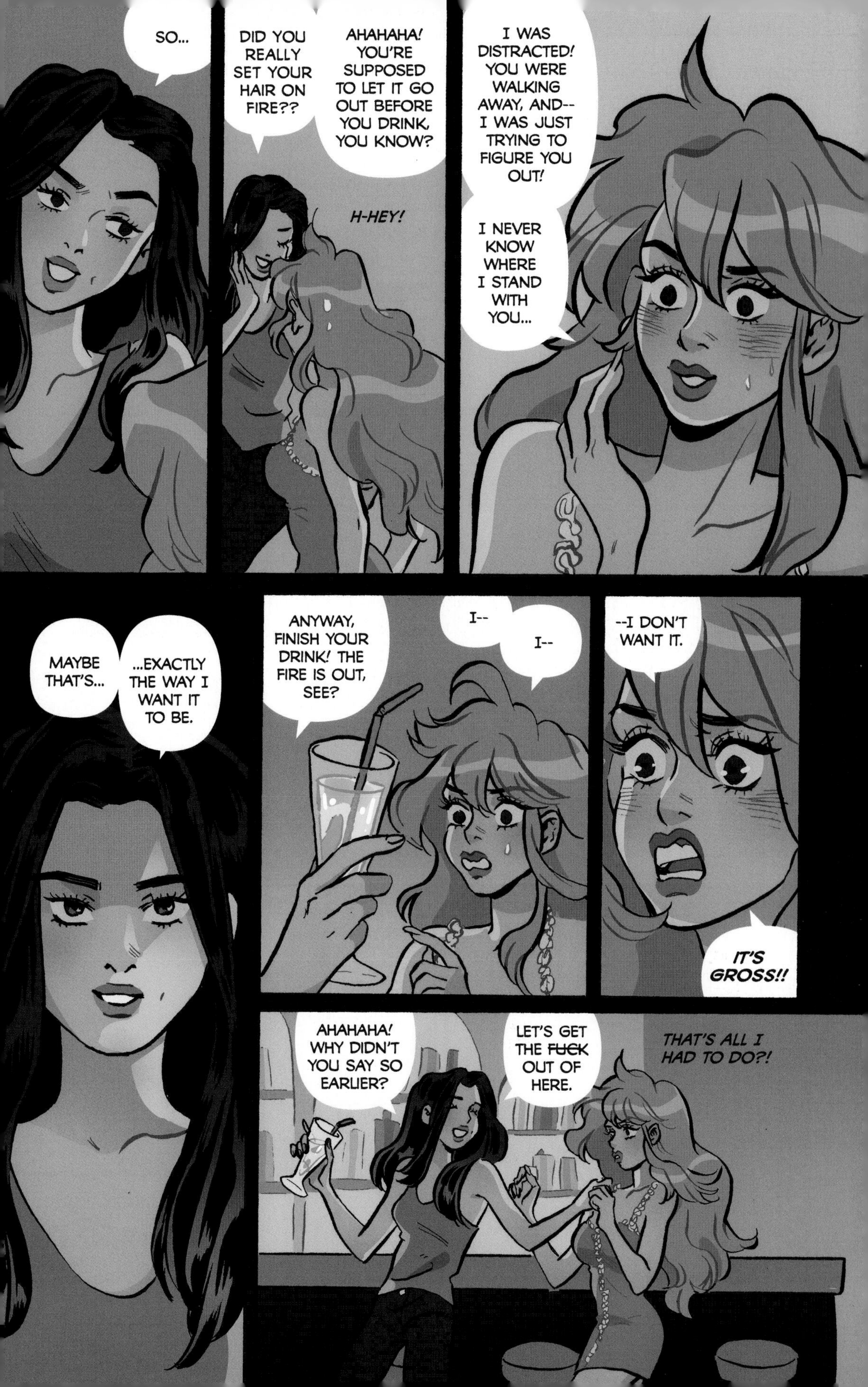
SO...
DID YOU REALLY SET YOUR HAIR ON FIRE??
AHAHAHA! YOU'RE SUPPOSED TO LET IT GO OUT BEFORE YOU DRINK, YOU KNOW?
H-HEY!
I WAS DISTRACTED! YOU WERE WALKING AWAY, AND-- I WAS JUST TRYING TO FIGURE YOU OUT!
I NEVER KNOW WHERE I STAND WITH YOU...
MAYBE THAT'S...
...EXACTLY THE WAY I WANT IT TO BE.
ANYWAY, FINISH YOUR DRINK! THE FIRE IS OUT, SEE?
I--
I--
--I DON'T WANT IT.
IT'S GROSS!!
AHAHAHA! WHY DIDN'T YOU SAY SO EARLIER?
LET'S GET THE FUCK OUT OF HERE.
THAT'S ALL I HAD TO DO?!

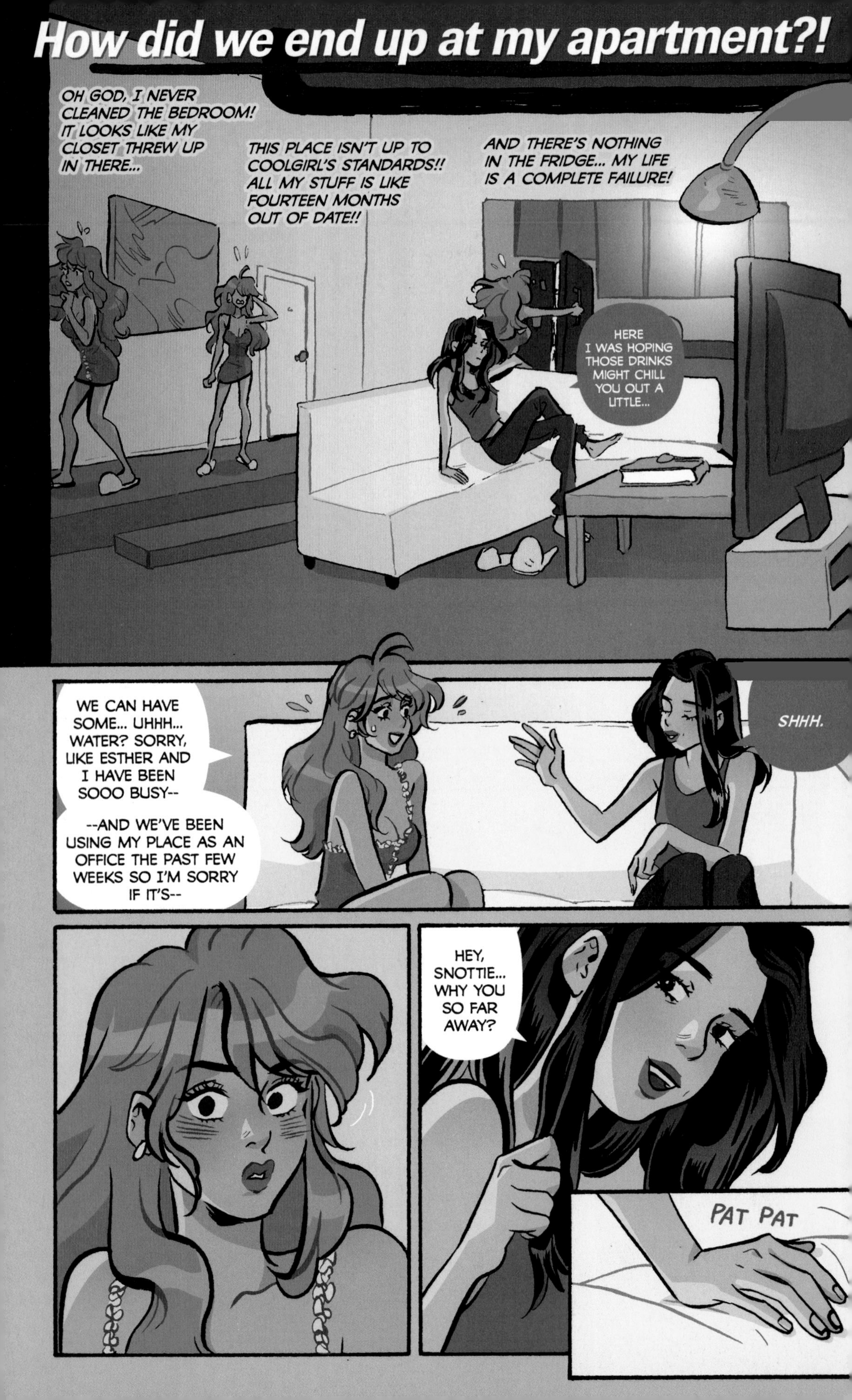
How did we end up at my apartment?!
OH GOD, I NEVER CLEANED THE BEDROOM! IT LOOKS LIKE MY CLOSET THREW UP IN THERE...
THIS PLACE ISN'T UP TO COOLGIRL'S STANDARDS!! ALL MY STUFF IS LIKE FOURTEEN MONTHS OUT OF DATE!!
AND THERE'S NOTHING IN THE FRIDGE... MY LIFE IS A COMPLETE FAILURE!
HERE I WAS HOPING THOSE DRINKS MIGHT CHILL YOU OUT A LITTLE...
WE CAN HAVE SOME... UHHH... WATER? SORRY, LIKE ESTHER AND I HAVE BEEN SOOO BUSY--
--AND WE'VE BEEN USING MY PLACE AS AN OFFICE THE PAST FEW WEEKS SO I'M SORRY IF IT'S--
SHHH.
HEY, SNOTTIE... WHY YOU SO FAR AWAY?
PAT PAT

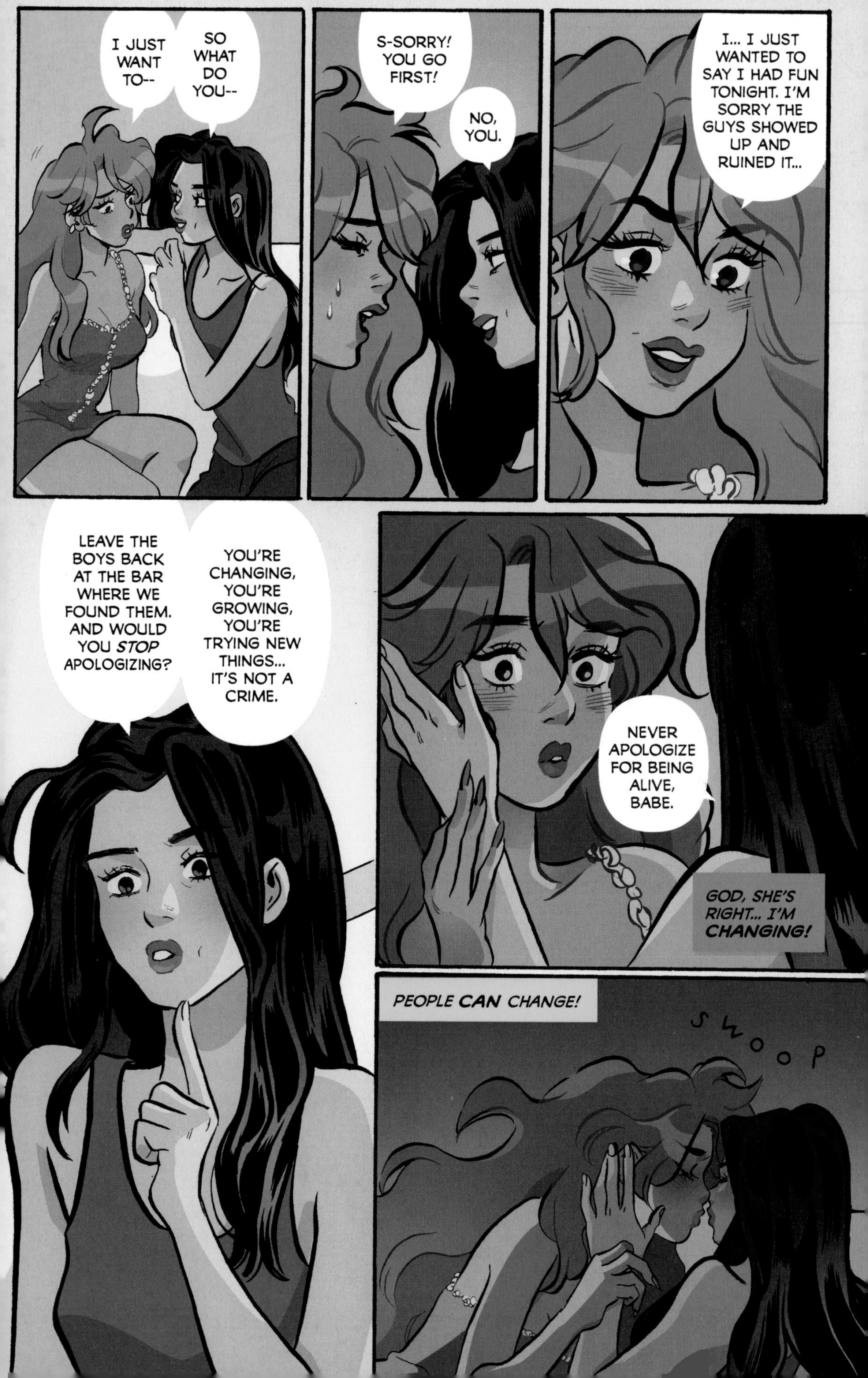

I JUST WANT TO--
SO WHAT DO YOU--
S-SORRY! YOU GO FIRST!
NO, YOU.
I... I JUST WANTED TO SAY I HAD FUN TONIGHT. I'M SORRY THE GUYS SHOWED UP AND RUINED IT...
LEAVE THE BOYS BACK AT THE BAR WHERE WE FOUND THEM. AND WOULD YOU *STOP* APOLOGIZING?
YOU'RE CHANGING, YOU'RE GROWING, YOU'RE TRYING NEW THINGS... IT'S NOT A CRIME.
NEVER APOLOGIZE FOR BEING ALIVE, BABE.
*GOD, SHE'S RIGHT... I'M **CHANGING!***
*PEOPLE **CAN** CHANGE!*
SWOOP

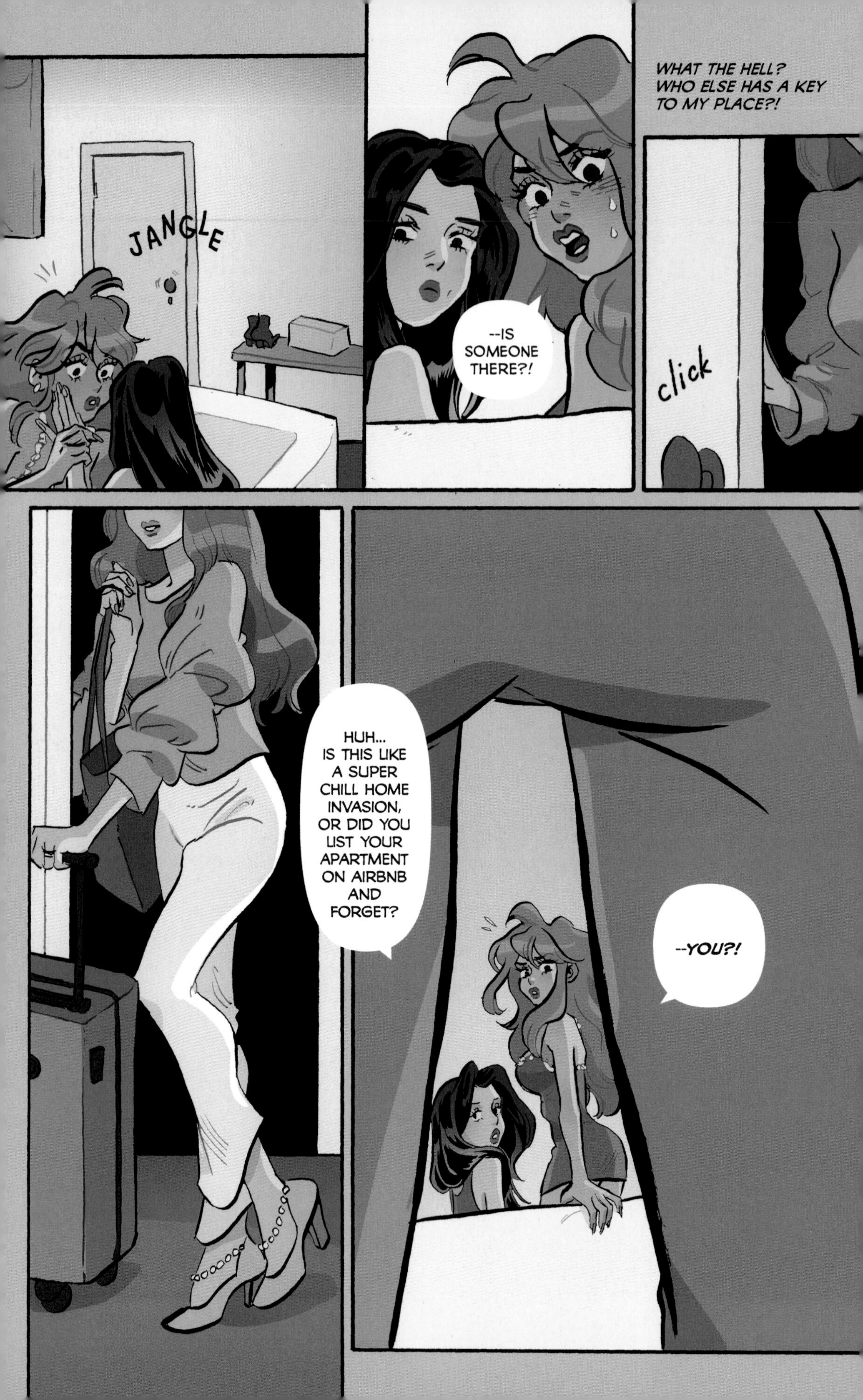
JANGLE
--IS SOMEONE THERE?!
WHAT THE HELL? WHO ELSE HAS A KEY TO MY PLACE?!
click
HUH... IS THIS LIKE A SUPER CHILL HOME INVASION, OR DID YOU LIST YOUR APARTMENT ON AIRBNB AND FORGET?
--YOU?!

12. HEAT WAVE

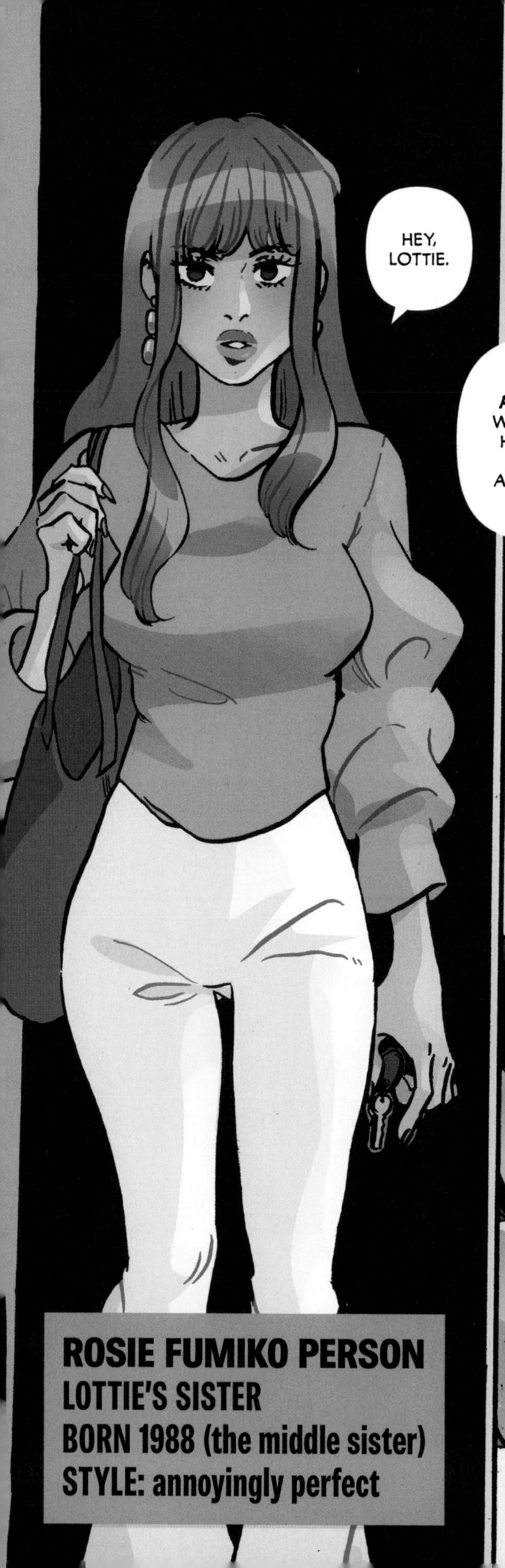
HEY, LOTTIE.
ROSIE FUMIKO PERSON
LOTTIE'S SISTER
BORN 1988 (the middle sister)
STYLE: annoyingly perfect

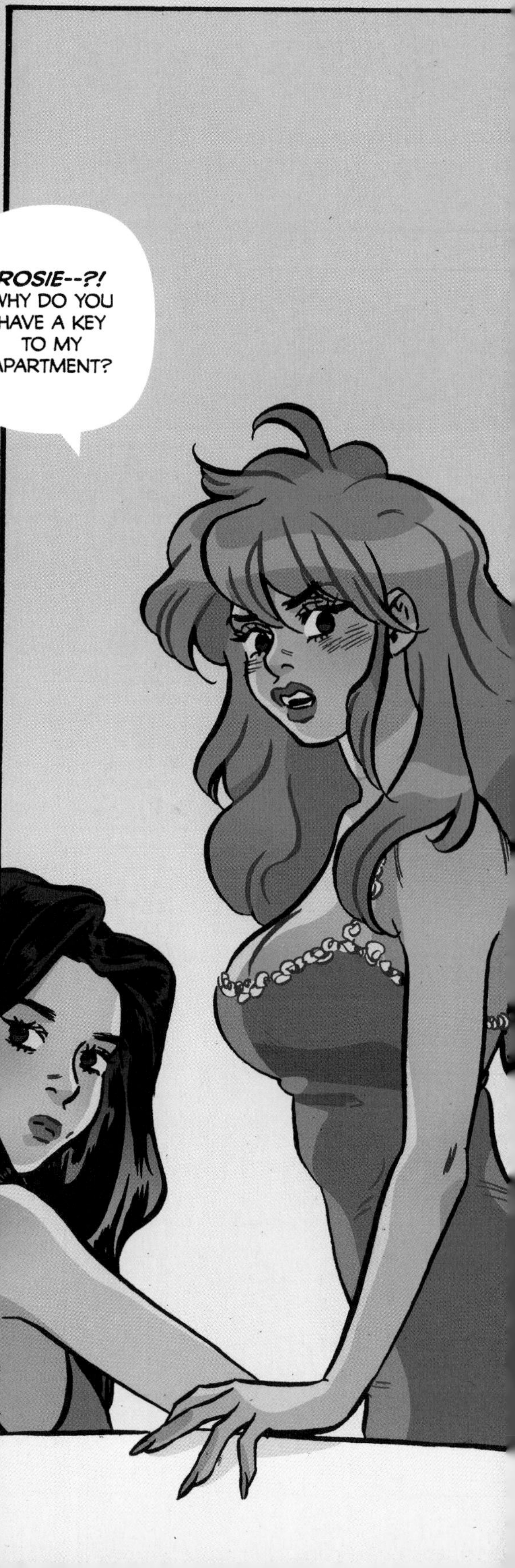
ROSIE--?! WHY DO YOU HAVE A KEY TO MY APARTMENT?

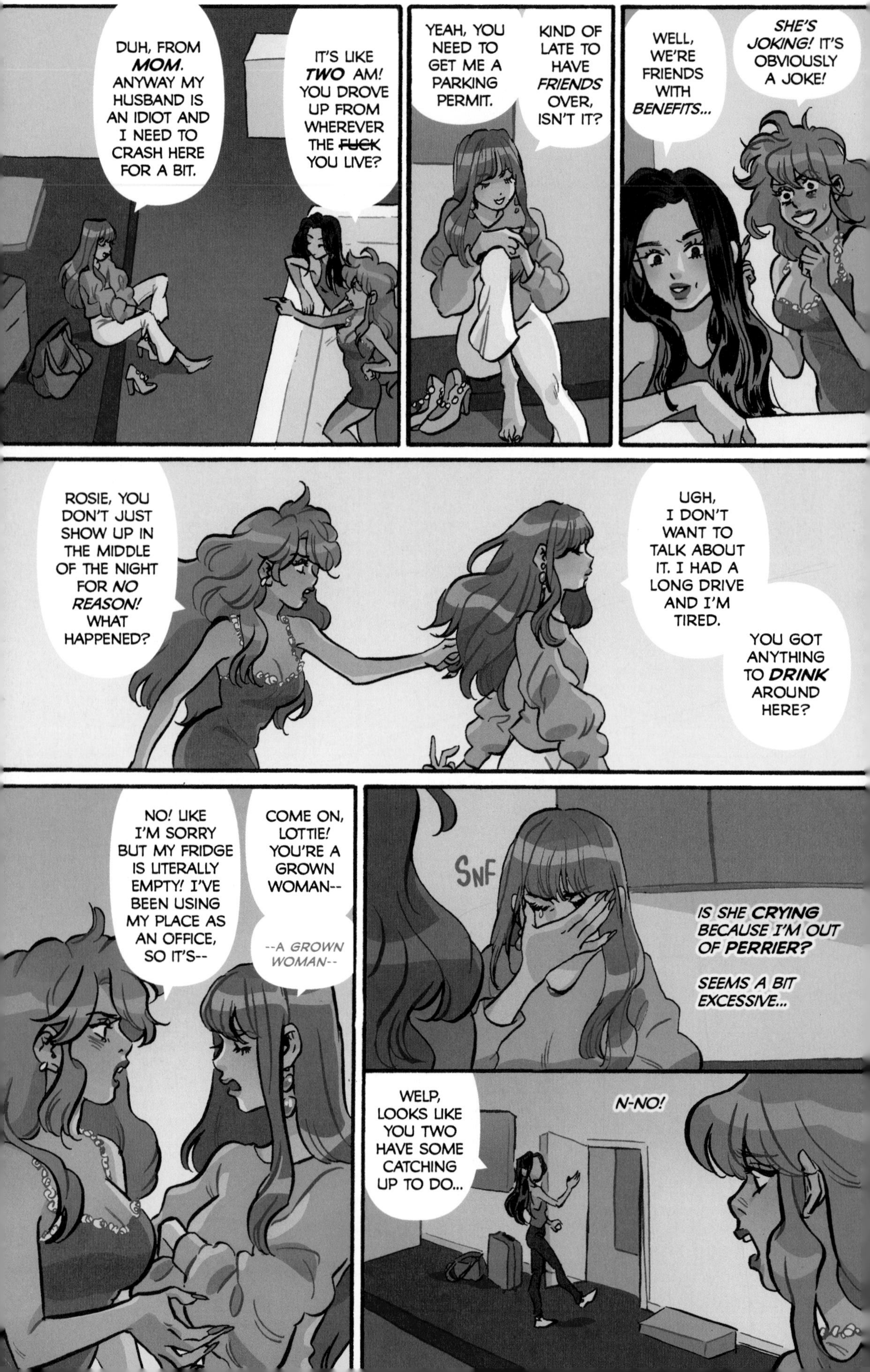
DUH, FROM MOM. ANYWAY MY HUSBAND IS AN IDIOT AND I NEED TO CRASH HERE FOR A BIT.
IT'S LIKE TWO AM! YOU DROVE UP FROM WHEREVER THE FUCK YOU LIVE?
YEAH, YOU NEED TO GET ME A PARKING PERMIT.
KIND OF LATE TO HAVE FRIENDS OVER, ISN'T IT?
WELL, WE'RE FRIENDS WITH BENEFITS...
SHE'S JOKING! IT'S OBVIOUSLY A JOKE!
ROSIE, YOU DON'T JUST SHOW UP IN THE MIDDLE OF THE NIGHT FOR NO REASON! WHAT HAPPENED?
UGH, I DON'T WANT TO TALK ABOUT IT. I HAD A LONG DRIVE AND I'M TIRED.
YOU GOT ANYTHING TO DRINK AROUND HERE?
NO! LIKE I'M SORRY BUT MY FRIDGE IS LITERALLY EMPTY! I'VE BEEN USING MY PLACE AS AN OFFICE, SO IT'S--
COME ON, LOTTIE! YOU'RE A GROWN WOMAN--
--A GROWN WOMAN--
SNF
IS SHE CRYING BECAUSE I'M OUT OF PERRIER?
SEEMS A BIT EXCESSIVE...
WELP, LOOKS LIKE YOU TWO HAVE SOME CATCHING UP TO DO...
N-NO!

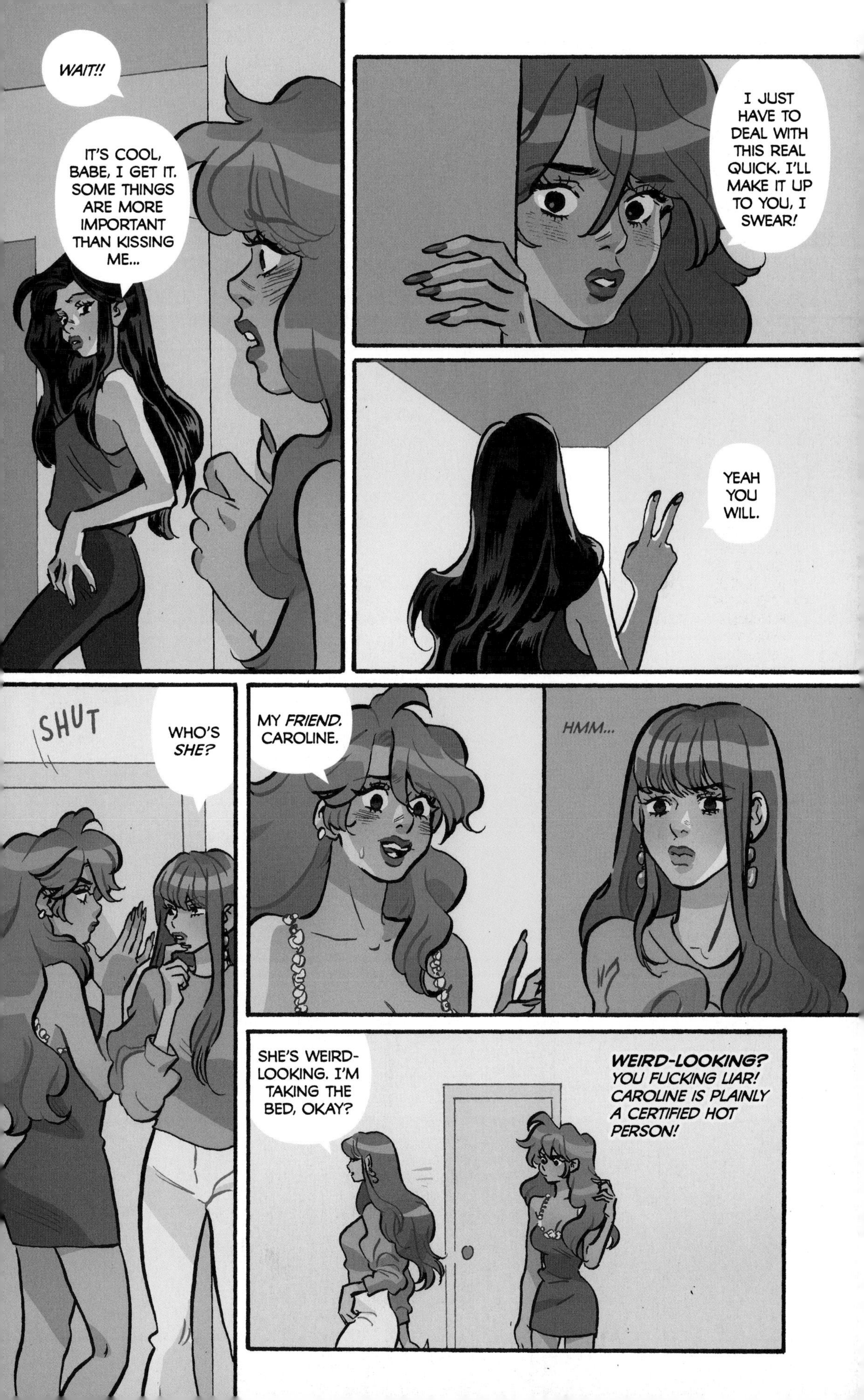
WAIT!!
IT'S COOL, BABE, I GET IT. SOME THINGS ARE MORE IMPORTANT THAN KISSING ME...
I JUST HAVE TO DEAL WITH THIS REAL QUICK. I'LL MAKE IT UP TO YOU, I SWEAR!
YEAH YOU WILL.
SHUT
WHO'S *SHE?*
MY *FRIEND.* CAROLINE.
HMM...
SHE'S WEIRD-LOOKING. I'M TAKING THE BED, OKAY?
WEIRD-LOOKING? *YOU FUCKING LIAR! CAROLINE IS PLAINLY A CERTIFIED HOT PERSON!*

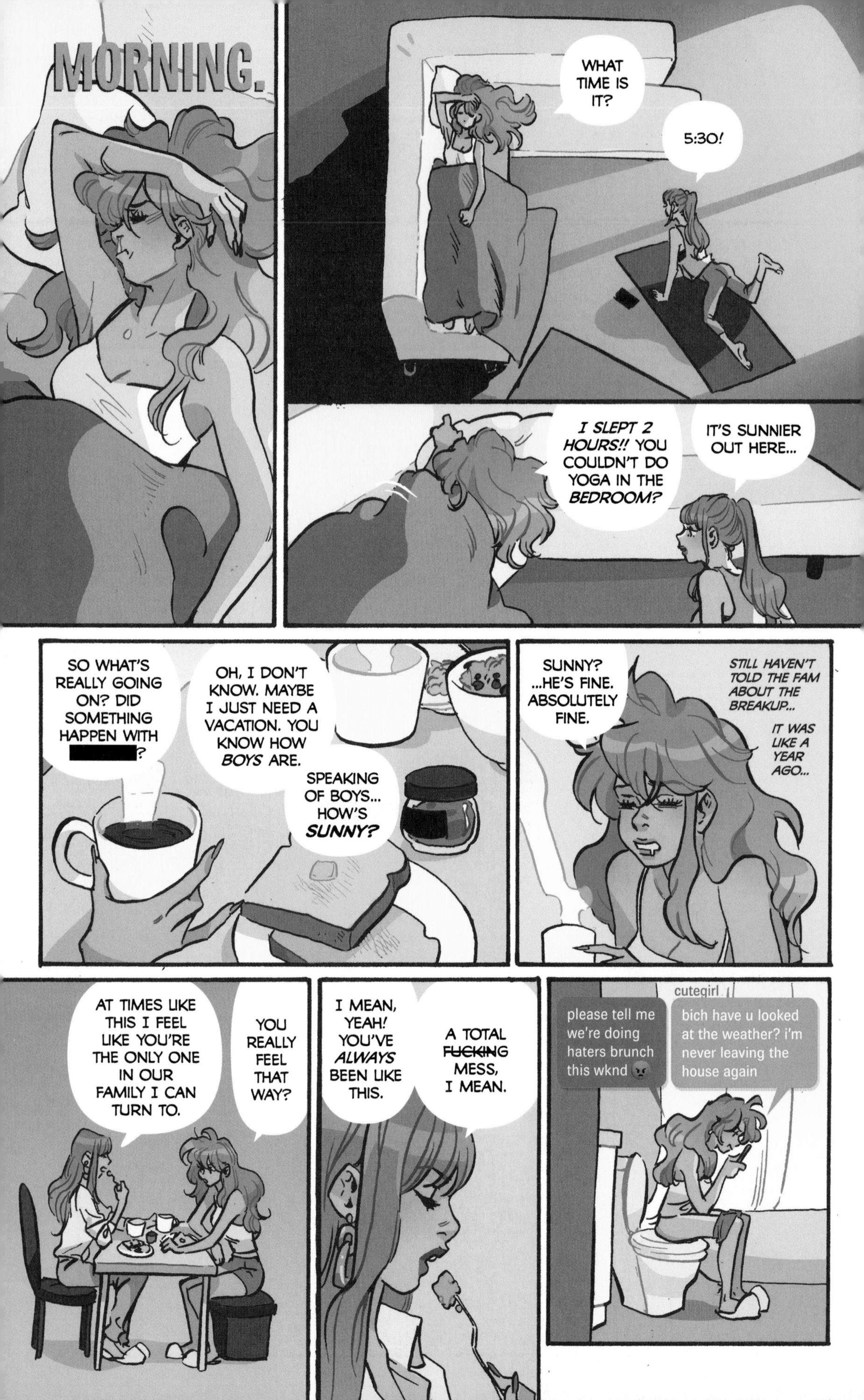
MORNING.
WHAT TIME IS IT?
5:30!
I SLEPT 2 HOURS!! YOU COULDN'T DO YOGA IN THE BEDROOM?
IT'S SUNNIER OUT HERE...
SO WHAT'S REALLY GOING ON? DID SOMETHING HAPPEN WITH [redacted]?
OH, I DON'T KNOW. MAYBE I JUST NEED A VACATION. YOU KNOW HOW BOYS ARE.
SPEAKING OF BOYS... HOW'S SUNNY?
SUNNY? ...HE'S FINE. ABSOLUTELY FINE.
STILL HAVEN'T TOLD THE FAM ABOUT THE BREAKUP...
IT WAS LIKE A YEAR AGO...
AT TIMES LIKE THIS I FEEL LIKE YOU'RE THE ONLY ONE IN OUR FAMILY I CAN TURN TO.
YOU REALLY FEEL THAT WAY?
I MEAN, YEAH! YOU'VE ALWAYS BEEN LIKE THIS.
A TOTAL ~~FUCKIN~~G MESS, I MEAN.
cutegirl
please tell me we're doing haters brunch this wknd 😡
bich have u looked at the weather? i'm never leaving the house again

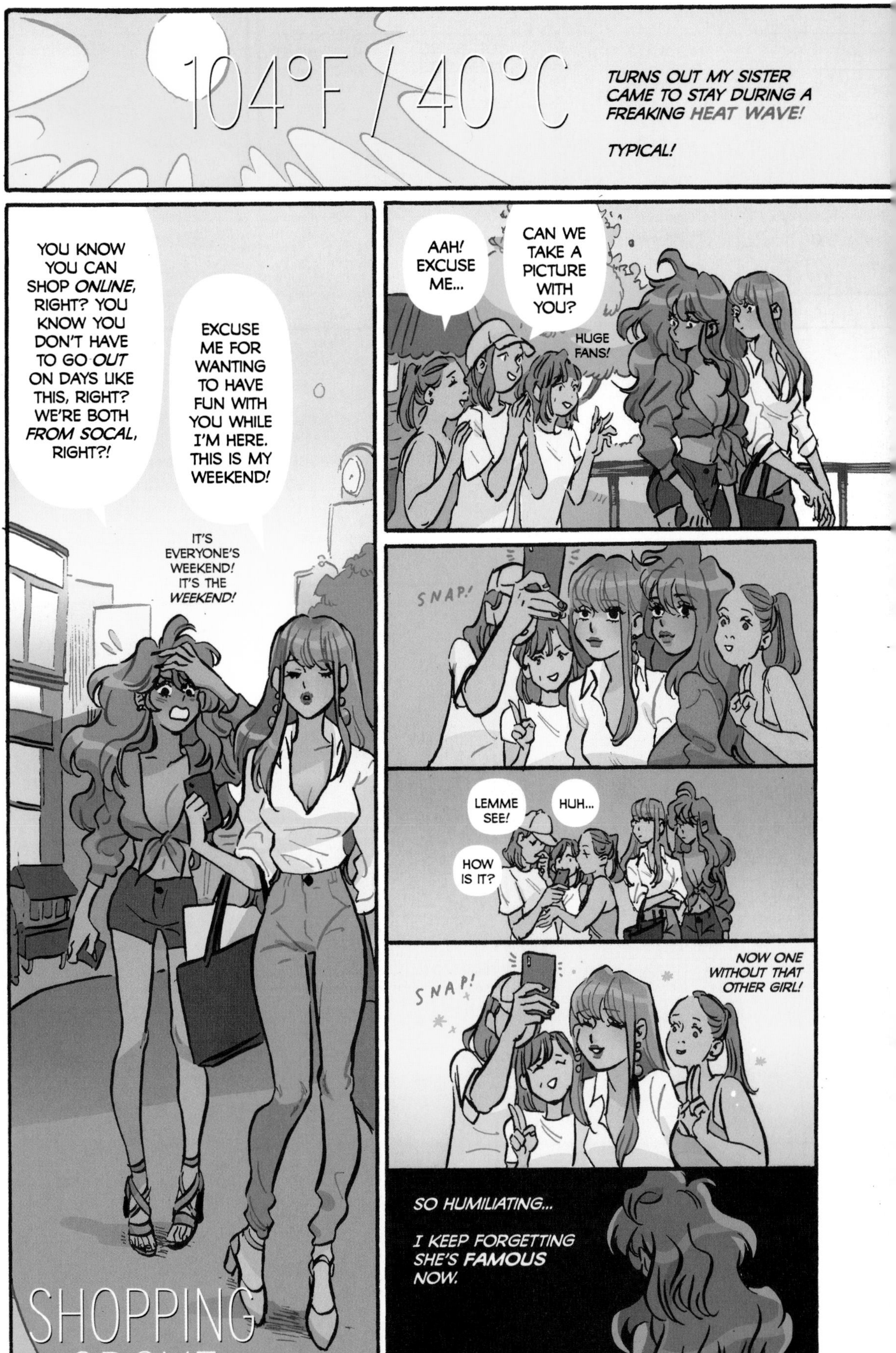
104°F / 40°C
TURNS OUT MY SISTER CAME TO STAY DURING A FREAKING HEAT WAVE!
TYPICAL!
YOU KNOW YOU CAN SHOP ONLINE, RIGHT? YOU KNOW YOU DON'T HAVE TO GO OUT ON DAYS LIKE THIS, RIGHT? WE'RE BOTH FROM SOCAL, RIGHT?!
EXCUSE ME FOR WANTING TO HAVE FUN WITH YOU WHILE I'M HERE. THIS IS MY WEEKEND!
IT'S EVERYONE'S WEEKEND! IT'S THE WEEKEND!
SHOPPING AT THE GROVE
AAH! EXCUSE ME...
CAN WE TAKE A PICTURE WITH YOU?
HUGE FANS!
SNAP!
LEMME SEE!
HUH...
HOW IS IT?
SNAP!
NOW ONE WITHOUT THAT OTHER GIRL!
SO HUMILIATING...
I KEEP FORGETTING SHE'S FAMOUS NOW.

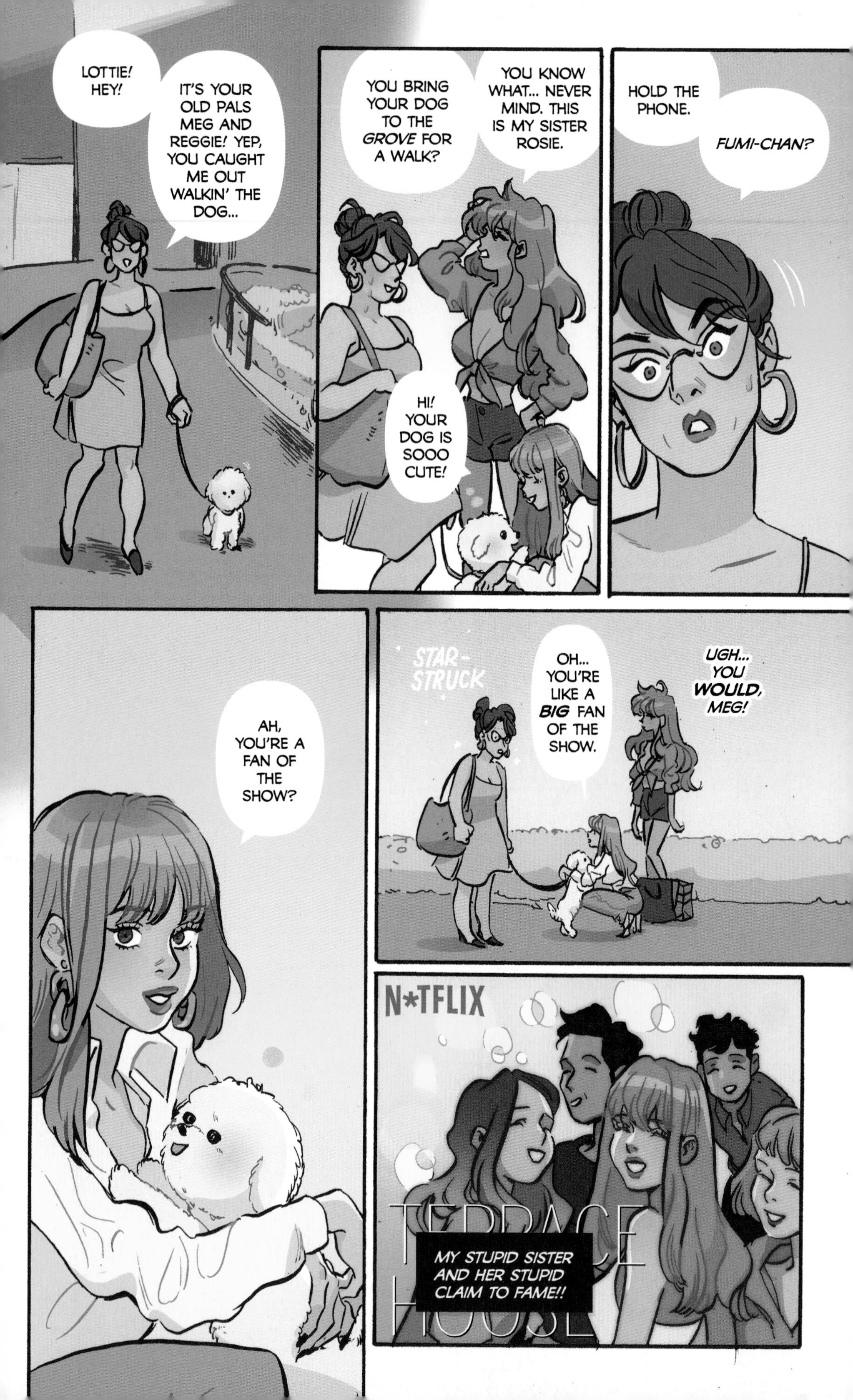
LOTTIE! HEY!
IT'S YOUR OLD PALS MEG AND REGGIE! YEP, YOU CAUGHT ME OUT WALKIN' THE DOG...
YOU BRING YOUR DOG TO THE *GROVE* FOR A WALK?
YOU KNOW WHAT... NEVER MIND. THIS IS MY SISTER ROSIE.
HI! YOUR DOG IS SOOO CUTE!
HOLD THE PHONE.
FUMI-CHAN?
AH, YOU'RE A FAN OF THE SHOW?
STAR-STRUCK
OH... YOU'RE LIKE A *BIG* FAN OF THE SHOW.
UGH... YOU WOULD, MEG!
N*TFLIX
TERRACE HOUSE
MY STUPID SISTER AND HER STUPID CLAIM TO FAME!!

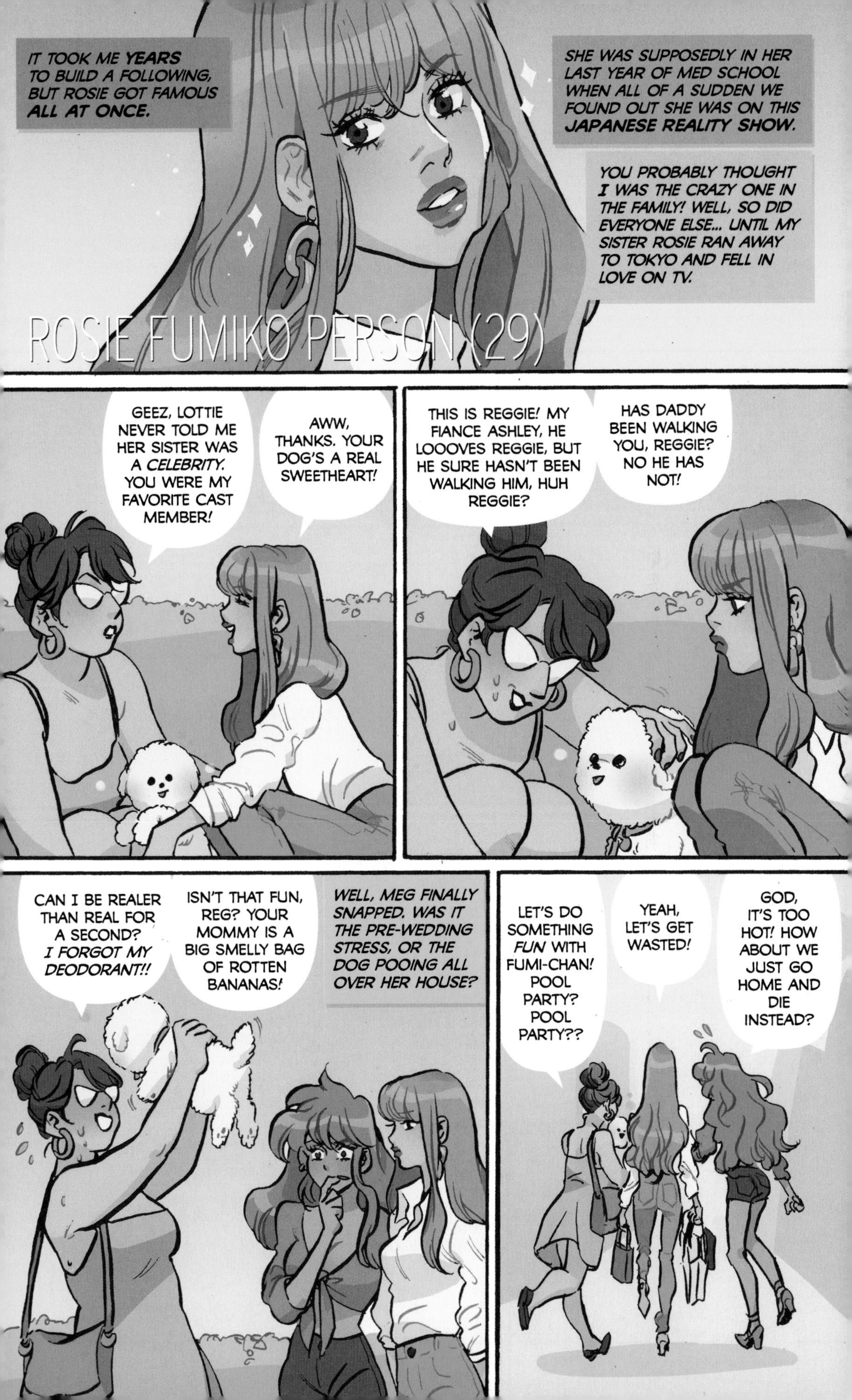
IT TOOK ME YEARS TO BUILD A FOLLOWING, BUT ROSIE GOT FAMOUS ALL AT ONCE.
SHE WAS SUPPOSEDLY IN HER LAST YEAR OF MED SCHOOL WHEN ALL OF A SUDDEN WE FOUND OUT SHE WAS ON THIS JAPANESE REALITY SHOW.
YOU PROBABLY THOUGHT I WAS THE CRAZY ONE IN THE FAMILY! WELL, SO DID EVERYONE ELSE... UNTIL MY SISTER ROSIE RAN AWAY TO TOKYO AND FELL IN LOVE ON TV.
ROSIE FUMIKO PERSON (29)
GEEZ, LOTTIE NEVER TOLD ME HER SISTER WAS A CELEBRITY. YOU WERE MY FAVORITE CAST MEMBER!
AWW, THANKS. YOUR DOG'S A REAL SWEETHEART!
THIS IS REGGIE! MY FIANCE ASHLEY, HE LOOOVES REGGIE, BUT HE SURE HASN'T BEEN WALKING HIM, HUH REGGIE?
HAS DADDY BEEN WALKING YOU, REGGIE? NO HE HAS NOT!
CAN I BE REALER THAN REAL FOR A SECOND? I FORGOT MY DEODORANT!!
ISN'T THAT FUN, REG? YOUR MOMMY IS A BIG SMELLY BAG OF ROTTEN BANANAS!
WELL, MEG FINALLY SNAPPED. WAS IT THE PRE-WEDDING STRESS, OR THE DOG POOING ALL OVER HER HOUSE?
LET'S DO SOMETHING FUN WITH FUMI-CHAN! POOL PARTY? POOL PARTY??
YEAH, LET'S GET WASTED!
GOD, IT'S TOO HOT! HOW ABOUT WE JUST GO HOME AND DIE INSTEAD?

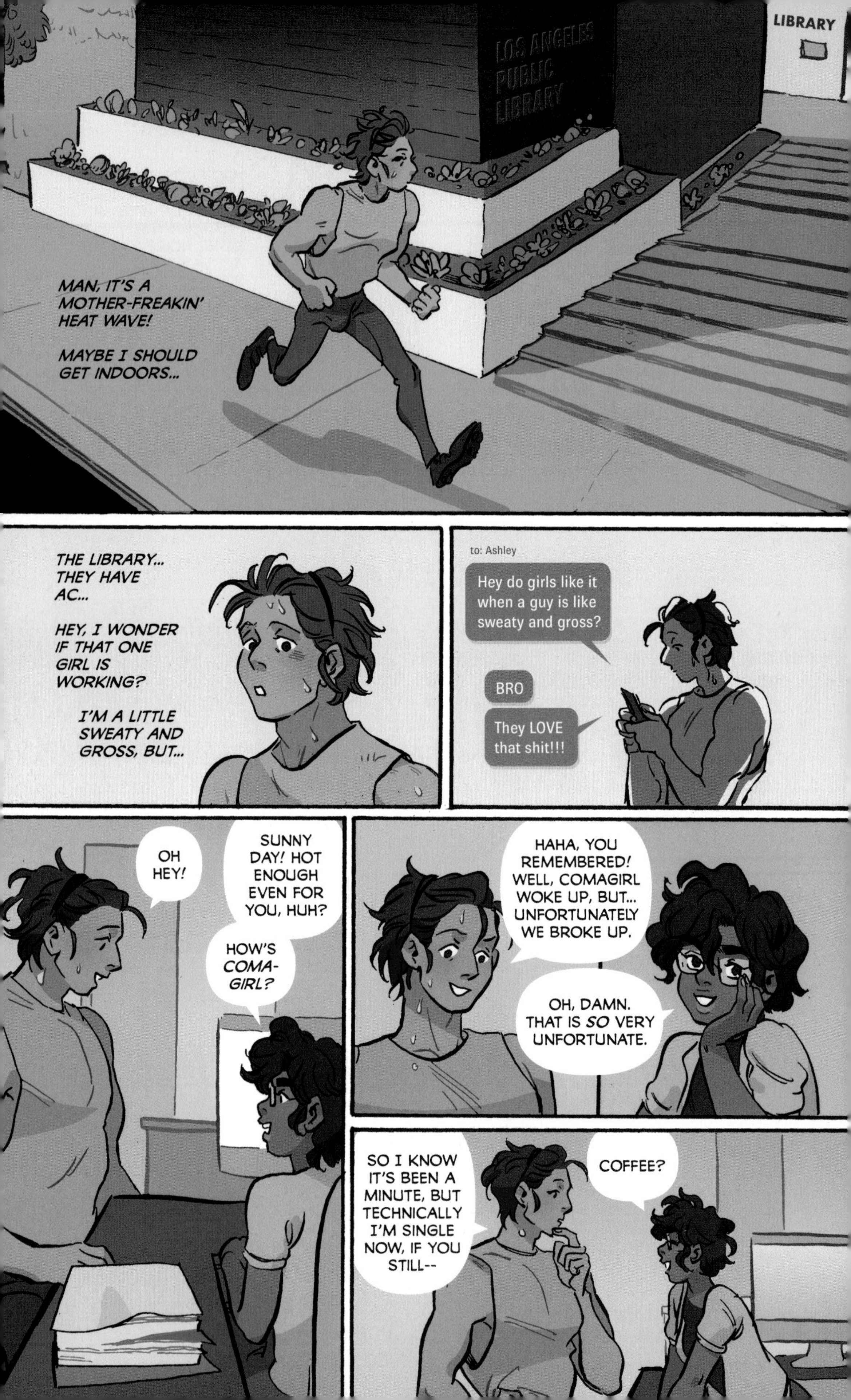
LOS ANGELES PUBLIC LIBRARY
LIBRARY
MAN, IT'S A MOTHER-FREAKIN' HEAT WAVE!
MAYBE I SHOULD GET INDOORS...
THE LIBRARY... THEY HAVE AC...
HEY, I WONDER IF THAT ONE GIRL IS WORKING?
I'M A LITTLE SWEATY AND GROSS, BUT...
to: Ashley
Hey do girls like it when a guy is like sweaty and gross?
BRO
They LOVE that shit!!!
OH HEY!
SUNNY DAY! HOT ENOUGH EVEN FOR YOU, HUH?
HOW'S COMA-GIRL?
HAHA, YOU REMEMBERED! WELL, COMAGIRL WOKE UP, BUT... UNFORTUNATELY WE BROKE UP.
OH, DAMN. THAT IS *SO* VERY UNFORTUNATE.
SO I KNOW IT'S BEEN A MINUTE, BUT TECHNICALLY I'M SINGLE NOW, IF YOU STILL--
COFFEE?

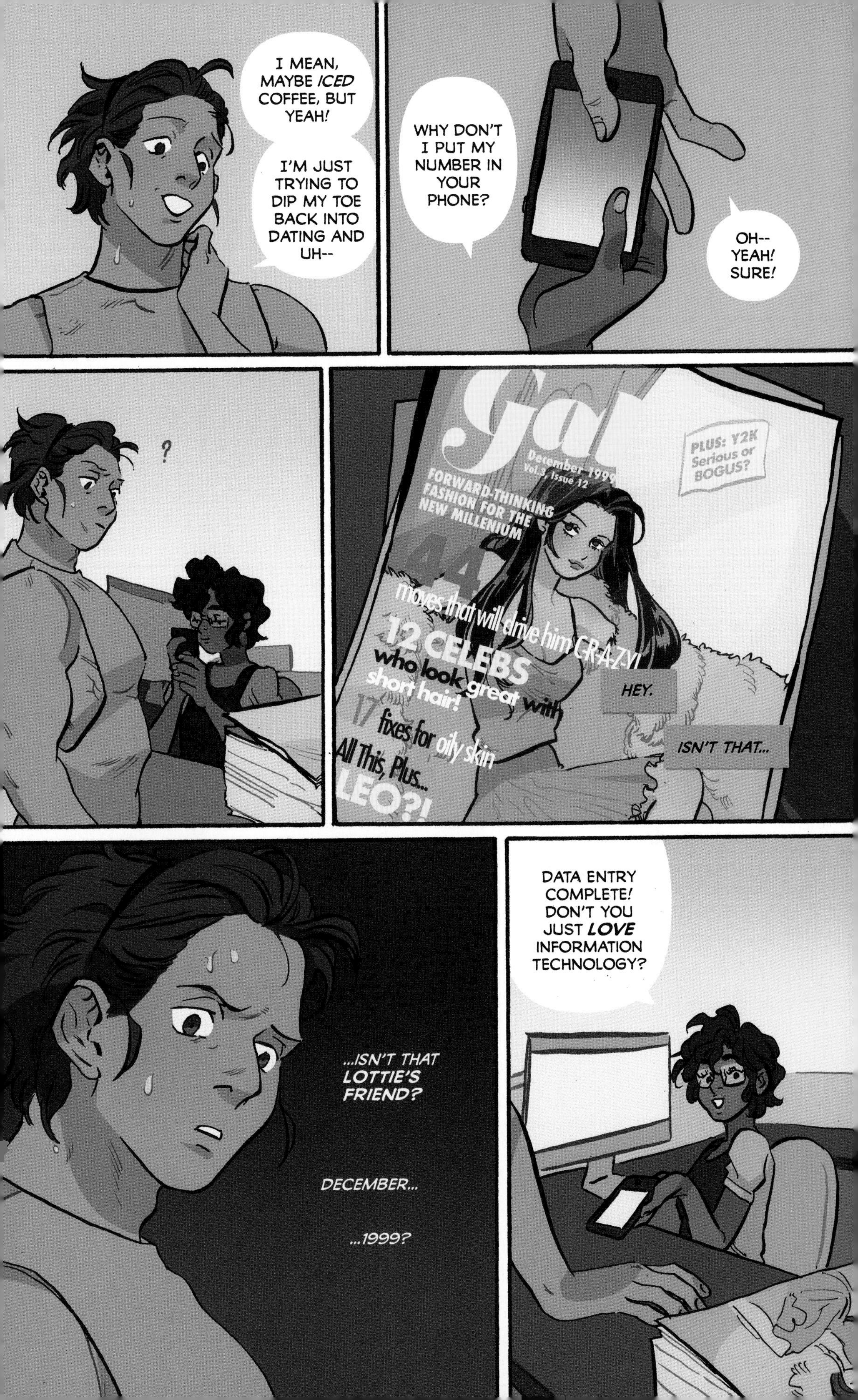
I MEAN, MAYBE *ICED* COFFEE, BUT YEAH!
I'M JUST TRYING TO DIP MY TOE BACK INTO DATING AND UH--
WHY DON'T I PUT MY NUMBER IN YOUR PHONE?
OH-- YEAH! SURE!
?
December 1999
Vol.3, Issue 12
PLUS: Y2K Serious or BOGUS?
FORWARD-THINKING FASHION FOR THE NEW MILLENIUM
44 moves that will drive him CR-A-Z-Y!
12 CELEBS who look great with short hair!
17 fixes for oily skin
All This, Plus... LEO?!
HEY.
ISN'T THAT...
...ISN'T THAT LOTTIE'S FRIEND?
DECEMBER...
...1999?
DATA ENTRY COMPLETE! DON'T YOU JUST *LOVE* INFORMATION TECHNOLOGY?

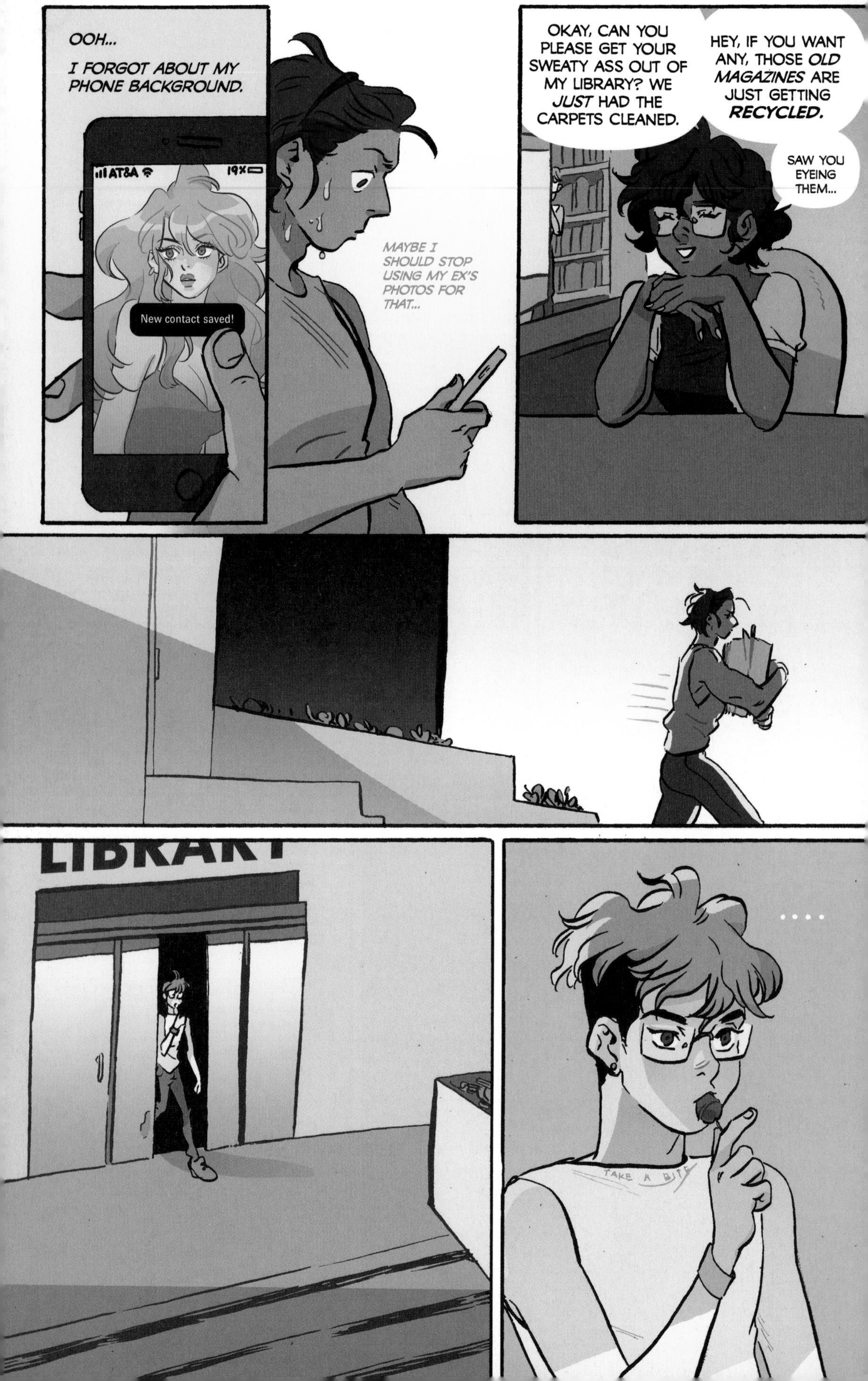

OOH...
I FORGOT ABOUT MY PHONE BACKGROUND.
AT&A
New contact saved!
MAYBE I SHOULD STOP USING MY EX'S PHOTOS FOR THAT...
OKAY, CAN YOU PLEASE GET YOUR SWEATY ASS OUT OF MY LIBRARY? WE JUST HAD THE CARPETS CLEANED.
HEY, IF YOU WANT ANY, THOSE OLD MAGAZINES ARE JUST GETTING RECYCLED.
SAW YOU EYEING THEM...
LIBRARY
....
TAKE A BITE

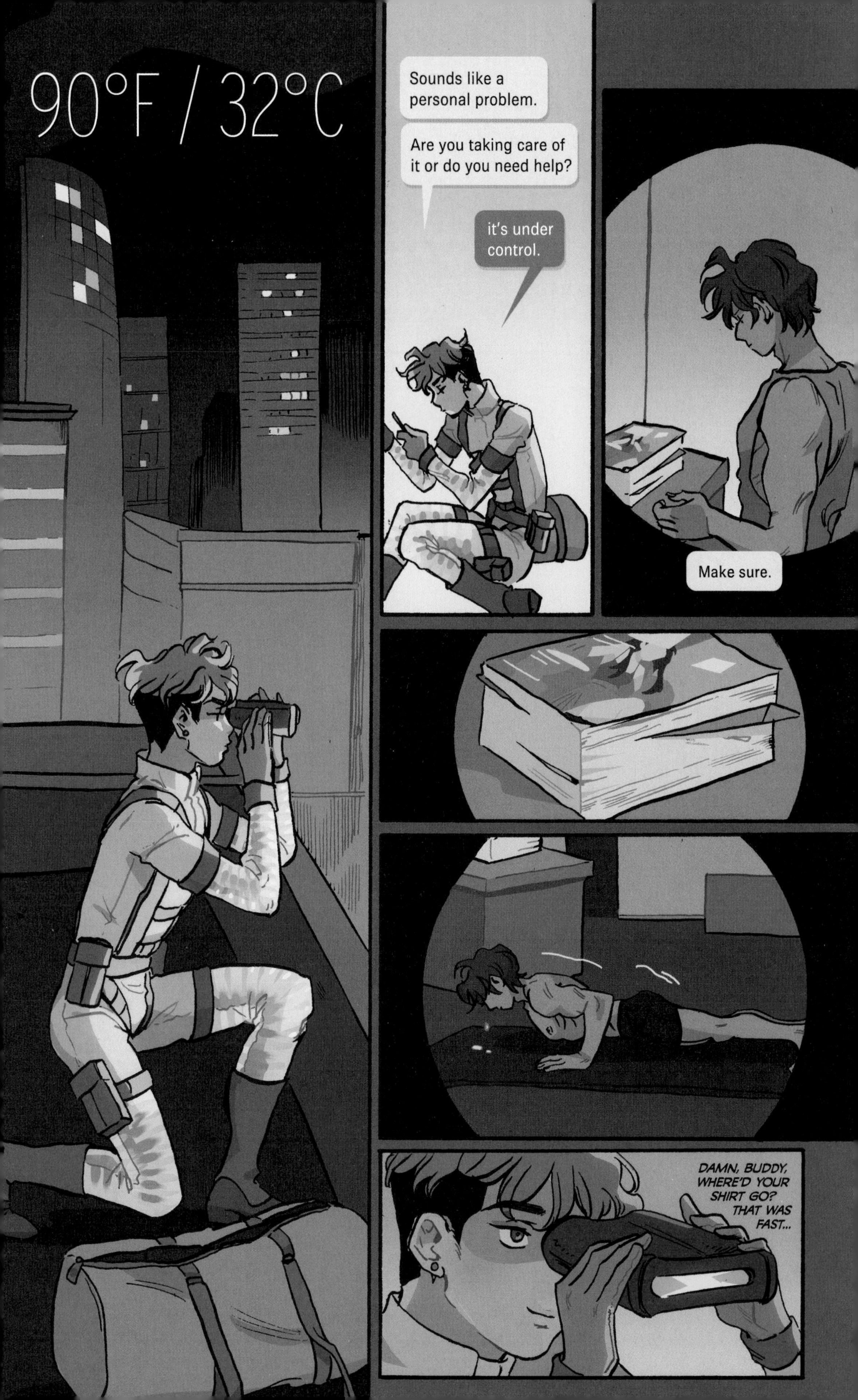
90°F / 32°C
Sounds like a personal problem.
Are you taking care of it or do you need help?
it's under control.
Make sure.
DAMN, BUDDY, WHERE'D YOUR SHIRT GO? THAT WAS FAST...

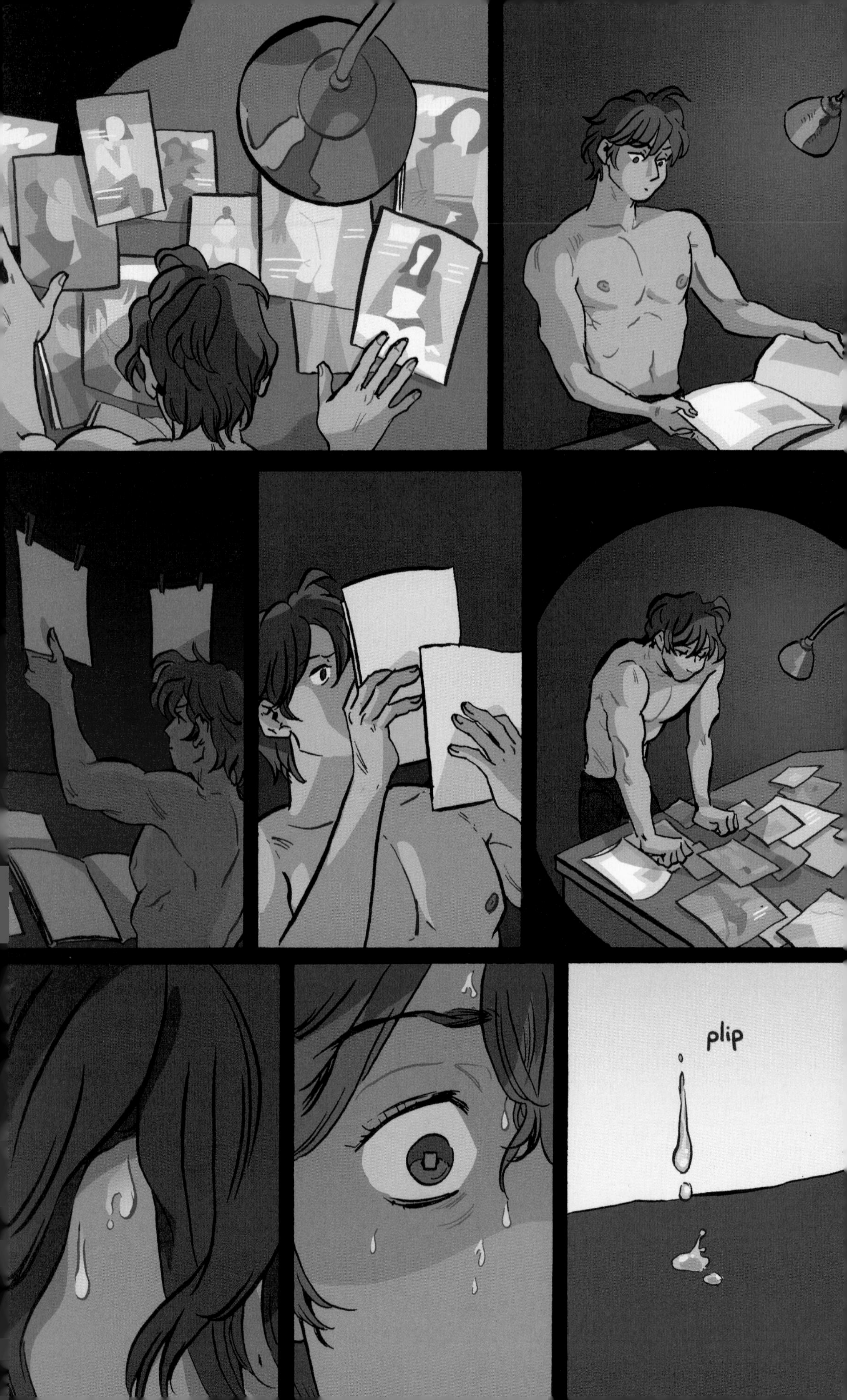
plip

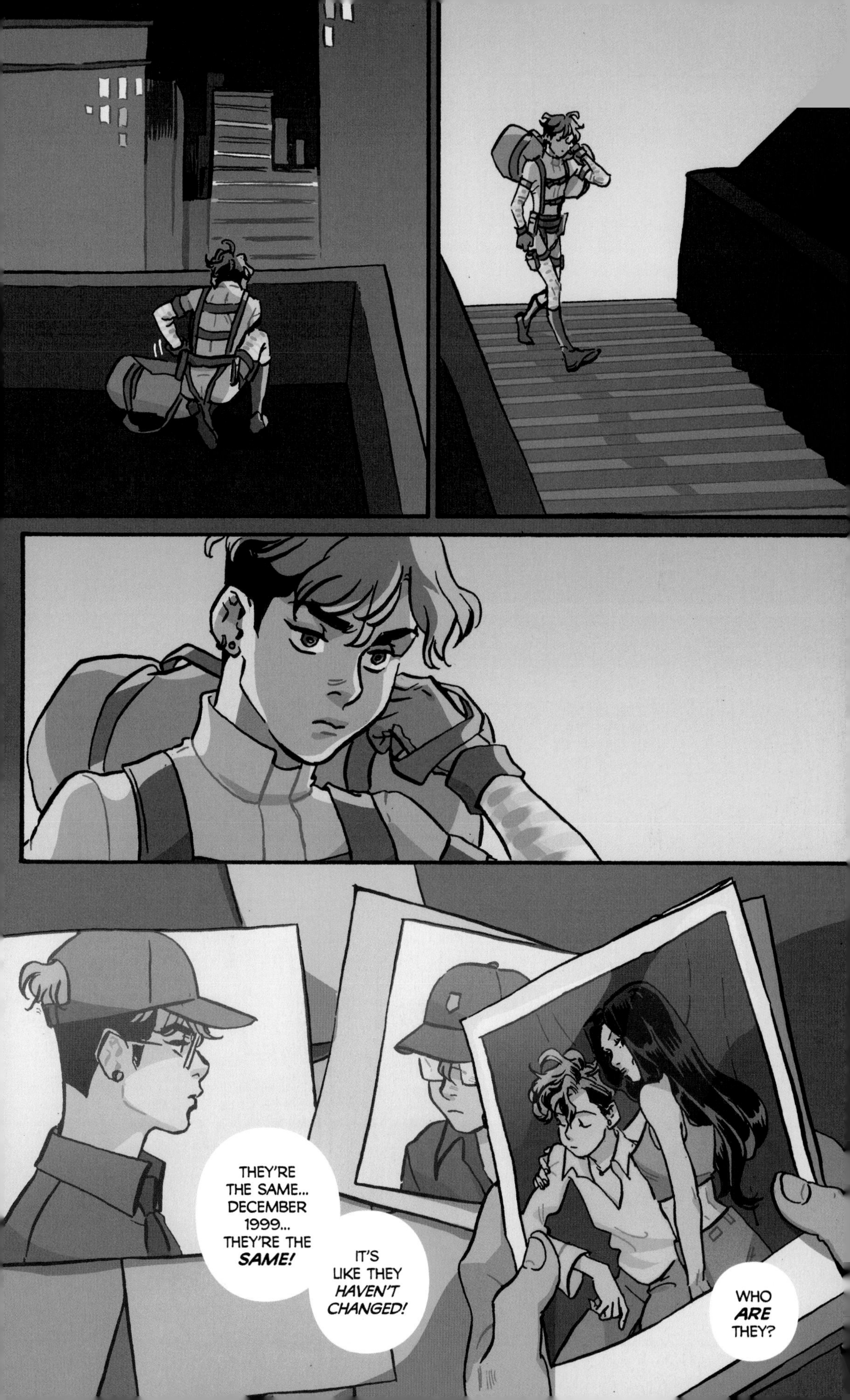
THEY'RE THE SAME... DECEMBER 1999... THEY'RE THE *SAME!*
IT'S LIKE THEY *HAVEN'T CHANGED!*
WHO *ARE* THEY?

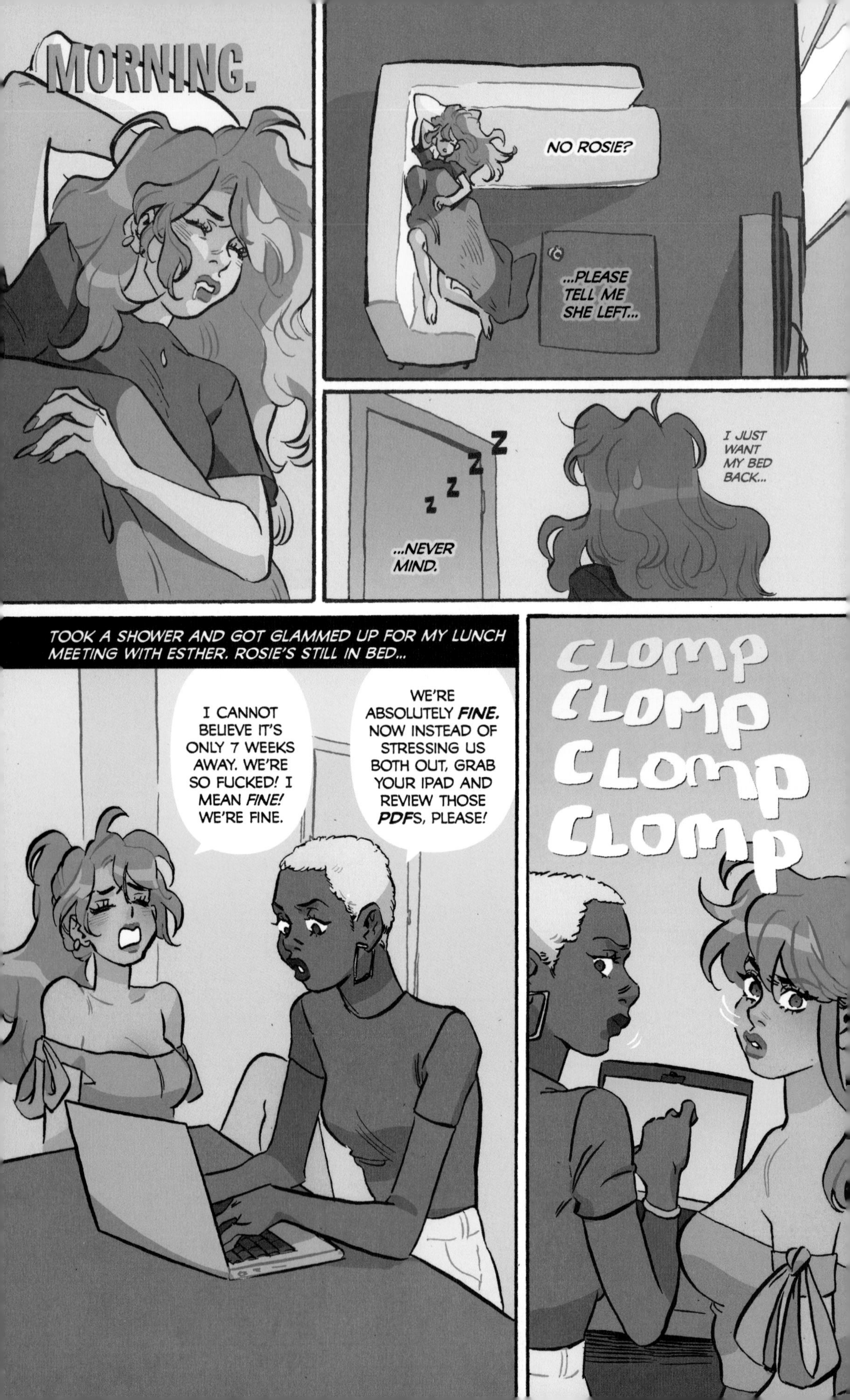
MORNING.
NO ROSIE?
...PLEASE TELL ME SHE LEFT...
Z Z Z Z
...NEVER MIND.
I JUST WANT MY BED BACK...
TOOK A SHOWER AND GOT GLAMMED UP FOR MY LUNCH MEETING WITH ESTHER. ROSIE'S STILL IN BED...
I CANNOT BELIEVE IT'S ONLY 7 WEEKS AWAY. WE'RE SO FUCKED! I MEAN FINE! WE'RE FINE.
WE'RE ABSOLUTELY FINE. NOW INSTEAD OF STRESSING US BOTH OUT, GRAB YOUR IPAD AND REVIEW THOSE PDFS, PLEASE!
CLOMP CLOMP CLOMP CLOMP

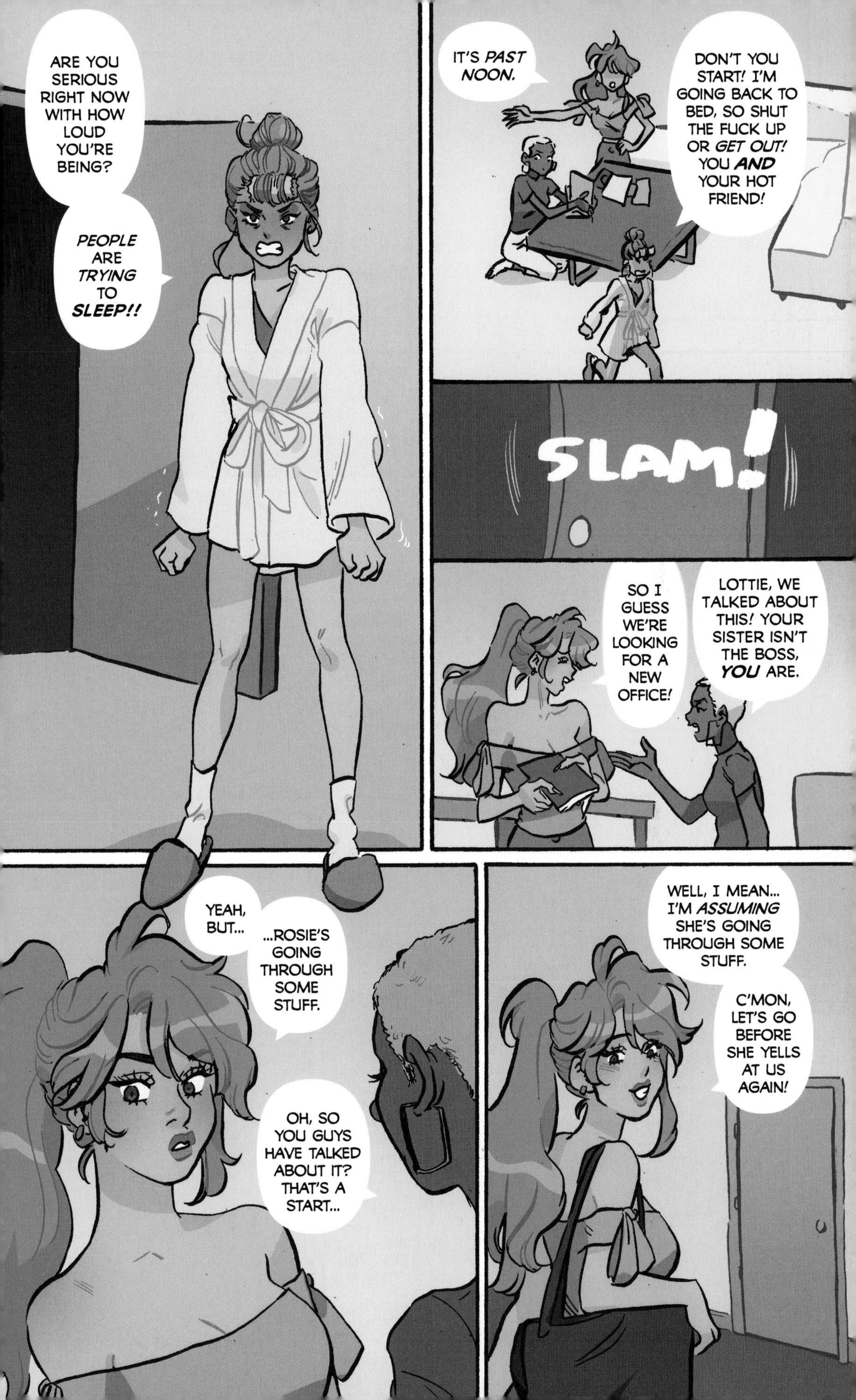
ARE YOU SERIOUS RIGHT NOW WITH HOW LOUD YOU'RE BEING?
PEOPLE ARE *TRYING* TO ***SLEEP!!***
IT'S *PAST NOON.*
DON'T YOU START! I'M GOING BACK TO BED, SO SHUT THE FUCK UP OR *GET OUT!* YOU ***AND*** YOUR HOT FRIEND!
SLAM!
SO I GUESS WE'RE LOOKING FOR A NEW OFFICE!
LOTTIE, WE TALKED ABOUT THIS! YOUR SISTER ISN'T THE BOSS, ***YOU*** ARE.
YEAH, BUT...
...ROSIE'S GOING THROUGH SOME STUFF.
OH, SO YOU GUYS HAVE TALKED ABOUT IT? THAT'S A START...
WELL, I MEAN... I'M *ASSUMING* SHE'S GOING THROUGH SOME STUFF.
C'MON, LET'S GO BEFORE SHE YELLS AT US AGAIN!

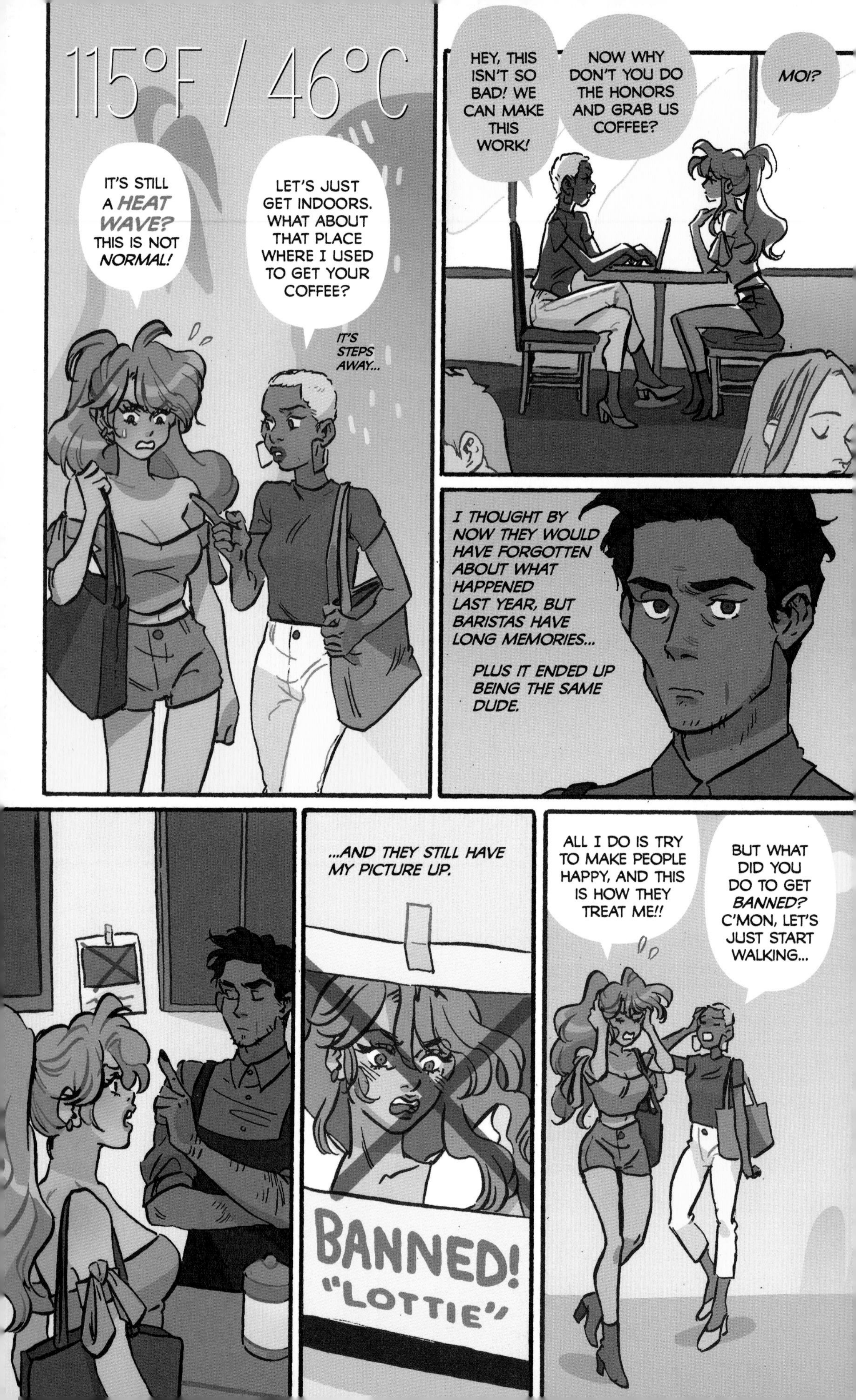
115°F / 46°C
IT'S STILL A HEAT WAVE? THIS IS NOT NORMAL!
LET'S JUST GET INDOORS. WHAT ABOUT THAT PLACE WHERE I USED TO GET YOUR COFFEE?
IT'S STEPS AWAY...
HEY, THIS ISN'T SO BAD! WE CAN MAKE THIS WORK!
NOW WHY DON'T YOU DO THE HONORS AND GRAB US COFFEE?
MOI?
I THOUGHT BY NOW THEY WOULD HAVE FORGOTTEN ABOUT WHAT HAPPENED LAST YEAR, BUT BARISTAS HAVE LONG MEMORIES...
PLUS IT ENDED UP BEING THE SAME DUDE.
...AND THEY STILL HAVE MY PICTURE UP.
BANNED!
"LOTTIE"
ALL I DO IS TRY TO MAKE PEOPLE HAPPY, AND THIS IS HOW THEY TREAT ME!!
BUT WHAT DID YOU DO TO GET BANNED? C'MON, LET'S JUST START WALKING...

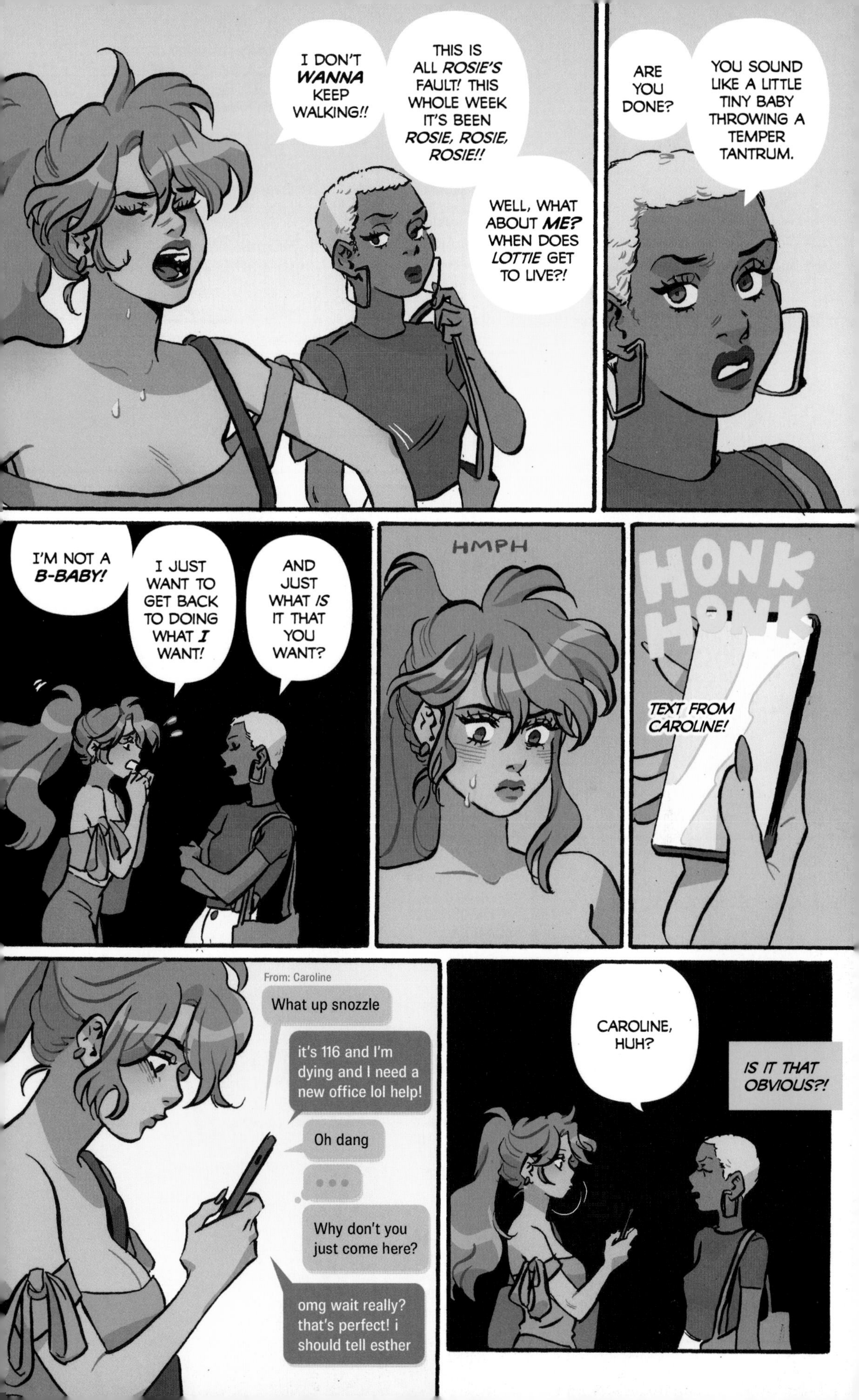

I DON'T *WANNA* KEEP WALKING!!
THIS IS ALL *ROSIE'S* FAULT! THIS WHOLE WEEK IT'S BEEN *ROSIE, ROSIE, ROSIE!!*
WELL, WHAT ABOUT *ME?* WHEN DOES *LOTTIE* GET TO LIVE?!
ARE YOU DONE?
YOU SOUND LIKE A LITTLE TINY BABY THROWING A TEMPER TANTRUM.
I'M NOT A *B-BABY!*
I JUST WANT TO GET BACK TO DOING WHAT *I* WANT!
AND JUST WHAT *IS* IT THAT YOU WANT?
HMPH
HONK HONK
TEXT FROM CAROLINE!
From: Caroline
What up snozzle
it's 116 and I'm dying and I need a new office lol help!
Oh dang
Why don't you just come here?
omg wait really? that's perfect! i should tell esther
CAROLINE, HUH?
IS IT THAT OBVIOUS?!

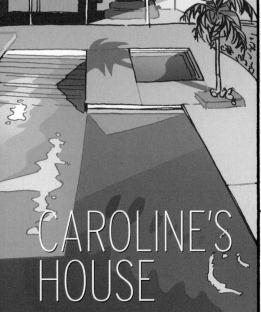

CAROLINE'S
HOUSE

THIS ISN'T SO BAD, RIGHT? WE CAN MAKE THIS WORK, RIGHT?

ARE YOU KIDDING? THIS HOUSE IS *COOL!*

I FEEL LIKE I'M IN AN IN-FLIGHT MAGAZINE.

I STILL CAN'T BELIEVE MY SISTER KICKED US OUT. WHY IS SHE *LIKE* THIS?

LOTTIE, YOU *LET* HER DO IT. YOU HAVE TO START ASSERTING YOURSELF WITH HER!

BUT... SHE'S MY *BIG SISTER.*

YOU MAY BE THE BABY OF THE FAMILY, BUT SOMETIMES YOU GOTTA TAKE RESPONSIBILITY FOR YOUR ELDERS.

YOU AREN'T KIDS ANYMORE. YOU'RE BOTH *GROWN WOMEN* AND SHE'S BEING A *DUMBASS B*TCH!*

YOU *HAVE* TO STAND UP TO HER.

SHE'S RIGHT, BABE.

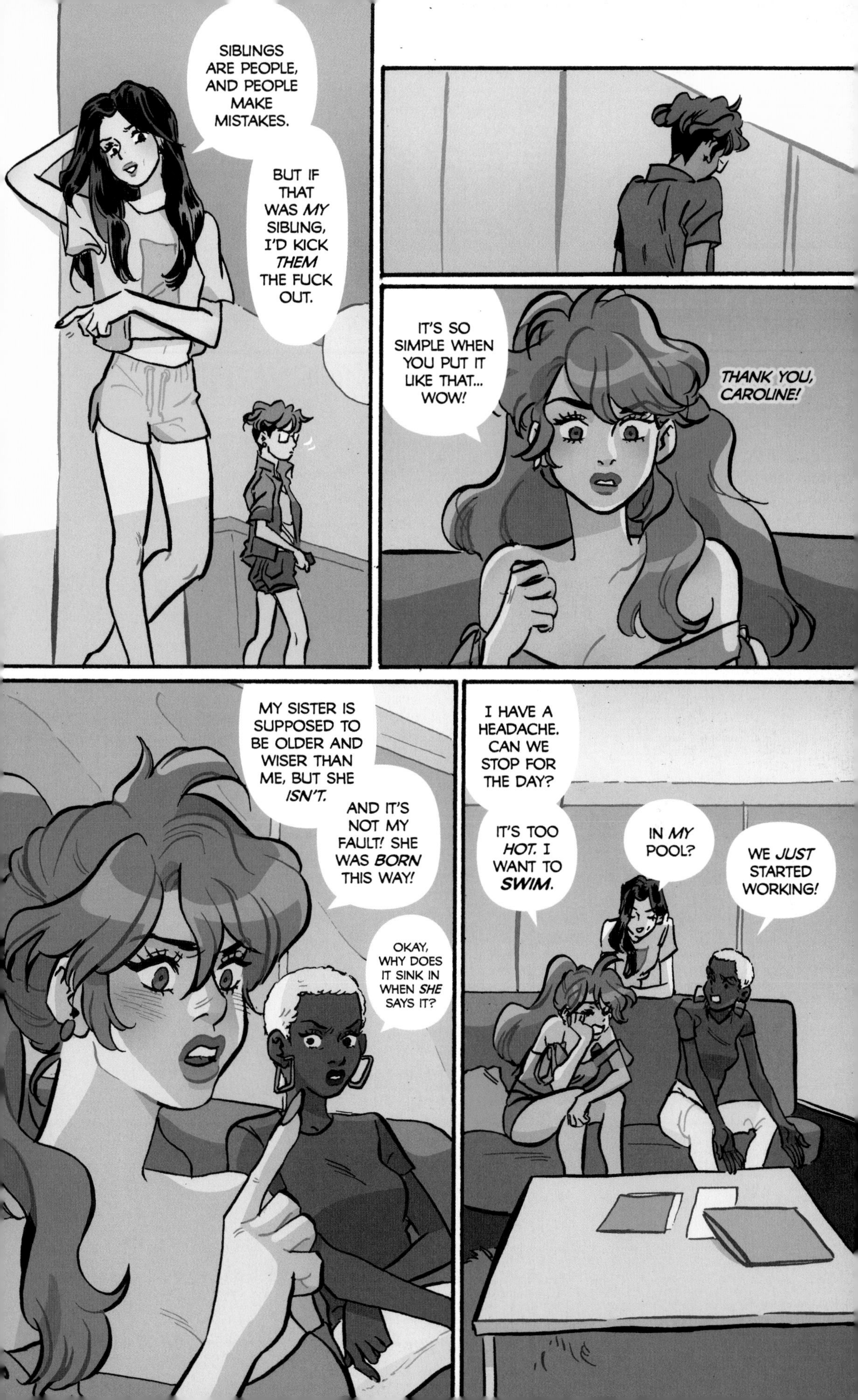
SIBLINGS ARE PEOPLE, AND PEOPLE MAKE MISTAKES.
BUT IF THAT WAS *MY* SIBLING, I'D KICK *THEM* THE FUCK OUT.
IT'S SO SIMPLE WHEN YOU PUT IT LIKE THAT... WOW!
THANK YOU, CAROLINE!
MY SISTER IS SUPPOSED TO BE OLDER AND WISER THAN ME, BUT SHE *ISN'T.*
AND IT'S NOT MY FAULT! SHE WAS *BORN* THIS WAY!
OKAY, WHY DOES IT SINK IN WHEN *SHE* SAYS IT?
I HAVE A HEADACHE. CAN WE STOP FOR THE DAY?
IT'S TOO *HOT.* I WANT TO ***SWIM***.
IN *MY* POOL?
WE *JUST* STARTED WORKING!

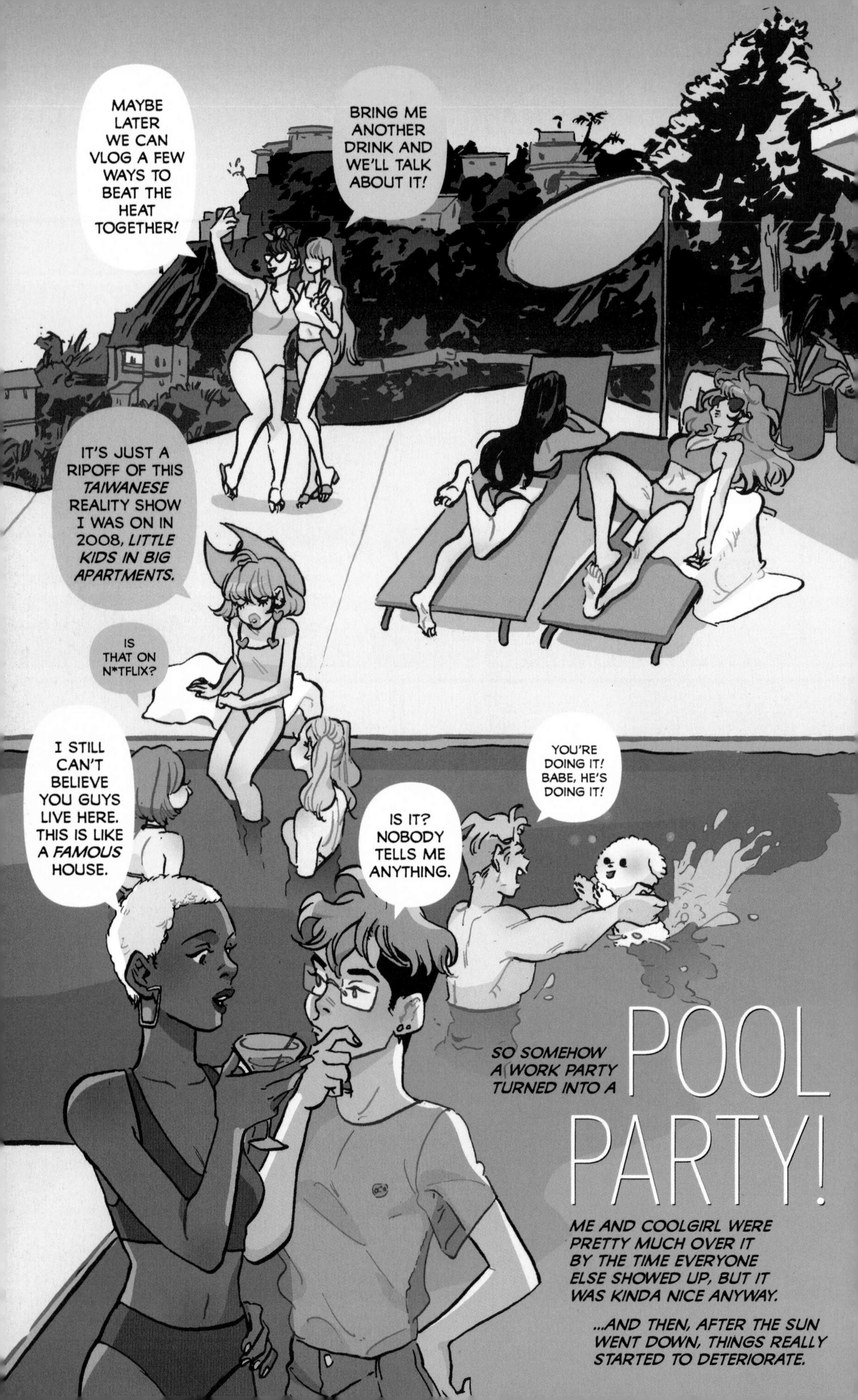
MAYBE LATER WE CAN VLOG A FEW WAYS TO BEAT THE HEAT TOGETHER!
BRING ME ANOTHER DRINK AND WE'LL TALK ABOUT IT!
IT'S JUST A RIPOFF OF THIS *TAIWANESE* REALITY SHOW I WAS ON IN 2008, *LITTLE KIDS IN BIG APARTMENTS.*
IS THAT ON N*TFLIX?
I STILL CAN'T BELIEVE YOU GUYS LIVE HERE. THIS IS LIKE A *FAMOUS* HOUSE.
IS IT? NOBODY TELLS ME ANYTHING.
YOU'RE DOING IT! BABE, HE'S DOING IT!
SO SOMEHOW A WORK PARTY TURNED INTO A POOL PARTY!
ME AND COOLGIRL WERE PRETTY MUCH OVER IT BY THE TIME EVERYONE ELSE SHOWED UP, BUT IT WAS KINDA NICE ANYWAY.
...AND THEN, AFTER THE SUN WENT DOWN, THINGS REALLY STARTED TO DETERIORATE.

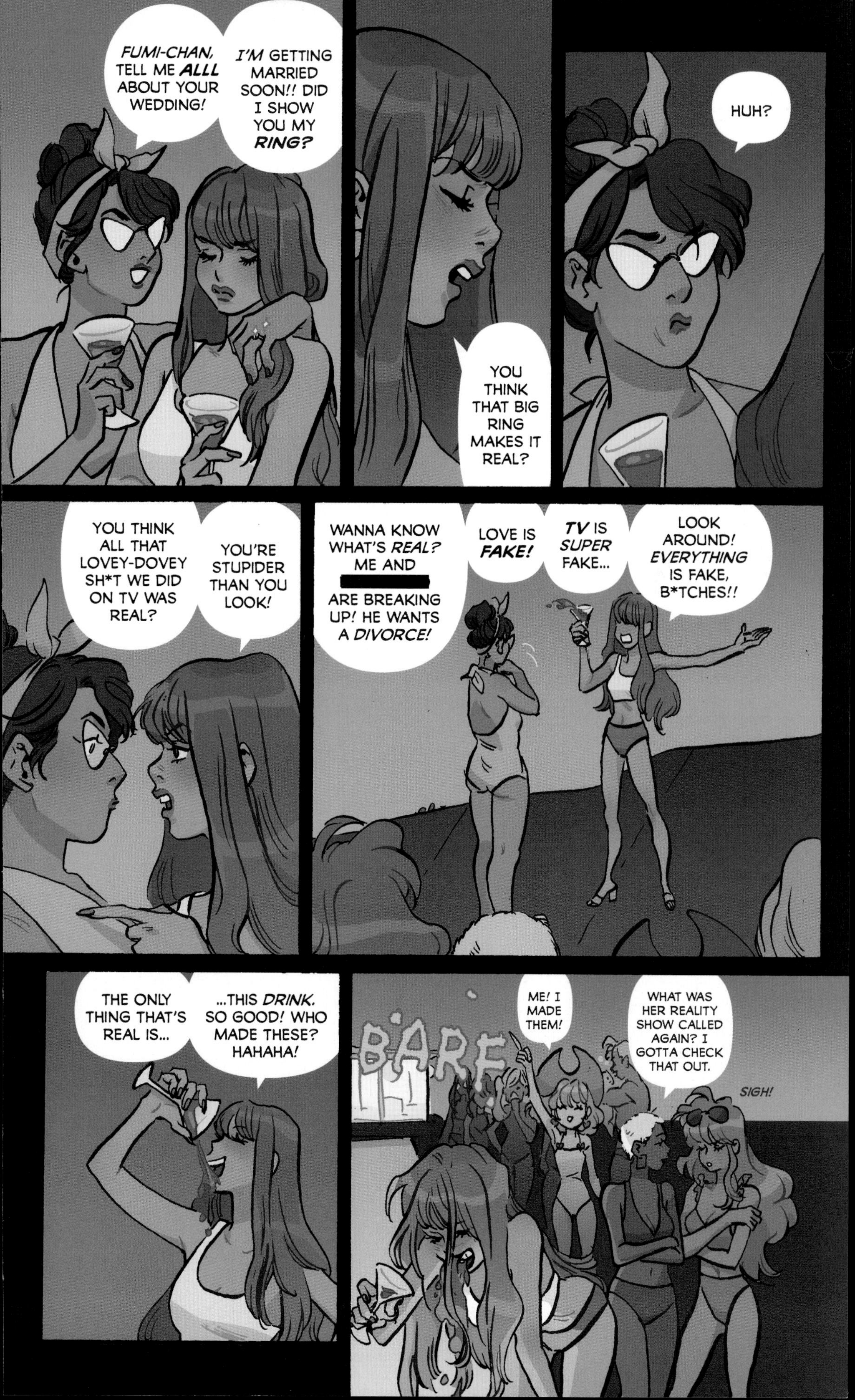
FUMI-CHAN, TELL ME ALLL ABOUT YOUR WEDDING!
I'M GETTING MARRIED SOON!! DID I SHOW YOU MY RING?
YOU THINK THAT BIG RING MAKES IT REAL?
HUH?
YOU THINK ALL THAT LOVEY-DOVEY SH*T WE DID ON TV WAS REAL?
YOU'RE STUPIDER THAN YOU LOOK!
WANNA KNOW WHAT'S REAL? ME AND [redacted] ARE BREAKING UP! HE WANTS A DIVORCE!
LOVE IS FAKE!
TV IS SUPER FAKE...
LOOK AROUND! EVERYTHING IS FAKE, B*TCHES!!
THE ONLY THING THAT'S REAL IS...
...THIS DRINK. SO GOOD! WHO MADE THESE? HAHAHA!
BARE
ME! I MADE THEM!
WHAT WAS HER REALITY SHOW CALLED AGAIN? I GOTTA CHECK THAT OUT.
SIGH!

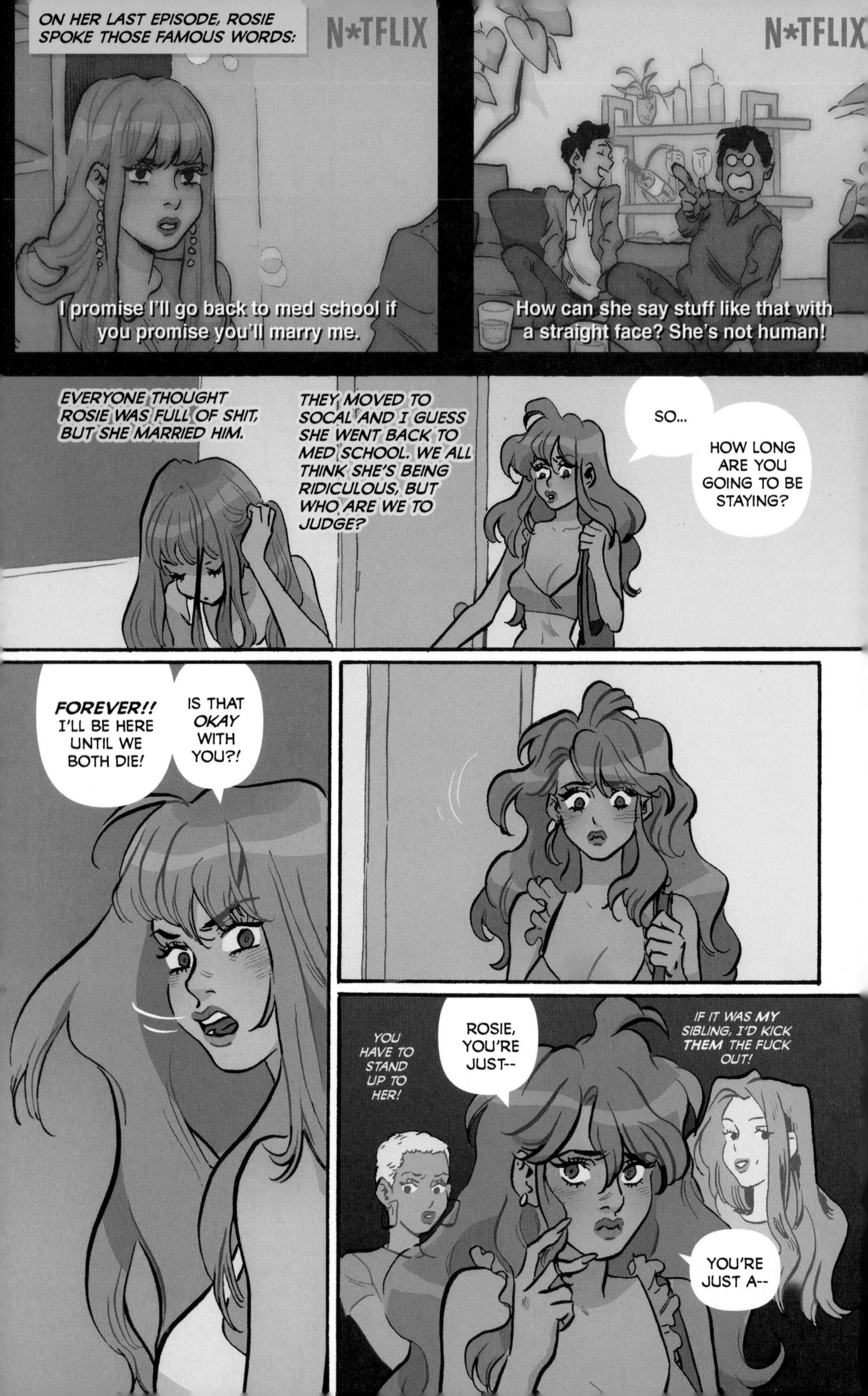
ON HER LAST EPISODE, ROSIE SPOKE THOSE FAMOUS WORDS:
N*TFLIX
I promise I'll go back to med school if you promise you'll marry me.
N*TFLIX
How can she say stuff like that with a straight face? She's not human!
EVERYONE THOUGHT ROSIE WAS FULL OF SHIT, BUT SHE MARRIED HIM.
THEY MOVED TO SOCAL AND I GUESS SHE WENT BACK TO MED SCHOOL. WE ALL THINK SHE'S BEING RIDICULOUS, BUT WHO ARE WE TO JUDGE?
SO...
HOW LONG ARE YOU GOING TO BE STAYING?
FOREVER!! I'LL BE HERE UNTIL WE BOTH DIE!
IS THAT OKAY WITH YOU?!
YOU HAVE TO STAND UP TO HER!
ROSIE, YOU'RE JUST--
IF IT WAS MY SIBLING, I'D KICK THEM THE FUCK OUT!
YOU'RE JUST A--

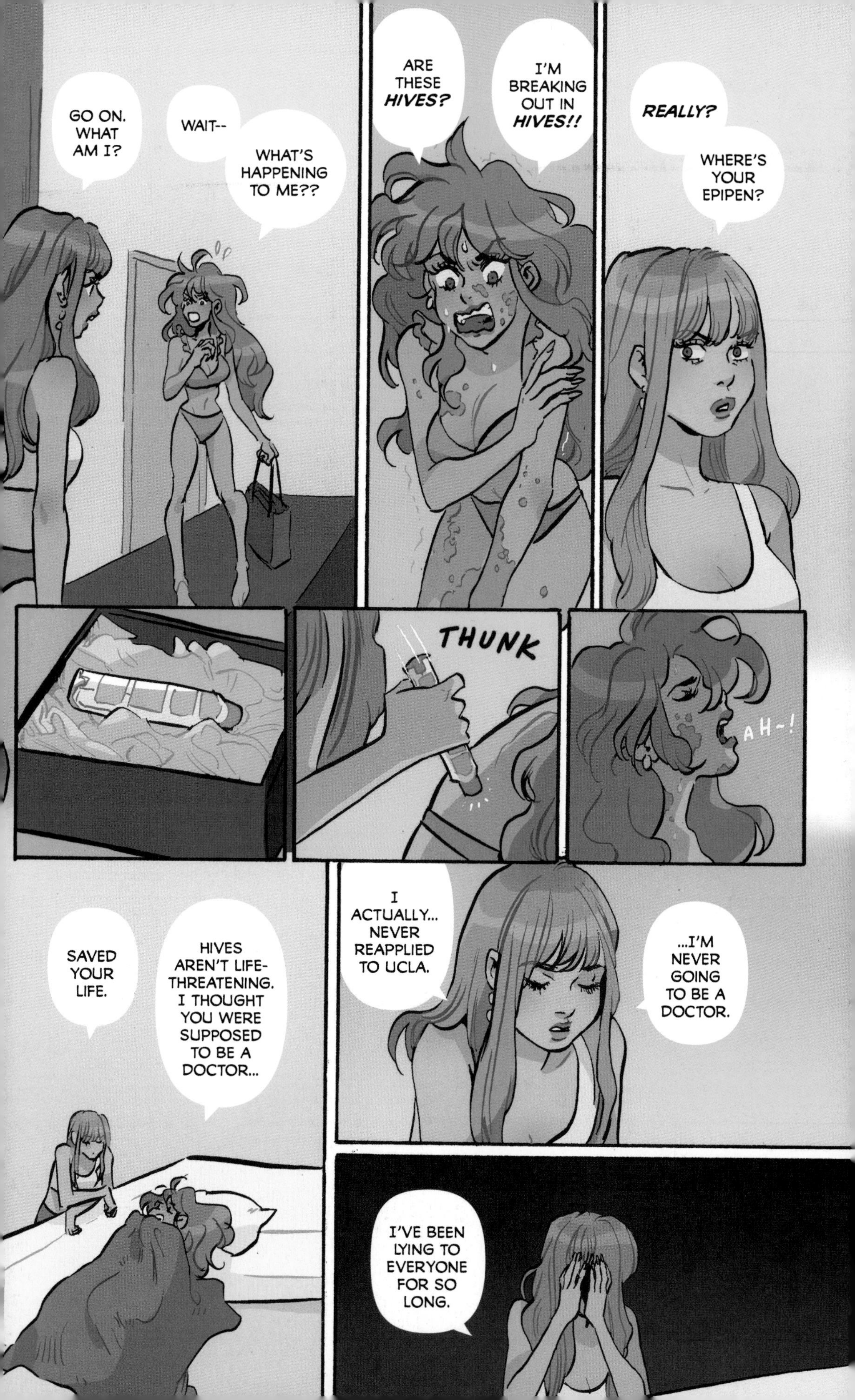
GO ON. WHAT AM I?
WAIT--
WHAT'S HAPPENING TO ME??
ARE THESE *HIVES?*
I'M BREAKING OUT IN *HIVES!!*
REALLY?
WHERE'S YOUR EPIPEN?
THUNK
AH-!
SAVED YOUR LIFE.
HIVES AREN'T LIFE-THREATENING. I THOUGHT YOU WERE SUPPOSED TO BE A DOCTOR...
I ACTUALLY... NEVER REAPPLIED TO UCLA.
...I'M NEVER GOING TO BE A DOCTOR.
I'VE BEEN LYING TO EVERYONE FOR SO LONG.

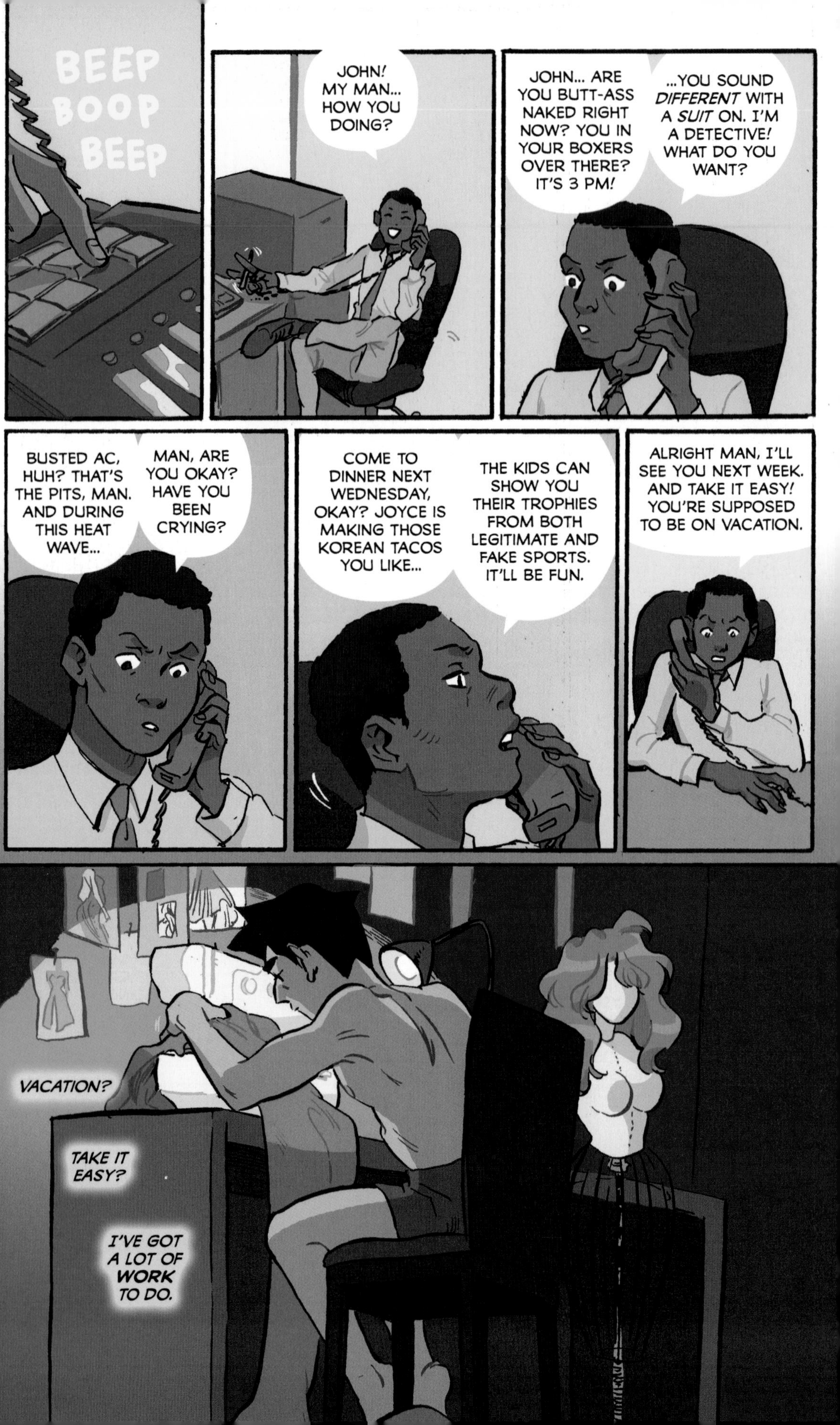
BEEP
BOOP
BEEP
JOHN! MY MAN... HOW YOU DOING?
JOHN... ARE YOU BUTT-ASS NAKED RIGHT NOW? YOU IN YOUR BOXERS OVER THERE? IT'S 3 PM!
...YOU SOUND *DIFFERENT* WITH A *SUIT* ON. I'M A DETECTIVE! WHAT DO YOU WANT?
BUSTED AC, HUH? THAT'S THE PITS, MAN. AND DURING THIS HEAT WAVE...
MAN, ARE YOU OKAY? HAVE YOU BEEN CRYING?
COME TO DINNER NEXT WEDNESDAY, OKAY? JOYCE IS MAKING THOSE KOREAN TACOS YOU LIKE...
THE KIDS CAN SHOW YOU THEIR TROPHIES FROM BOTH LEGITIMATE AND FAKE SPORTS. IT'LL BE FUN.
ALRIGHT MAN, I'LL SEE YOU NEXT WEEK. AND TAKE IT EASY! YOU'RE SUPPOSED TO BE ON VACATION.
VACATION?
TAKE IT EASY?
I'VE GOT A LOT OF ***WORK*** *TO DO.*

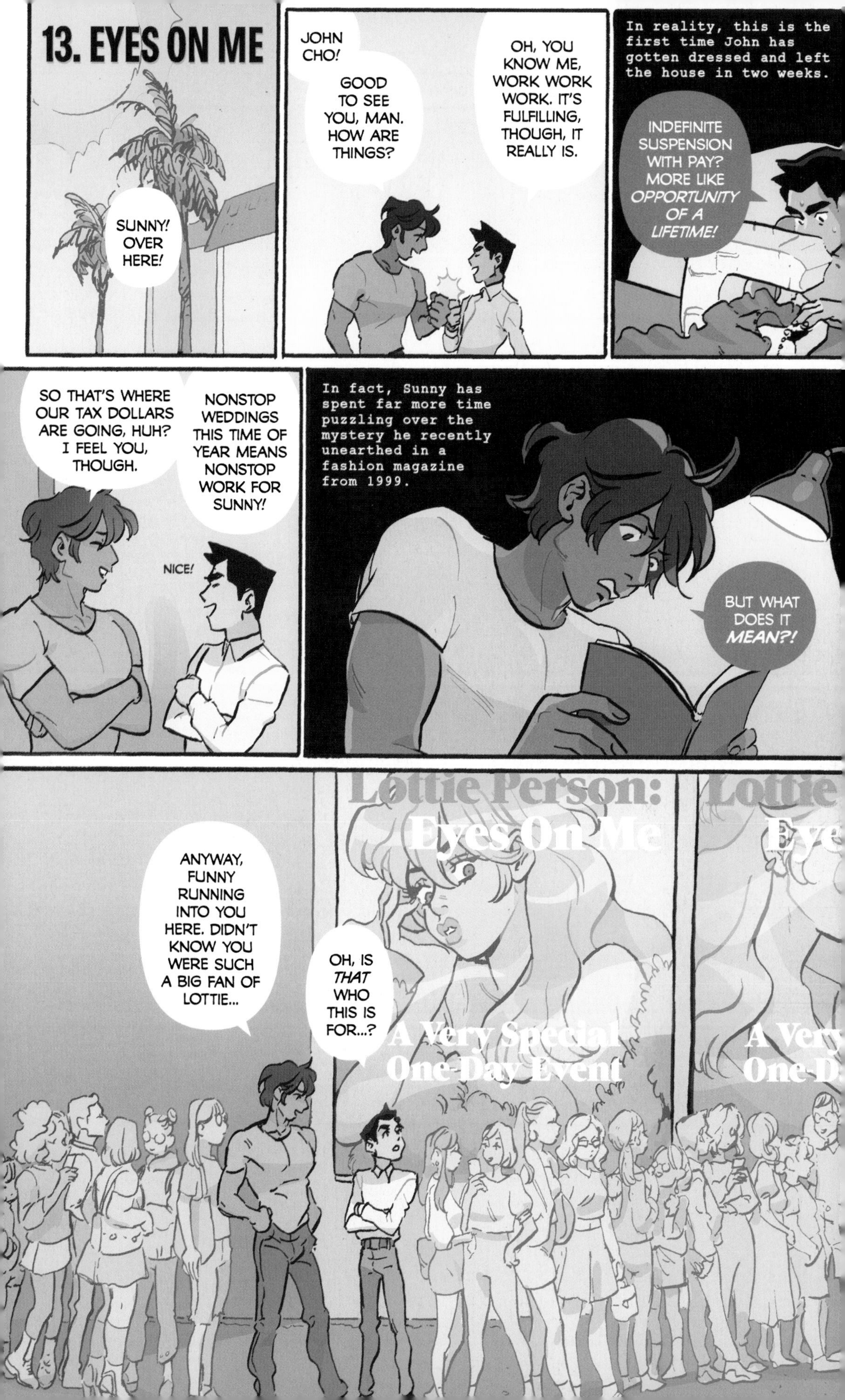

13. EYES ON ME
SUNNY! OVER HERE!
JOHN CHO!
GOOD TO SEE YOU, MAN. HOW ARE THINGS?
OH, YOU KNOW ME, WORK WORK WORK. IT'S FULFILLING, THOUGH, IT REALLY IS.
In reality, this is the first time John has gotten dressed and left the house in two weeks.
INDEFINITE SUSPENSION WITH PAY? MORE LIKE *OPPORTUNITY OF A LIFETIME!*
SO THAT'S WHERE OUR TAX DOLLARS ARE GOING, HUH? I FEEL YOU, THOUGH.
NONSTOP WEDDINGS THIS TIME OF YEAR MEANS NONSTOP WORK FOR SUNNY!
NICE!
In fact, Sunny has spent far more time puzzling over the mystery he recently unearthed in a fashion magazine from 1999.
BUT WHAT DOES IT *MEAN?!*
Lottie Person:
Eyes On Me
A Very Special
One-Day Event
ANYWAY, FUNNY RUNNING INTO YOU HERE. DIDN'T KNOW YOU WERE SUCH A BIG FAN OF LOTTIE...
OH, IS *THAT* WHO THIS IS FOR...?

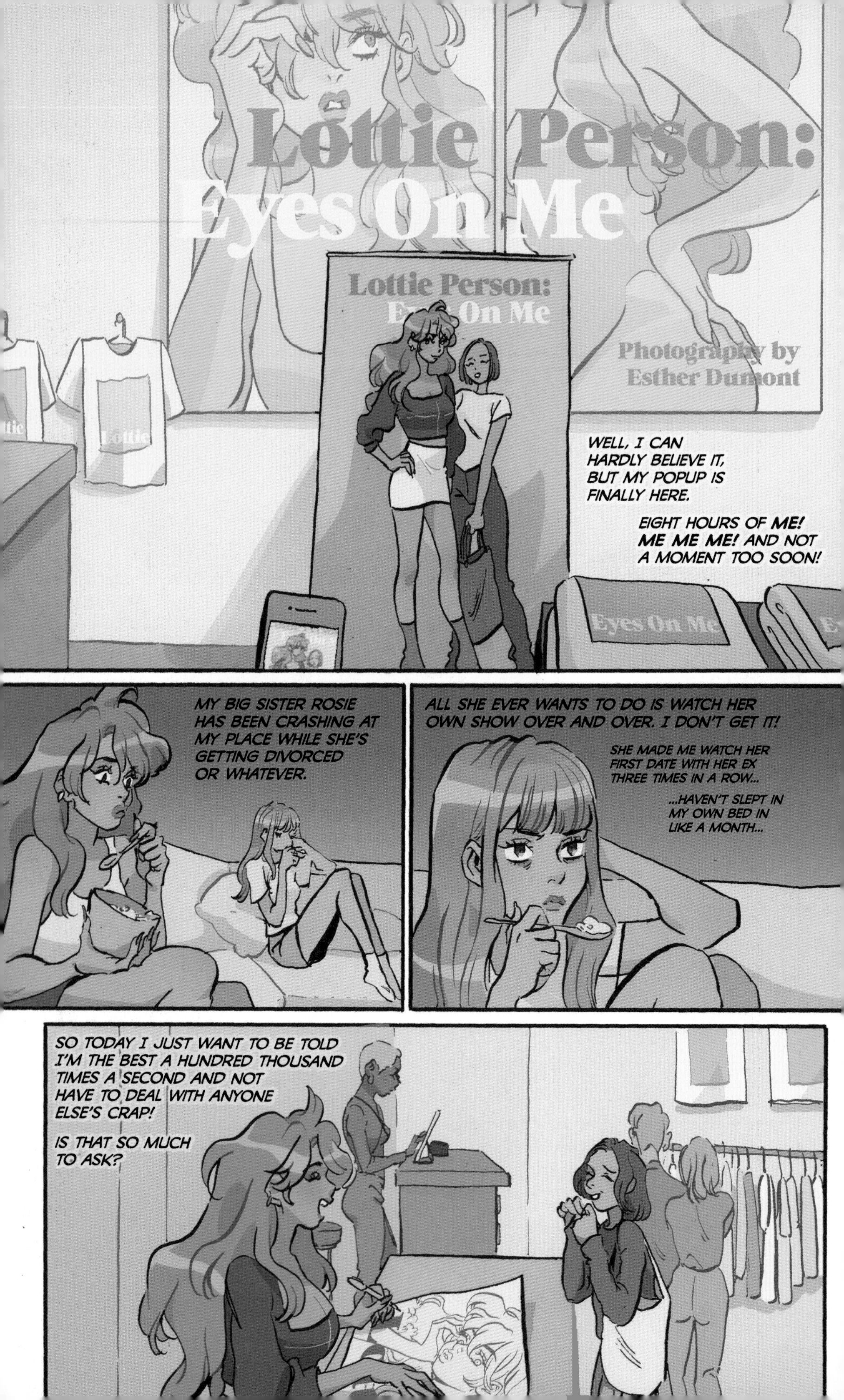
Lottie Person:
Eyes On Me
Lottie Person:
Eyes On Me
Photography by
Esther Dumont
Lottie
Lottie
Eyes On Me
WELL, I CAN HARDLY BELIEVE IT, BUT MY POPUP IS FINALLY HERE.
EIGHT HOURS OF ME! ME ME ME! AND NOT A MOMENT TOO SOON!
MY BIG SISTER ROSIE HAS BEEN CRASHING AT MY PLACE WHILE SHE'S GETTING DIVORCED OR WHATEVER.
ALL SHE EVER WANTS TO DO IS WATCH HER OWN SHOW OVER AND OVER. I DON'T GET IT!
SHE MADE ME WATCH HER FIRST DATE WITH HER EX THREE TIMES IN A ROW...
...HAVEN'T SLEPT IN MY OWN BED IN LIKE A MONTH...
SO TODAY I JUST WANT TO BE TOLD I'M THE BEST A HUNDRED THOUSAND TIMES A SECOND AND NOT HAVE TO DEAL WITH ANYONE ELSE'S CRAP!
IS THAT SO MUCH TO ASK?

Phone Time

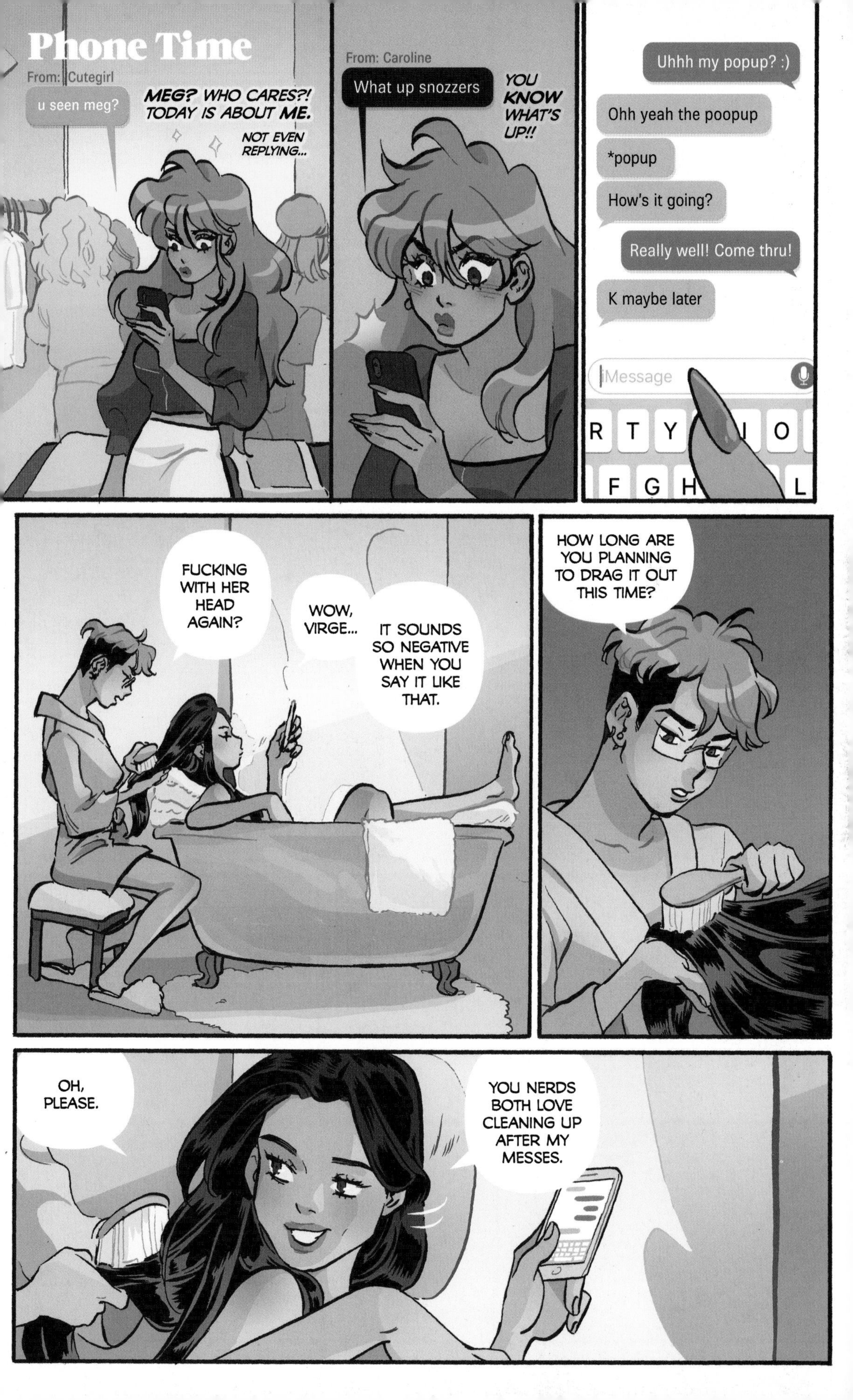

From: Cutegirl
u seen meg?
MEG? WHO CARES?! TODAY IS ABOUT ME.
NOT EVEN REPLYING...
From: Caroline
What up snozzers
YOU KNOW WHAT'S UP!!
Uhhh my popup? :)
Ohh yeah the poopup
*popup
How's it going?
Really well! Come thru!
K maybe later
iMessage
R T Y I O
F G H L
FUCKING WITH HER HEAD AGAIN?
WOW, VIRGE...
IT SOUNDS SO NEGATIVE WHEN YOU SAY IT LIKE THAT.
HOW LONG ARE YOU PLANNING TO DRAG IT OUT THIS TIME?
OH, PLEASE.
YOU NERDS BOTH LOVE CLEANING UP AFTER MY MESSES.

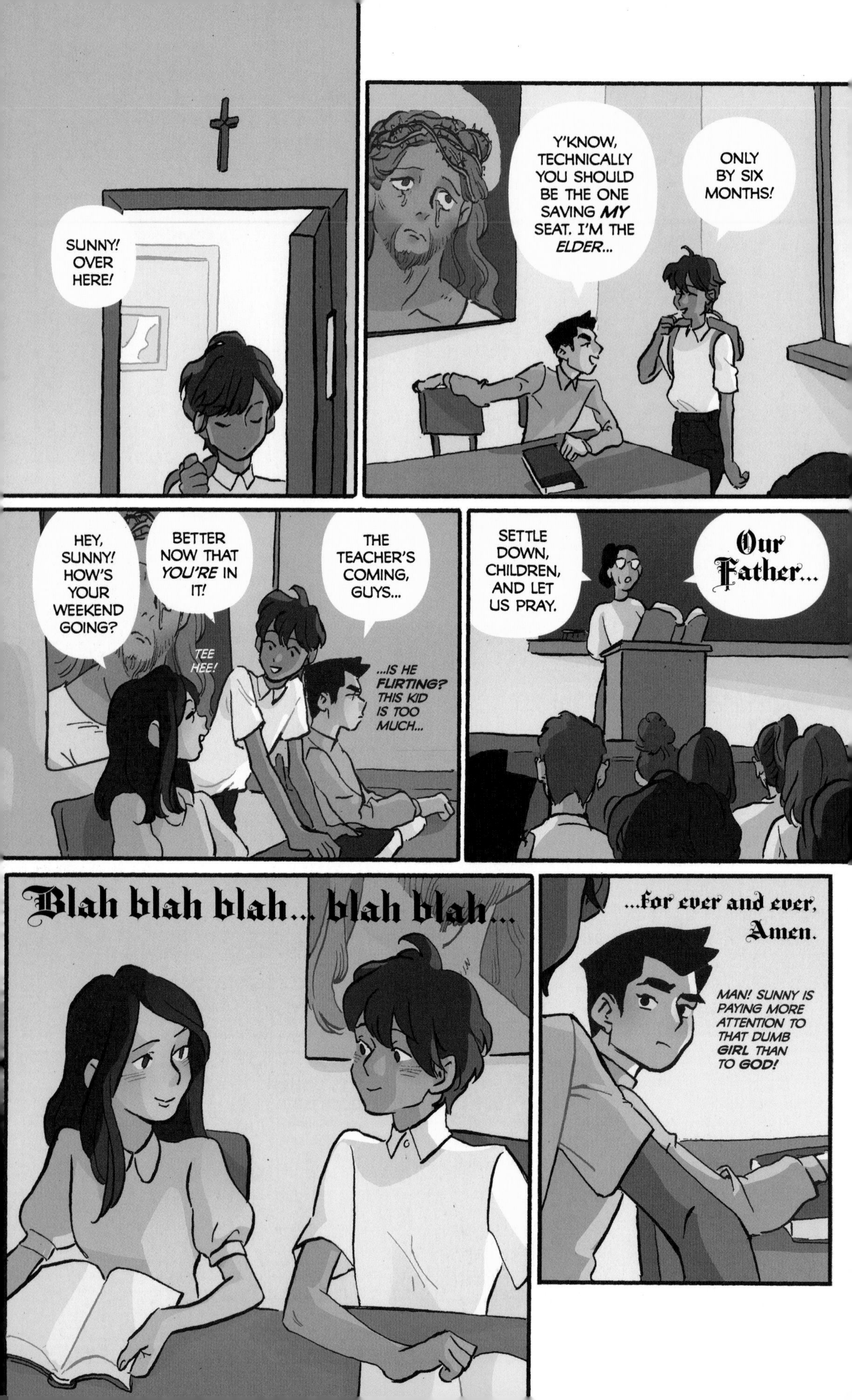
SUNNY! OVER HERE!
Y'KNOW, TECHNICALLY YOU SHOULD BE THE ONE SAVING *MY* SEAT. I'M THE *ELDER*...
ONLY BY SIX MONTHS!
HEY, SUNNY! HOW'S YOUR WEEKEND GOING?
BETTER NOW THAT *YOU'RE* IN IT!
TEE HEE!
THE TEACHER'S COMING, GUYS...
...IS HE *FLIRTING?* THIS KID IS TOO MUCH...
SETTLE DOWN, CHILDREN, AND LET US PRAY.
Our Father...
Blah blah blah... blah blah...
...for ever and ever, Amen.
MAN! SUNNY IS PAYING MORE ATTENTION TO THAT DUMB *GIRL* THAN TO *GOD!*

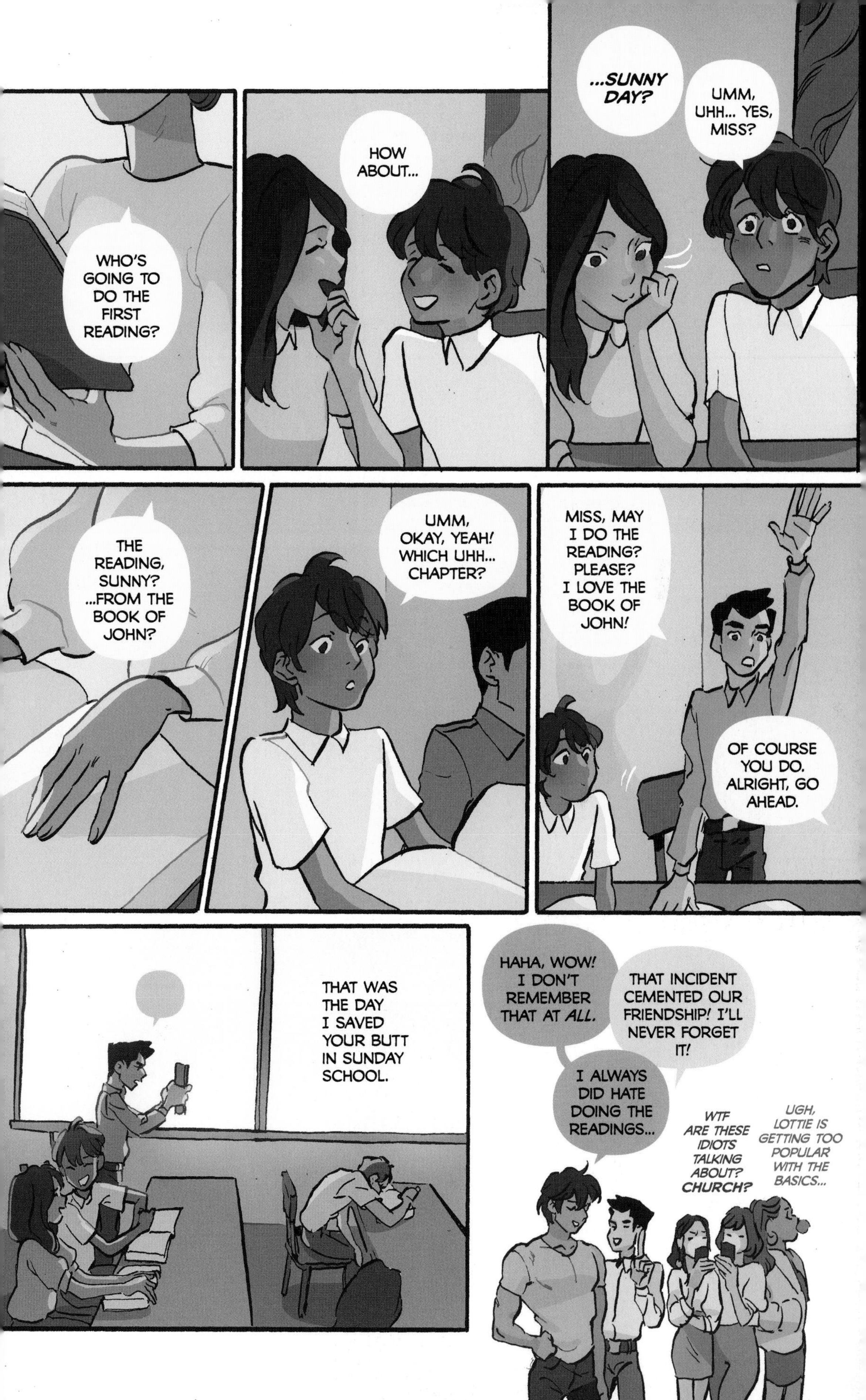
WHO'S GOING TO DO THE FIRST READING?
HOW ABOUT...
...SUNNY DAY?
UMM, UHH... YES, MISS?
THE READING, SUNNY? ...FROM THE BOOK OF JOHN?
UMM, OKAY, YEAH! WHICH UHH... CHAPTER?
MISS, MAY I DO THE READING? PLEASE? I LOVE THE BOOK OF JOHN!
OF COURSE YOU DO. ALRIGHT, GO AHEAD.
THAT WAS THE DAY I SAVED YOUR BUTT IN SUNDAY SCHOOL.
HAHA, WOW! I DON'T REMEMBER THAT AT ALL.
THAT INCIDENT CEMENTED OUR FRIENDSHIP! I'LL NEVER FORGET IT!
I ALWAYS DID HATE DOING THE READINGS...
WTF ARE THESE IDIOTS TALKING ABOUT? CHURCH?
UGH, LOTTIE IS GETTING TOO POPULAR WITH THE BASICS...

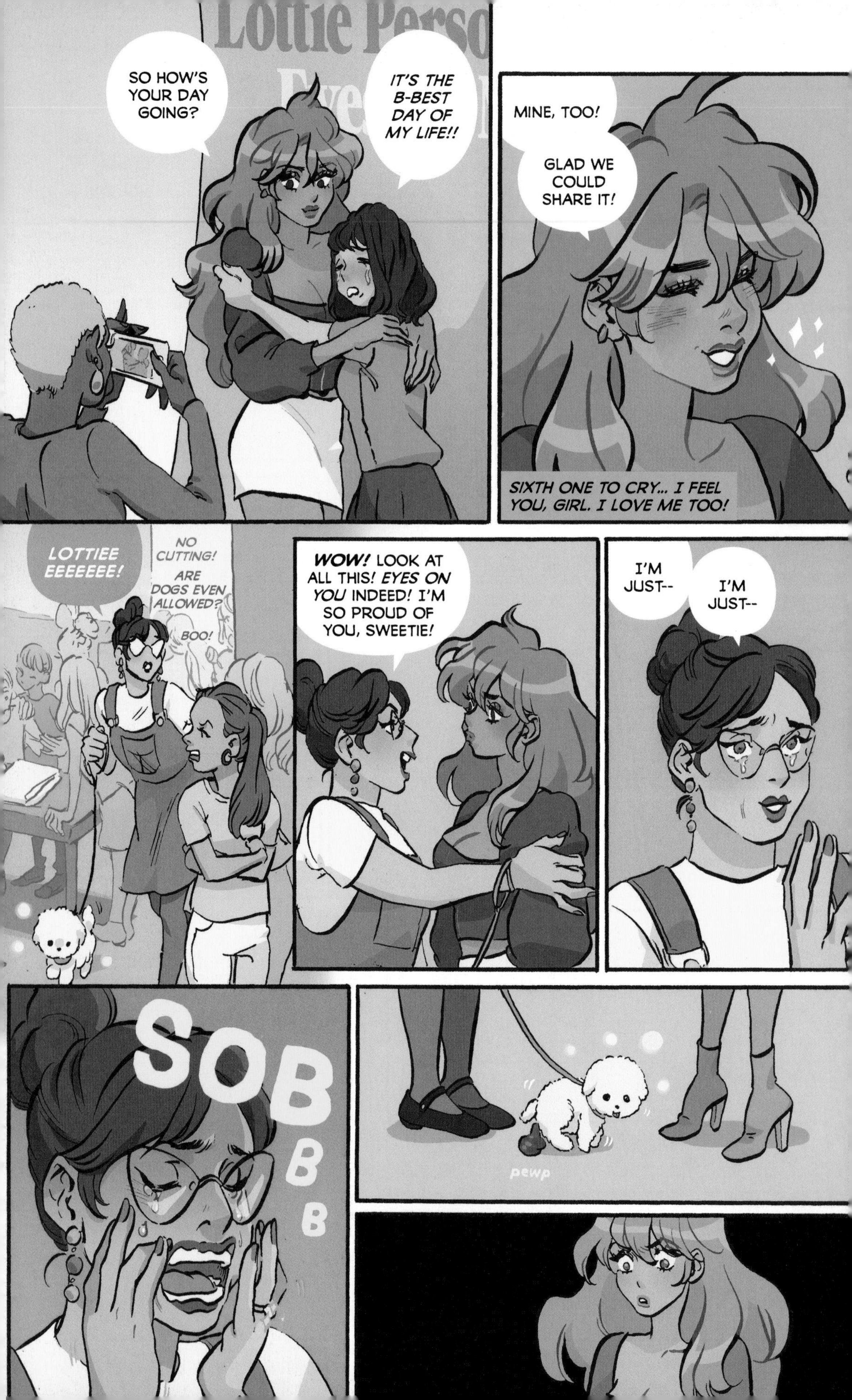

Lottie Perso
SO HOW'S YOUR DAY GOING?
IT'S THE B-BEST DAY OF MY LIFE!!
MINE, TOO!
GLAD WE COULD SHARE IT!
SIXTH ONE TO CRY... I FEEL YOU, GIRL. I LOVE ME TOO!
LOTTIEE EEEEEEE!
NO CUTTING!
ARE DOGS EVEN ALLOWED?
BOO!
WOW! LOOK AT ALL THIS! EYES ON YOU INDEED! I'M SO PROUD OF YOU, SWEETIE!
I'M JUST--
I'M JUST--
SOBBB
pewp

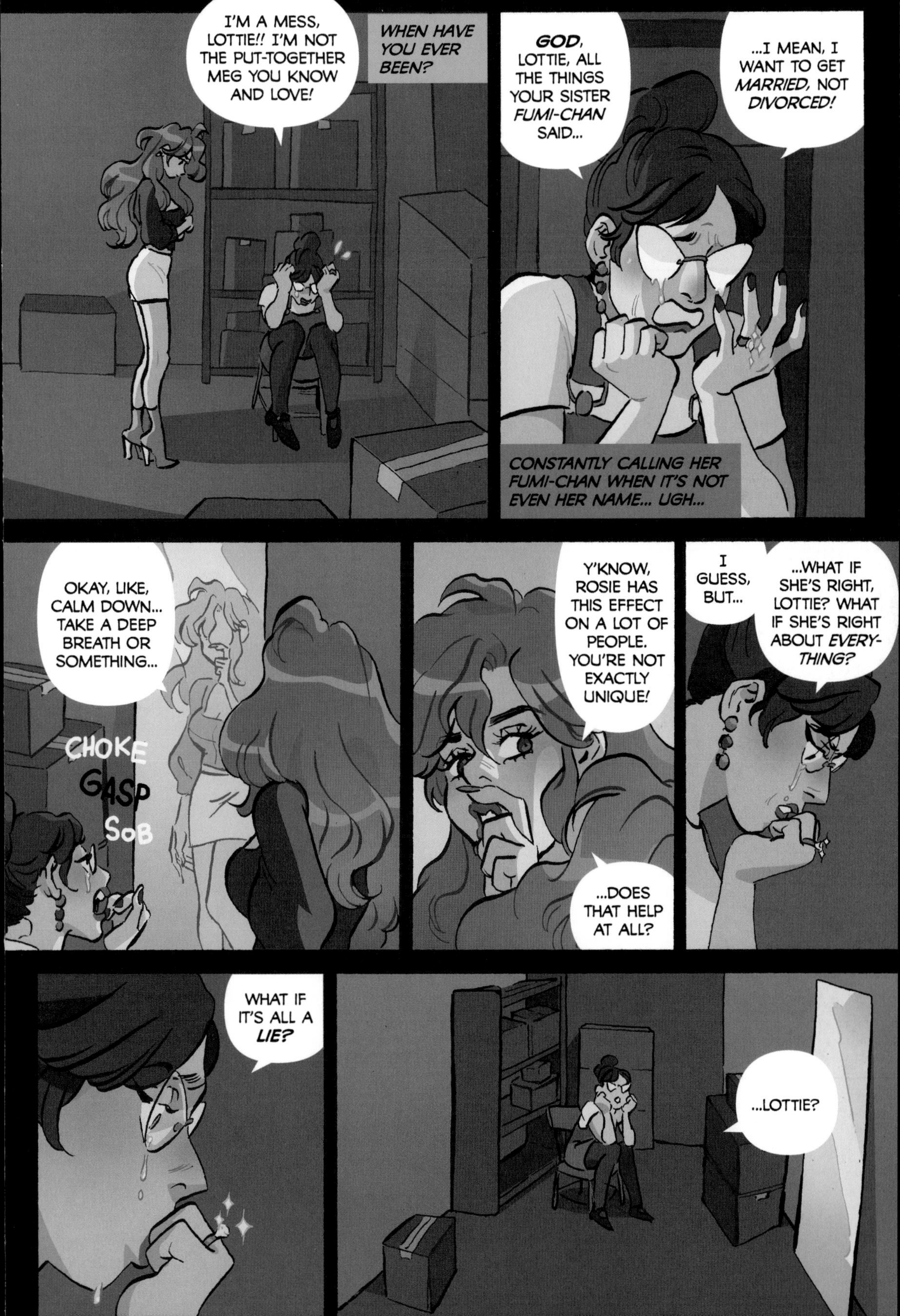
I'M A MESS, LOTTIE!! I'M NOT THE PUT-TOGETHER MEG YOU KNOW AND LOVE!
WHEN HAVE YOU EVER BEEN?
GOD, LOTTIE, ALL THE THINGS YOUR SISTER FUMI-CHAN SAID...
...I MEAN, I WANT TO GET MARRIED, NOT DIVORCED!
CONSTANTLY CALLING HER FUMI-CHAN WHEN IT'S NOT EVEN HER NAME... UGH...
OKAY, LIKE, CALM DOWN... TAKE A DEEP BREATH OR SOMETHING...
CHOKE
GASP
SOB
Y'KNOW, ROSIE HAS THIS EFFECT ON A LOT OF PEOPLE. YOU'RE NOT EXACTLY UNIQUE!
...DOES THAT HELP AT ALL?
I GUESS, BUT...
...WHAT IF SHE'S RIGHT, LOTTIE? WHAT IF SHE'S RIGHT ABOUT EVERYTHING?
WHAT IF IT'S ALL A LIE?
...LOTTIE?

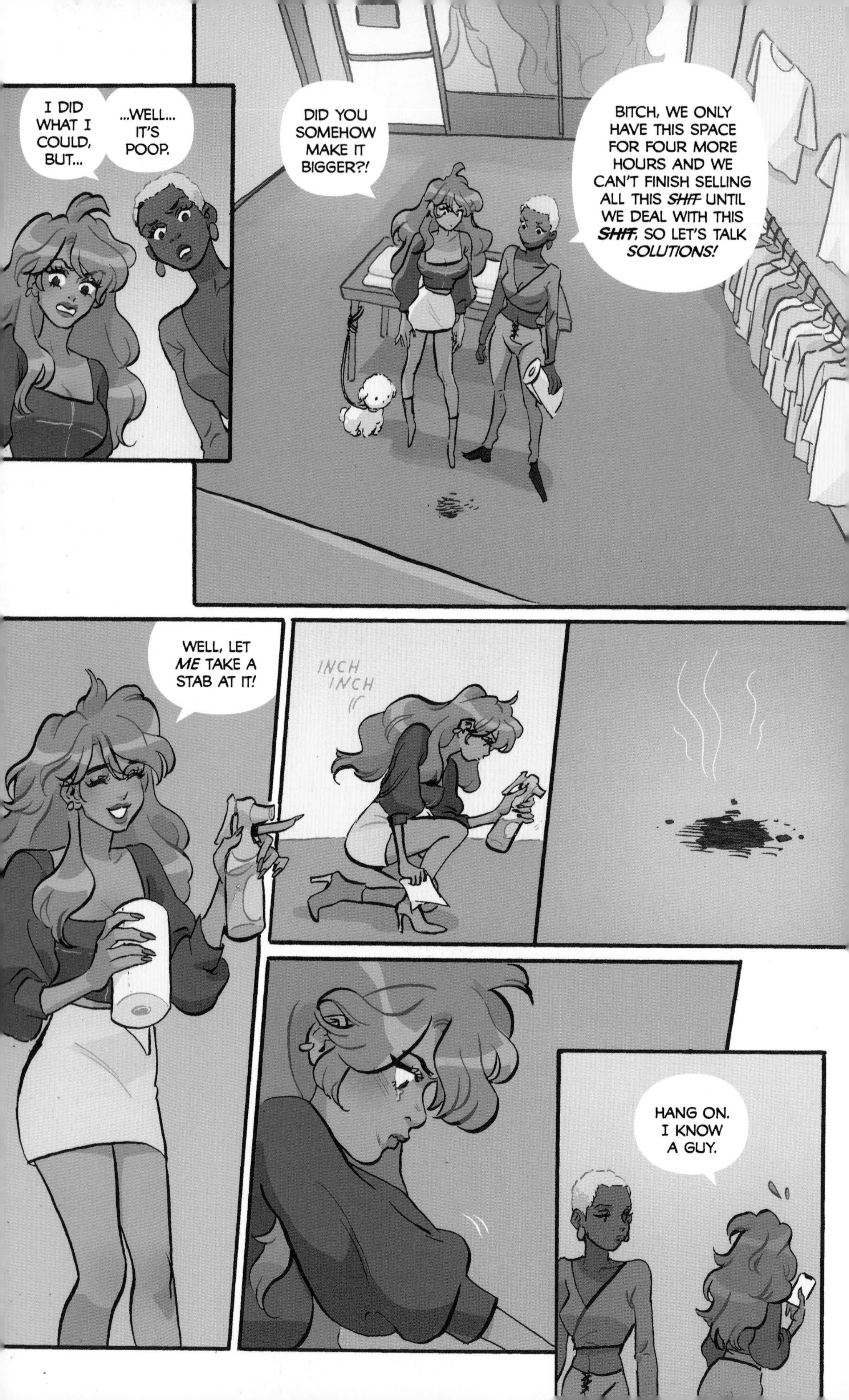
I DID WHAT I COULD, BUT...
...WELL... IT'S POOP.
DID YOU SOMEHOW MAKE IT BIGGER?!
BITCH, WE ONLY HAVE THIS SPACE FOR FOUR MORE HOURS AND WE CAN'T FINISH SELLING ALL THIS *SHIT* UNTIL WE DEAL WITH THIS ***SHIT***, SO LET'S TALK *SOLUTIONS!*
WELL, LET *ME* TAKE A STAB AT IT!
INCH INCH
HANG ON. I KNOW A GUY.

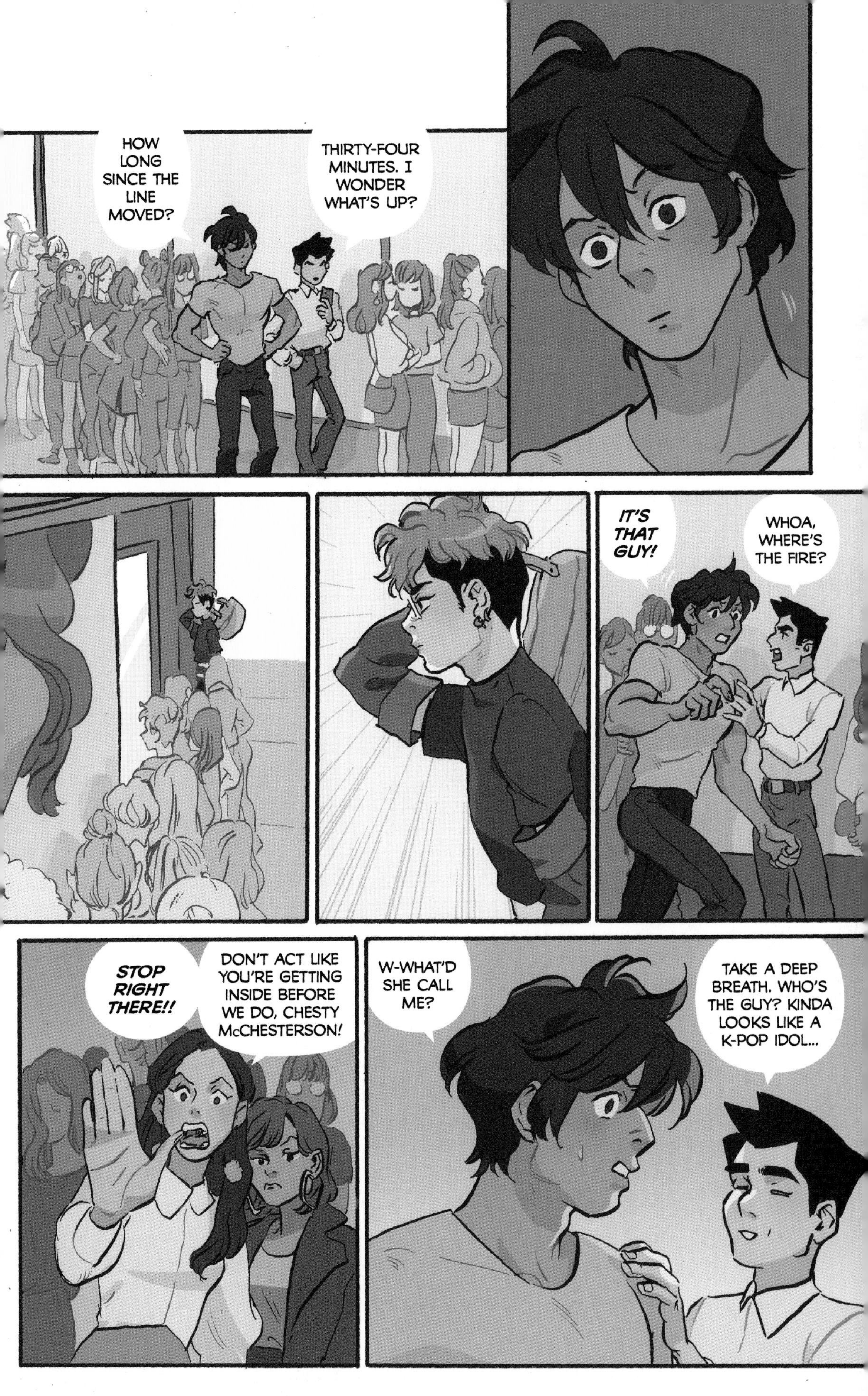
HOW LONG SINCE THE LINE MOVED?
THIRTY-FOUR MINUTES. I WONDER WHAT'S UP?
IT'S THAT GUY!
WHOA, WHERE'S THE FIRE?
STOP RIGHT THERE!!
DON'T ACT LIKE YOU'RE GETTING INSIDE BEFORE WE DO, CHESTY McCHESTERSON!
W-WHAT'D SHE CALL ME?
TAKE A DEEP BREATH. WHO'S THE GUY? KINDA LOOKS LIKE A K-POP IDOL...

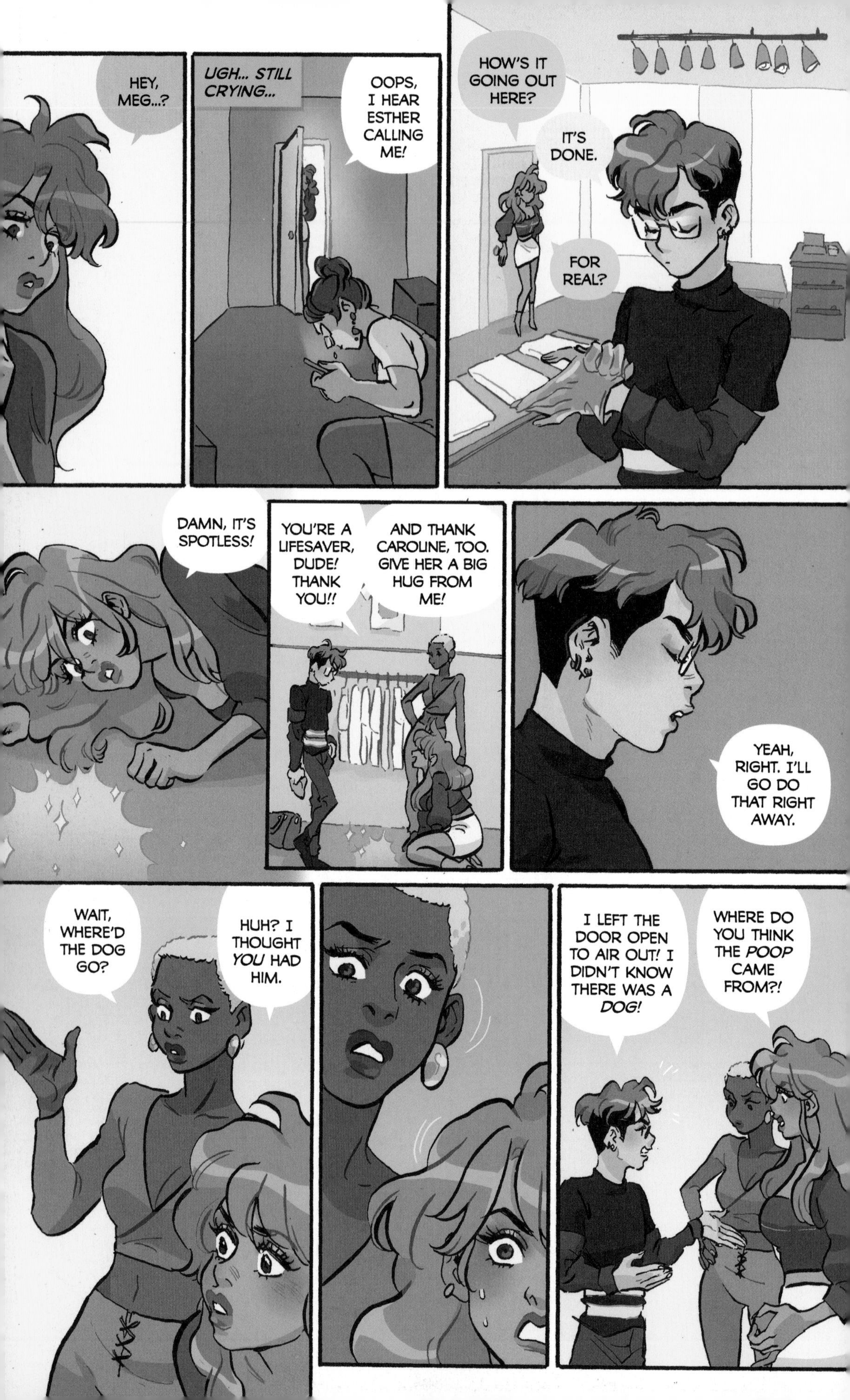
HEY, MEG...?
UGH... STILL CRYING...
OOPS, I HEAR ESTHER CALLING ME!
HOW'S IT GOING OUT HERE?
IT'S DONE.
FOR REAL?
DAMN, IT'S SPOTLESS!
YOU'RE A LIFESAVER, DUDE! THANK YOU!!
AND THANK CAROLINE, TOO. GIVE HER A BIG HUG FROM ME!
YEAH, RIGHT. I'LL GO DO THAT RIGHT AWAY.
WAIT, WHERE'D THE DOG GO?
HUH? I THOUGHT YOU HAD HIM.
I LEFT THE DOOR OPEN TO AIR OUT! I DIDN'T KNOW THERE WAS A DOG!
WHERE DO YOU THINK THE POOP CAME FROM?!

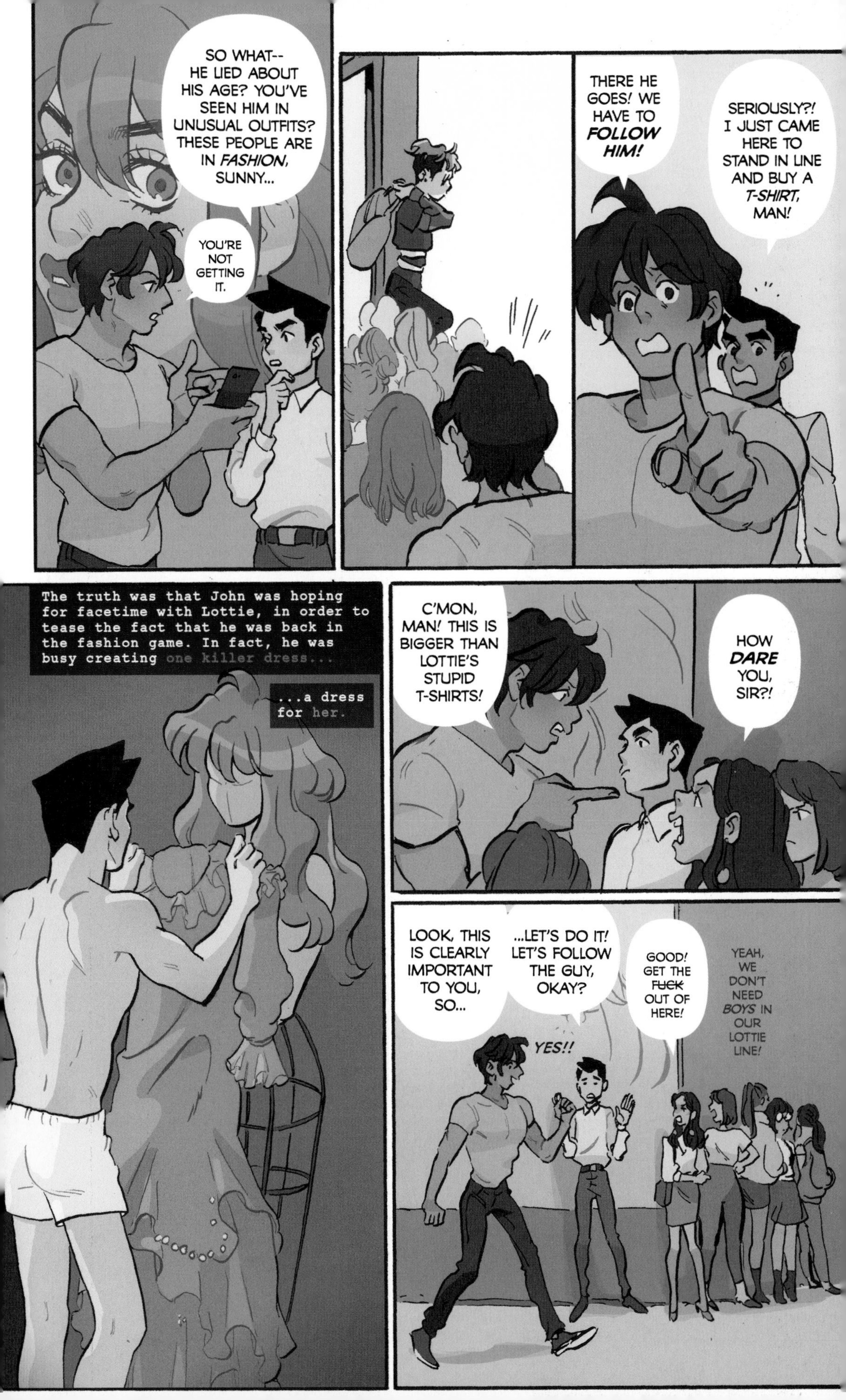
SO WHAT-- HE LIED ABOUT HIS AGE? YOU'VE SEEN HIM IN UNUSUAL OUTFITS? THESE PEOPLE ARE IN *FASHION*, SUNNY...
YOU'RE NOT GETTING IT.
THERE HE GOES! WE HAVE TO ***FOLLOW HIM!***
SERIOUSLY?! I JUST CAME HERE TO STAND IN LINE AND BUY A *T-SHIRT*, MAN!
The truth was that John was hoping for facetime with Lottie, in order to tease the fact that he was back in the fashion game. In fact, he was busy creating one killer dress...
...a dress for her.
C'MON, MAN! THIS IS BIGGER THAN LOTTIE'S STUPID T-SHIRTS!
HOW ***DARE*** YOU, SIR?!
LOOK, THIS IS CLEARLY IMPORTANT TO YOU, SO...
...LET'S DO IT! LET'S FOLLOW THE GUY, OKAY?
YES!!
GOOD! GET THE ~~FUCK~~ OUT OF HERE!
YEAH, WE DON'T NEED *BOYS* IN OUR LOTTIE LINE!

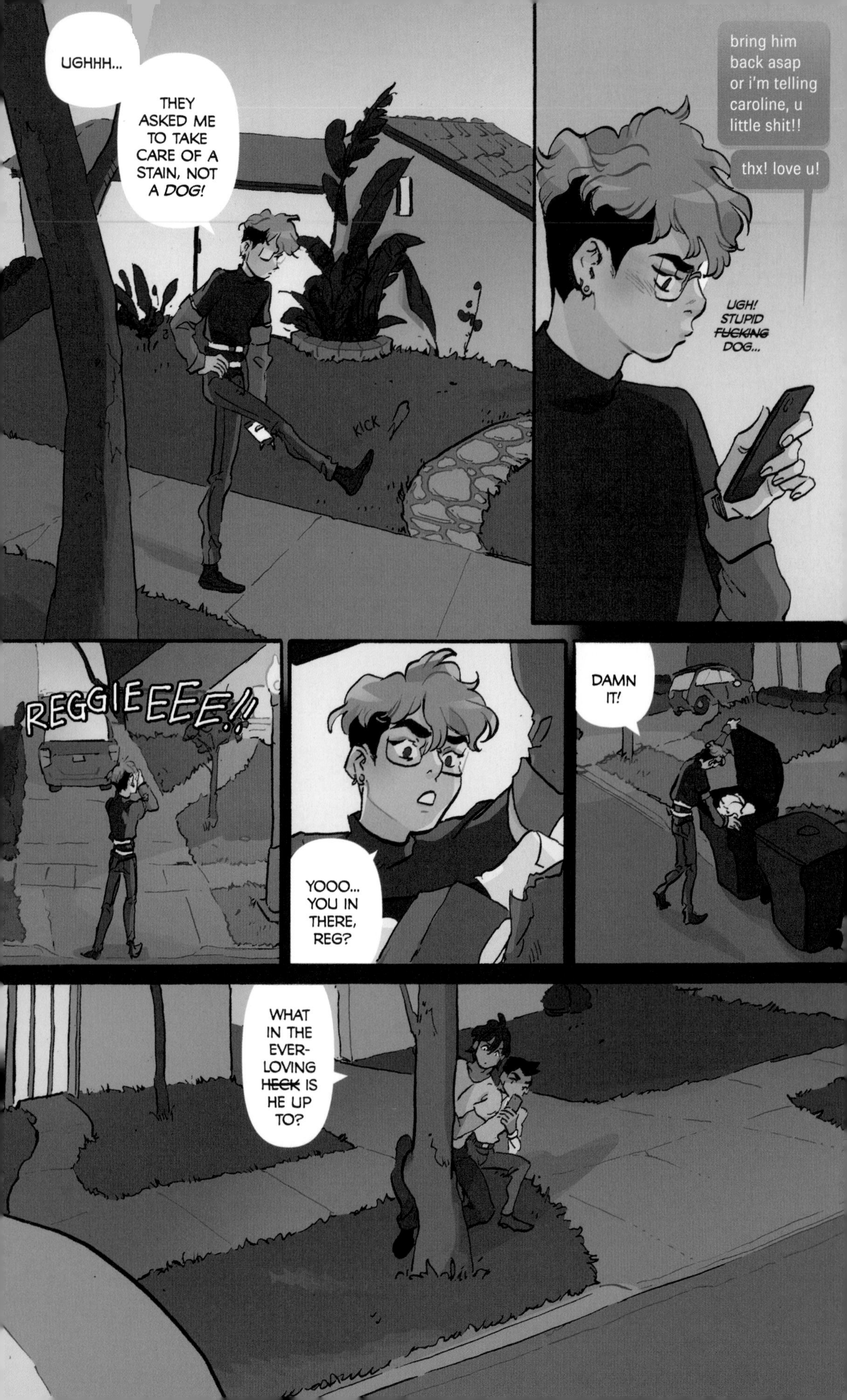
UGHHH...
THEY ASKED ME TO TAKE CARE OF A STAIN, NOT A *DOG!*
KICK
bring him back asap or i'm telling caroline, u little shit!!
thx! love u!
UGH! STUPID ~~FUCKING~~ DOG...
REGGIEEEEE!!
YOOO... YOU IN THERE, REG?
DAMN IT!
WHAT IN THE EVER-LOVING ~~HECK~~ IS HE UP TO?

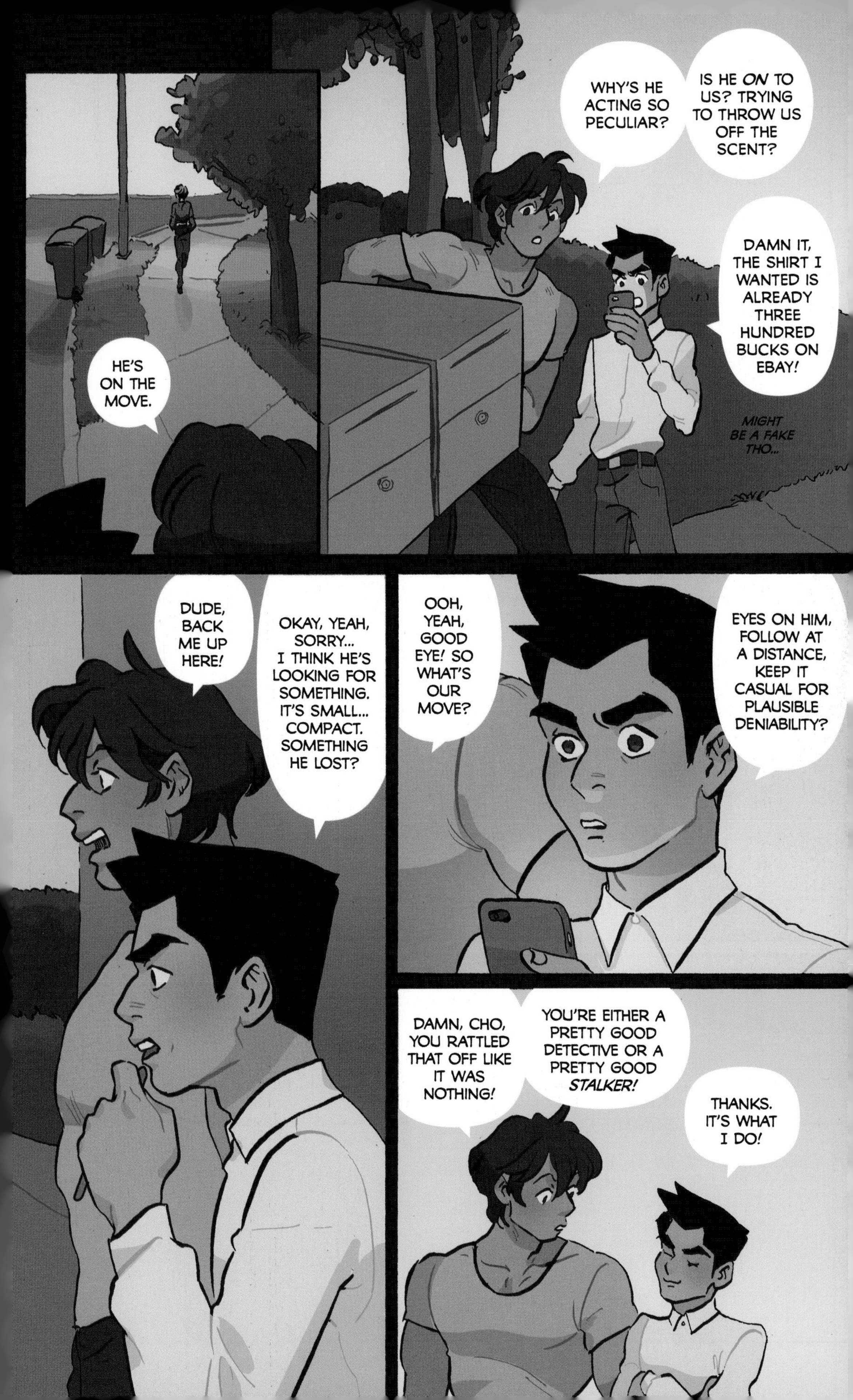
HE'S ON THE MOVE.
WHY'S HE ACTING SO PECULIAR?
IS HE *ON* TO US? TRYING TO THROW US OFF THE SCENT?
DAMN IT, THE SHIRT I WANTED IS ALREADY THREE HUNDRED BUCKS ON EBAY!
MIGHT BE A FAKE THO...
DUDE, BACK ME UP HERE!
OKAY, YEAH, SORRY... I THINK HE'S LOOKING FOR SOMETHING. IT'S SMALL... COMPACT. SOMETHING HE LOST?
OOH, YEAH, GOOD EYE! SO WHAT'S OUR MOVE?
EYES ON HIM, FOLLOW AT A DISTANCE, KEEP IT CASUAL FOR PLAUSIBLE DENIABILITY?
DAMN, CHO, YOU RATTLED THAT OFF LIKE IT WAS NOTHING!
YOU'RE EITHER A PRETTY GOOD DETECTIVE OR A PRETTY GOOD *STALKER!*
THANKS. IT'S WHAT I DO!

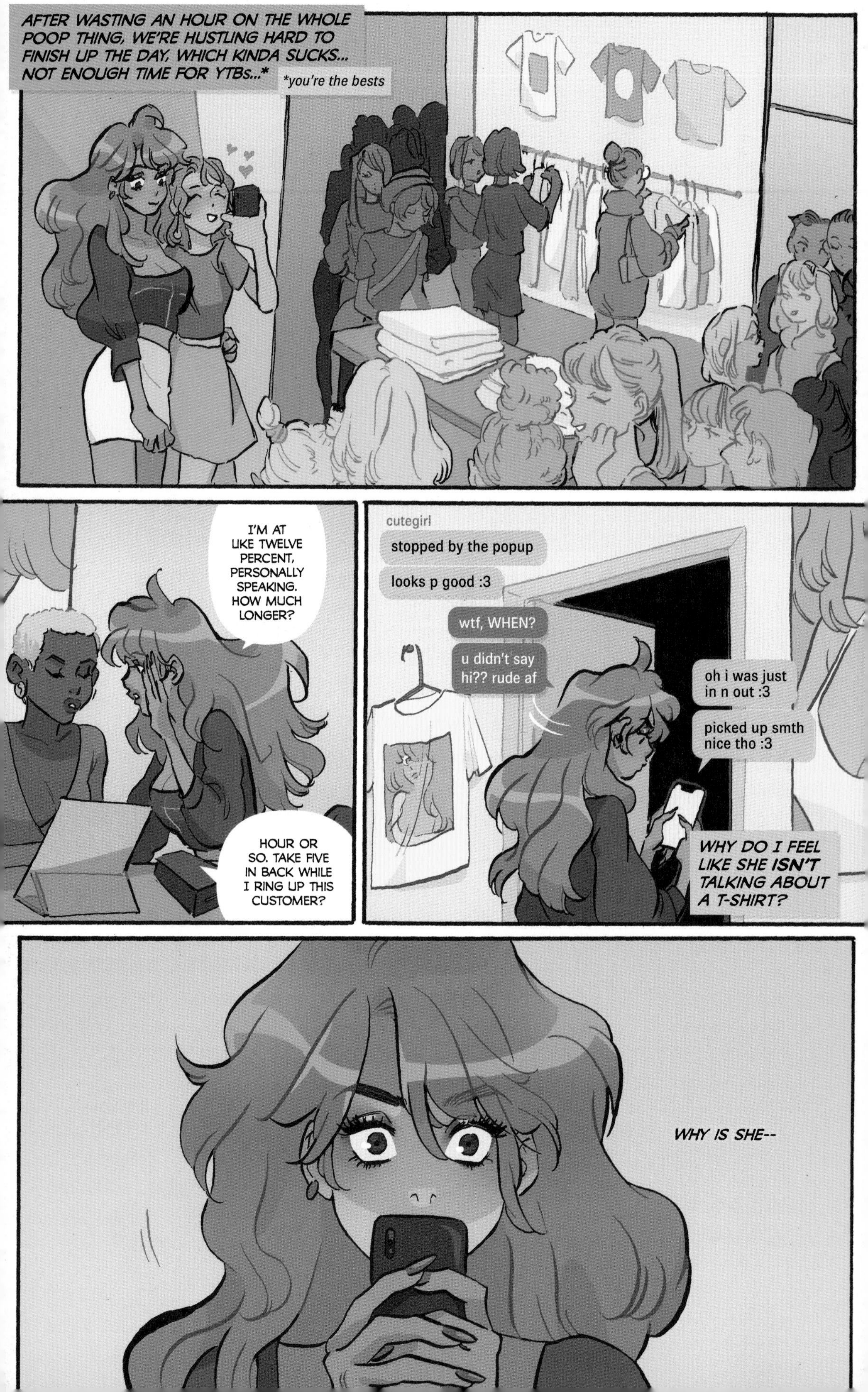
AFTER WASTING AN HOUR ON THE WHOLE POOP THING, WE'RE HUSTLING HARD TO FINISH UP THE DAY, WHICH KINDA SUCKS... NOT ENOUGH TIME FOR YTBs...*
*you're the bests
I'M AT LIKE TWELVE PERCENT, PERSONALLY SPEAKING. HOW MUCH LONGER?
HOUR OR SO. TAKE FIVE IN BACK WHILE I RING UP THIS CUSTOMER?
cutegirl
stopped by the popup
looks p good :3
wtf, WHEN?
u didn't say hi?? rude af
oh i was just in n out :3
picked up smth nice tho :3
WHY DO I FEEL LIKE SHE ISN'T TALKING ABOUT A T-SHIRT?
WHY IS SHE--

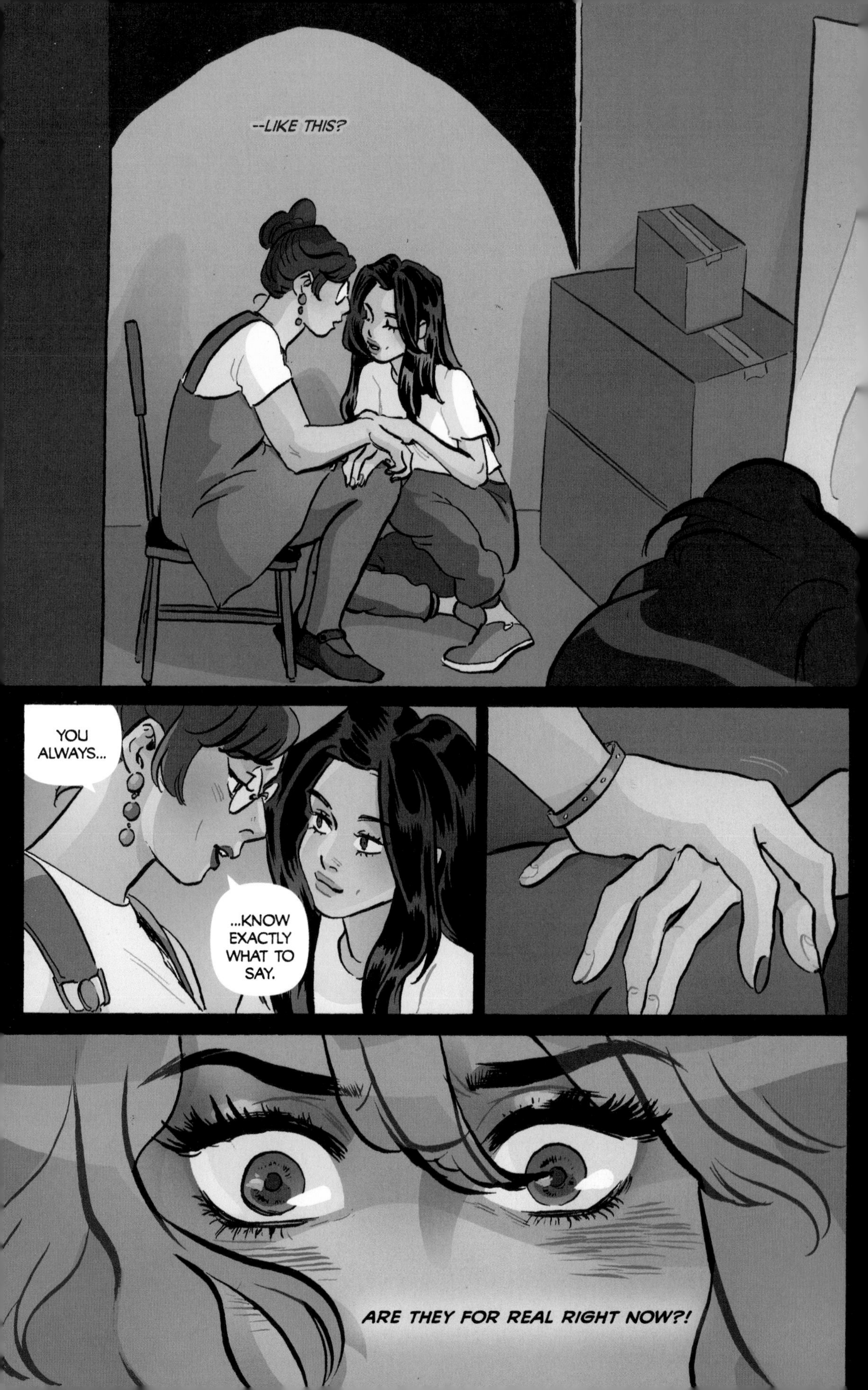
--LIKE THIS?
YOU ALWAYS...
...KNOW EXACTLY WHAT TO SAY.
ARE THEY FOR REAL RIGHT NOW?!

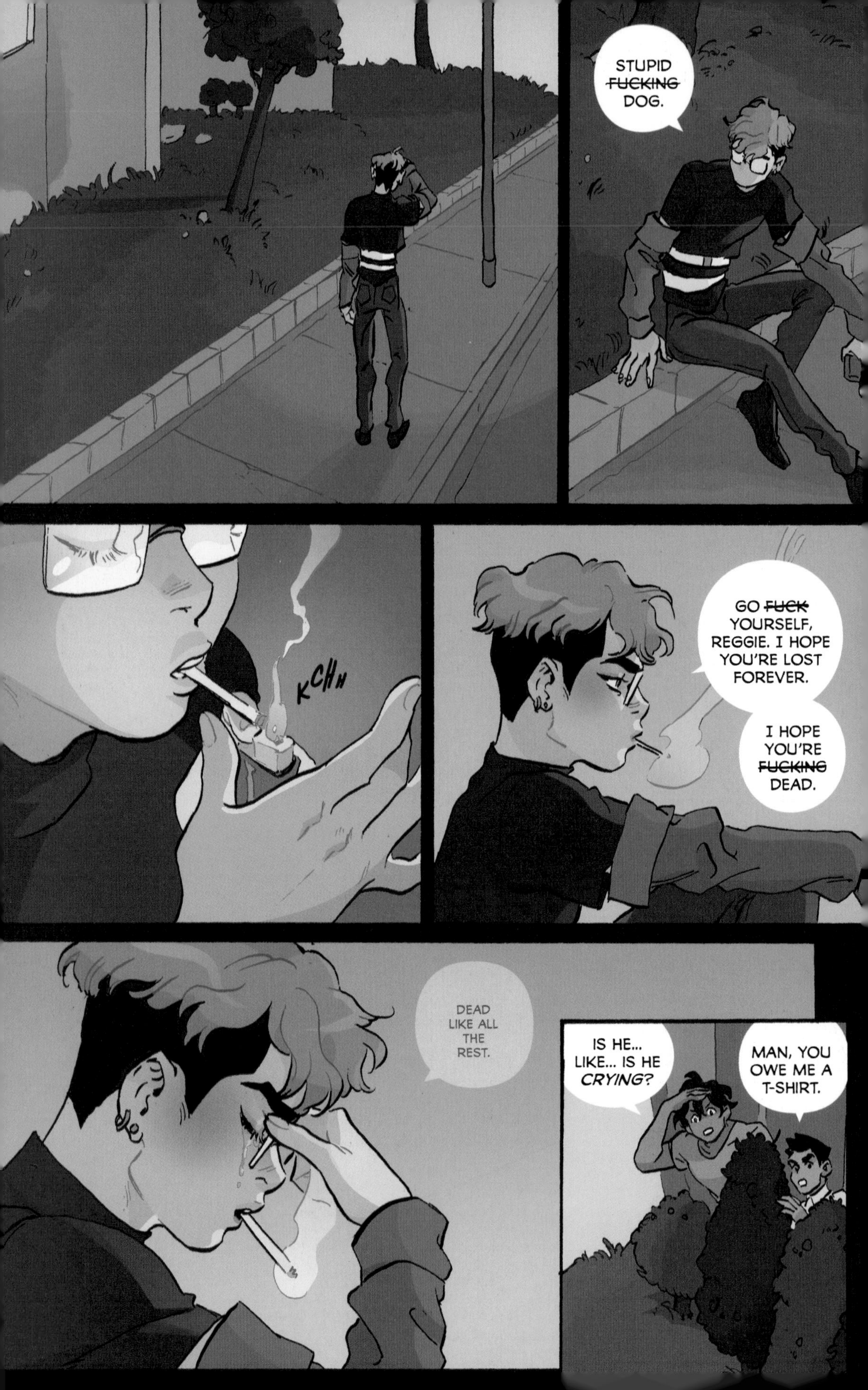
STUPID ~~FUCKING~~ DOG.
KCHH
GO ~~FUCK~~ YOURSELF, REGGIE. I HOPE YOU'RE LOST FOREVER.
I HOPE YOU'RE ~~FUCKING~~ DEAD.
DEAD LIKE ALL THE REST.
IS HE... LIKE... IS HE *CRYING*?
MAN, YOU OWE ME A T-SHIRT.

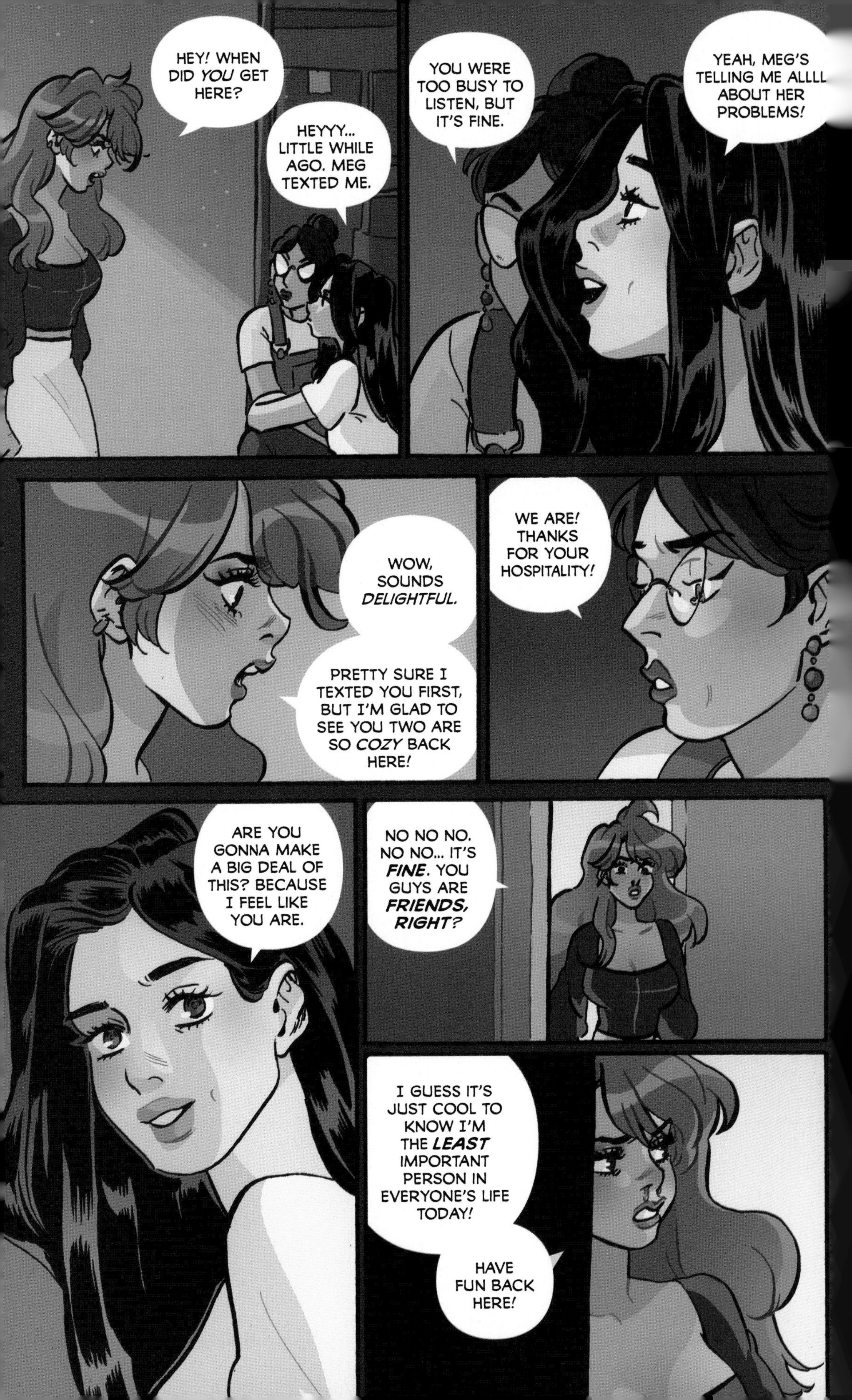
HEY! WHEN DID YOU GET HERE?
HEYYY... LITTLE WHILE AGO. MEG TEXTED ME.
YOU WERE TOO BUSY TO LISTEN, BUT IT'S FINE.
YEAH, MEG'S TELLING ME ALLLL ABOUT HER PROBLEMS!
WOW, SOUNDS DELIGHTFUL.
PRETTY SURE I TEXTED YOU FIRST, BUT I'M GLAD TO SEE YOU TWO ARE SO COZY BACK HERE!
WE ARE! THANKS FOR YOUR HOSPITALITY!
ARE YOU GONNA MAKE A BIG DEAL OF THIS? BECAUSE I FEEL LIKE YOU ARE.
NO NO NO. NO NO... IT'S FINE. YOU GUYS ARE FRIENDS, RIGHT?
I GUESS IT'S JUST COOL TO KNOW I'M THE LEAST IMPORTANT PERSON IN EVERYONE'S LIFE TODAY!
HAVE FUN BACK HERE!

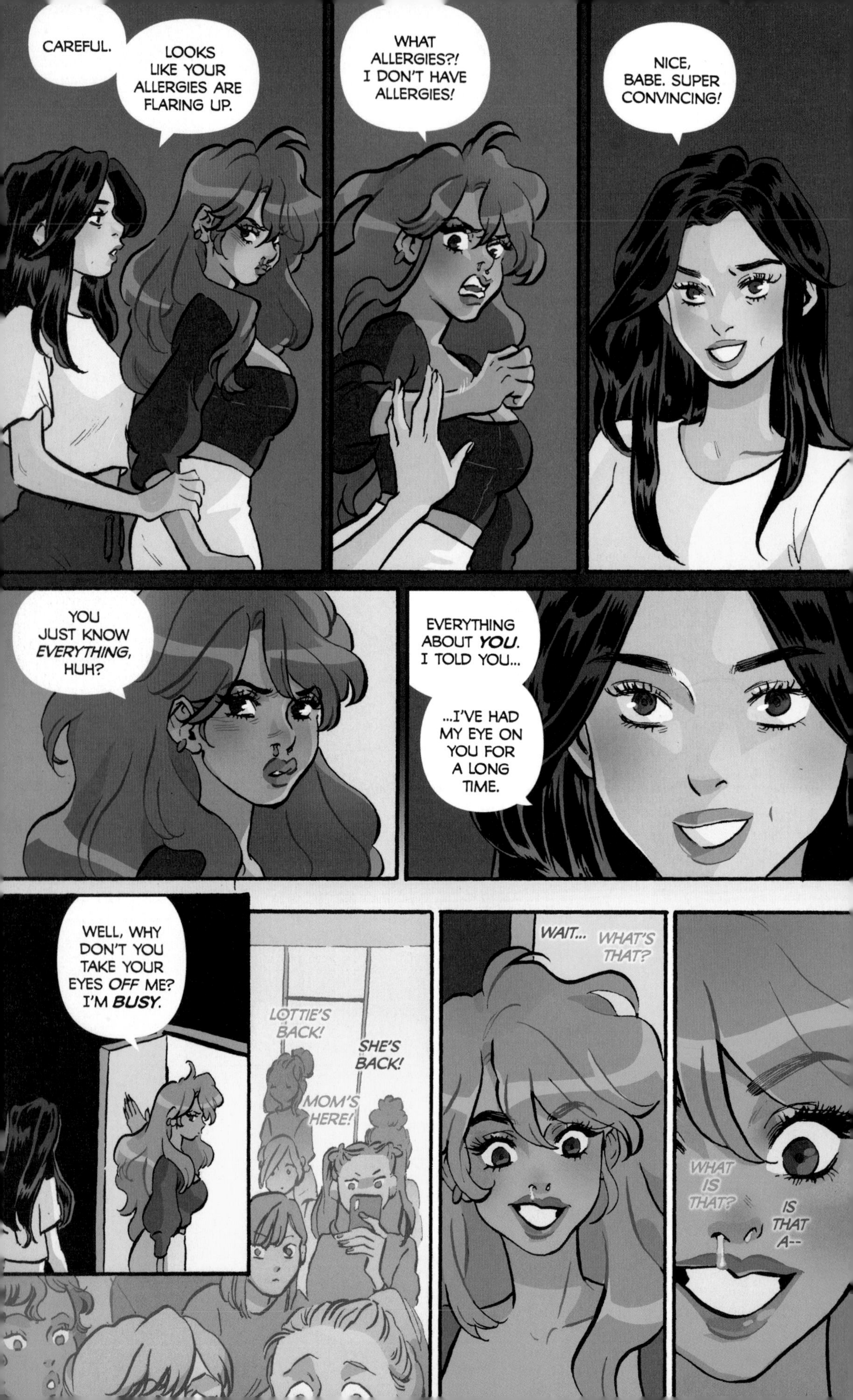
CAREFUL.
LOOKS LIKE YOUR ALLERGIES ARE FLARING UP.
WHAT ALLERGIES?! I DON'T HAVE ALLERGIES!
NICE, BABE. SUPER CONVINCING!
YOU JUST KNOW EVERYTHING, HUH?
EVERYTHING ABOUT YOU. I TOLD YOU...
...I'VE HAD MY EYE ON YOU FOR A LONG TIME.
WELL, WHY DON'T YOU TAKE YOUR EYES OFF ME? I'M BUSY.
LOTTIE'S BACK!
SHE'S BACK!
MOM'S HERE!
WAIT...
WHAT'S THAT?
WHAT IS THAT?
IS THAT A--

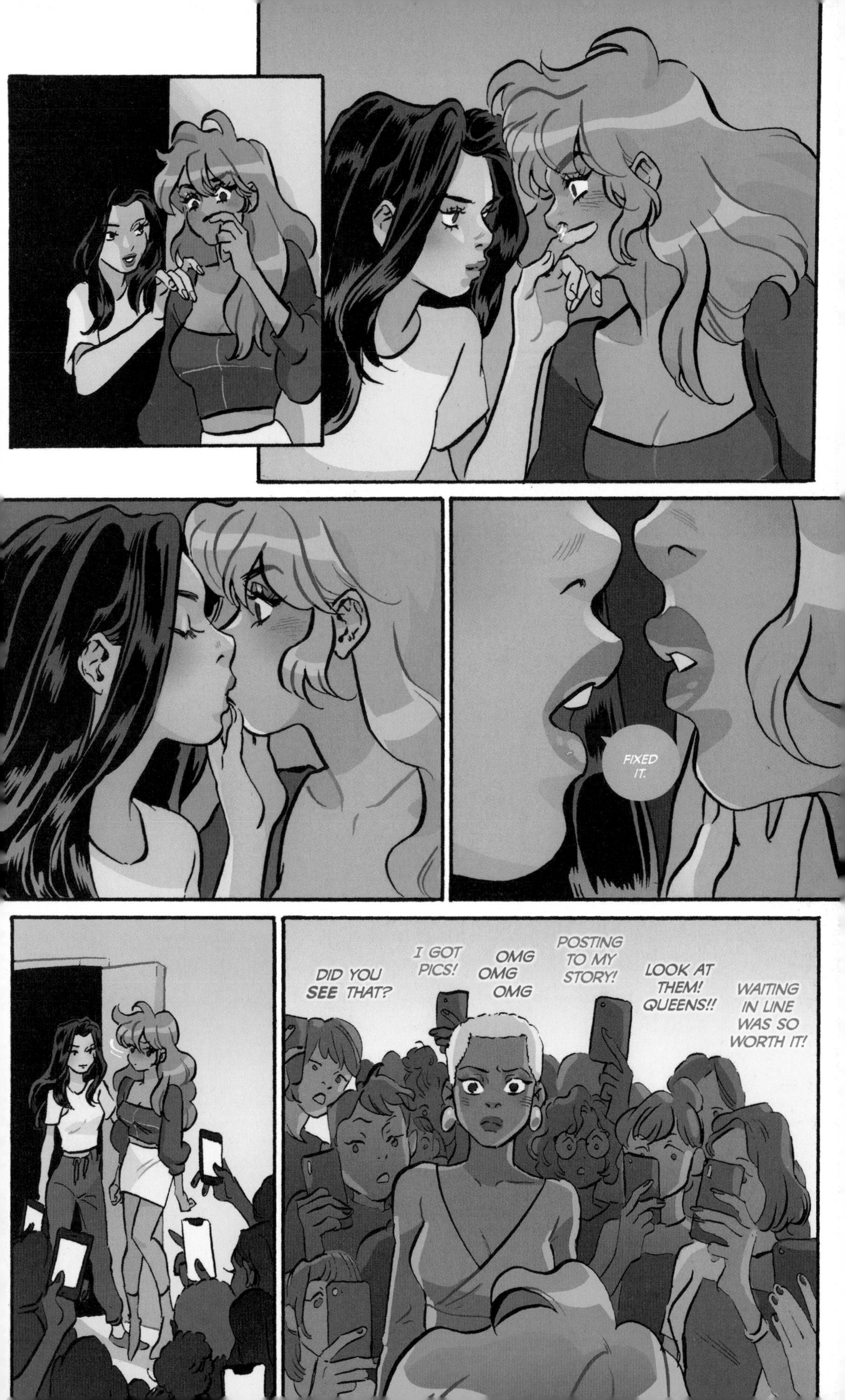
FIXED IT.
DID YOU SEE THAT?
I GOT PICS!
OMG OMG OMG
POSTING TO MY STORY!
LOOK AT THEM! QUEENS!!
WAITING IN LINE WAS SO WORTH IT!

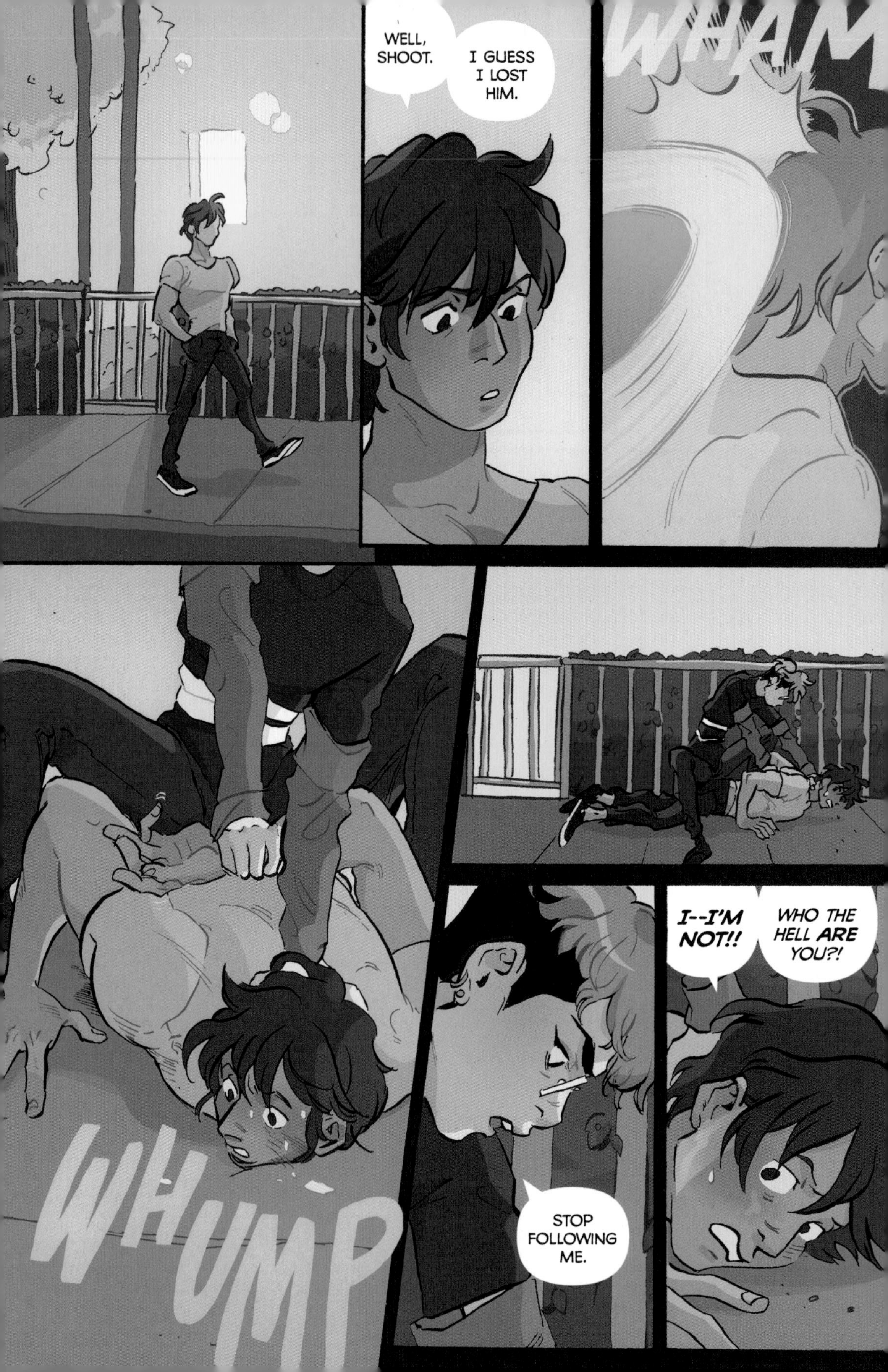
WELL, SHOOT.
I GUESS I LOST HIM.
WHAM
WHUMP
STOP FOLLOWING ME.
I--I'M NOT!!
WHO THE HELL ARE YOU?!

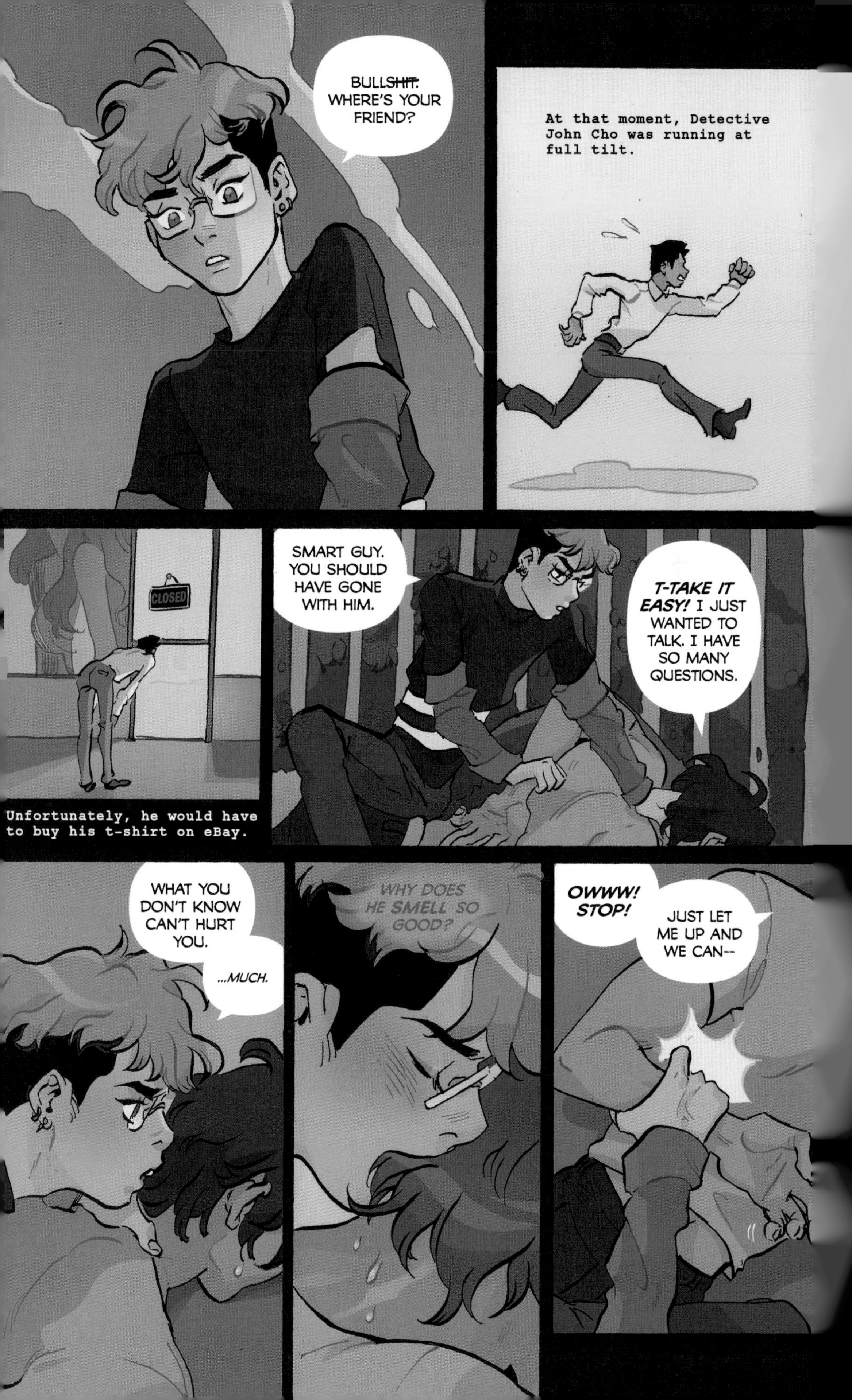
BULLSHIT. WHERE'S YOUR FRIEND?
At that moment, Detective John Cho was running at full tilt.
CLOSED
Unfortunately, he would have to buy his t-shirt on eBay.
SMART GUY. YOU SHOULD HAVE GONE WITH HIM.
T-TAKE IT EASY! I JUST WANTED TO TALK. I HAVE SO MANY QUESTIONS.
WHAT YOU DON'T KNOW CAN'T HURT YOU.
...MUCH.
WHY DOES HE SMELL SO GOOD?
OWWW! STOP!
JUST LET ME UP AND WE CAN--

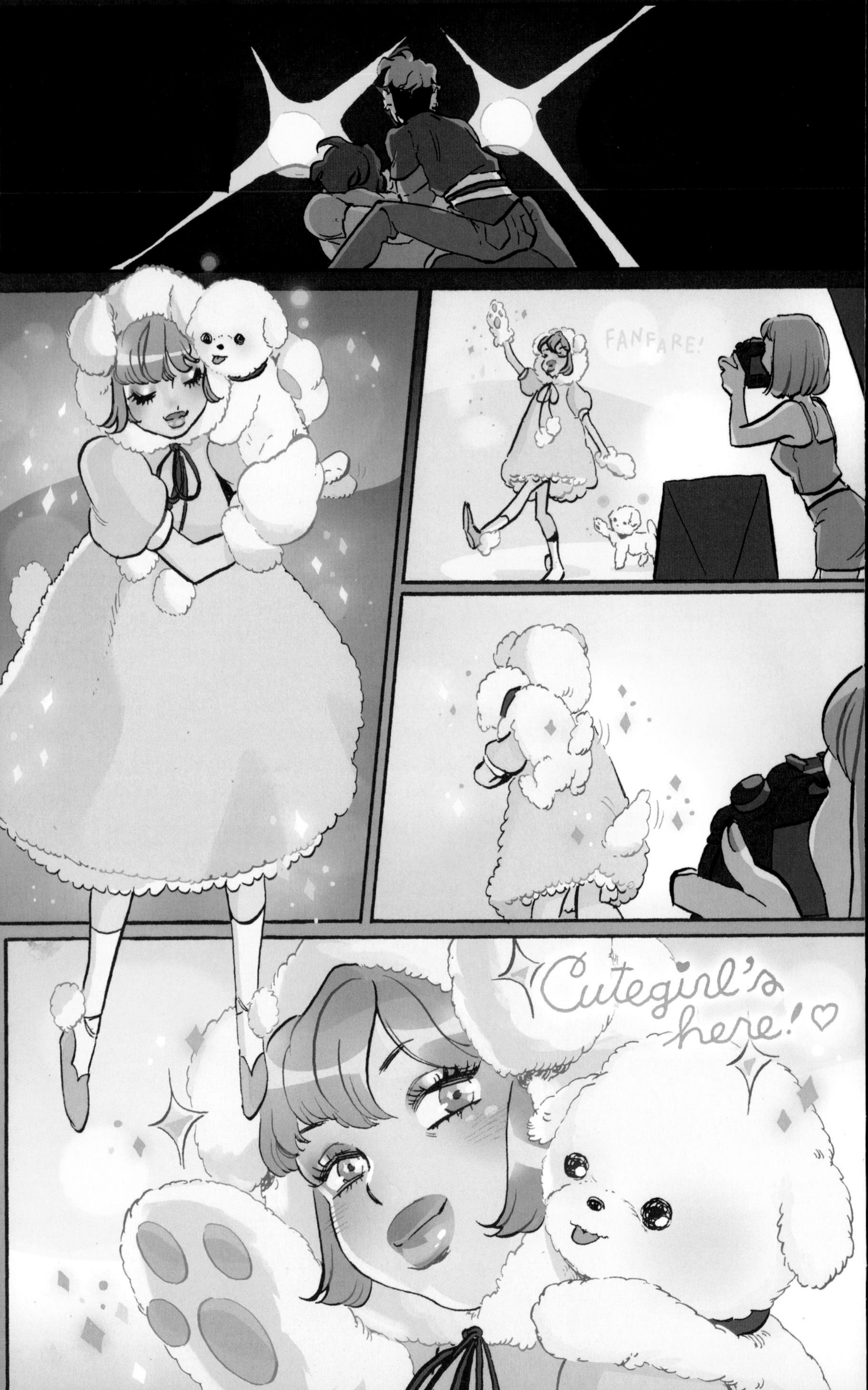
FANFARE!
Cutegirl's here! ♡

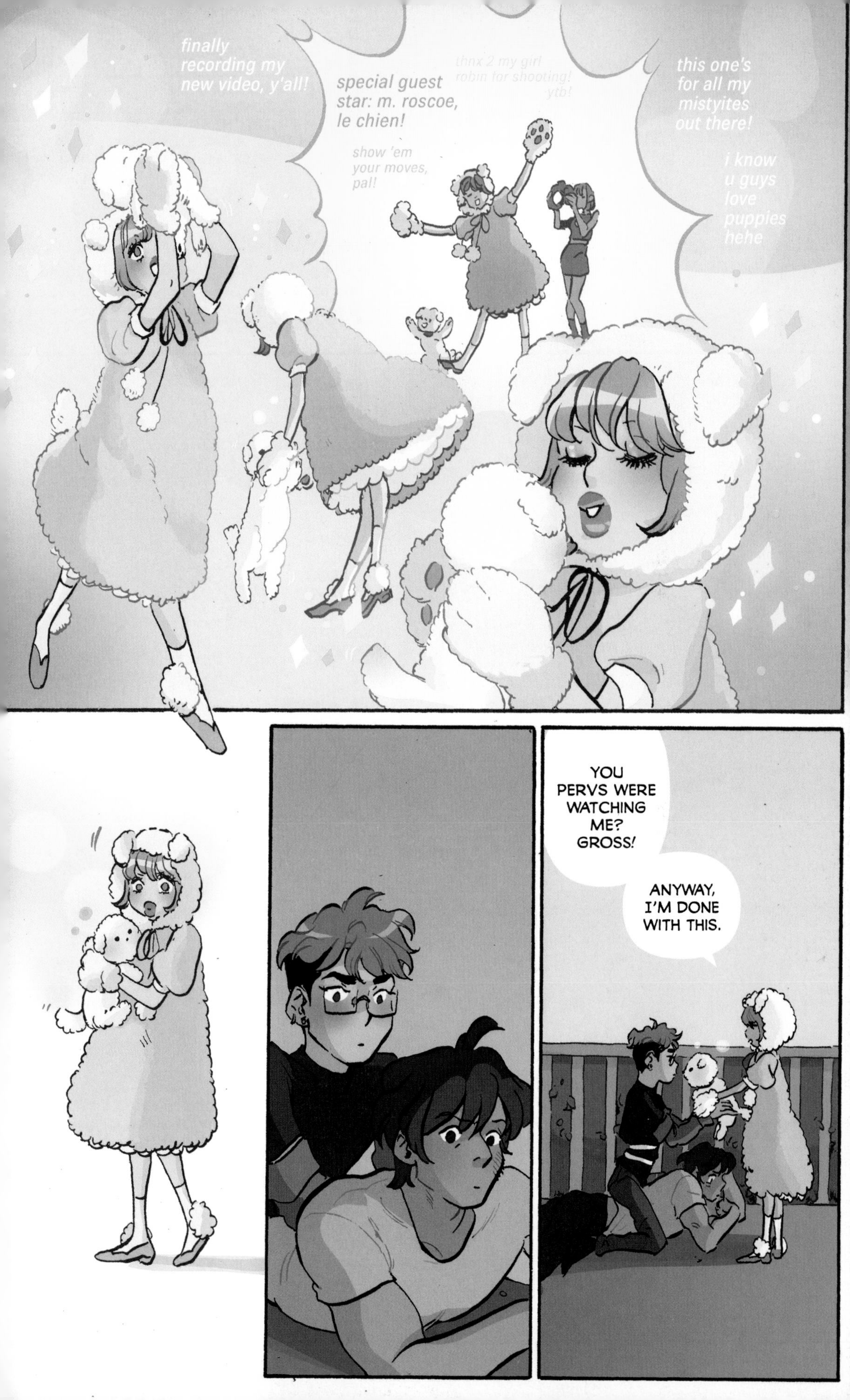
finally recording my new video, y'all!
special guest star: m. roscoe, le chien!
thnx 2 my girl robin for shooting! ytb!
this one's for all my mistyites out there!
show 'em your moves, pal!
i know u guys love puppies hehe
YOU PERVS WERE WATCHING ME? GROSS!
ANYWAY, I'M DONE WITH THIS.

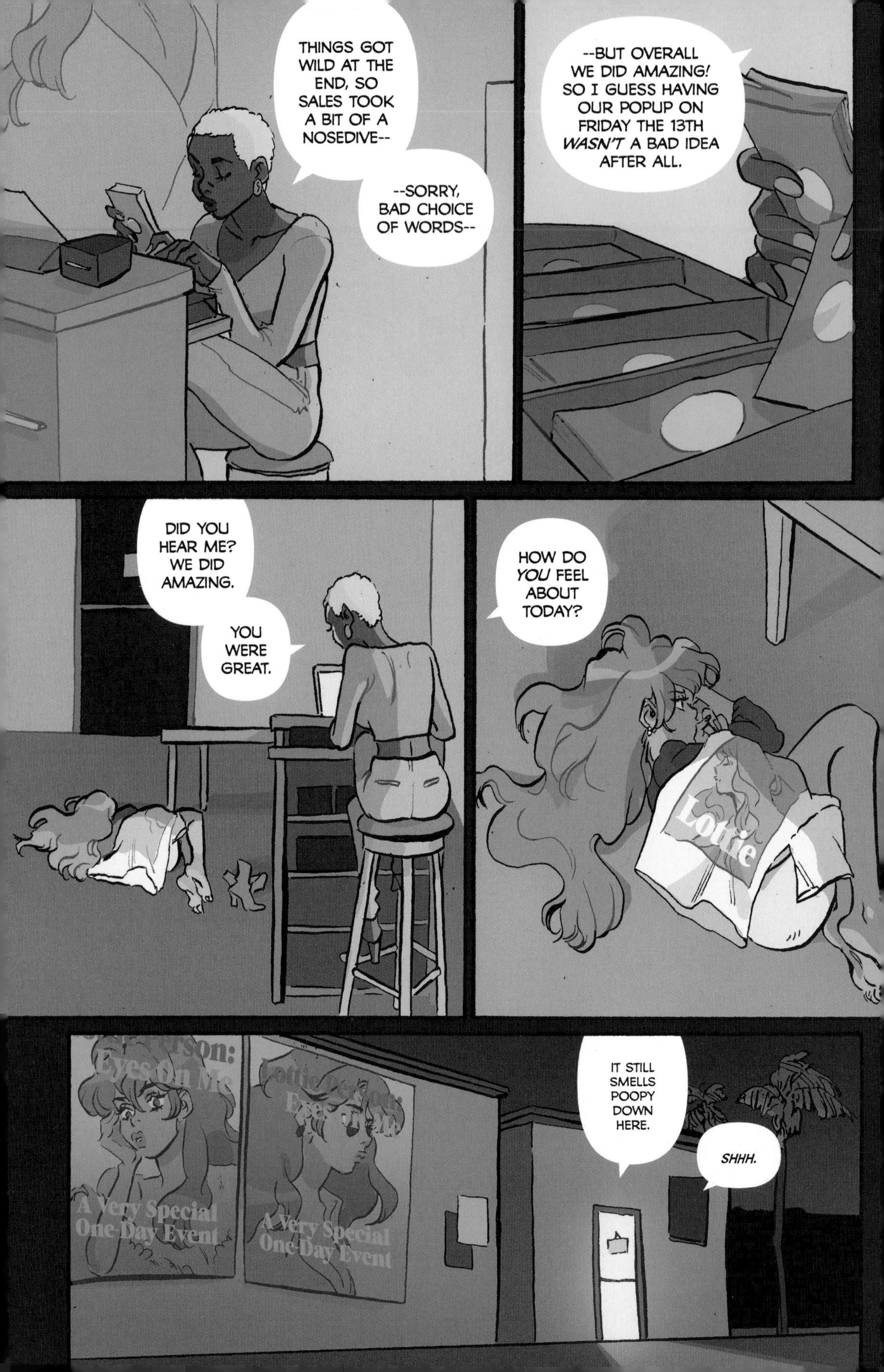
THINGS GOT WILD AT THE END, SO SALES TOOK A BIT OF A NOSEDIVE--
--SORRY, BAD CHOICE OF WORDS--
--BUT OVERALL WE DID AMAZING! SO I GUESS HAVING OUR POPUP ON FRIDAY THE 13TH *WASN'T* A BAD IDEA AFTER ALL.
DID YOU HEAR ME? WE DID AMAZING.
YOU WERE GREAT.
HOW DO *YOU* FEEL ABOUT TODAY?
Lottie
A Very Special One-Day Event
A Very Special One-Day Event
IT STILL SMELLS POOPY DOWN HERE.
SHHH.

14. TOO MUCH?

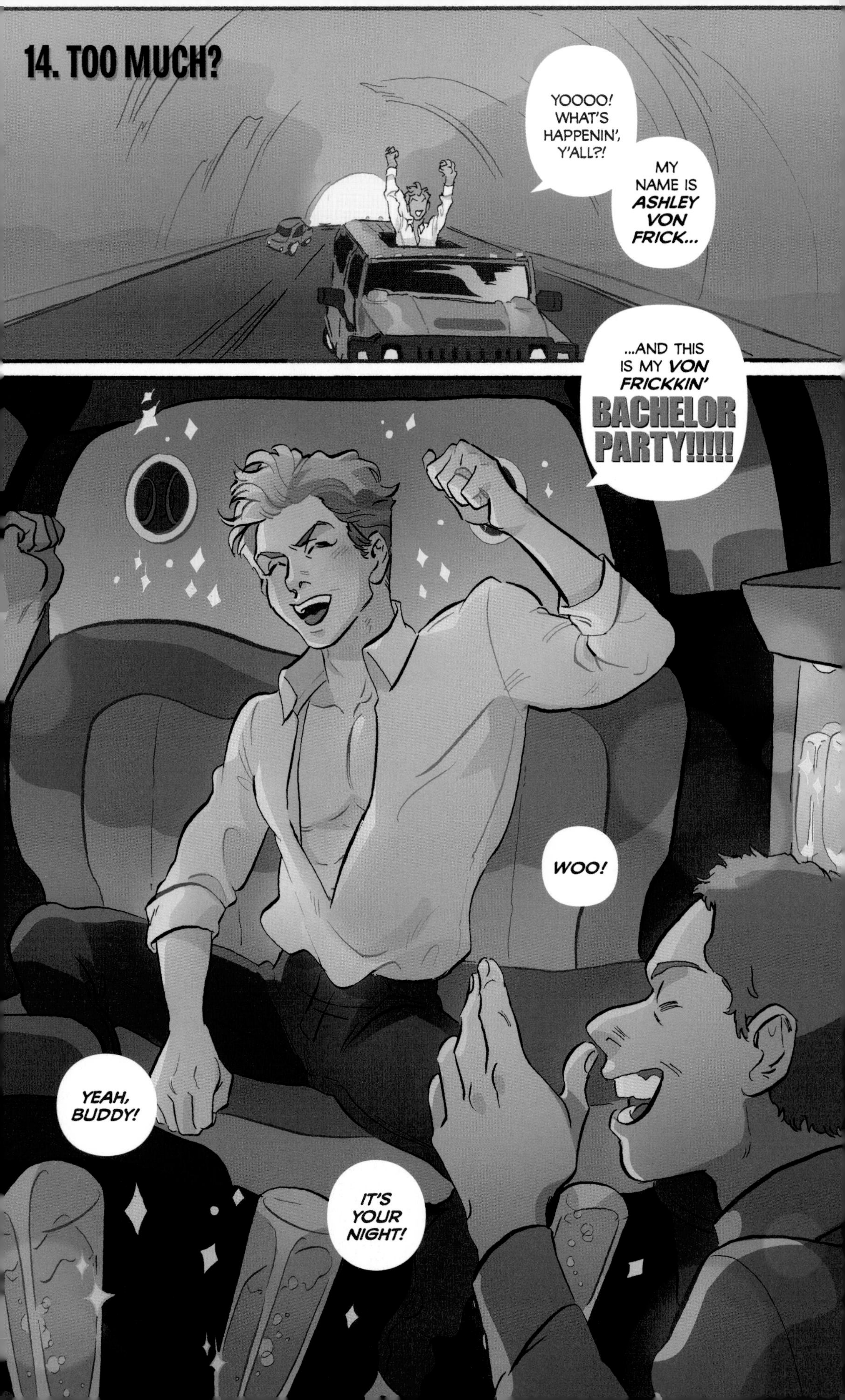

YOOOO! WHAT'S HAPPENIN', Y'ALL?!
MY NAME IS ASHLEY VON FRICK...
...AND THIS IS MY VON FRICKKIN' BACHELOR PARTY!!!!!
WOO!
YEAH, BUDDY!
IT'S YOUR NIGHT!

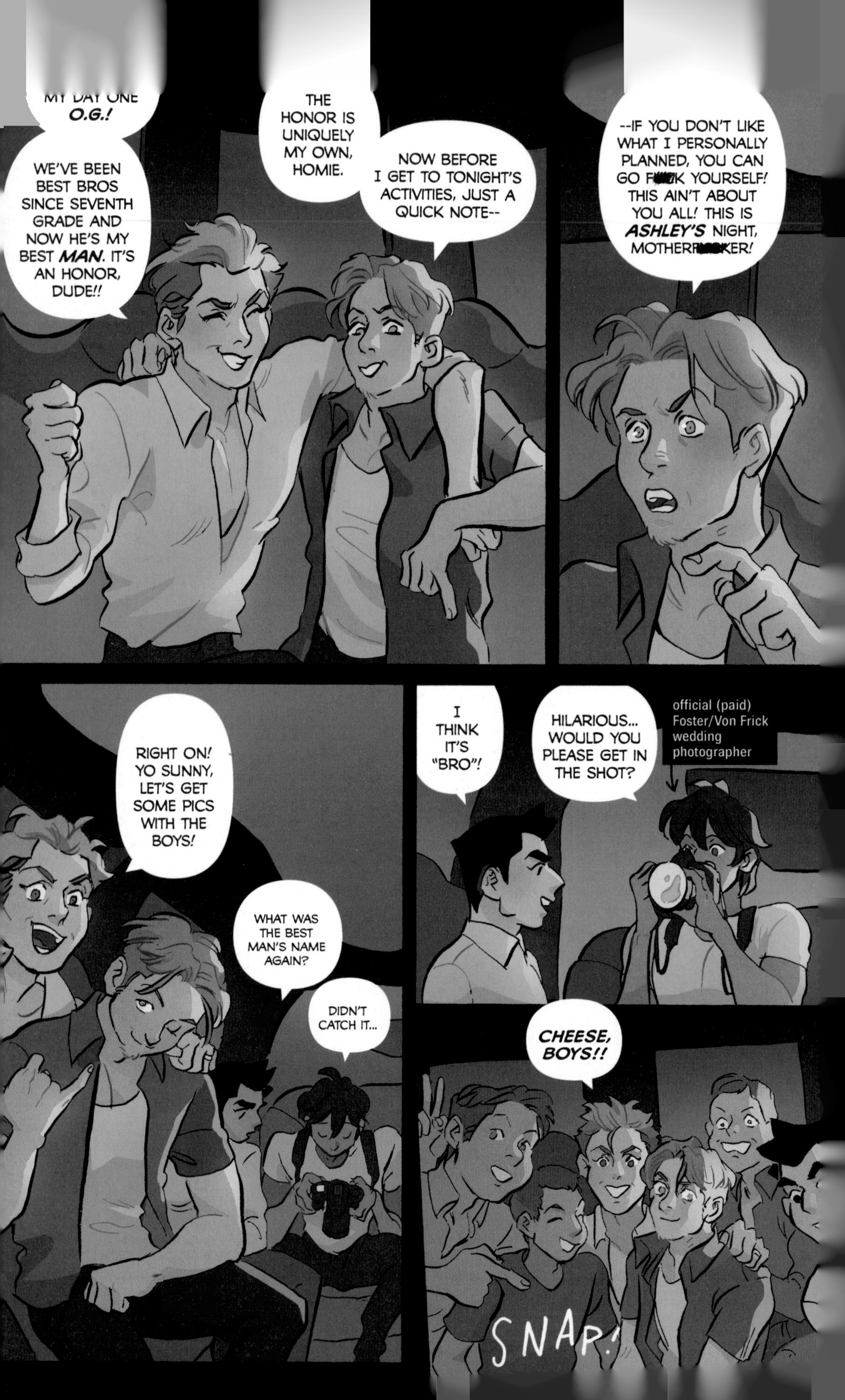

MY DAY ONE O.G.!
WE'VE BEEN BEST BROS SINCE SEVENTH GRADE AND NOW HE'S MY BEST MAN. IT'S AN HONOR, DUDE!!
THE HONOR IS UNIQUELY MY OWN, HOMIE.
NOW BEFORE I GET TO TONIGHT'S ACTIVITIES, JUST A QUICK NOTE--
--IF YOU DON'T LIKE WHAT I PERSONALLY PLANNED, YOU CAN GO F[redacted]K YOURSELF! THIS AIN'T ABOUT YOU ALL! THIS IS ASHLEY'S NIGHT, MOTHERF[redacted]KER!
RIGHT ON! YO SUNNY, LET'S GET SOME PICS WITH THE BOYS!
WHAT WAS THE BEST MAN'S NAME AGAIN?
DIDN'T CATCH IT...
I THINK IT'S "BRO"!
HILARIOUS... WOULD YOU PLEASE GET IN THE SHOT?
official (paid) Foster/Von Frick wedding photographer
CHEESE, BOYS!!
SNAP!

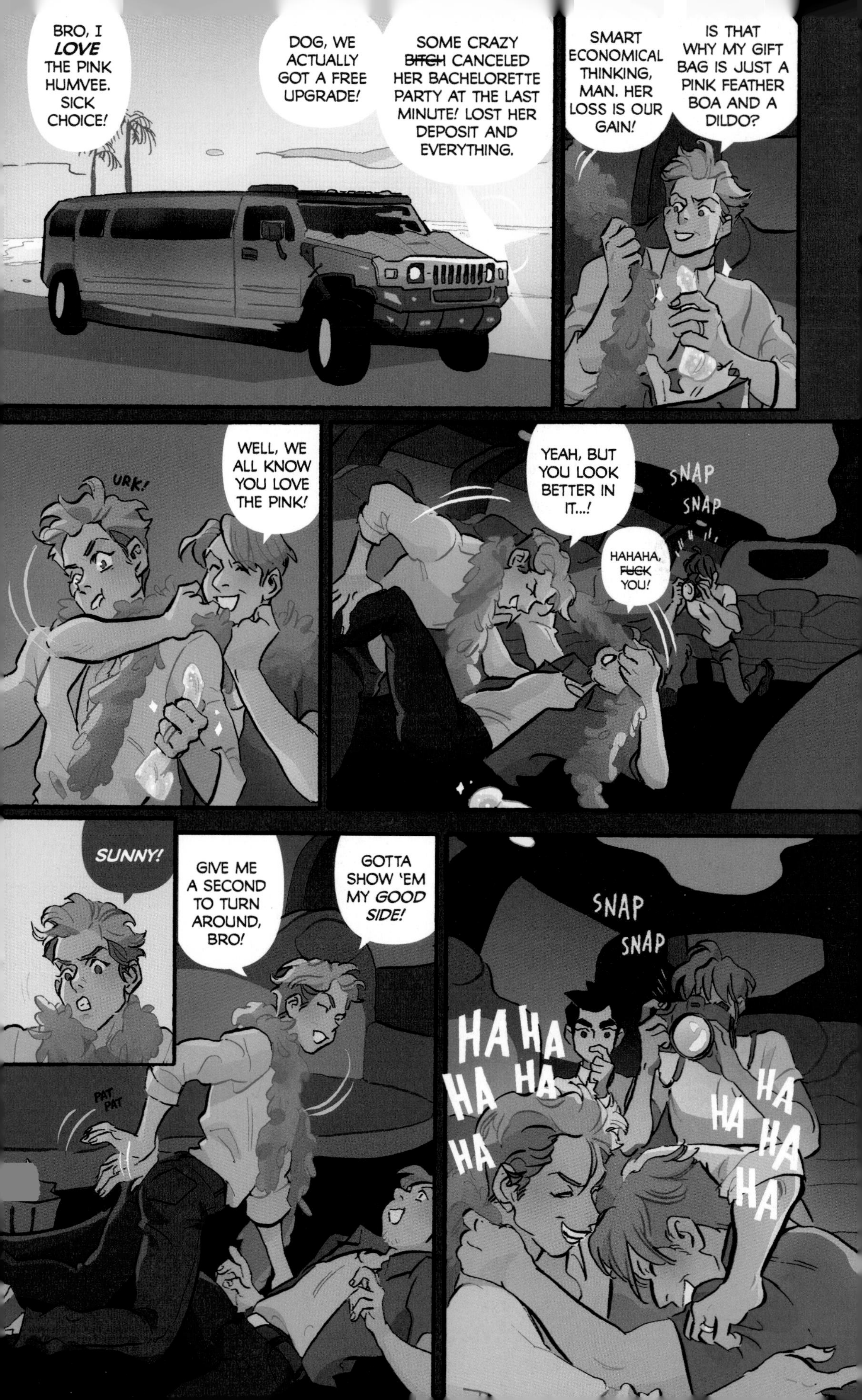
BRO, I *LOVE* THE PINK HUMVEE. SICK CHOICE!
DOG, WE ACTUALLY GOT A FREE UPGRADE!
SOME CRAZY ~~BITCH~~ CANCELED HER BACHELORETTE PARTY AT THE LAST MINUTE! LOST HER DEPOSIT AND EVERYTHING.
SMART ECONOMICAL THINKING, MAN. HER LOSS IS OUR GAIN!
IS THAT WHY MY GIFT BAG IS JUST A PINK FEATHER BOA AND A DILDO?
URK!
WELL, WE ALL KNOW YOU LOVE THE PINK!
YEAH, BUT YOU LOOK BETTER IN IT...!
SNAP
SNAP
HAHAHA, ~~FUCK~~ YOU!
SUNNY!
GIVE ME A SECOND TO TURN AROUND, BRO!
GOTTA SHOW 'EM MY *GOOD SIDE!*
PAT PAT
SNAP
SNAP
HA HA HA HA HA HA
HA HA HA HA HA HA

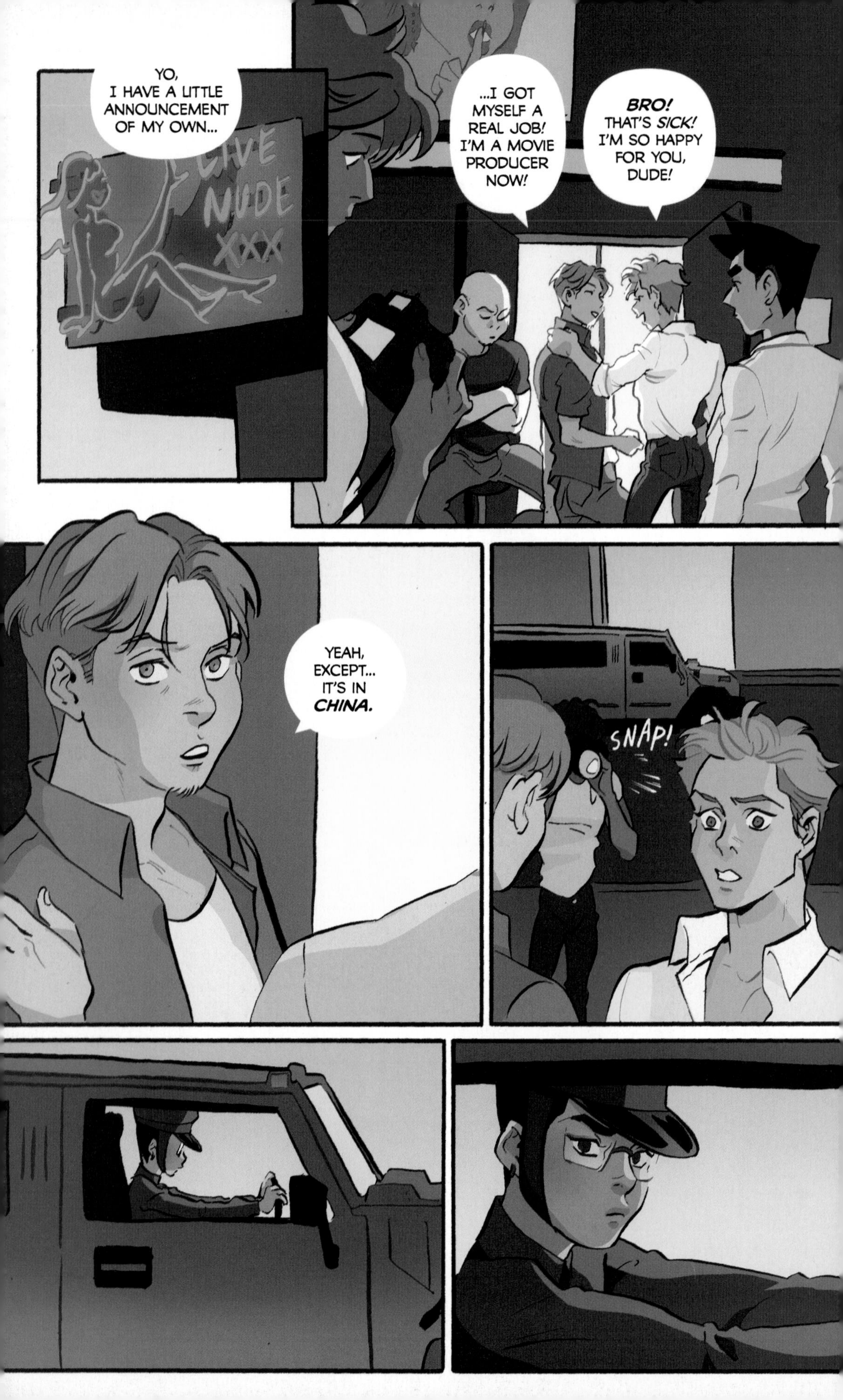
YO, I HAVE A LITTLE ANNOUNCEMENT OF MY OWN...
LIVE NUDE XXX
...I GOT MYSELF A REAL JOB! I'M A MOVIE PRODUCER NOW!
BRO! THAT'S SICK! I'M SO HAPPY FOR YOU, DUDE!
YEAH, EXCEPT... IT'S IN CHINA.
SNAP!

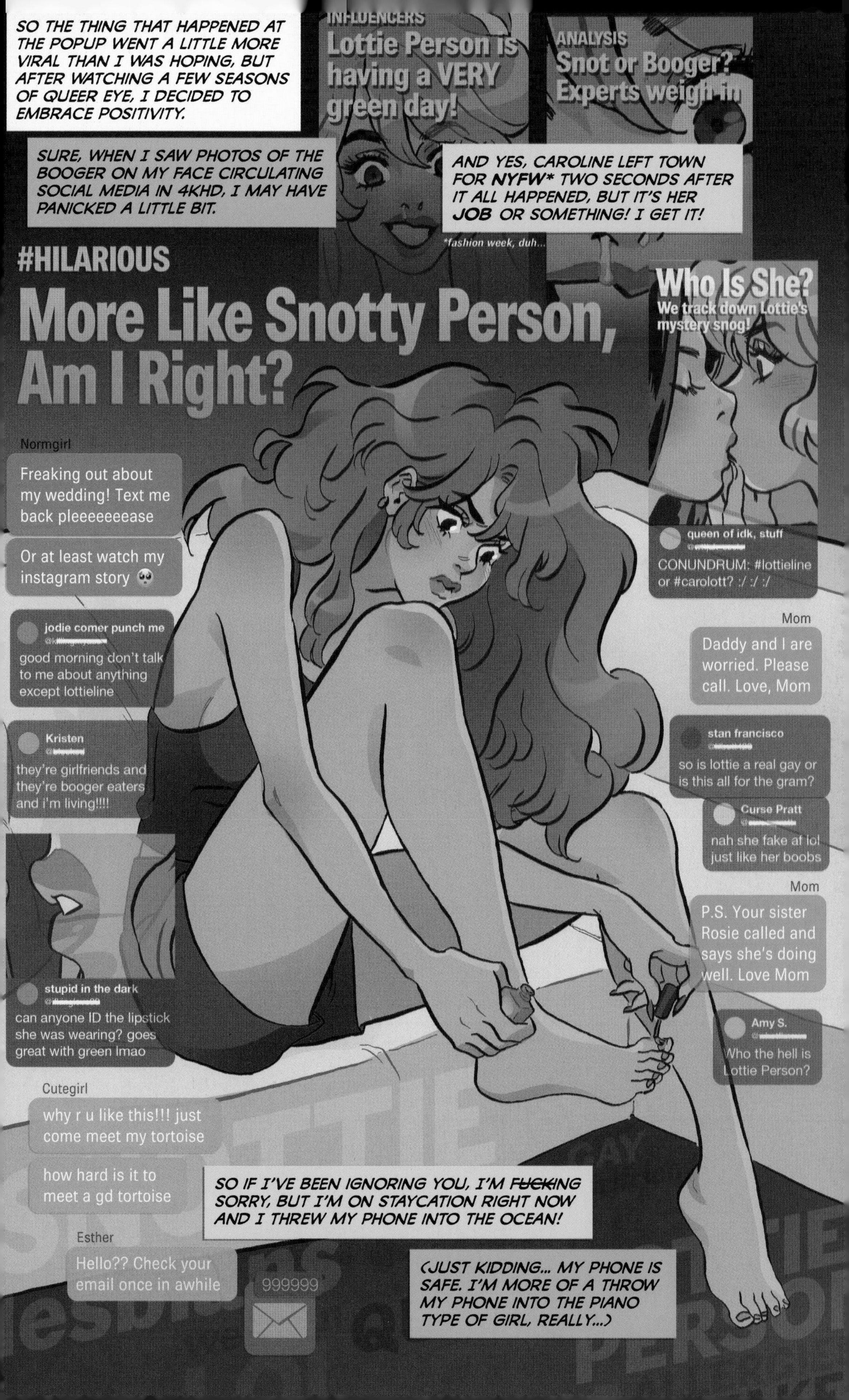
SO THE THING THAT HAPPENED AT THE POPUP WENT A LITTLE MORE VIRAL THAN I WAS HOPING, BUT AFTER WATCHING A FEW SEASONS OF QUEER EYE, I DECIDED TO EMBRACE POSITIVITY.
INFLUENCERS
Lottie Person is having a VERY green day!
ANALYSIS
Snot or Booger? Experts weigh in
SURE, WHEN I SAW PHOTOS OF THE BOOGER ON MY FACE CIRCULATING SOCIAL MEDIA IN 4KHD, I MAY HAVE PANICKED A LITTLE BIT.
AND YES, CAROLINE LEFT TOWN FOR NYFW* TWO SECONDS AFTER IT ALL HAPPENED, BUT IT'S HER JOB OR SOMETHING! I GET IT!
*fashion week, duh...
#HILARIOUS
More Like Snotty Person, Am I Right?
Who Is She?
We track down Lottie's mystery snog!
Normgirl
Freaking out about my wedding! Text me back pleeeeeeease
Or at least watch my instagram story 🥺
queen of idk, stuff
@[redacted]
CONUNDRUM: #lottieline or #carolott? :/ :/ :/
jodie comer punch me
@[redacted]
good morning don't talk to me about anything except lottieline
Mom
Daddy and I are worried. Please call. Love, Mom
Kristen
@[redacted]
they're girlfriends and they're booger eaters and i'm living!!!!
stan francisco
@[redacted]
so is lottie a real gay or is this all for the gram?
Curse Pratt
@[redacted]
nah she fake af lol just like her boobs
Mom
P.S. Your sister Rosie called and says she's doing well. Love Mom
stupid in the dark
@[redacted]
can anyone ID the lipstick she was wearing? goes great with green lmao
Amy S.
@[redacted]
Who the hell is Lottie Person?
Cutegirl
why r u like this!!! just come meet my tortoise
how hard is it to meet a gd tortoise
SO IF I'VE BEEN IGNORING YOU, I'M FUCKING SORRY, BUT I'M ON STAYCATION RIGHT NOW AND I THREW MY PHONE INTO THE OCEAN!
Esther
Hello?? Check your email once in awhile
999999
(JUST KIDDING... MY PHONE IS SAFE. I'M MORE OF A THROW MY PHONE INTO THE PIANO TYPE OF GIRL, REALLY...)

YOU KNOW, THIS STAYCATION WOULD BE A HELL OF A LOT MORE RELAXING IF **ROSIE** WASN'T STILL HERE.

LAST WEEK SHE WAS A PERMANENT FIXTURE ON MY COUCH, THIS WEEK SHE'S BOUNCING ALL OVER THE PLACE... BIG SIS HAS NO CHILL!

THE INTERNET SAYS CAROLINE IS YOUR GIRLFRIEND.

My mood right n...? Apocalyptic

WELL, THE INTERNET NEVER LIES, SO...

PFFF, THERE'S NO WAY. GIRLS LIKE THAT CAN'T STAND THE SMELL OF *DESPERATION.*

EXCUSE ME??

SHHH.

I WANT TO HEAR THIS PART.

YOU'VE SEEN IT *LITERALLY* A MILLION TIMES...

-Do you think Fumichan will strangle him?
-That would be a first for the show!

AHAHAHA! I LOVE THEM!

...I'M *LITERALLY* GOING CRAZY, HUH?

I MEAN...

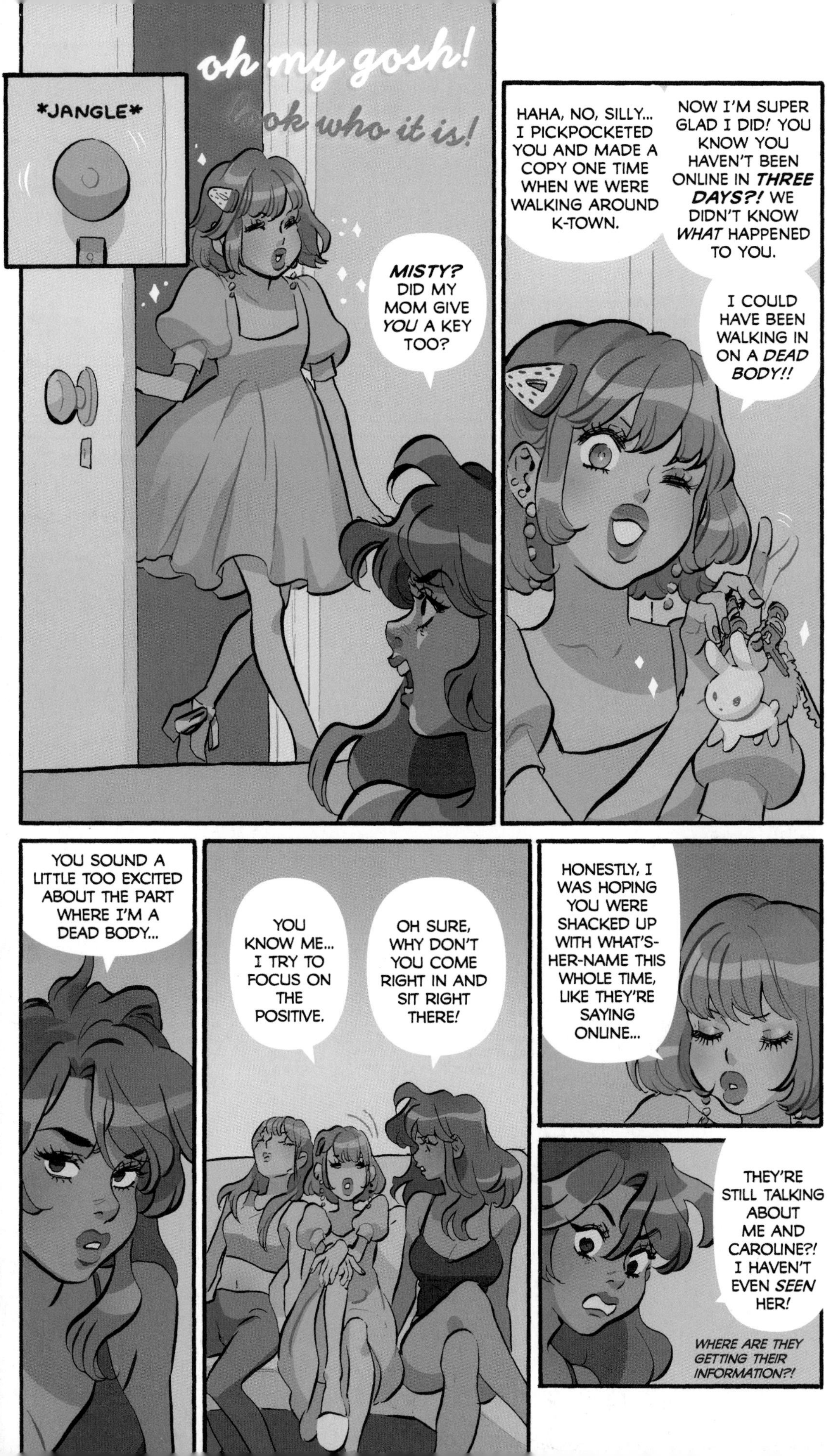

JANGLE
oh my gosh!
look who it is!
MISTY? DID MY MOM GIVE YOU A KEY TOO?
HAHA, NO, SILLY... I PICKPOCKETED YOU AND MADE A COPY ONE TIME WHEN WE WERE WALKING AROUND K-TOWN.
NOW I'M SUPER GLAD I DID! YOU KNOW YOU HAVEN'T BEEN ONLINE IN THREE DAYS?! WE DIDN'T KNOW WHAT HAPPENED TO YOU.
I COULD HAVE BEEN WALKING IN ON A DEAD BODY!!
YOU SOUND A LITTLE TOO EXCITED ABOUT THE PART WHERE I'M A DEAD BODY...
YOU KNOW ME... I TRY TO FOCUS ON THE POSITIVE.
OH SURE, WHY DON'T YOU COME RIGHT IN AND SIT RIGHT THERE!
HONESTLY, I WAS HOPING YOU WERE SHACKED UP WITH WHAT'S-HER-NAME THIS WHOLE TIME, LIKE THEY'RE SAYING ONLINE...
THEY'RE STILL TALKING ABOUT ME AND CAROLINE?! I HAVEN'T EVEN SEEN HER!
WHERE ARE THEY GETTING THEIR INFORMATION?!

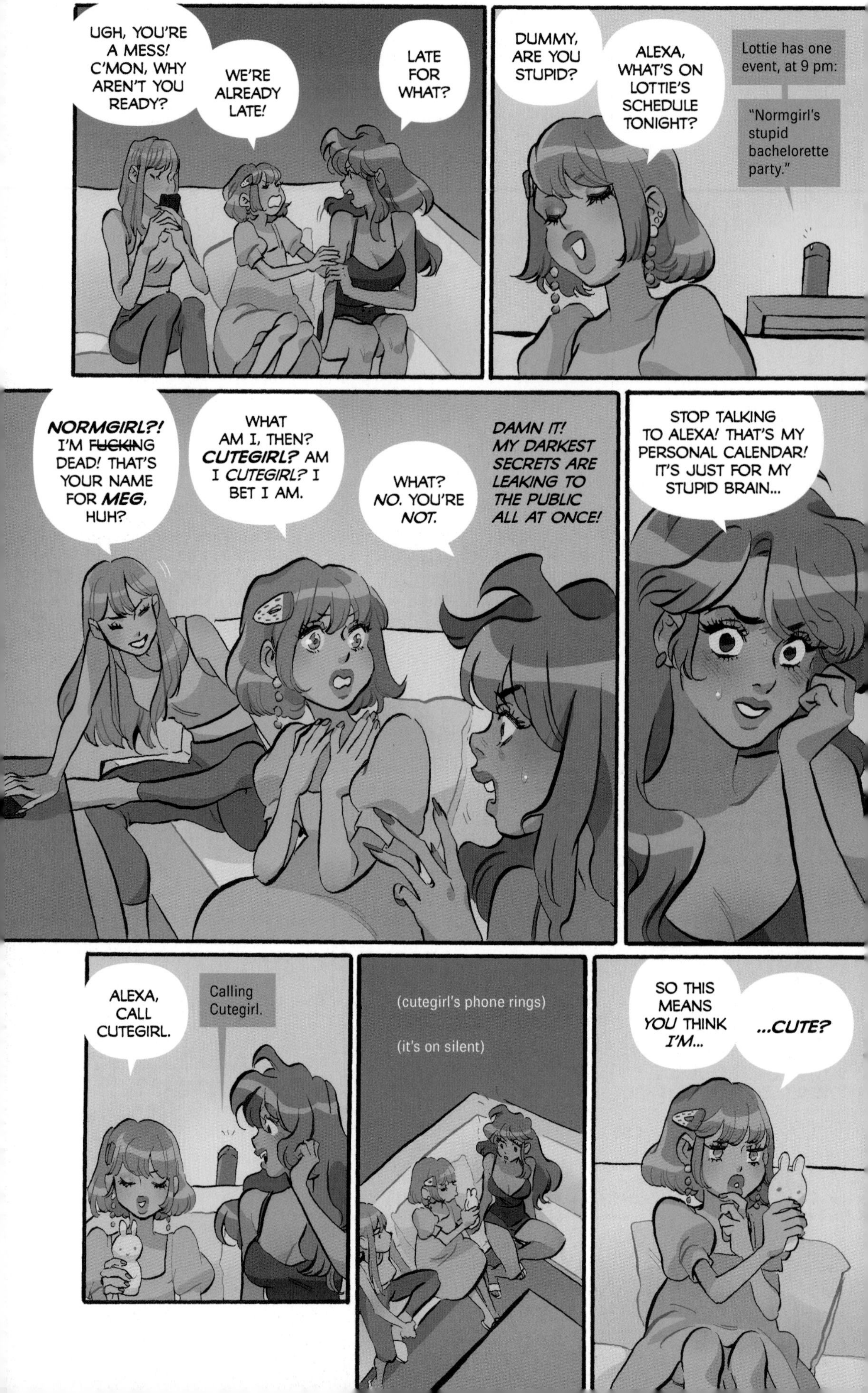
UGH, YOU'RE A MESS! C'MON, WHY AREN'T YOU READY?
WE'RE ALREADY LATE!
LATE FOR WHAT?
DUMMY, ARE YOU STUPID?
ALEXA, WHAT'S ON LOTTIE'S SCHEDULE TONIGHT?
Lottie has one event, at 9 pm:
"Normgirl's stupid bachelorette party."
NORMGIRL?! I'M FUCKING DEAD! THAT'S YOUR NAME FOR MEG, HUH?
WHAT AM I, THEN? CUTEGIRL? AM I CUTEGIRL? I BET I AM.
WHAT? NO. YOU'RE NOT.
DAMN IT! MY DARKEST SECRETS ARE LEAKING TO THE PUBLIC ALL AT ONCE!
STOP TALKING TO ALEXA! THAT'S MY PERSONAL CALENDAR! IT'S JUST FOR MY STUPID BRAIN...
ALEXA, CALL CUTEGIRL.
Calling Cutegirl.
(cutegirl's phone rings)
(it's on silent)
SO THIS MEANS YOU THINK I'M...
...CUTE?

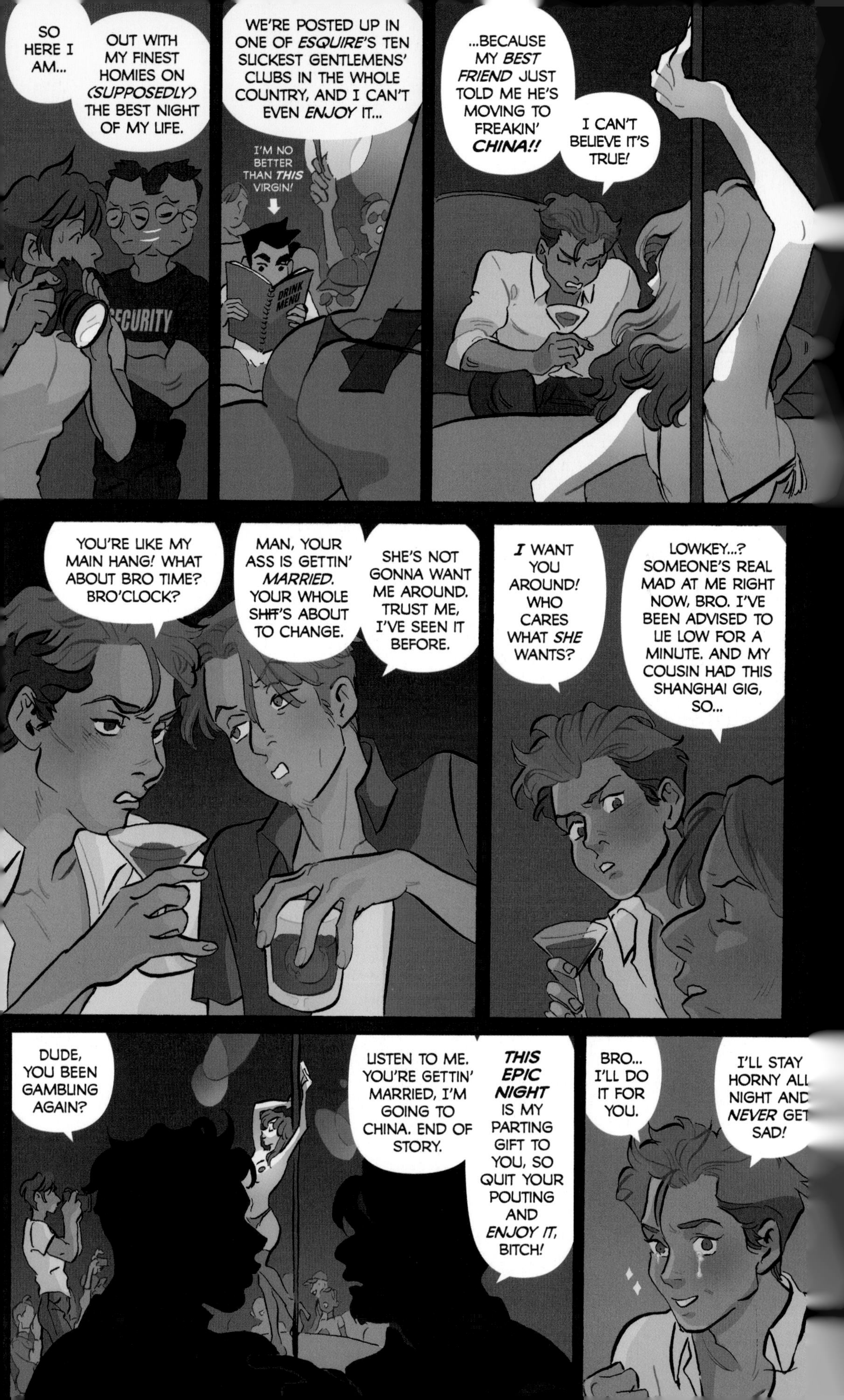
SO HERE I AM...
OUT WITH MY FINEST HOMIES ON (SUPPOSEDLY) THE BEST NIGHT OF MY LIFE.
SECURITY
WE'RE POSTED UP IN ONE OF ESQUIRE'S TEN SLICKEST GENTLEMENS' CLUBS IN THE WHOLE COUNTRY, AND I CAN'T EVEN ENJOY IT...
I'M NO BETTER THAN THIS VIRGIN!
DRINK MENU
...BECAUSE MY BEST FRIEND JUST TOLD ME HE'S MOVING TO FREAKIN' CHINA!!
I CAN'T BELIEVE IT'S TRUE!
YOU'RE LIKE MY MAIN HANG! WHAT ABOUT BRO TIME? BRO'CLOCK?
MAN, YOUR ASS IS GETTIN' MARRIED. YOUR WHOLE SHIT'S ABOUT TO CHANGE.
SHE'S NOT GONNA WANT ME AROUND. TRUST ME, I'VE SEEN IT BEFORE.
I WANT YOU AROUND! WHO CARES WHAT SHE WANTS?
LOWKEY...? SOMEONE'S REAL MAD AT ME RIGHT NOW, BRO. I'VE BEEN ADVISED TO LIE LOW FOR A MINUTE. AND MY COUSIN HAD THIS SHANGHAI GIG, SO...
DUDE, YOU BEEN GAMBLING AGAIN?
LISTEN TO ME. YOU'RE GETTIN' MARRIED, I'M GOING TO CHINA. END OF STORY.
THIS EPIC NIGHT IS MY PARTING GIFT TO YOU, SO QUIT YOUR POUTING AND ENJOY IT, BITCH!
BRO... I'LL DO IT FOR YOU.
I'LL STAY HORNY ALL NIGHT AND NEVER GET SAD!

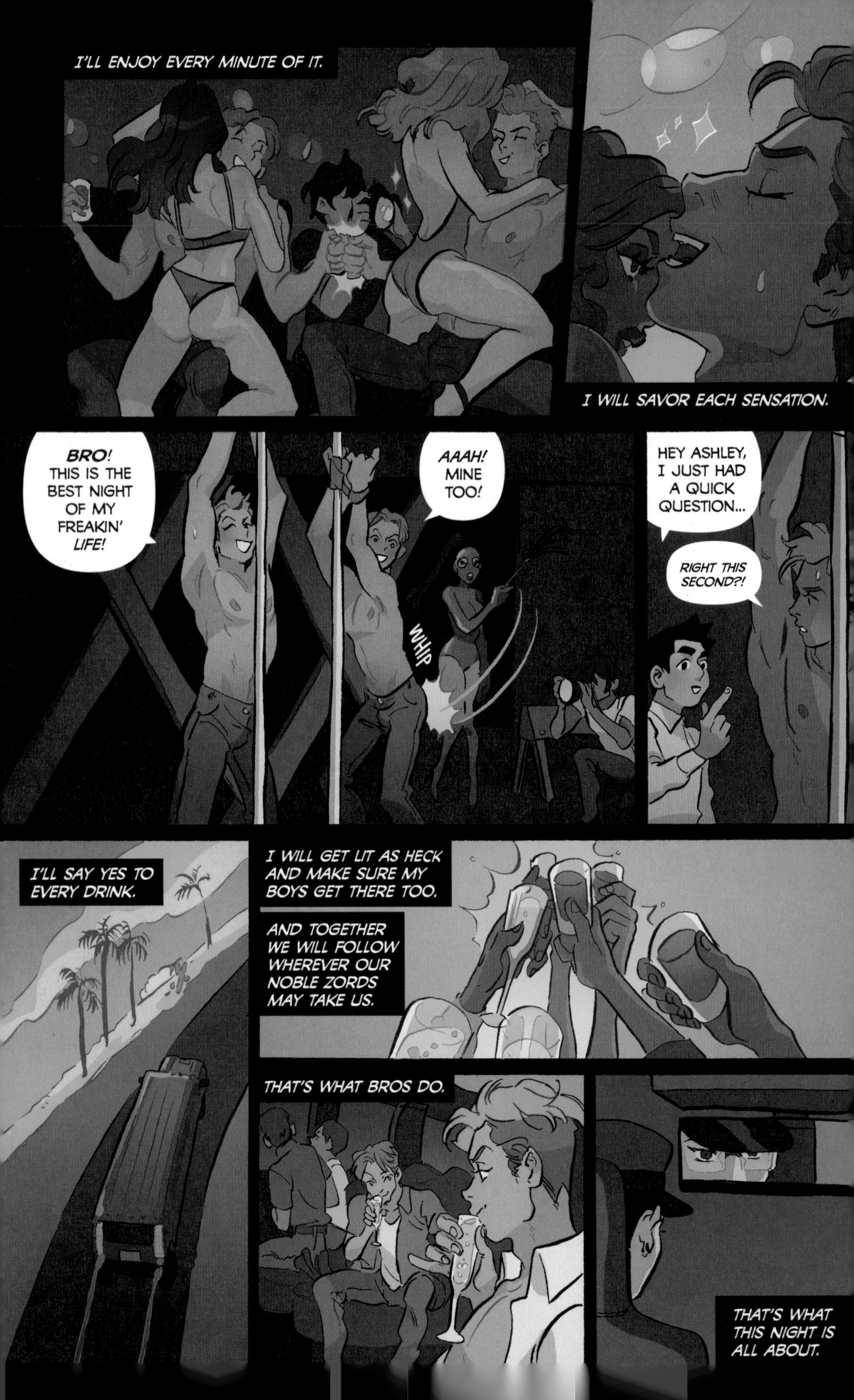
I'LL ENJOY EVERY MINUTE OF IT.
I WILL SAVOR EACH SENSATION.
BRO! THIS IS THE BEST NIGHT OF MY FREAKIN' LIFE!
AAAH! MINE TOO!
WHIP
HEY ASHLEY, I JUST HAD A QUICK QUESTION...
RIGHT THIS SECOND?!
I'LL SAY YES TO EVERY DRINK.
I WILL GET LIT AS HECK AND MAKE SURE MY BOYS GET THERE TOO.
AND TOGETHER WE WILL FOLLOW WHEREVER OUR NOBLE ZORDS MAY TAKE US.
THAT'S WHAT BROS DO.
THAT'S WHAT THIS NIGHT IS ALL ABOUT.

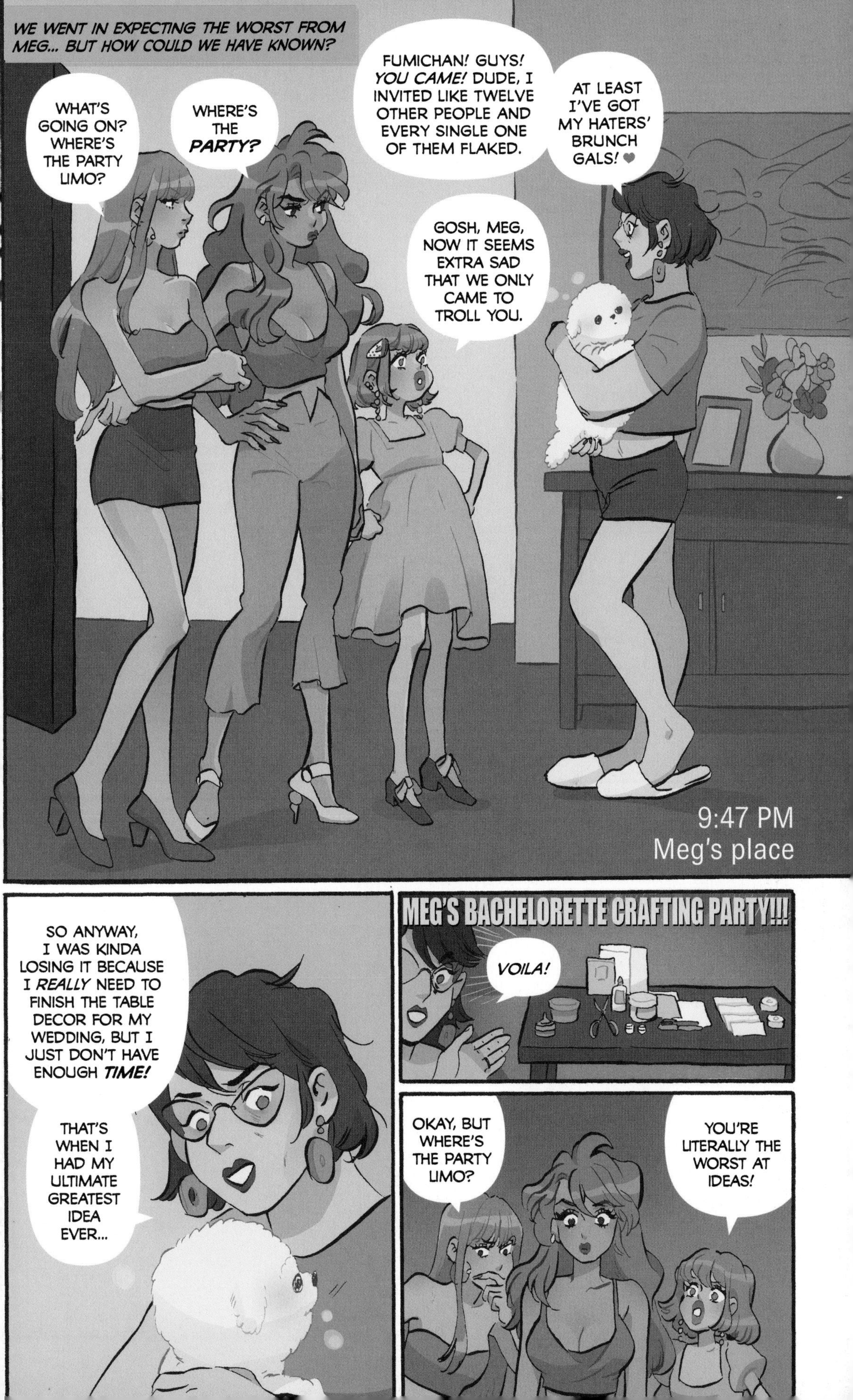
WE WENT IN EXPECTING THE WORST FROM MEG... BUT HOW COULD WE HAVE KNOWN?
WHAT'S GOING ON? WHERE'S THE PARTY LIMO?
WHERE'S THE PARTY?
FUMICHAN! GUYS! YOU CAME! DUDE, I INVITED LIKE TWELVE OTHER PEOPLE AND EVERY SINGLE ONE OF THEM FLAKED.
AT LEAST I'VE GOT MY HATERS' BRUNCH GALS! ♥
GOSH, MEG, NOW IT SEEMS EXTRA SAD THAT WE ONLY CAME TO TROLL YOU.
9:47 PM
Meg's place
SO ANYWAY, I WAS KINDA LOSING IT BECAUSE I REALLY NEED TO FINISH THE TABLE DECOR FOR MY WEDDING, BUT I JUST DON'T HAVE ENOUGH TIME!
THAT'S WHEN I HAD MY ULTIMATE GREATEST IDEA EVER...
MEG'S BACHELORETTE CRAFTING PARTY!!!
VOILA!
OKAY, BUT WHERE'S THE PARTY LIMO?
YOU'RE LITERALLY THE WORST AT IDEAS!

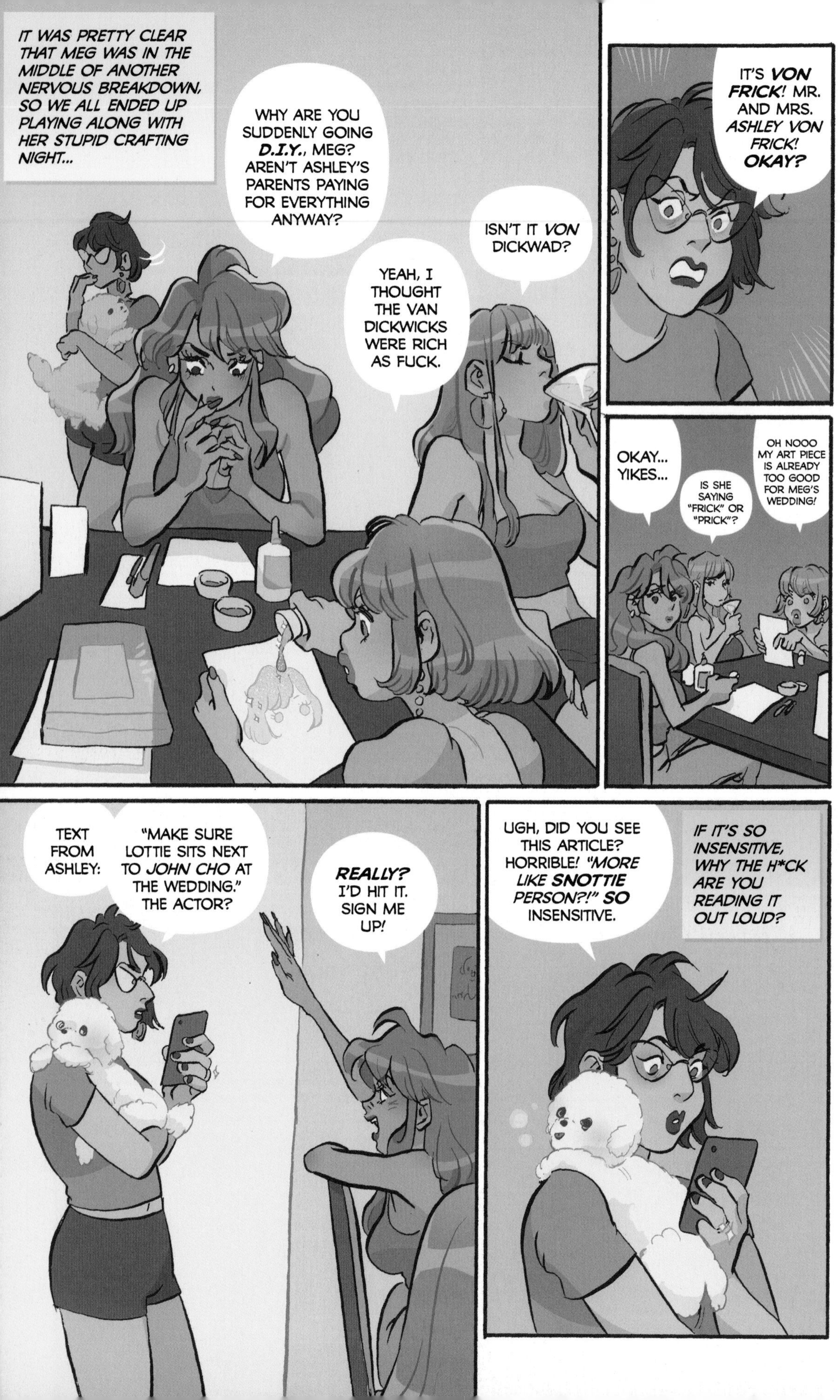
IT WAS PRETTY CLEAR THAT MEG WAS IN THE MIDDLE OF ANOTHER NERVOUS BREAKDOWN, SO WE ALL ENDED UP PLAYING ALONG WITH HER STUPID CRAFTING NIGHT...
WHY ARE YOU SUDDENLY GOING D.I.Y., MEG? AREN'T ASHLEY'S PARENTS PAYING FOR EVERYTHING ANYWAY?
YEAH, I THOUGHT THE VAN DICKWICKS WERE RICH AS FUCK.
ISN'T IT VON DICKWAD?
IT'S VON FRICK! MR. AND MRS. ASHLEY VON FRICK! OKAY?
OKAY... YIKES...
IS SHE SAYING "FRICK" OR "PRICK"?
OH NOOO MY ART PIECE IS ALREADY TOO GOOD FOR MEG'S WEDDING!
TEXT FROM ASHLEY:
"MAKE SURE LOTTIE SITS NEXT TO JOHN CHO AT THE WEDDING." THE ACTOR?
REALLY? I'D HIT IT. SIGN ME UP!
UGH, DID YOU SEE THIS ARTICLE? HORRIBLE! "MORE LIKE SNOTTIE PERSON?!" SO INSENSITIVE.
IF IT'S SO INSENSITIVE, WHY THE H*CK ARE YOU READING IT OUT LOUD?

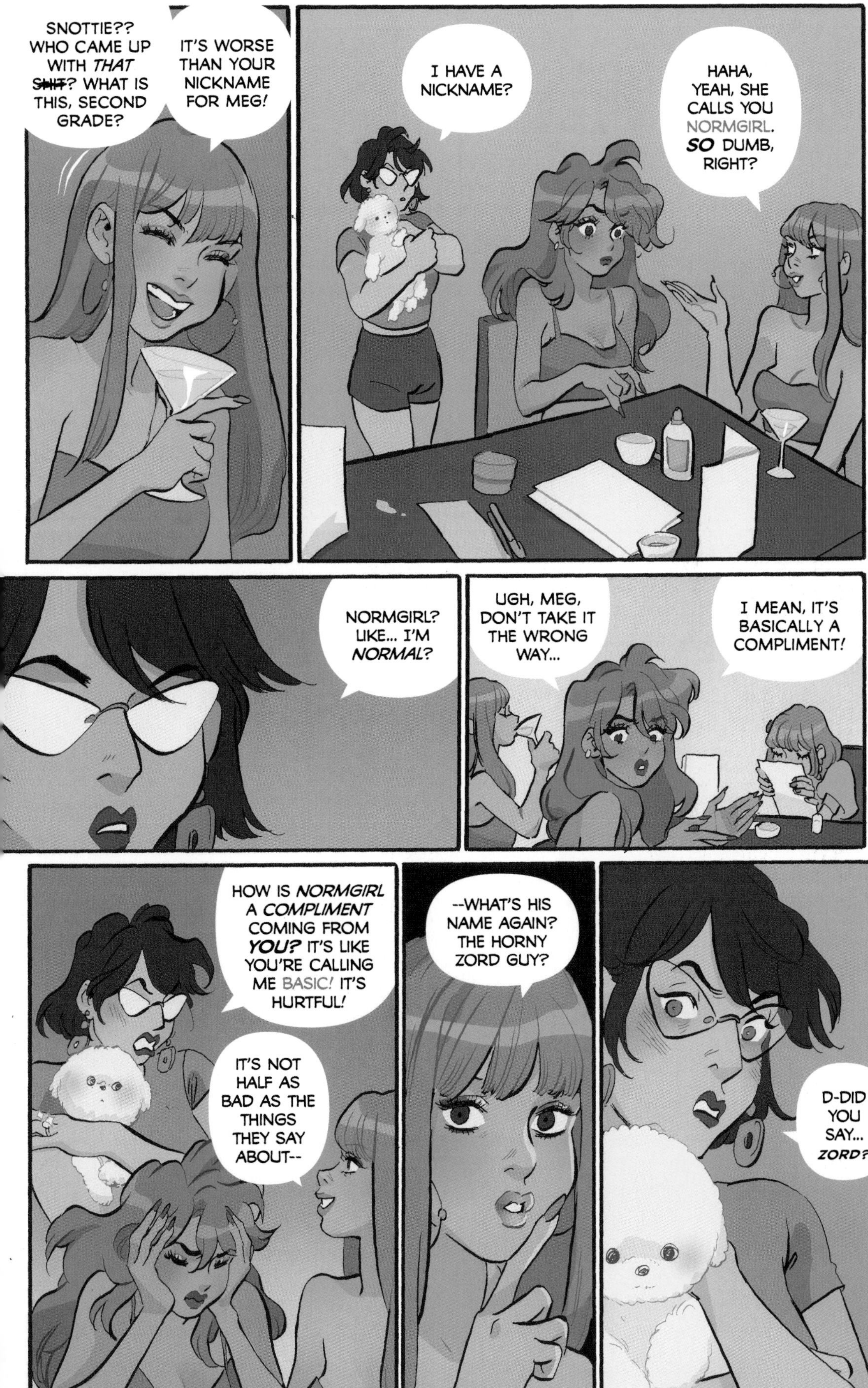

SNOTTIE?? WHO CAME UP WITH *THAT* SHIT? WHAT IS THIS, SECOND GRADE?
IT'S WORSE THAN YOUR NICKNAME FOR MEG!
I HAVE A NICKNAME?
HAHA, YEAH, SHE CALLS YOU NORMGIRL. ***SO*** DUMB, RIGHT?
NORMGIRL? LIKE... I'M *NORMAL*?
UGH, MEG, DON'T TAKE IT THE WRONG WAY...
I MEAN, IT'S BASICALLY A COMPLIMENT!
HOW IS *NORMGIRL* A *COMPLIMENT* COMING FROM ***YOU?*** IT'S LIKE YOU'RE CALLING ME BASIC! IT'S HURTFUL!
IT'S NOT HALF AS BAD AS THE THINGS THEY SAY ABOUT--
--WHAT'S HIS NAME AGAIN? THE HORNY ZORD GUY?
D-DID YOU SAY... ***ZORD?***

...YOU GUYS ALL KNOW ABOUT THAT? EVERYONE KNOWS ABOUT THE ZORD DOCKING PROCEDURE?

AAAAH WE KNOW ENOUGH! WE DON'T NEED ANY MORE DETAILS!

KNOW ABOUT IT? GIRL, HALF OF US HAVE *SEEN* IT!

SO I MAY HAVE GOTTEN BORED AT SOME POINT AND TOLD ROSIE A BUNCH OF FRIEND GOSSIP THAT I PROBABLY SHOULD HAVE KEPT TO MYSELF... OOPS?

W-WHO SAW WHAT? WHO, WHAT, WHEN?!

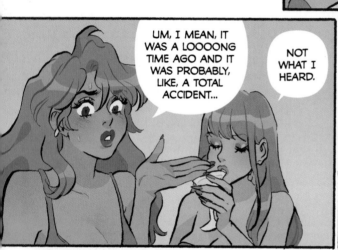

UM, I MEAN, IT WAS A LOOOONG TIME AGO AND IT WAS PROBABLY, LIKE, A TOTAL ACCIDENT...

NOT WHAT I HEARD.

IT WAS THE FIRST TIME I MET HIM... AT YOUR ENGAGEMENT PARTY.

YOU KNOW I HATE PARTIES AND I *SUPER* HATE FLIRTING, BUT SOME SEMI-CUTE GUY WAS MAKING ~~FUCK~~ EYES AT ME ALL NIGHT AND MY RESISTANCE WAS STARTING TO WAVER.

SO I'M LOWKEY KINDA FEELING IT, WHEN ALL OF A SUDDEN YOU COME OUT LIKE:

Y'ALL, THIS HORNY GOAT IS MY *FIANCÉ!*

LONG STORY SHORT, I STEERED CLEAR OF HIM FOR THE REST OF THE NIGHT, UNTIL ME AND CAROLINE WALKED IN THE BATHROOM AND HE WAS WAITING FOR US IN THERE BUTT-ASS NAKED. SO WE RAN THE HECK AWAY! THE END!

LADIES. VOULEZ-VOUS UN PETIT F*CK SPORTIF?

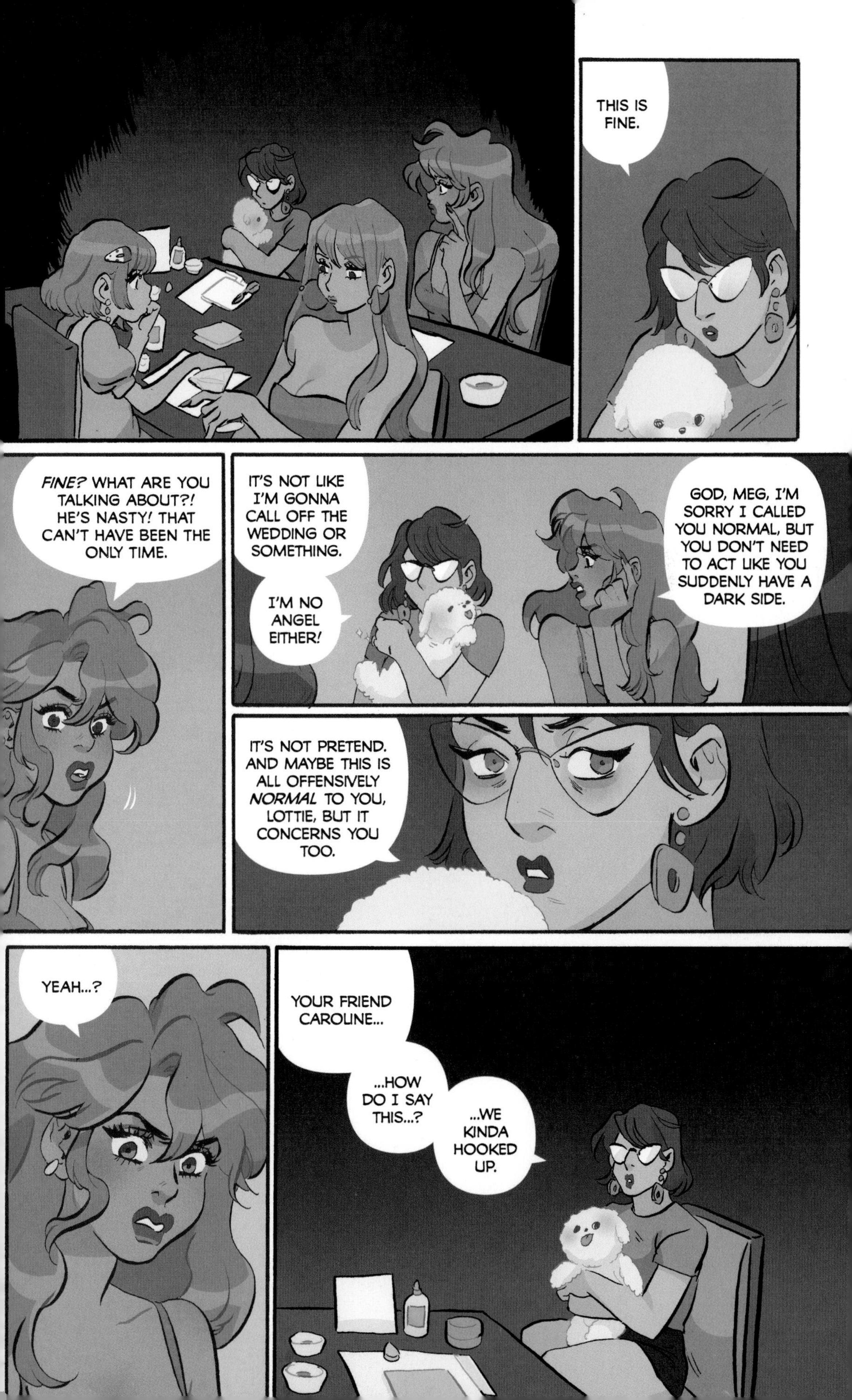
THIS IS FINE.
FINE? WHAT ARE YOU TALKING ABOUT?! HE'S NASTY! THAT CAN'T HAVE BEEN THE ONLY TIME.
IT'S NOT LIKE I'M GONNA CALL OFF THE WEDDING OR SOMETHING.
I'M NO ANGEL EITHER!
GOD, MEG, I'M SORRY I CALLED YOU NORMAL, BUT YOU DON'T NEED TO ACT LIKE YOU SUDDENLY HAVE A DARK SIDE.
IT'S NOT PRETEND. AND MAYBE THIS IS ALL OFFENSIVELY NORMAL TO YOU, LOTTIE, BUT IT CONCERNS YOU TOO.
YEAH...?
YOUR FRIEND CAROLINE...
...HOW DO I SAY THIS...?
...WE KINDA HOOKED UP.

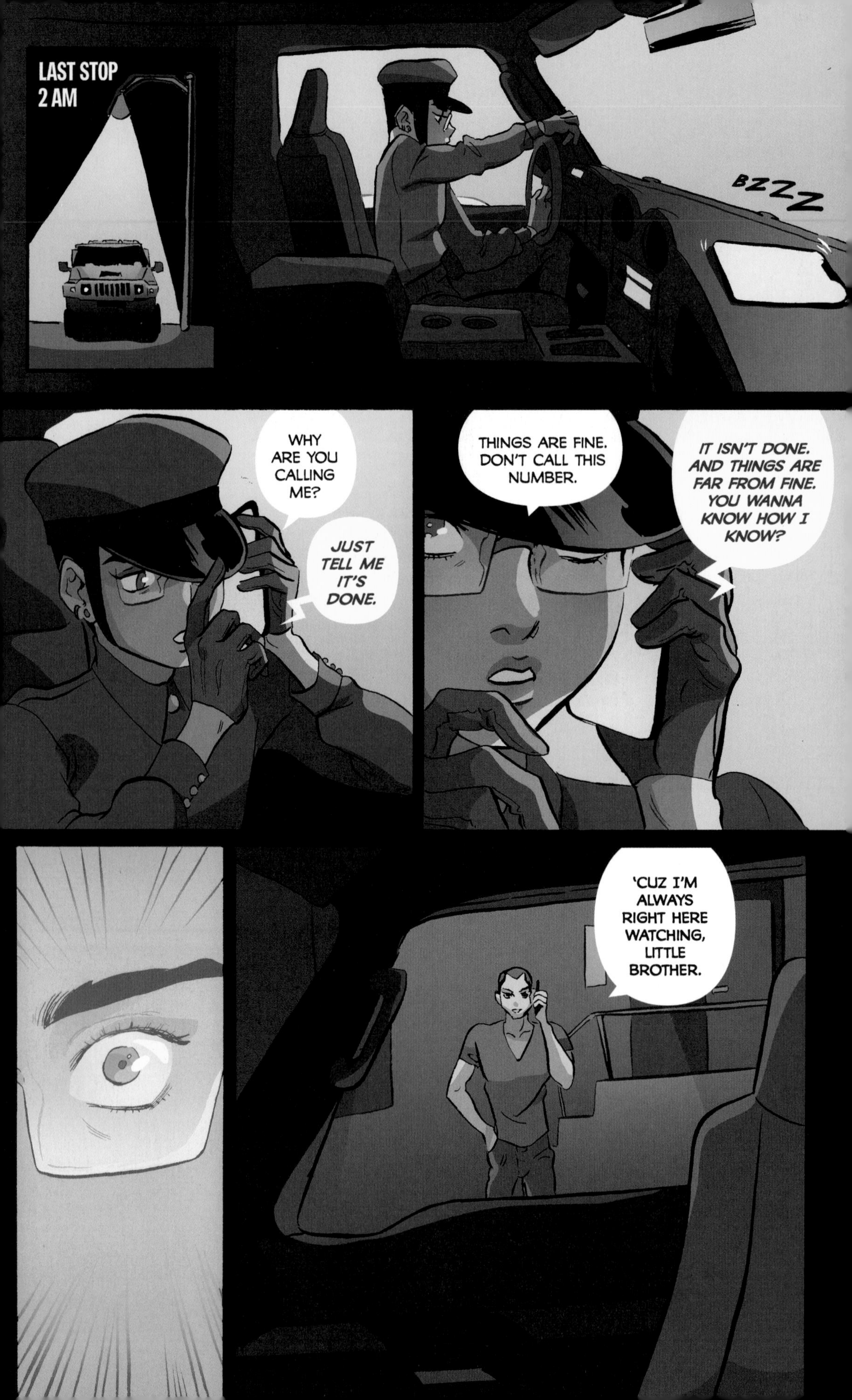
LAST STOP
2 AM
BZZZ
WHY ARE YOU CALLING ME?
JUST TELL ME IT'S DONE.
THINGS ARE FINE. DON'T CALL THIS NUMBER.
IT ISN'T DONE. AND THINGS ARE FAR FROM FINE. YOU WANNA KNOW HOW I KNOW?
'CUZ I'M ALWAYS RIGHT HERE WATCHING, LITTLE BROTHER.

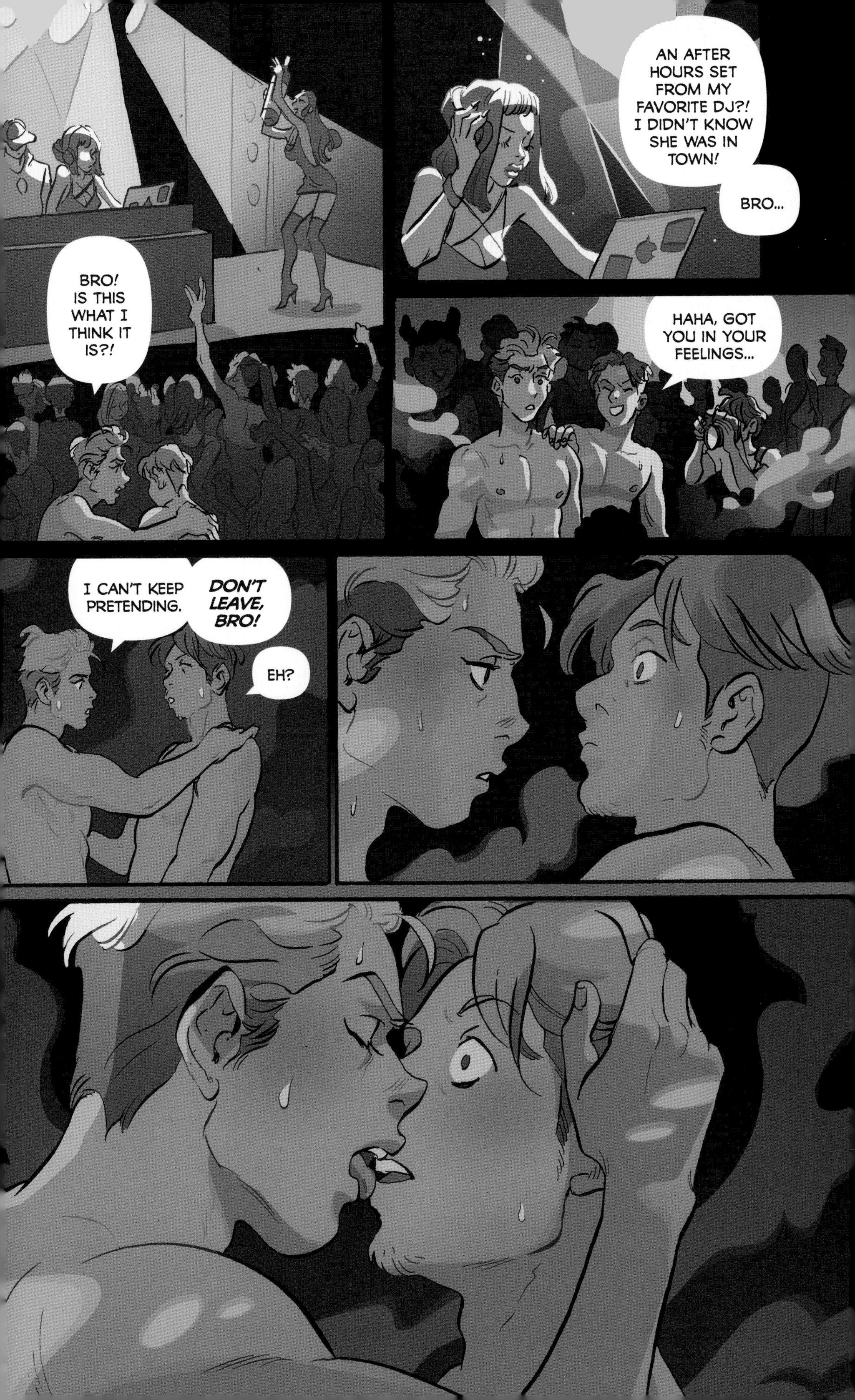
BRO! IS THIS WHAT I THINK IT IS?!
AN AFTER HOURS SET FROM MY FAVORITE DJ?! I DIDN'T KNOW SHE WAS IN TOWN!
BRO...
HAHA, GOT YOU IN YOUR FEELINGS...
I CAN'T KEEP PRETENDING.
DON'T LEAVE, BRO!
EH?

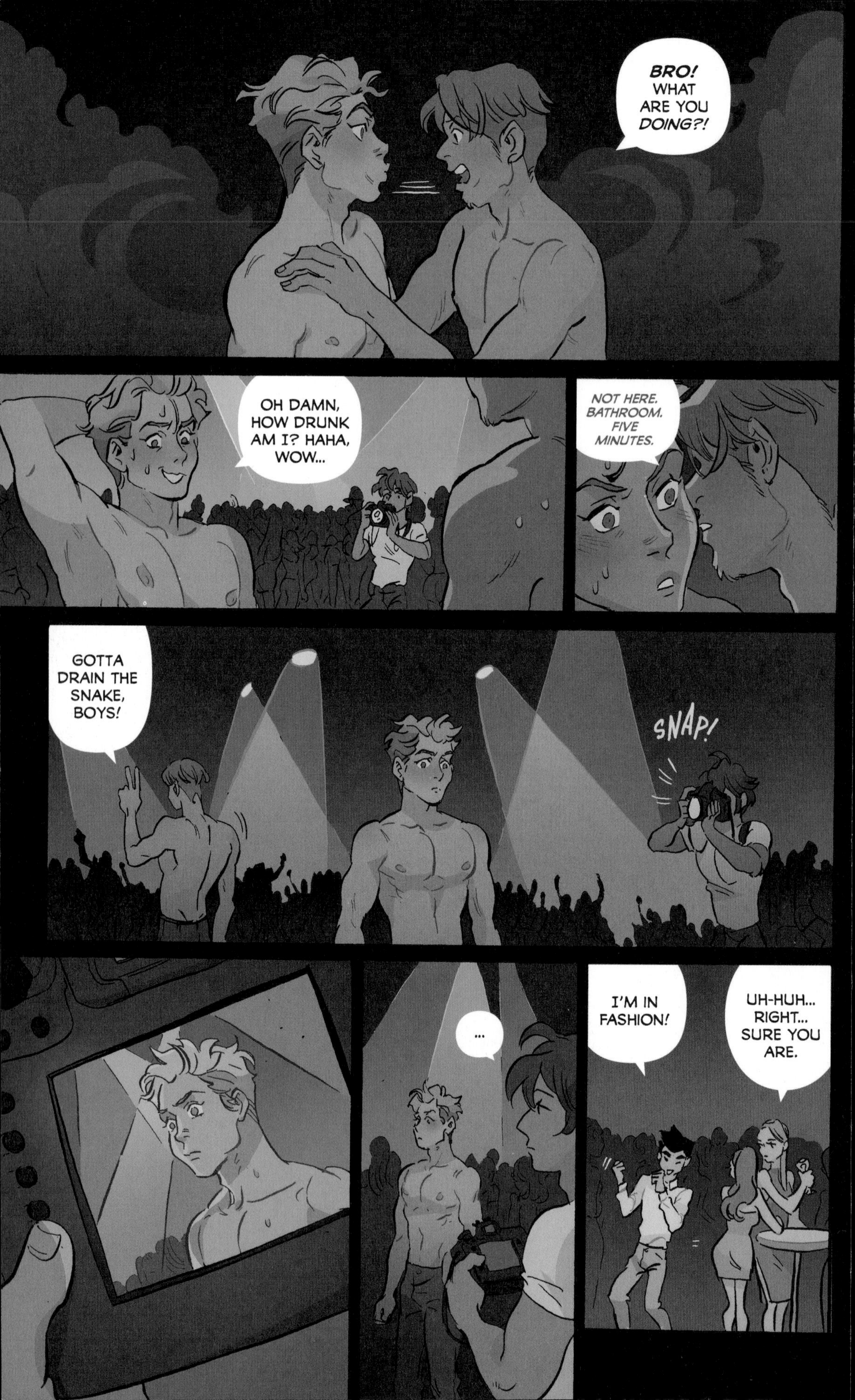
BRO! WHAT ARE YOU DOING?!
OH DAMN, HOW DRUNK AM I? HAHA, WOW...
NOT HERE. BATHROOM. FIVE MINUTES.
GOTTA DRAIN THE SNAKE, BOYS!
SNAP!
...
I'M IN FASHION!
UH-HUH... RIGHT... SURE YOU ARE.

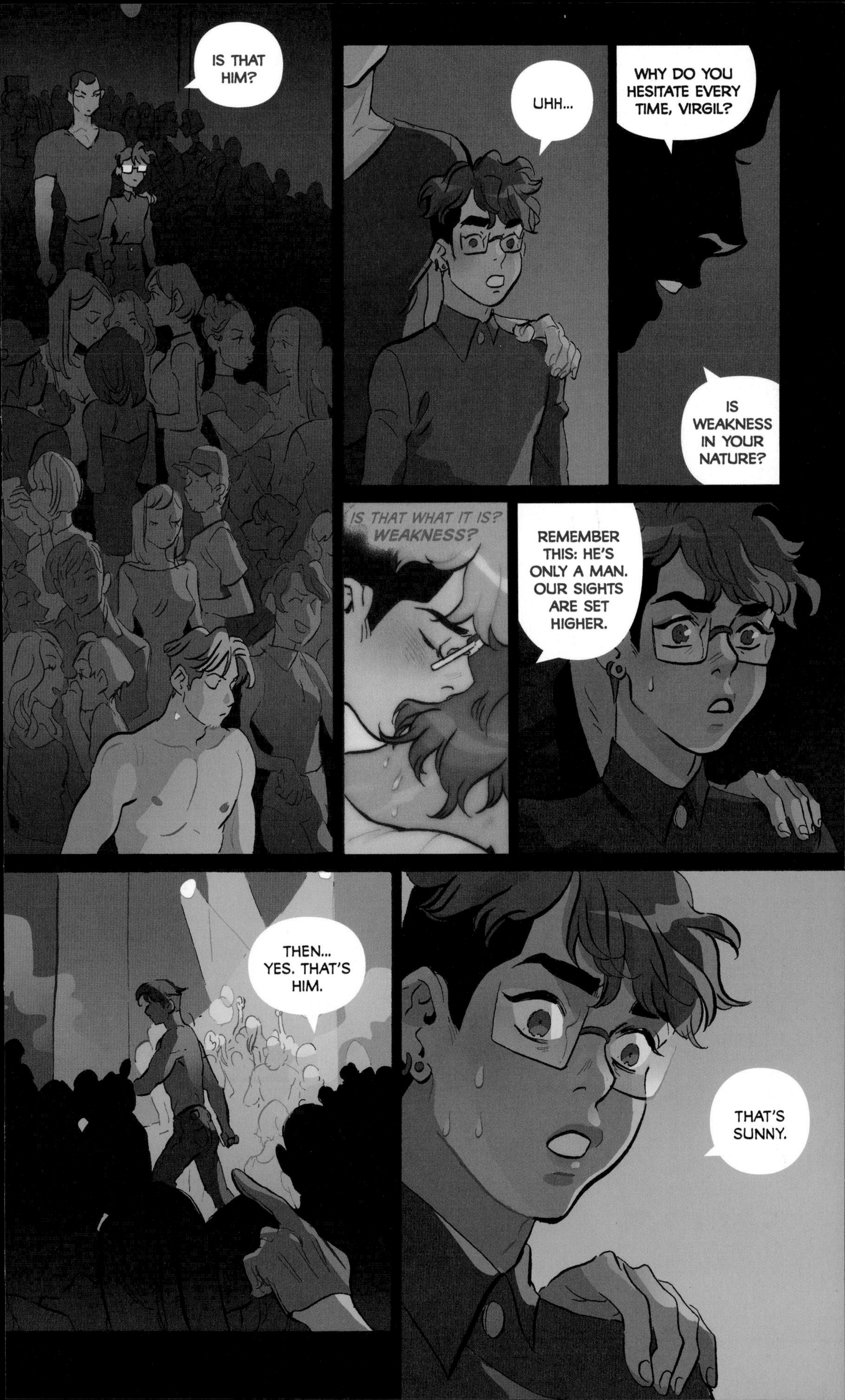
IS THAT HIM?
UHH...
WHY DO YOU HESITATE EVERY TIME, VIRGIL?
IS WEAKNESS IN YOUR NATURE?
IS THAT WHAT IT IS? WEAKNESS?
REMEMBER THIS: HE'S ONLY A MAN. OUR SIGHTS ARE SET HIGHER.
THEN... YES. THAT'S HIM.
THAT'S SUNNY.

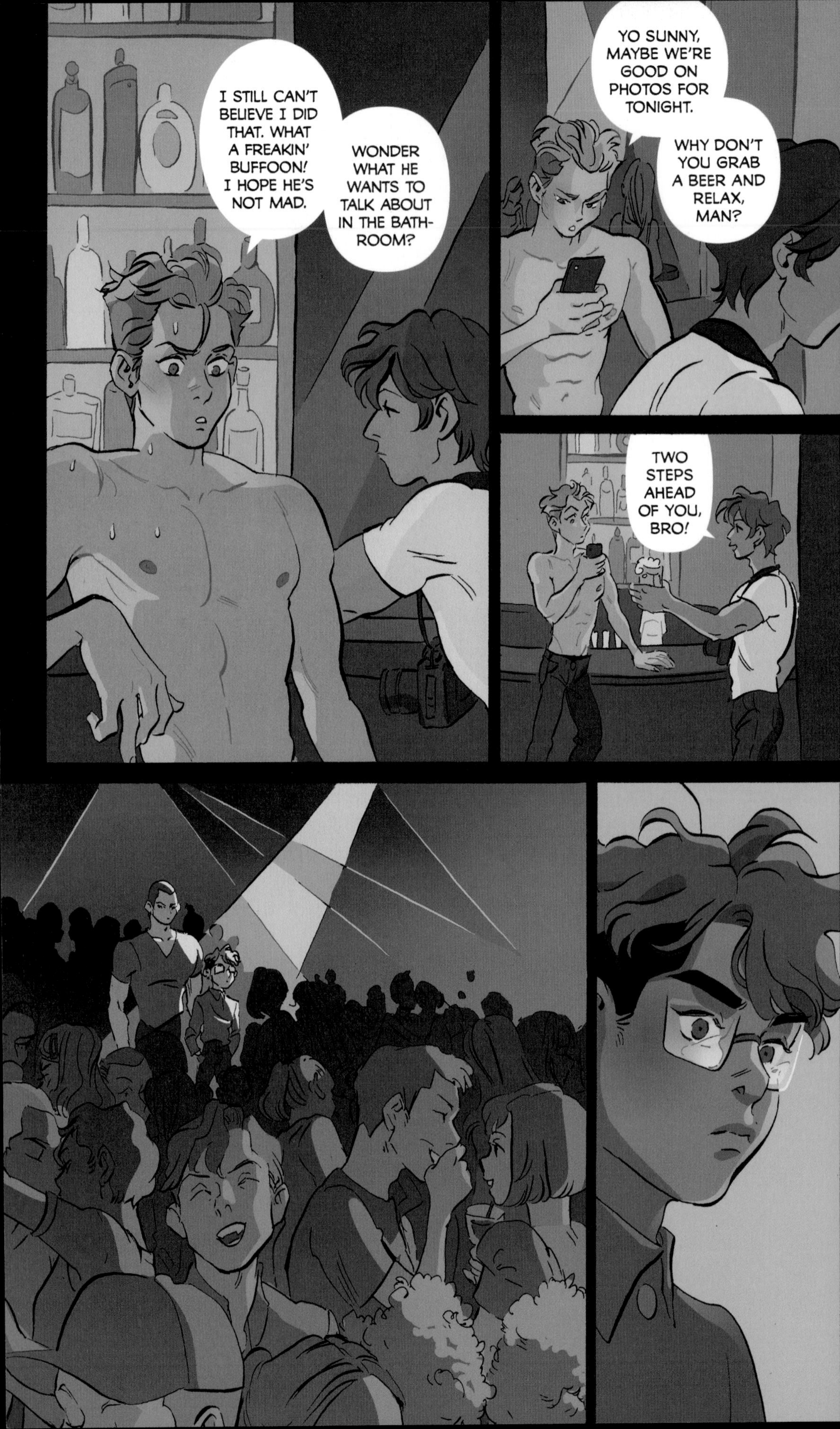
I STILL CAN'T BELIEVE I DID THAT. WHAT A FREAKIN' BUFFOON! I HOPE HE'S NOT MAD.
WONDER WHAT HE WANTS TO TALK ABOUT IN THE BATH-ROOM?
YO SUNNY, MAYBE WE'RE GOOD ON PHOTOS FOR TONIGHT.
WHY DON'T YOU GRAB A BEER AND RELAX, MAN?
TWO STEPS AHEAD OF YOU, BRO!

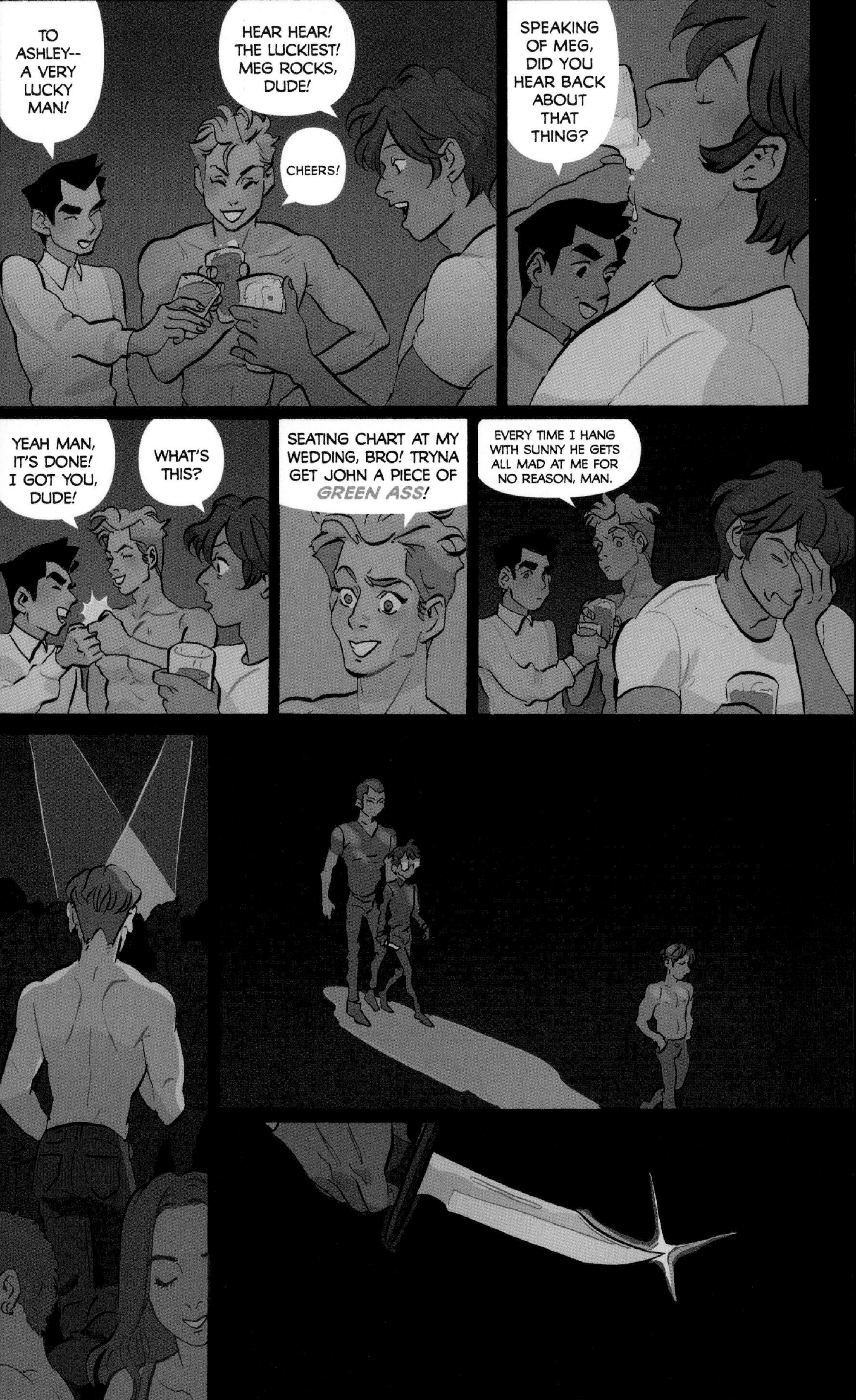
TO ASHLEY-- A VERY LUCKY MAN!
HEAR HEAR! THE LUCKIEST! MEG ROCKS, DUDE!
CHEERS!
SPEAKING OF MEG, DID YOU HEAR BACK ABOUT THAT THING?
YEAH MAN, IT'S DONE! I GOT YOU, DUDE!
WHAT'S THIS?
SEATING CHART AT MY WEDDING, BRO! TRYNA GET JOHN A PIECE OF GREEN ASS!
EVERY TIME I HANG WITH SUNNY HE GETS ALL MAD AT ME FOR NO REASON, MAN.

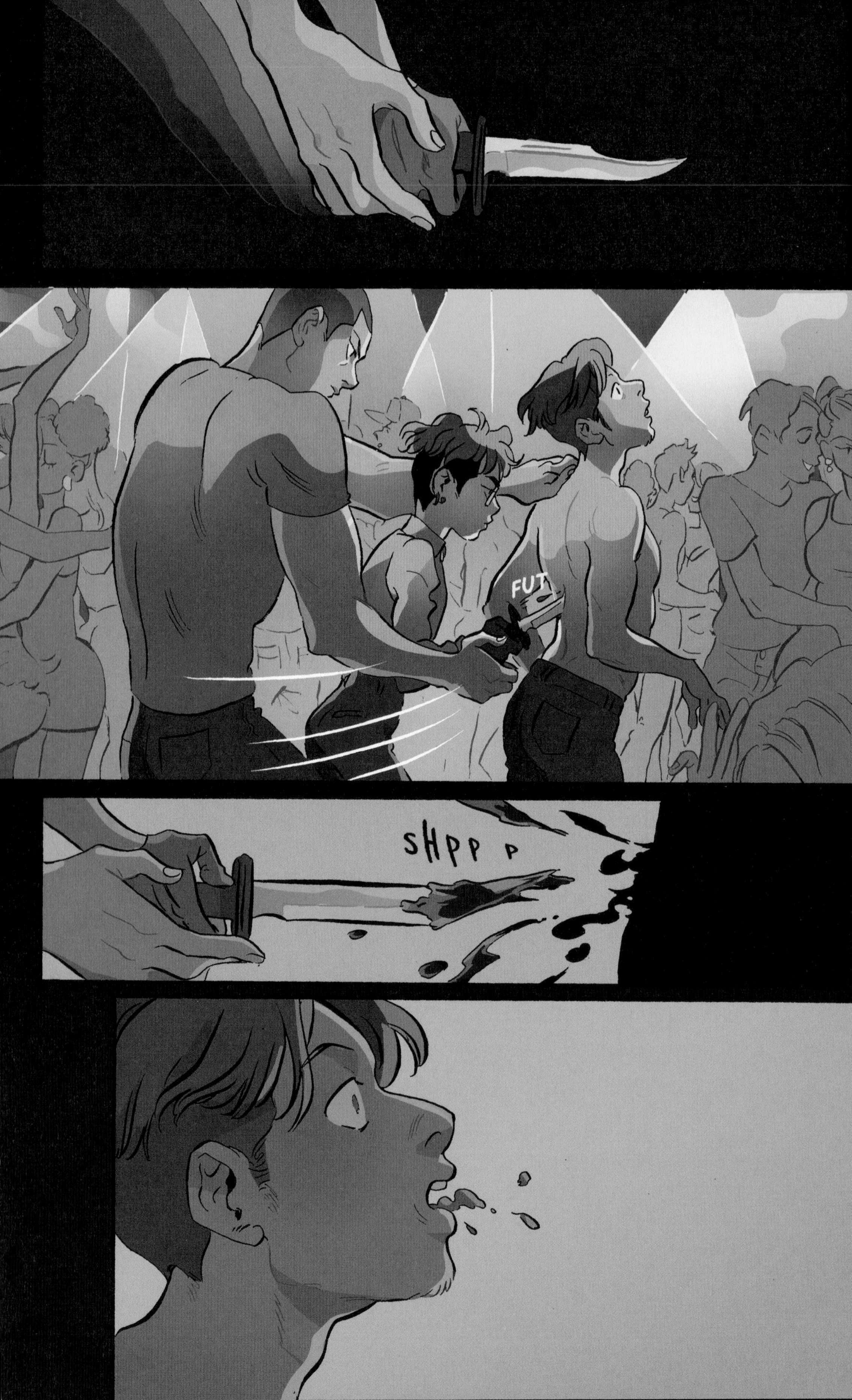
FUT
SHPP P

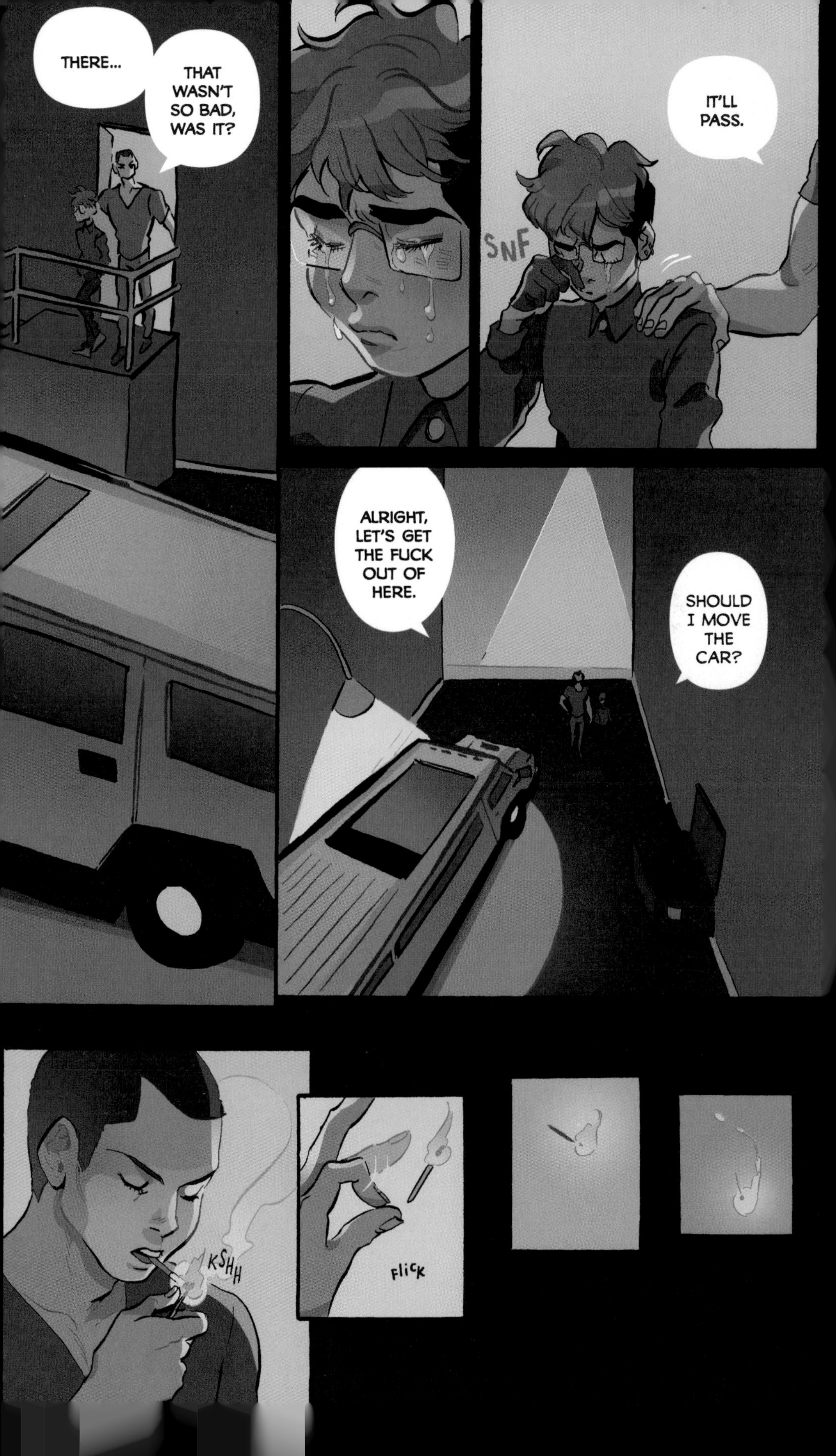
THERE...
THAT WASN'T SO BAD, WAS IT?
SNF
IT'LL PASS.
ALRIGHT, LET'S GET THE FUCK OUT OF HERE.
SHOULD I MOVE THE CAR?
KSHH
FLICK

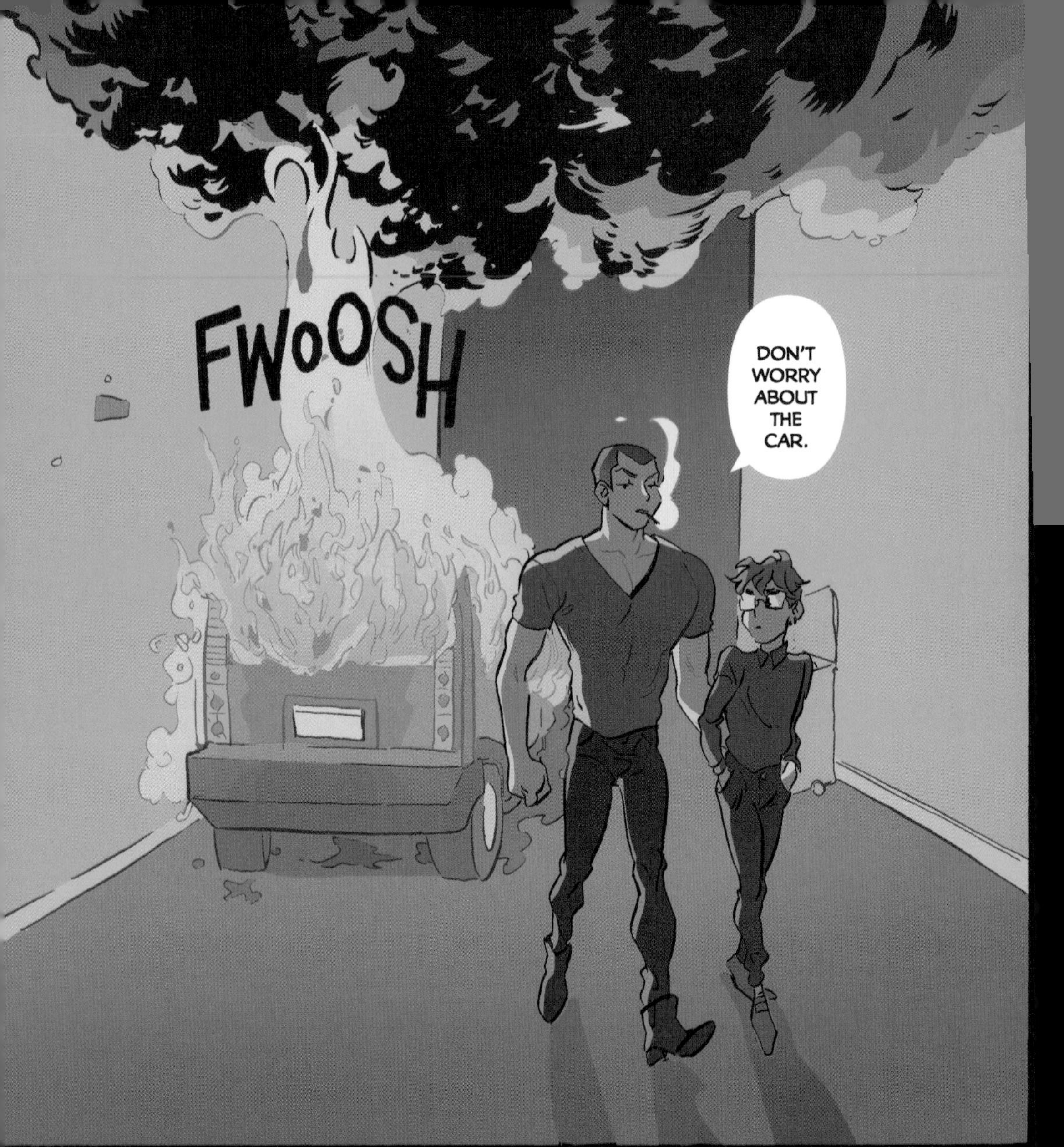
FWOOSH
DON'T WORRY ABOUT THE CAR.

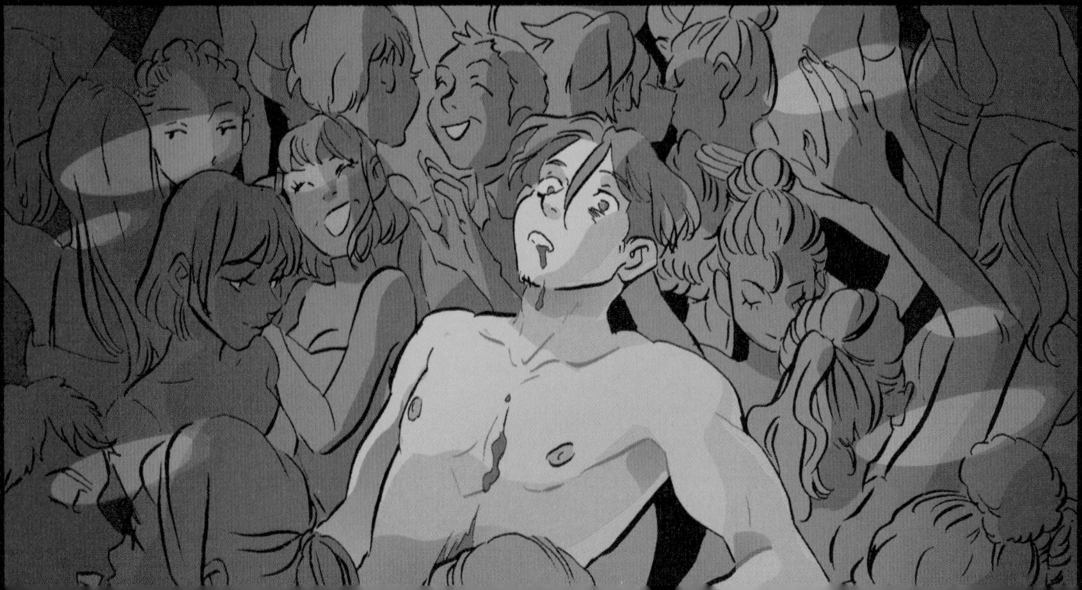

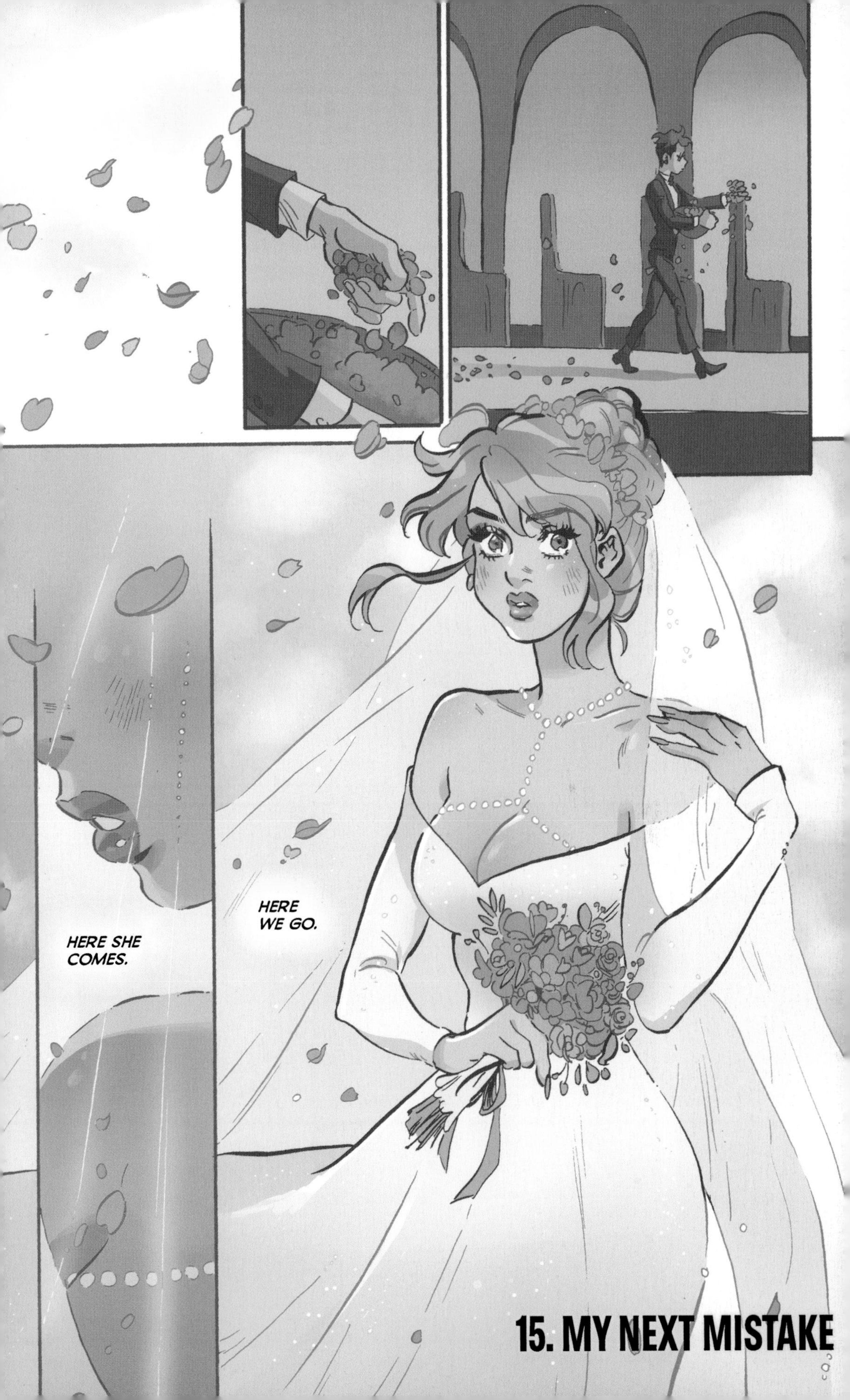
HERE SHE COMES.
HERE WE GO.
15. MY NEXT MISTAKE

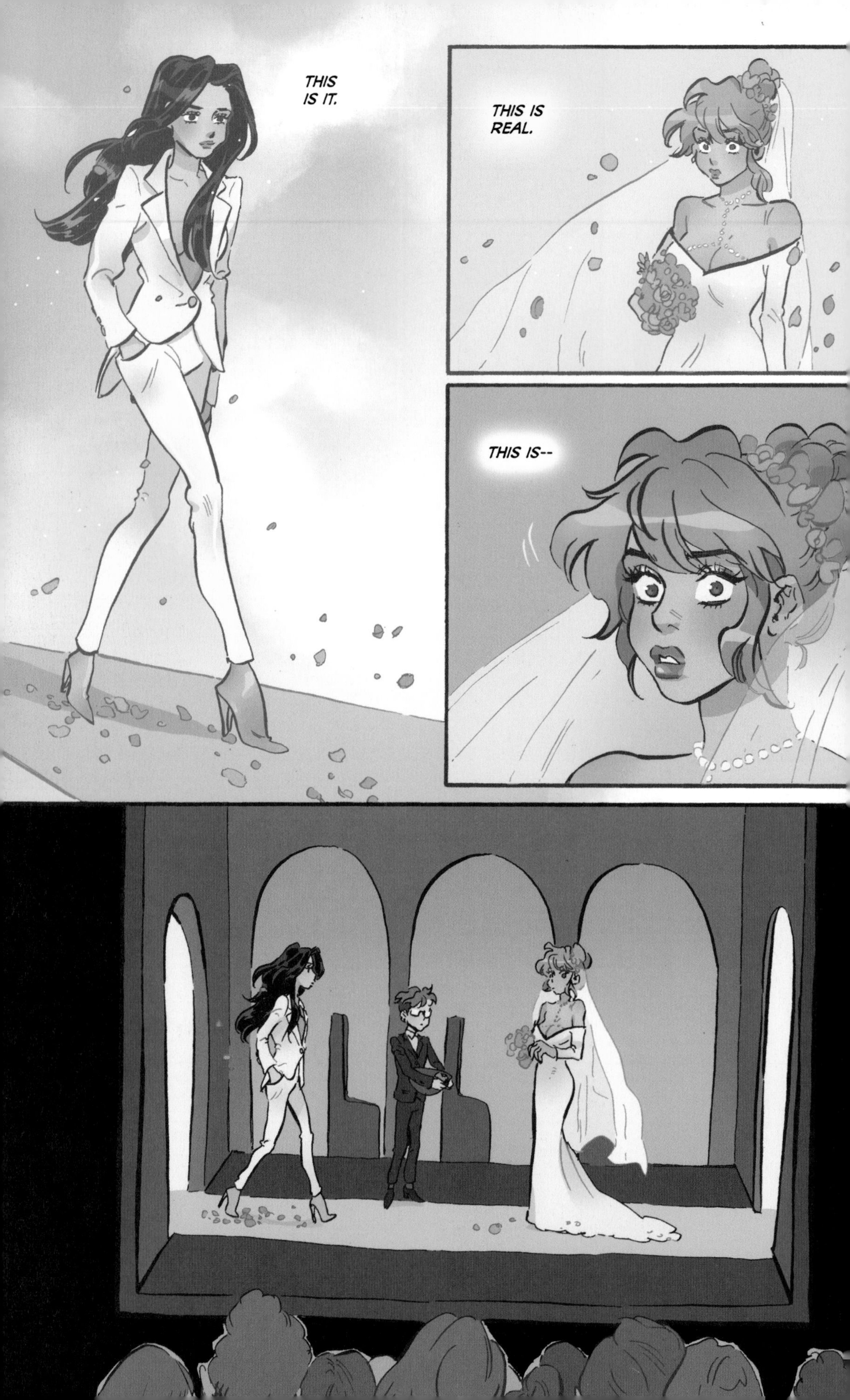
THIS IS IT.
THIS IS REAL.
THIS IS--

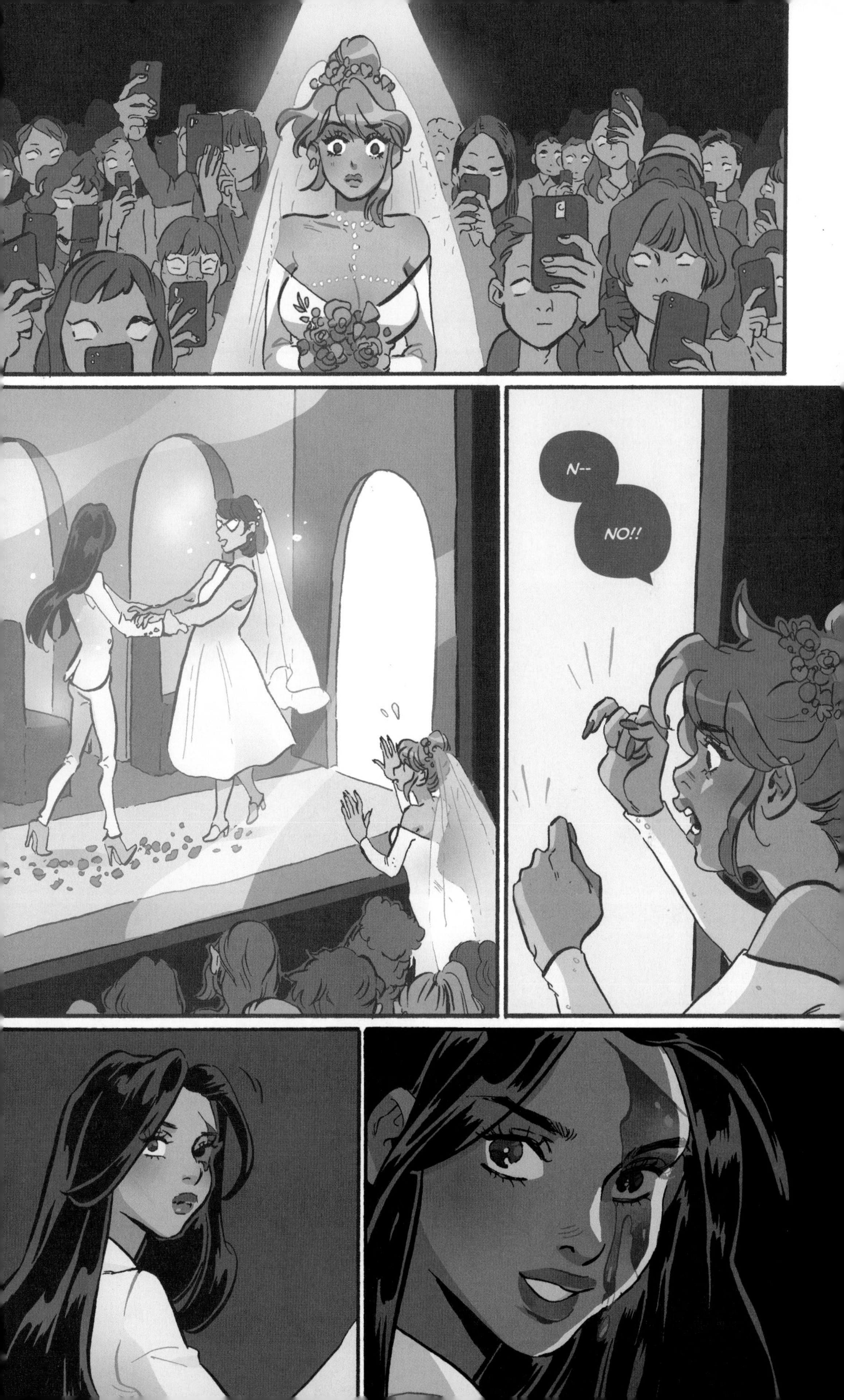
N--
NO!!

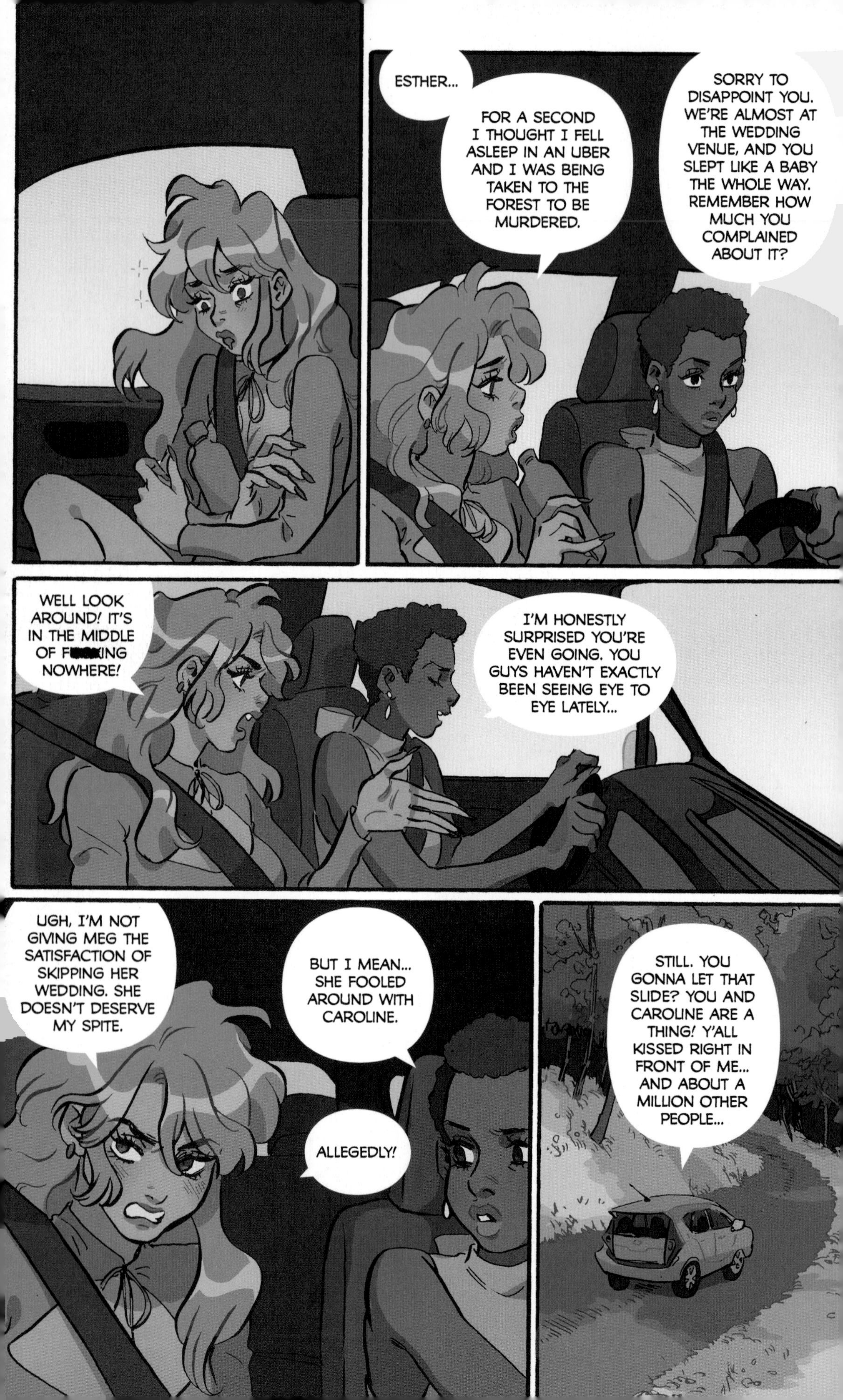
ESTHER...
FOR A SECOND I THOUGHT I FELL ASLEEP IN AN UBER AND I WAS BEING TAKEN TO THE FOREST TO BE MURDERED.
SORRY TO DISAPPOINT YOU. WE'RE ALMOST AT THE WEDDING VENUE, AND YOU SLEPT LIKE A BABY THE WHOLE WAY. REMEMBER HOW MUCH YOU COMPLAINED ABOUT IT?
WELL LOOK AROUND! IT'S IN THE MIDDLE OF F[redacted]ING NOWHERE!
I'M HONESTLY SURPRISED YOU'RE EVEN GOING. YOU GUYS HAVEN'T EXACTLY BEEN SEEING EYE TO EYE LATELY...
UGH, I'M NOT GIVING MEG THE SATISFACTION OF SKIPPING HER WEDDING. SHE DOESN'T DESERVE MY SPITE.
BUT I MEAN... SHE FOOLED AROUND WITH CAROLINE.
ALLEGEDLY!
STILL. YOU GONNA LET THAT SLIDE? YOU AND CAROLINE ARE A THING! Y'ALL KISSED RIGHT IN FRONT OF ME... AND ABOUT A MILLION OTHER PEOPLE...

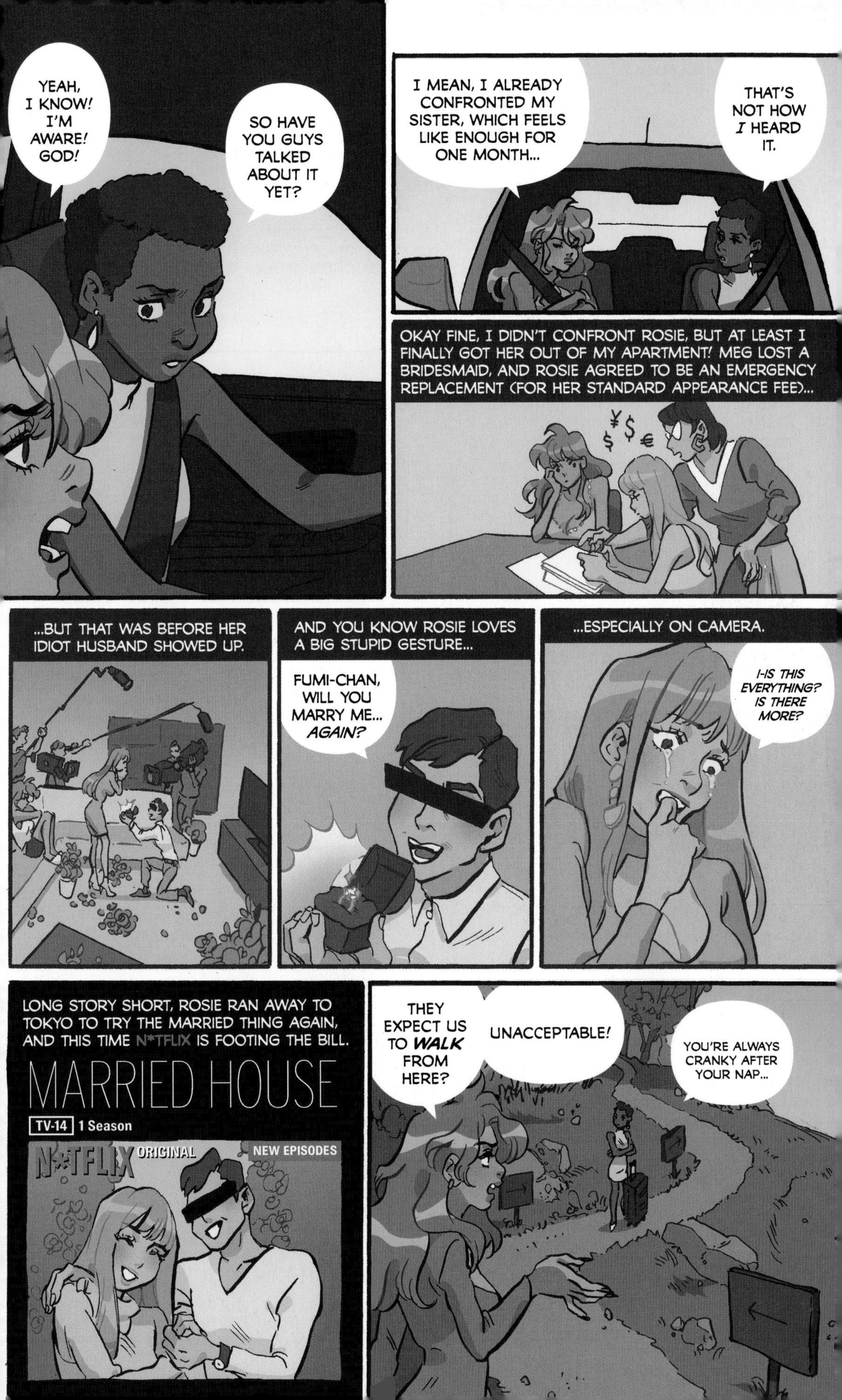
YEAH, I KNOW! I'M AWARE! GOD!
SO HAVE YOU GUYS TALKED ABOUT IT YET?
I MEAN, I ALREADY CONFRONTED MY SISTER, WHICH FEELS LIKE ENOUGH FOR ONE MONTH...
THAT'S NOT HOW *I* HEARD IT.
OKAY FINE, I DIDN'T CONFRONT ROSIE, BUT AT LEAST I FINALLY GOT HER OUT OF MY APARTMENT! MEG LOST A BRIDESMAID, AND ROSIE AGREED TO BE AN EMERGENCY REPLACEMENT (FOR HER STANDARD APPEARANCE FEE)...
¥ $ $ €
...BUT THAT WAS BEFORE HER IDIOT HUSBAND SHOWED UP.
AND YOU KNOW ROSIE LOVES A BIG STUPID GESTURE...
FUMI-CHAN, WILL YOU MARRY ME... *AGAIN?*
...ESPECIALLY ON CAMERA.
I-IS THIS EVERYTHING? IS THERE MORE?
LONG STORY SHORT, ROSIE RAN AWAY TO TOKYO TO TRY THE MARRIED THING AGAIN, AND THIS TIME N*TFLIX IS FOOTING THE BILL.
MARRIED HOUSE
TV-14 1 Season
N*TFLIX ORIGINAL
NEW EPISODES
THEY EXPECT US TO *WALK* FROM HERE?
UNACCEPTABLE!
YOU'RE ALWAYS CRANKY AFTER YOUR NAP...

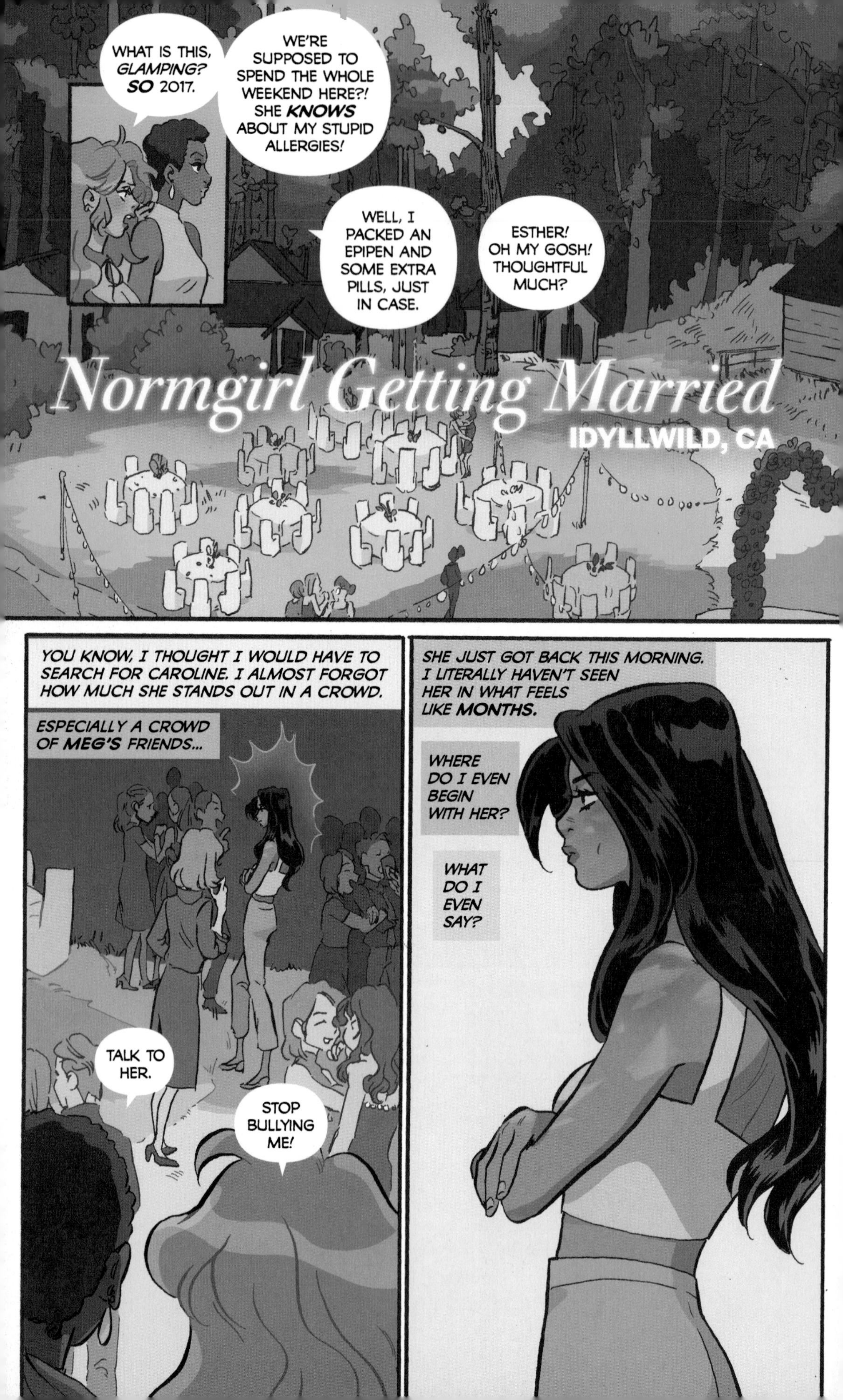
WHAT IS THIS, GLAMPING? SO 2017.
WE'RE SUPPOSED TO SPEND THE WHOLE WEEKEND HERE?! SHE KNOWS ABOUT MY STUPID ALLERGIES!
WELL, I PACKED AN EPIPEN AND SOME EXTRA PILLS, JUST IN CASE.
ESTHER! OH MY GOSH! THOUGHTFUL MUCH?
Normgirl Getting Married
IDYLLWILD, CA
YOU KNOW, I THOUGHT I WOULD HAVE TO SEARCH FOR CAROLINE. I ALMOST FORGOT HOW MUCH SHE STANDS OUT IN A CROWD.
ESPECIALLY A CROWD OF MEG'S FRIENDS...
TALK TO HER.
STOP BULLYING ME!
SHE JUST GOT BACK THIS MORNING. I LITERALLY HAVEN'T SEEN HER IN WHAT FEELS LIKE MONTHS.
WHERE DO I EVEN BEGIN WITH HER?
WHAT DO I EVEN SAY?

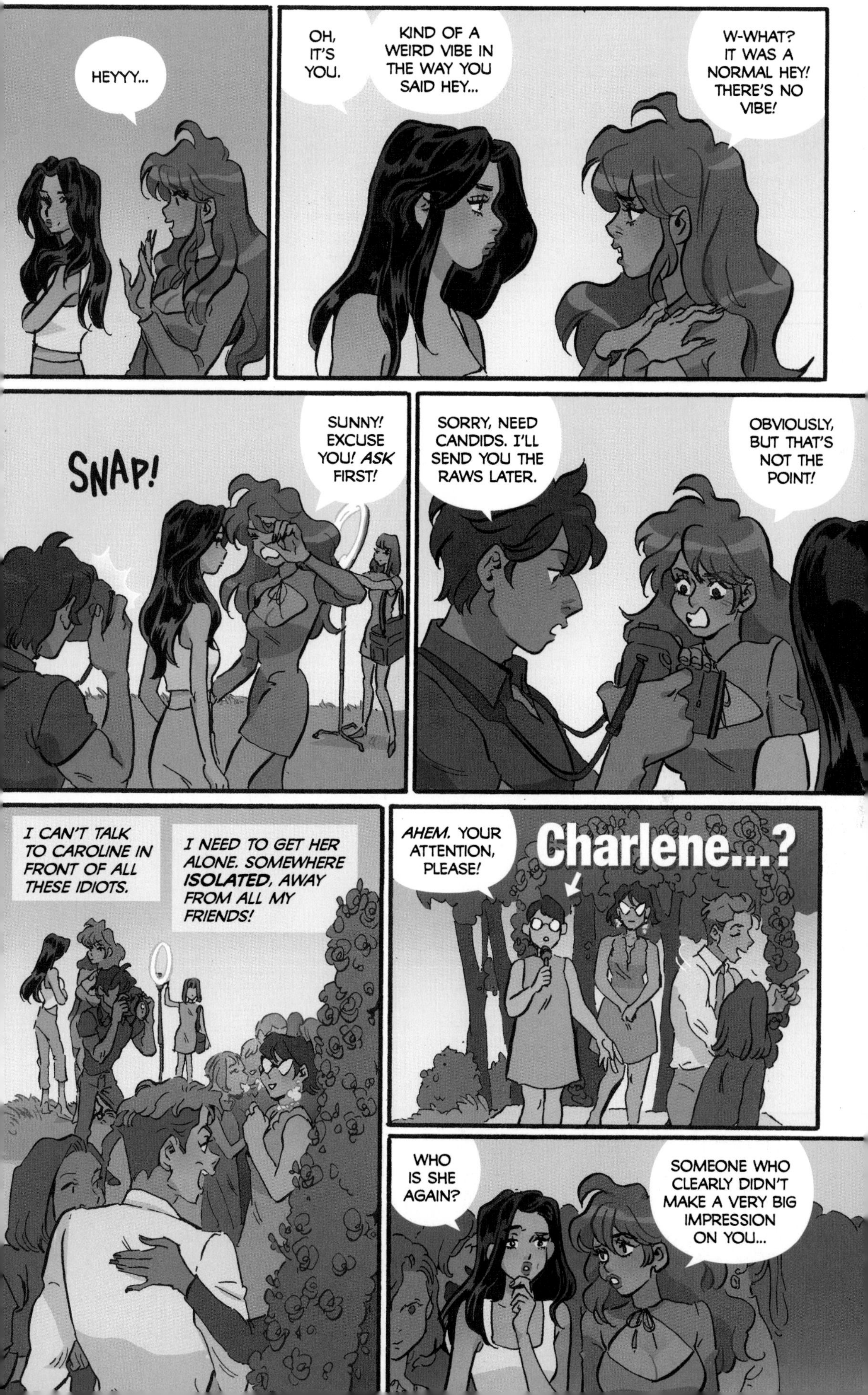
HEYYY...
OH, IT'S YOU.
KIND OF A WEIRD VIBE IN THE WAY YOU SAID HEY...
W-WHAT? IT WAS A NORMAL HEY! THERE'S NO VIBE!
SNAP!
SUNNY! EXCUSE YOU! ASK FIRST!
SORRY, NEED CANDIDS. I'LL SEND YOU THE RAWS LATER.
OBVIOUSLY, BUT THAT'S NOT THE POINT!
I CAN'T TALK TO CAROLINE IN FRONT OF ALL THESE IDIOTS.
I NEED TO GET HER ALONE. SOMEWHERE ISOLATED, AWAY FROM ALL MY FRIENDS!
AHEM. YOUR ATTENTION, PLEASE!
Charlene...?
WHO IS SHE AGAIN?
SOMEONE WHO CLEARLY DIDN'T MAKE A VERY BIG IMPRESSION ON YOU...

HELLO, FRIENDS, AND BY FRIENDS I MEAN MEG'S, BECAUSE I DON'T KNOW MOST OF YOU. I'M CHARLENE, THE MAID OF HONOR.

MEG HAS ASKED ME TO EXPLAIN WHY WE'VE BEEN WAITING SO LONG, AND IF POSSIBLE TO TAKE THE BLAME MYSELF, SO HERE GOES...

WOW, *SHE'S* MEG'S MAID OF HONOR? *HER*, REALLY?

YOU KNOW WHO MEG ASKED FIRST THOUGH, RIGHT?

OKAY, SO THE FAMILY IS SEATED, BUT WE RAN INTO A SLIGHT CHAIR SHORTAGE. SOMEONE MIGHT HAVE ▢ OUT TO TAR▢ I THINK ▢ 40 MILES ▢ IF YOU TA▢ LANE T▢ WAY ▢

YOU SAID NO! I HAVE IT ON *VIDEO*.

I DON'T MEAN TO BE RUDE TO YOU AT YOUR WEDDING, BUT DON'T YOU KNOW ANY OTHER PEOPLE?!

THERE HA▢ BEEN MA▢ CHALLENG▢ LIKE THIS ▢ ALONG TH▢ I JUST HA▢ SAY IT'S ▢ REWARDI▢ EXPERIENC▢ FOR ME...

CHARLENE IS A *GOOD FRIEND!* WHO ELSE WOULD SPEND EIGHTY HOURS FORAGING BERRIES WITH ME FOR TONIGHT'S TRIFLE?

THE ONLY TRIFLE HERE IS YOUR TRIFLING FRIENDSHIP WITH *HER!*

WHAT'S SHE EVEN *SAYING?* I CAN'T HEAR A WORD!

GOD, YOU'RE *SO* DRAMATIC.

SHE'S JUST TELLING EVERYONE NOT TO WORRY ABOUT THE FIRE, BECAUSE IT'S NOT AS CLOSE AS IT LOOKS!

ROAR

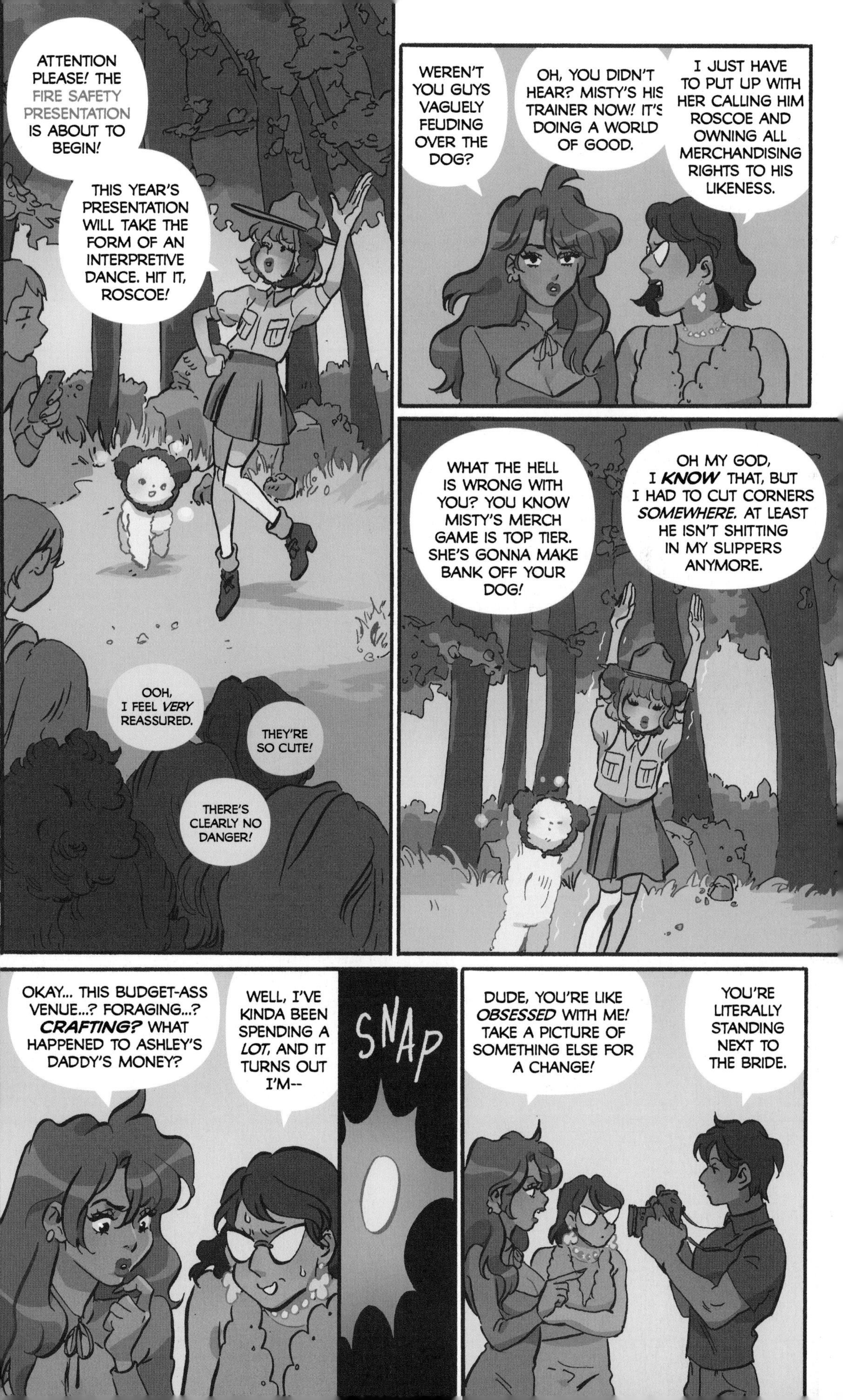
ATTENTION PLEASE! THE FIRE SAFETY PRESENTATION IS ABOUT TO BEGIN!
THIS YEAR'S PRESENTATION WILL TAKE THE FORM OF AN INTERPRETIVE DANCE. HIT IT, ROSCOE!
OOH, I FEEL VERY REASSURED.
THEY'RE SO CUTE!
THERE'S CLEARLY NO DANGER!
WEREN'T YOU GUYS VAGUELY FEUDING OVER THE DOG?
OH, YOU DIDN'T HEAR? MISTY'S HIS TRAINER NOW! IT'S DOING A WORLD OF GOOD.
I JUST HAVE TO PUT UP WITH HER CALLING HIM ROSCOE AND OWNING ALL MERCHANDISING RIGHTS TO HIS LIKENESS.
WHAT THE HELL IS WRONG WITH YOU? YOU KNOW MISTY'S MERCH GAME IS TOP TIER. SHE'S GONNA MAKE BANK OFF YOUR DOG!
OH MY GOD, I KNOW THAT, BUT I HAD TO CUT CORNERS SOMEWHERE. AT LEAST HE ISN'T SHITTING IN MY SLIPPERS ANYMORE.
OKAY... THIS BUDGET-ASS VENUE...? FORAGING...? CRAFTING? WHAT HAPPENED TO ASHLEY'S DADDY'S MONEY?
WELL, I'VE KINDA BEEN SPENDING A LOT, AND IT TURNS OUT I'M--
SNAP
DUDE, YOU'RE LIKE OBSESSED WITH ME! TAKE A PICTURE OF SOMETHING ELSE FOR A CHANGE!
YOU'RE LITERALLY STANDING NEXT TO THE BRIDE.

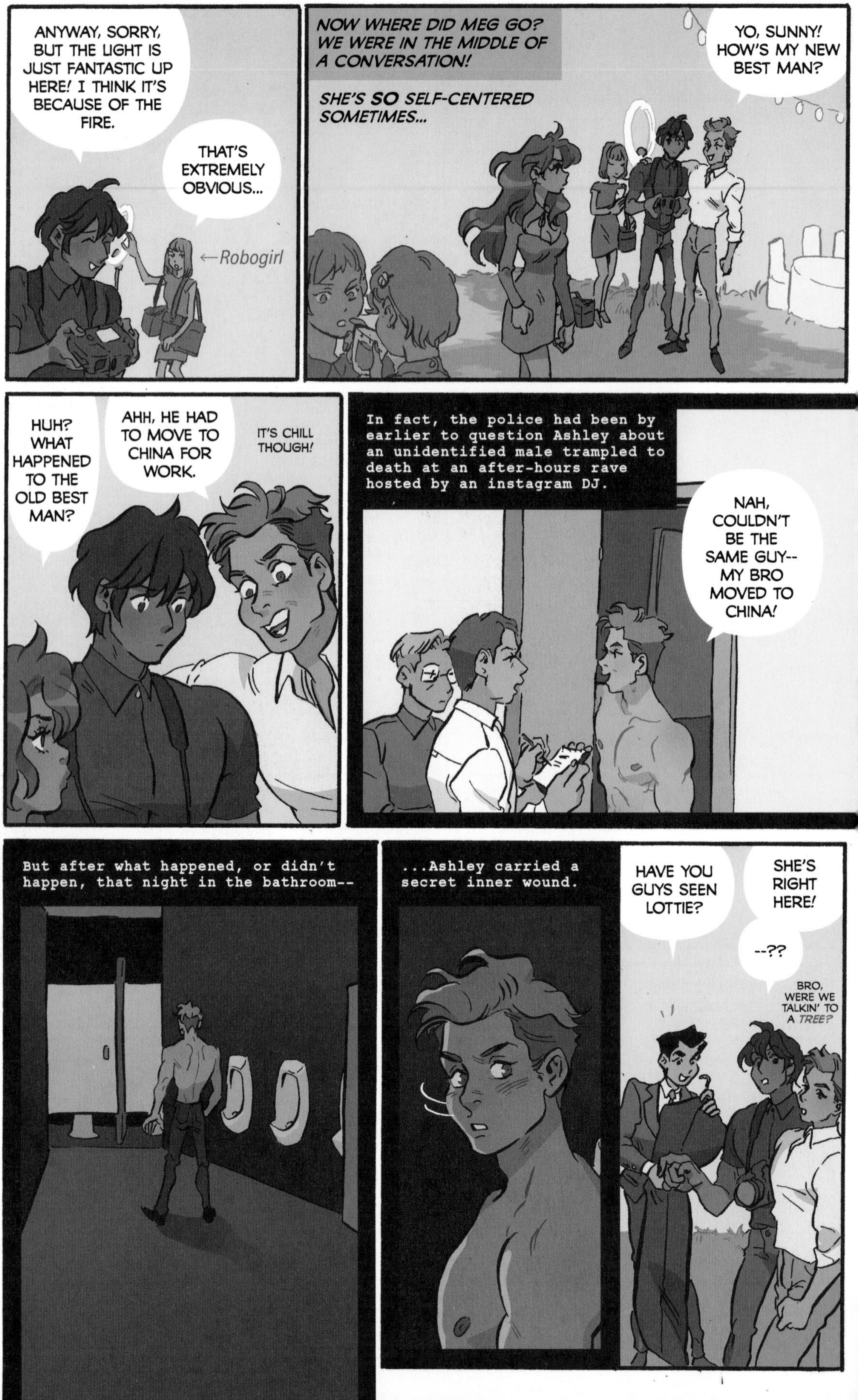

ANYWAY, SORRY, BUT THE LIGHT IS JUST FANTASTIC UP HERE! I THINK IT'S BECAUSE OF THE FIRE.
THAT'S EXTREMELY OBVIOUS...
←Robogirl
NOW WHERE DID MEG GO? WE WERE IN THE MIDDLE OF A CONVERSATION!
SHE'S SO SELF-CENTERED SOMETIMES...
YO, SUNNY! HOW'S MY NEW BEST MAN?
HUH? WHAT HAPPENED TO THE OLD BEST MAN?
AHH, HE HAD TO MOVE TO CHINA FOR WORK.
IT'S CHILL THOUGH!
In fact, the police had been by earlier to question Ashley about an unidentified male trampled to death at an after-hours rave hosted by an instagram DJ.
NAH, COULDN'T BE THE SAME GUY-- MY BRO MOVED TO CHINA!
But after what happened, or didn't happen, that night in the bathroom--
...Ashley carried a secret inner wound.
HAVE YOU GUYS SEEN LOTTIE?
SHE'S RIGHT HERE!
--??
BRO, WERE WE TALKIN' TO A TREE?

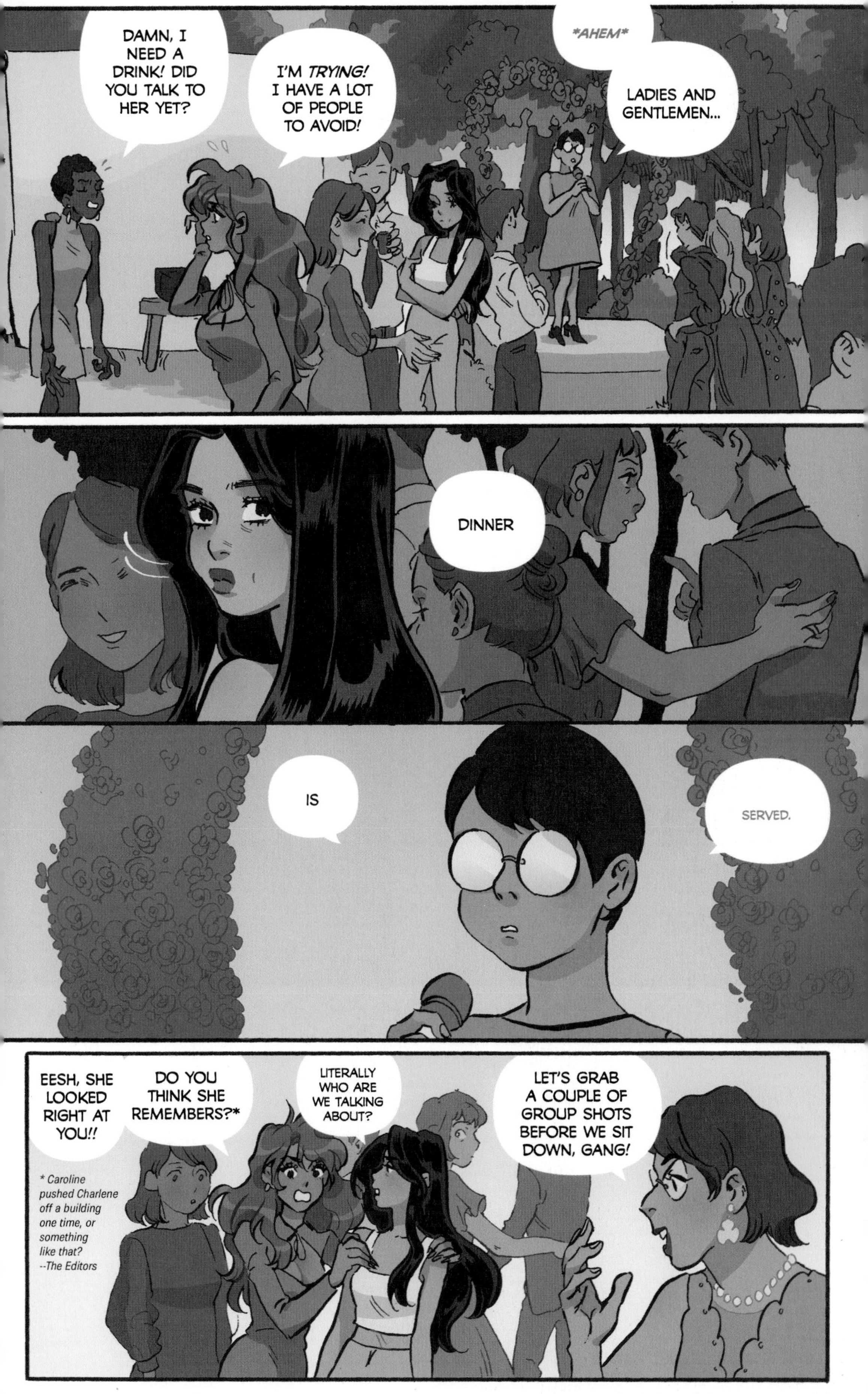
DAMN, I NEED A DRINK! DID YOU TALK TO HER YET?
I'M *TRYING!* I HAVE A LOT OF PEOPLE TO AVOID!
AHEM
LADIES AND GENTLEMEN...
DINNER
IS
SERVED.
EESH, SHE LOOKED RIGHT AT YOU!!
DO YOU THINK SHE REMEMBERS?*
LITERALLY WHO ARE WE TALKING ABOUT?
LET'S GRAB A COUPLE OF GROUP SHOTS BEFORE WE SIT DOWN, GANG!
* Caroline pushed Charlene off a building one time, or something like that? --The Editors

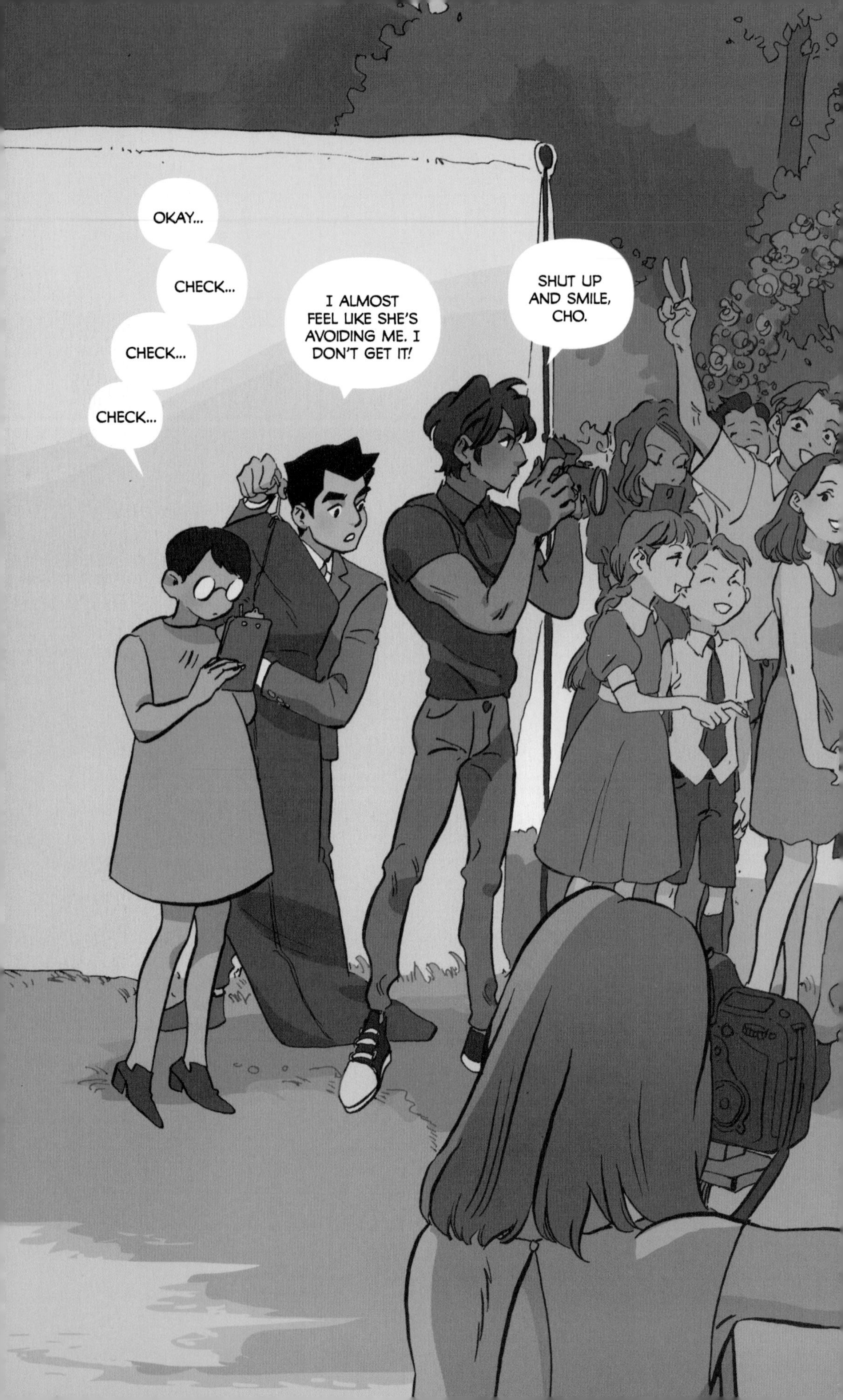
OKAY...
CHECK...
CHECK...
CHECK...
I ALMOST FEEL LIKE SHE'S AVOIDING ME. I DON'T GET IT!
SHUT UP AND SMILE, CHO.

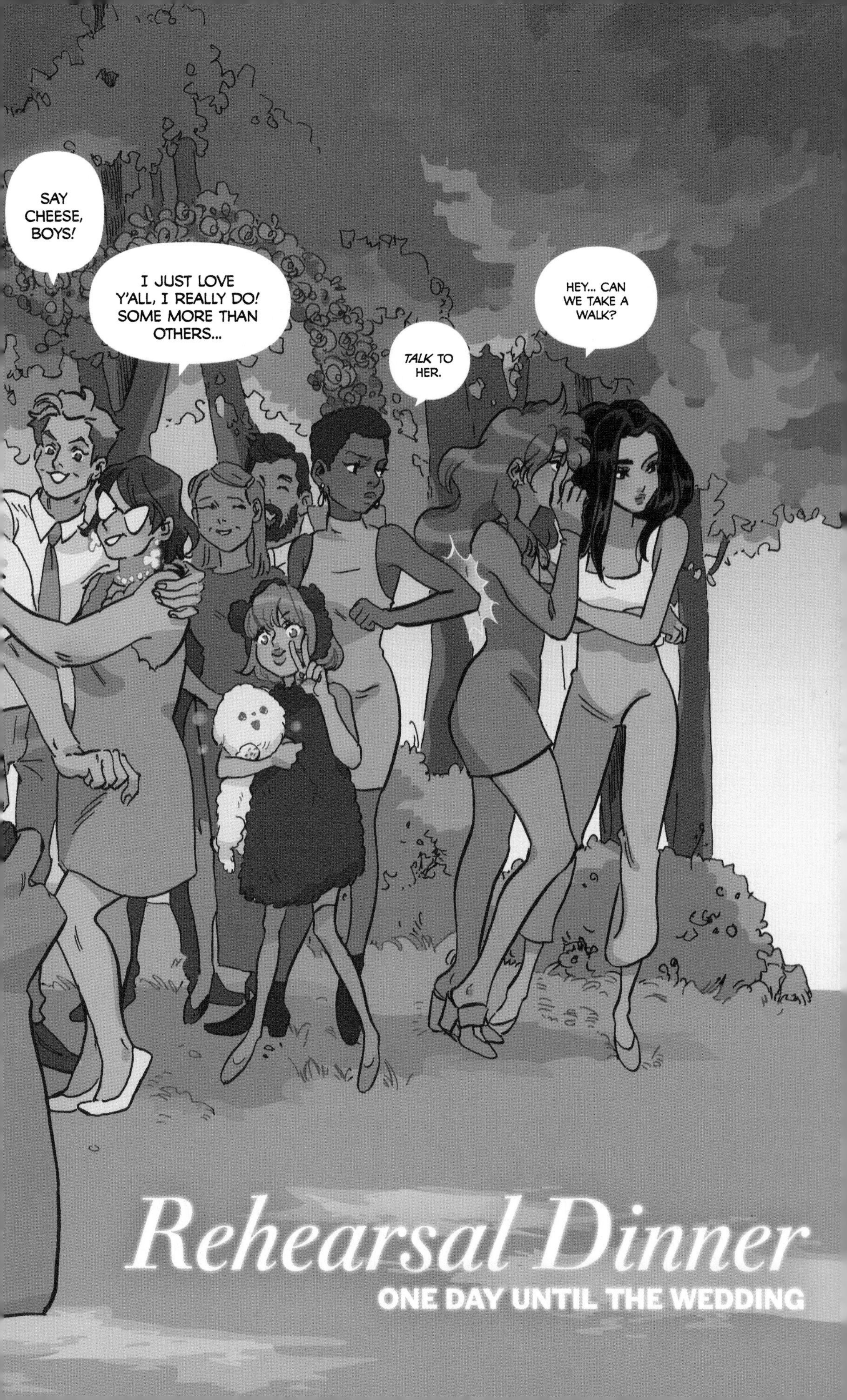
SAY CHEESE, BOYS!
I JUST LOVE Y'ALL, I REALLY DO! SOME MORE THAN OTHERS...
TALK TO HER.
HEY... CAN WE TAKE A WALK?
Rehearsal Dinner
ONE DAY UNTIL THE WEDDING

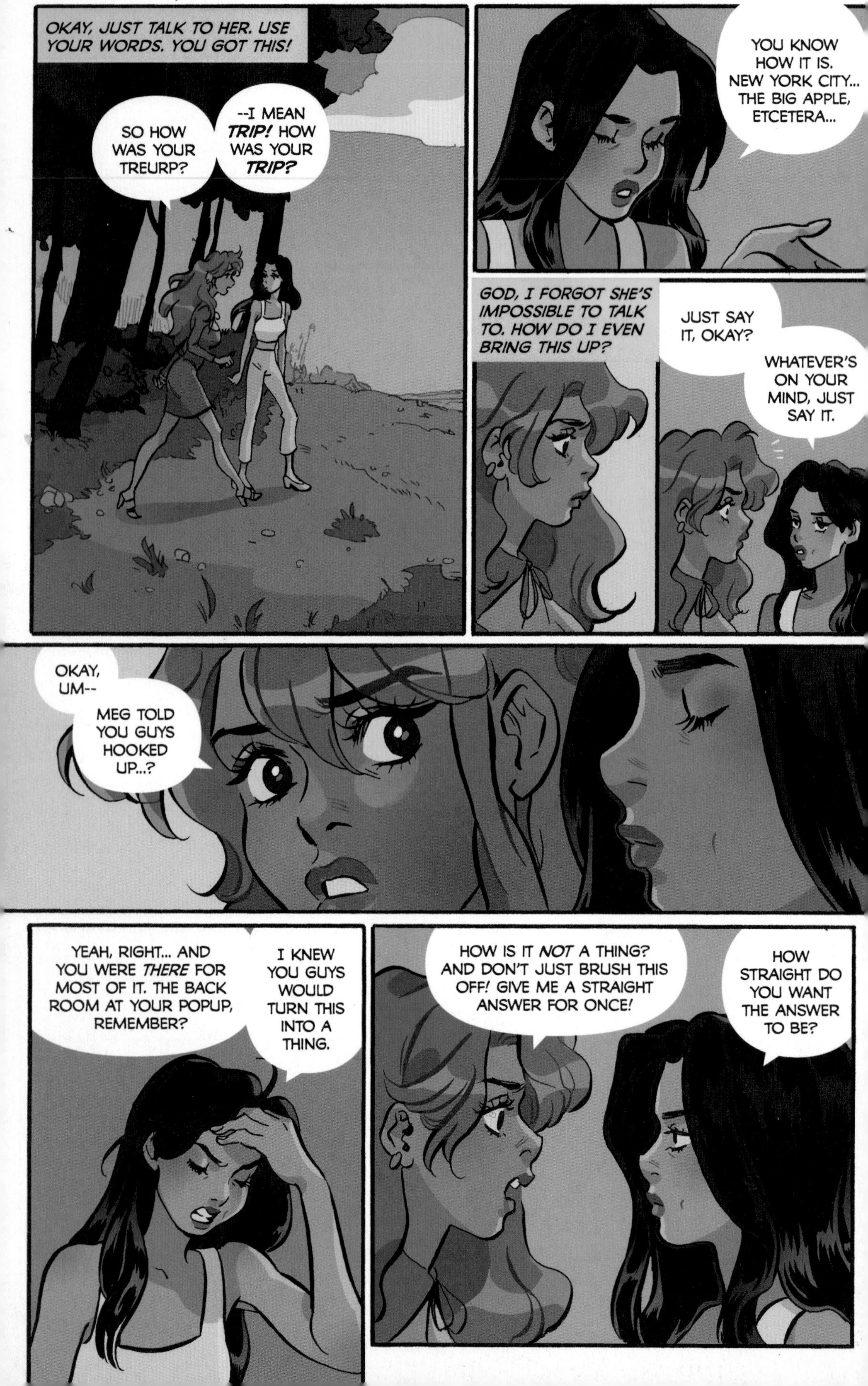
OKAY, JUST TALK TO HER. USE YOUR WORDS. YOU GOT THIS!
SO HOW WAS YOUR TREURP?
--I MEAN *TRIP!* HOW WAS YOUR *TRIP?*
YOU KNOW HOW IT IS. NEW YORK CITY... THE BIG APPLE, ETCETERA...
GOD, I FORGOT SHE'S IMPOSSIBLE TO TALK TO. HOW DO I EVEN BRING THIS UP?
JUST SAY IT, OKAY?
WHATEVER'S ON YOUR MIND, JUST SAY IT.
OKAY, UM--
MEG TOLD YOU GUYS HOOKED UP...?
YEAH, RIGHT... AND YOU WERE *THERE* FOR MOST OF IT. THE BACK ROOM AT YOUR POPUP, REMEMBER?
I KNEW YOU GUYS WOULD TURN THIS INTO A THING.
HOW IS IT *NOT* A THING? AND DON'T JUST BRUSH THIS OFF! GIVE ME A STRAIGHT ANSWER FOR ONCE!
HOW STRAIGHT DO YOU WANT THE ANSWER TO BE?

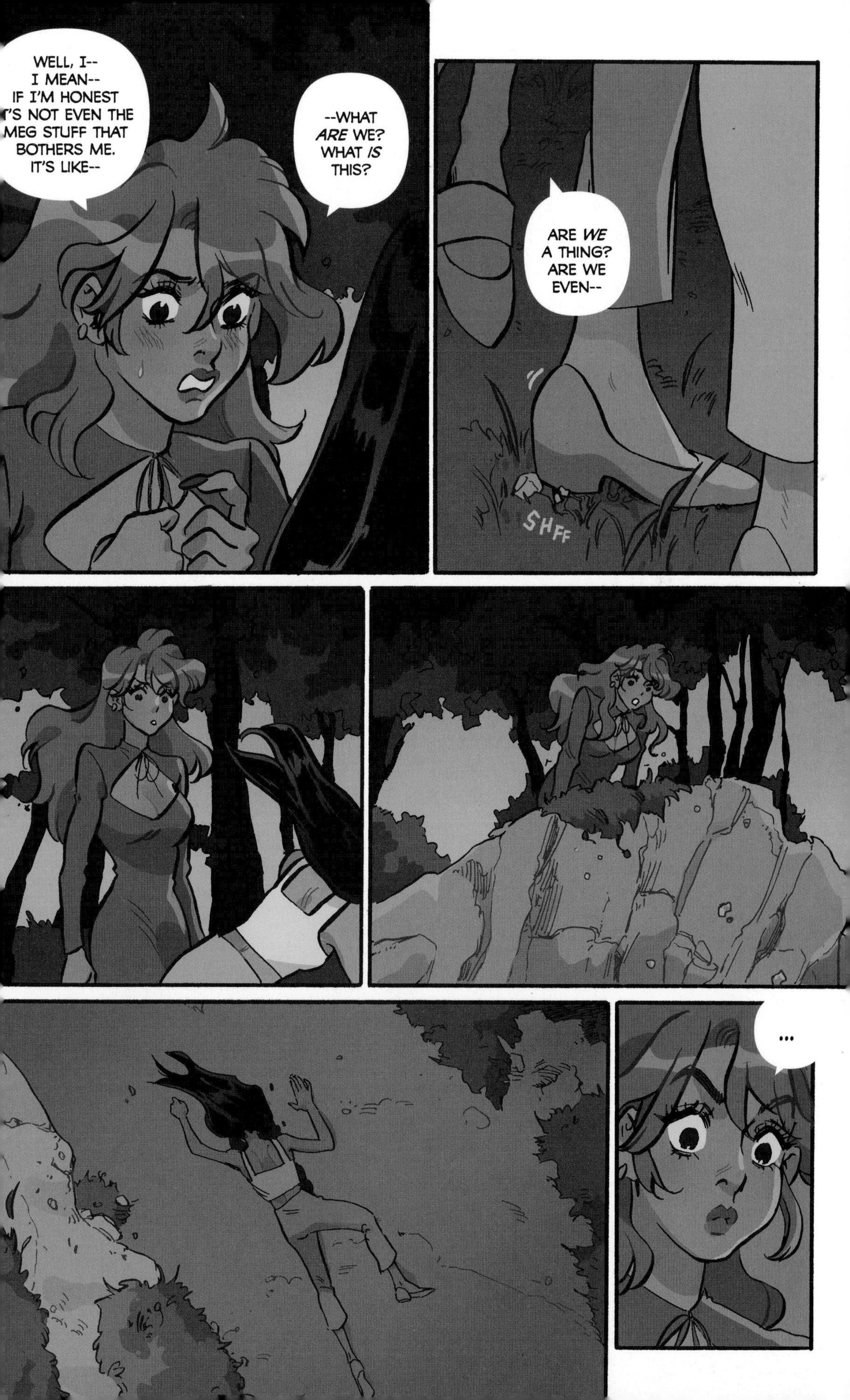
WELL, I-- I MEAN-- IF I'M HONEST 'S NOT EVEN THE MEG STUFF THAT BOTHERS ME. IT'S LIKE--
--WHAT *ARE* WE? WHAT *IS* THIS?
ARE *WE* A THING? ARE WE EVEN--
SHFF
...

CAROLINE...?

IS SHE...

IS SHE OKAY?

VIRGIL WILL KNOW WHAT TO DO.

VIRGIL WILL HELP.

NO BARS. JUST NEED A SIGNAL!

SIGNAL... SIGNAL...

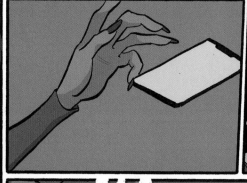

KLACK

FWUMP

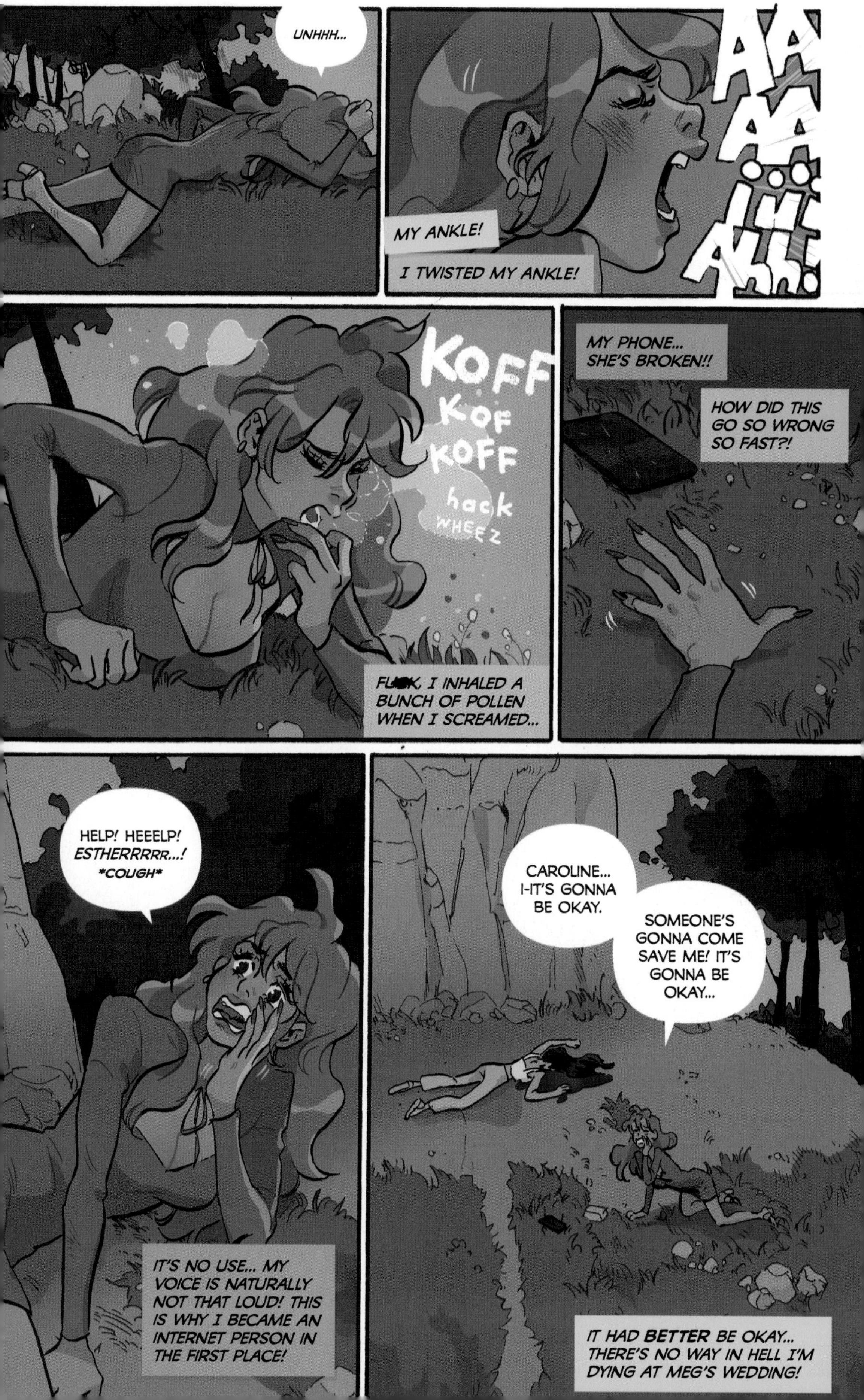
UNHHH...
MY ANKLE!
I TWISTED MY ANKLE!
KOFF
KOF
KOFF
hack
WHEEZ
F[redacted]K, I INHALED A BUNCH OF POLLEN WHEN I SCREAMED...
MY PHONE... SHE'S BROKEN!!
HOW DID THIS GO SO WRONG SO FAST?!
HELP! HEEELP! ESTHERRRRR...! *COUGH*
IT'S NO USE... MY VOICE IS NATURALLY NOT THAT LOUD! THIS IS WHY I BECAME AN INTERNET PERSON IN THE FIRST PLACE!
CAROLINE... I-IT'S GONNA BE OKAY.
SOMEONE'S GONNA COME SAVE ME! IT'S GONNA BE OKAY...
IT HAD BETTER BE OKAY... THERE'S NO WAY IN HELL I'M DYING AT MEG'S WEDDING!

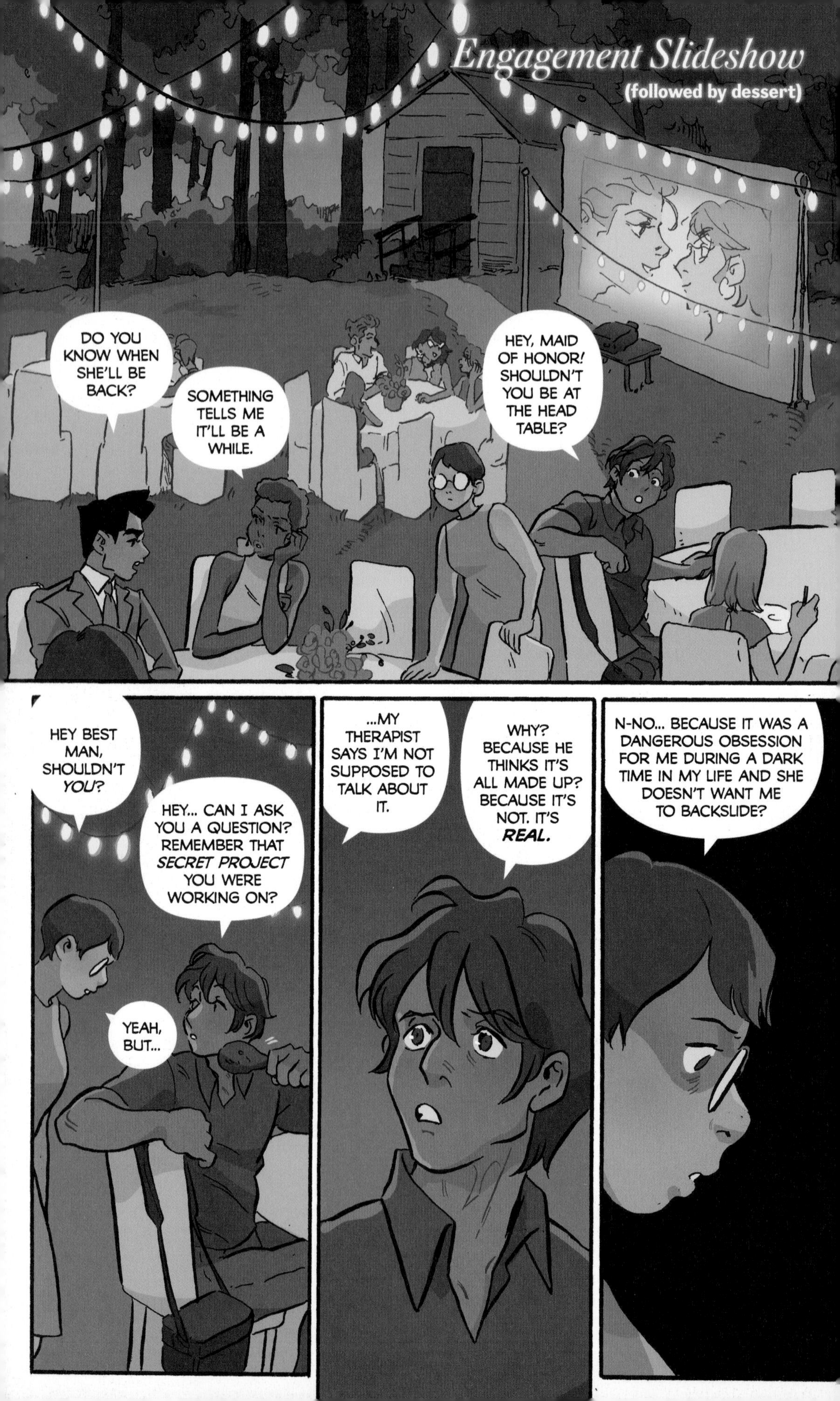
Engagement Slideshow
(followed by dessert)
DO YOU KNOW WHEN SHE'LL BE BACK?
SOMETHING TELLS ME IT'LL BE A WHILE.
HEY, MAID OF HONOR! SHOULDN'T YOU BE AT THE HEAD TABLE?
HEY BEST MAN, SHOULDN'T *YOU*?
HEY... CAN I ASK YOU A QUESTION? REMEMBER THAT *SECRET PROJECT* YOU WERE WORKING ON?
YEAH, BUT...
...MY THERAPIST SAYS I'M NOT SUPPOSED TO TALK ABOUT IT.
WHY? BECAUSE HE THINKS IT'S ALL MADE UP? BECAUSE IT'S NOT. IT'S ***REAL.***
N-NO... BECAUSE IT WAS A DANGEROUS OBSESSION FOR ME DURING A DARK TIME IN MY LIFE AND SHE DOESN'T WANT ME TO BACKSLIDE?

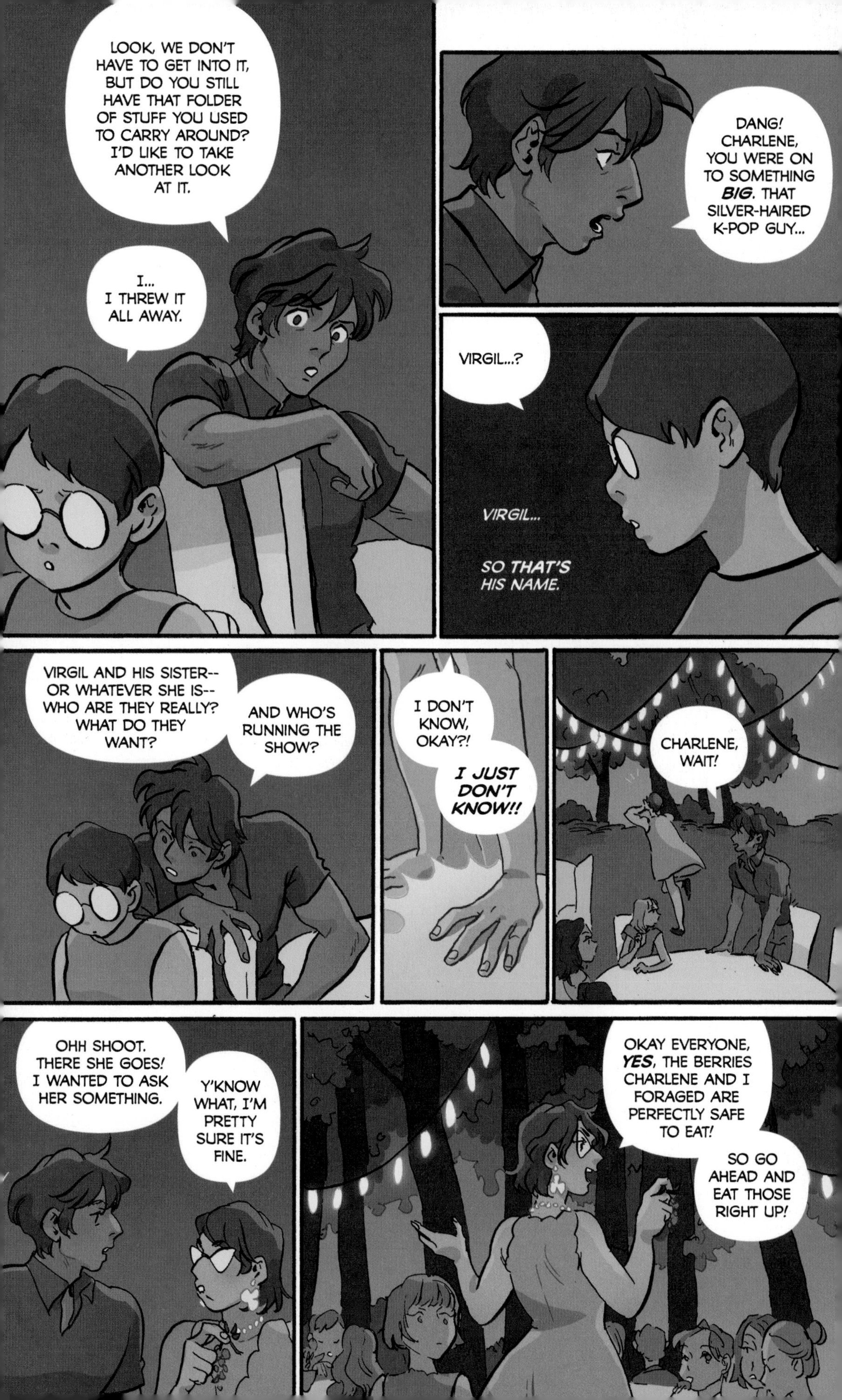
LOOK, WE DON'T HAVE TO GET INTO IT, BUT DO YOU STILL HAVE THAT FOLDER OF STUFF YOU USED TO CARRY AROUND? I'D LIKE TO TAKE ANOTHER LOOK AT IT.
I... I THREW IT ALL AWAY.
DANG! CHARLENE, YOU WERE ON TO SOMETHING BIG. THAT SILVER-HAIRED K-POP GUY...
VIRGIL...?
VIRGIL...
SO THAT'S HIS NAME.
VIRGIL AND HIS SISTER-- OR WHATEVER SHE IS-- WHO ARE THEY REALLY? WHAT DO THEY WANT?
AND WHO'S RUNNING THE SHOW?
I DON'T KNOW, OKAY?!
I JUST DON'T KNOW!!
CHARLENE, WAIT!
OHH SHOOT. THERE SHE GOES! I WANTED TO ASK HER SOMETHING.
Y'KNOW WHAT, I'M PRETTY SURE IT'S FINE.
OKAY EVERYONE, YES, THE BERRIES CHARLENE AND I FORAGED ARE PERFECTLY SAFE TO EAT!
SO GO AHEAD AND EAT THOSE RIGHT UP!

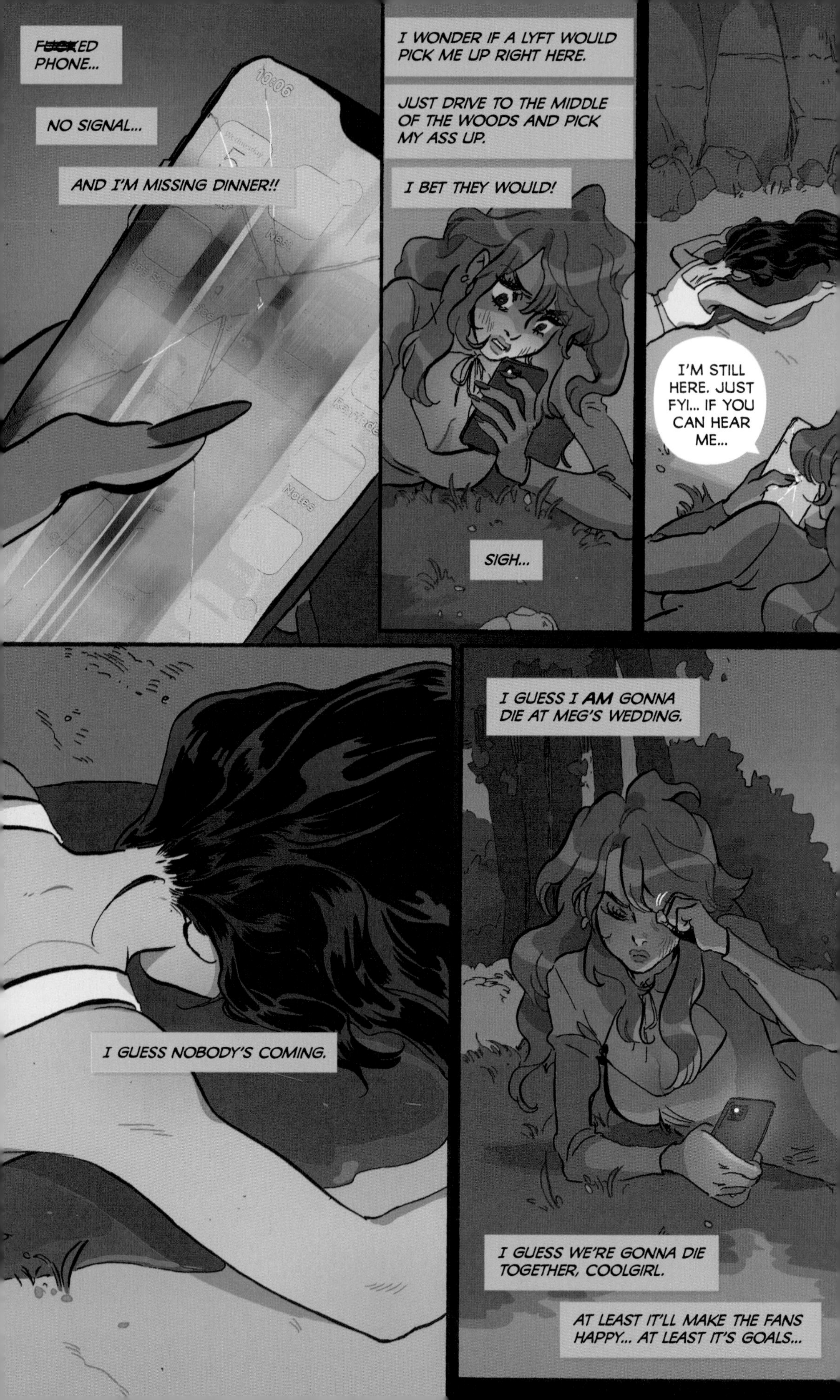
F[redacted]ED PHONE...
NO SIGNAL...
AND I'M MISSING DINNER!!
I WONDER IF A LYFT WOULD PICK ME UP RIGHT HERE.
JUST DRIVE TO THE MIDDLE OF THE WOODS AND PICK MY ASS UP.
I BET THEY WOULD!
SIGH...
I'M STILL HERE. JUST FYI... IF YOU CAN HEAR ME...
I GUESS NOBODY'S COMING.
I GUESS I **AM** GONNA DIE AT MEG'S WEDDING.
I GUESS WE'RE GONNA DIE TOGETHER, COOLGIRL.
AT LEAST IT'LL MAKE THE FANS HAPPY... AT LEAST IT'S GOALS...

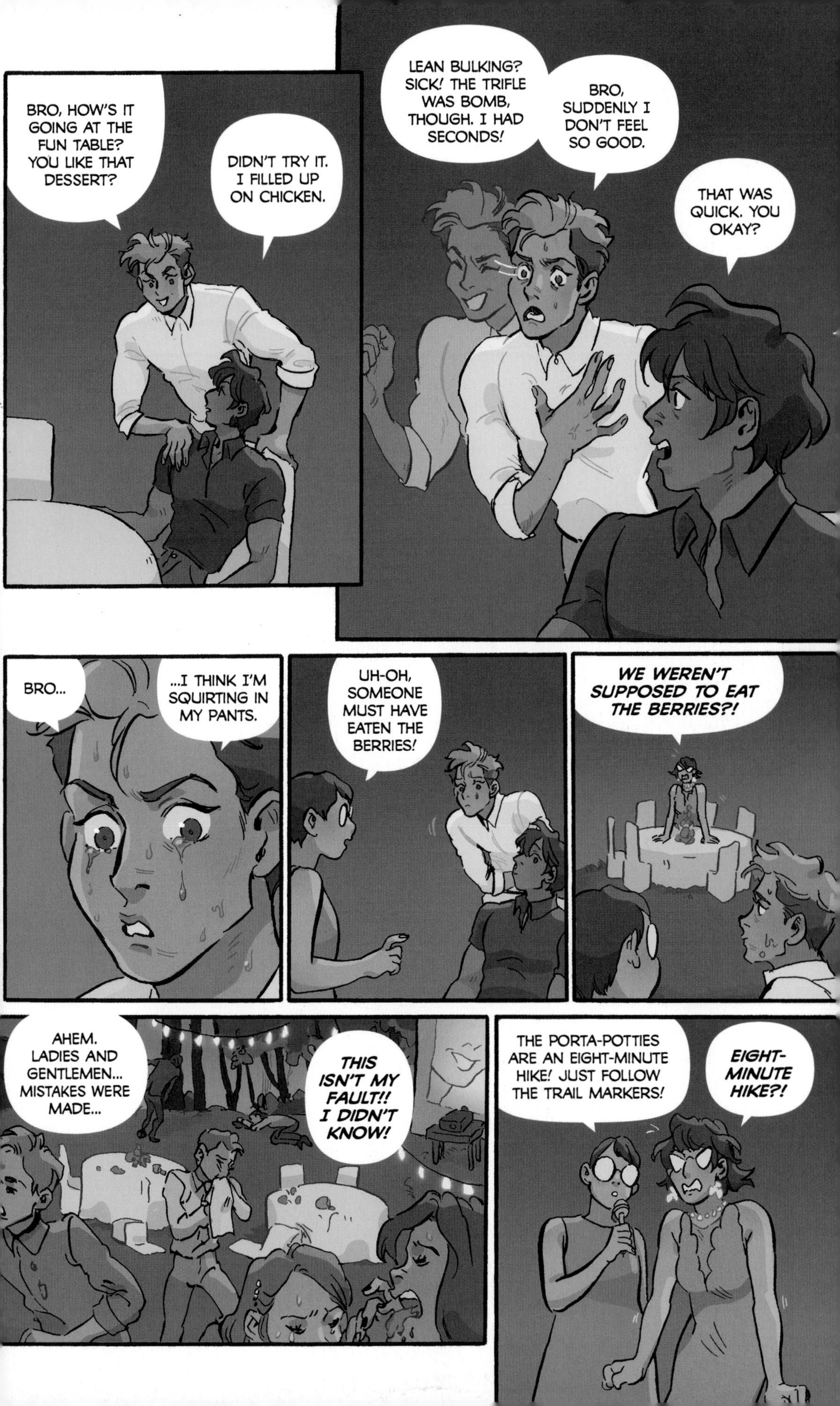
BRO, HOW'S IT GOING AT THE FUN TABLE? YOU LIKE THAT DESSERT?
DIDN'T TRY IT. I FILLED UP ON CHICKEN.
LEAN BULKING? SICK! THE TRIFLE WAS BOMB, THOUGH. I HAD SECONDS!
BRO, SUDDENLY I DON'T FEEL SO GOOD.
THAT WAS QUICK. YOU OKAY?
BRO...
...I THINK I'M SQUIRTING IN MY PANTS.
UH-OH, SOMEONE MUST HAVE EATEN THE BERRIES!
WE WEREN'T SUPPOSED TO EAT THE BERRIES?!
AHEM. LADIES AND GENTLEMEN... MISTAKES WERE MADE...
THIS ISN'T MY FAULT!! I DIDN'T KNOW!
THE PORTA-POTTIES ARE AN EIGHT-MINUTE HIKE! JUST FOLLOW THE TRAIL MARKERS!
EIGHT-MINUTE HIKE?!

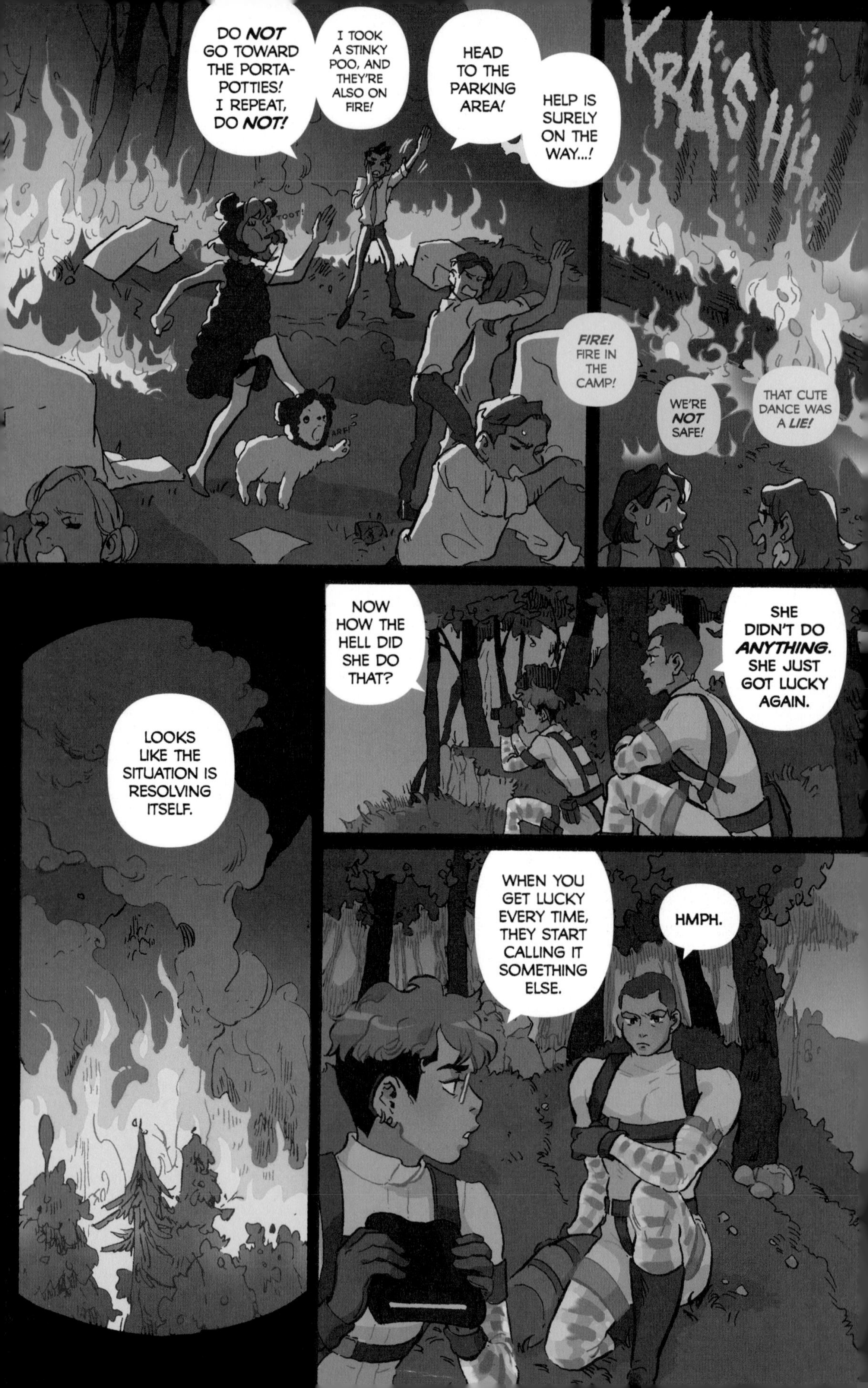
DO NOT GO TOWARD THE PORTA-POTTIES! I REPEAT, DO NOT!
I TOOK A STINKY POO, AND THEY'RE ALSO ON FIRE!
HEAD TO THE PARKING AREA!
HELP IS SURELY ON THE WAY...!
TOOT!
ARF!
FIRE! FIRE IN THE CAMP!
KRASHHH
WE'RE NOT SAFE!
THAT CUTE DANCE WAS A LIE!
LOOKS LIKE THE SITUATION IS RESOLVING ITSELF.
NOW HOW THE HELL DID SHE DO THAT?
SHE DIDN'T DO ANYTHING. SHE JUST GOT LUCKY AGAIN.
WHEN YOU GET LUCKY EVERY TIME, THEY START CALLING IT SOMETHING ELSE.
HMPH.

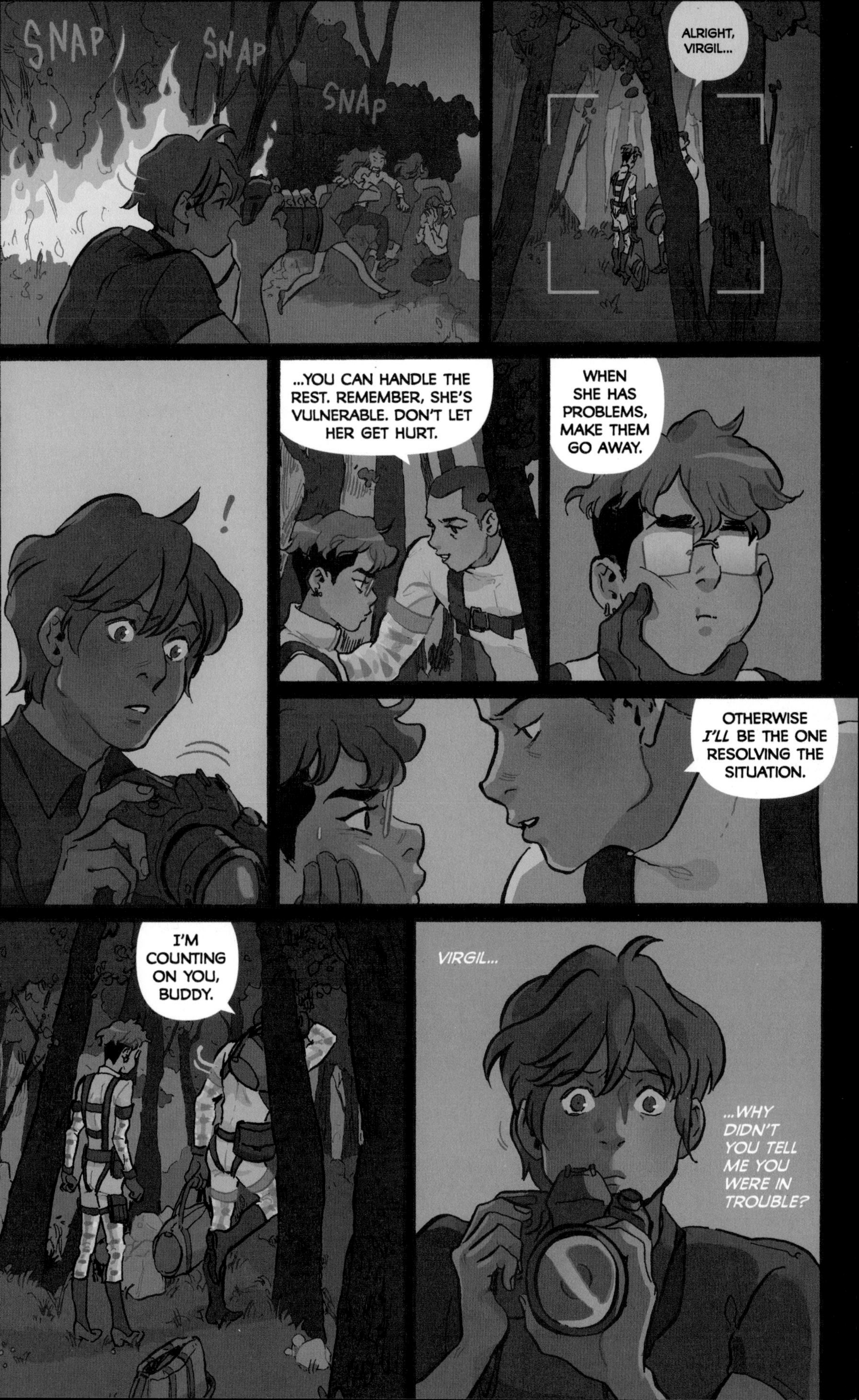
SNAP
SNAP
SNAP
ALRIGHT, VIRGIL...
...YOU CAN HANDLE THE REST. REMEMBER, SHE'S VULNERABLE. DON'T LET HER GET HURT.
WHEN SHE HAS PROBLEMS, MAKE THEM GO AWAY.
!
OTHERWISE *I'LL* BE THE ONE RESOLVING THE SITUATION.
I'M COUNTING ON YOU, BUDDY.
VIRGIL...
...WHY DIDN'T YOU TELL ME YOU WERE IN TROUBLE?

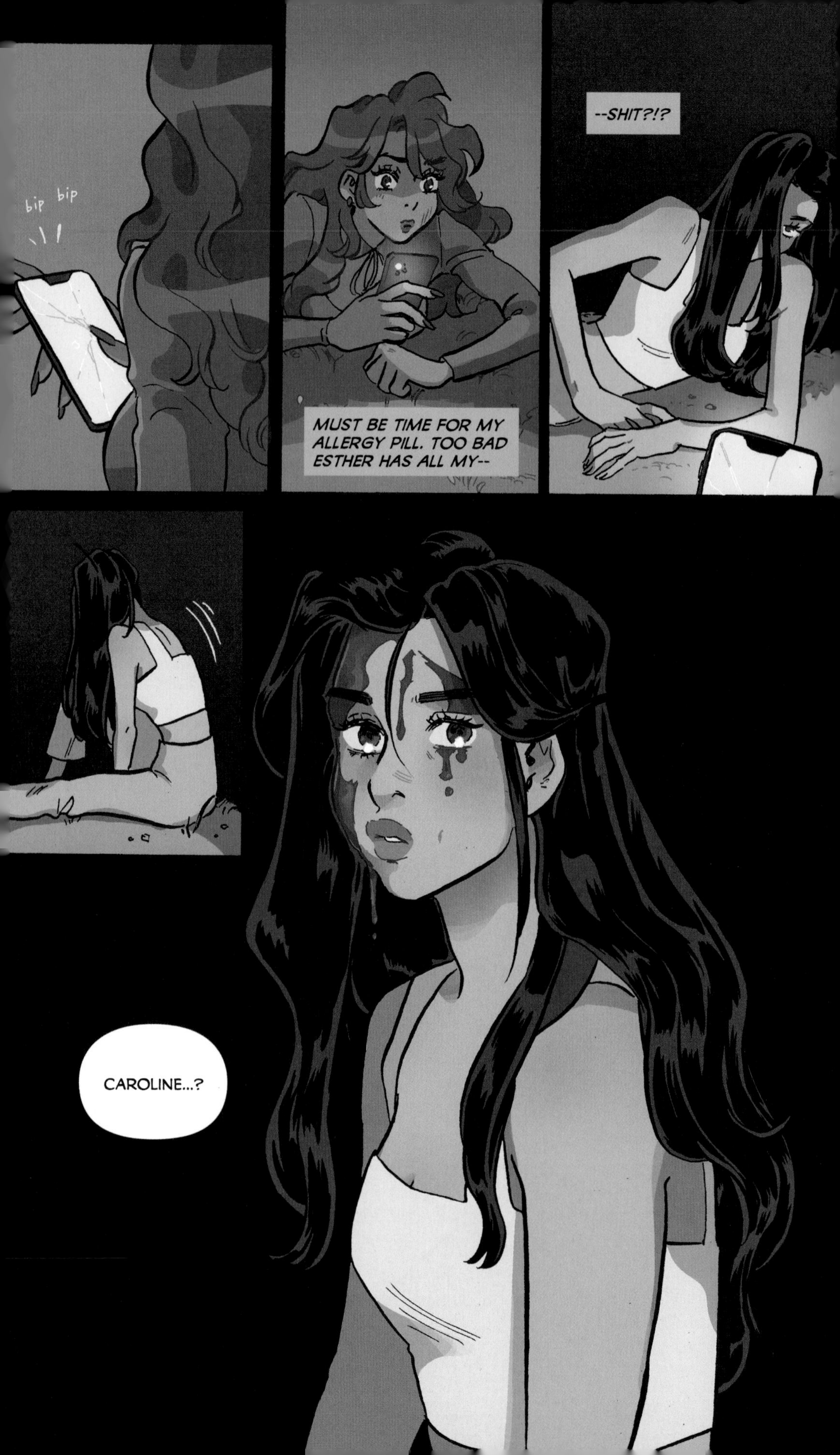
bip bip
MUST BE TIME FOR MY ALLERGY PILL. TOO BAD ESTHER HAS ALL MY--
--SHIT?!?
CAROLINE...?

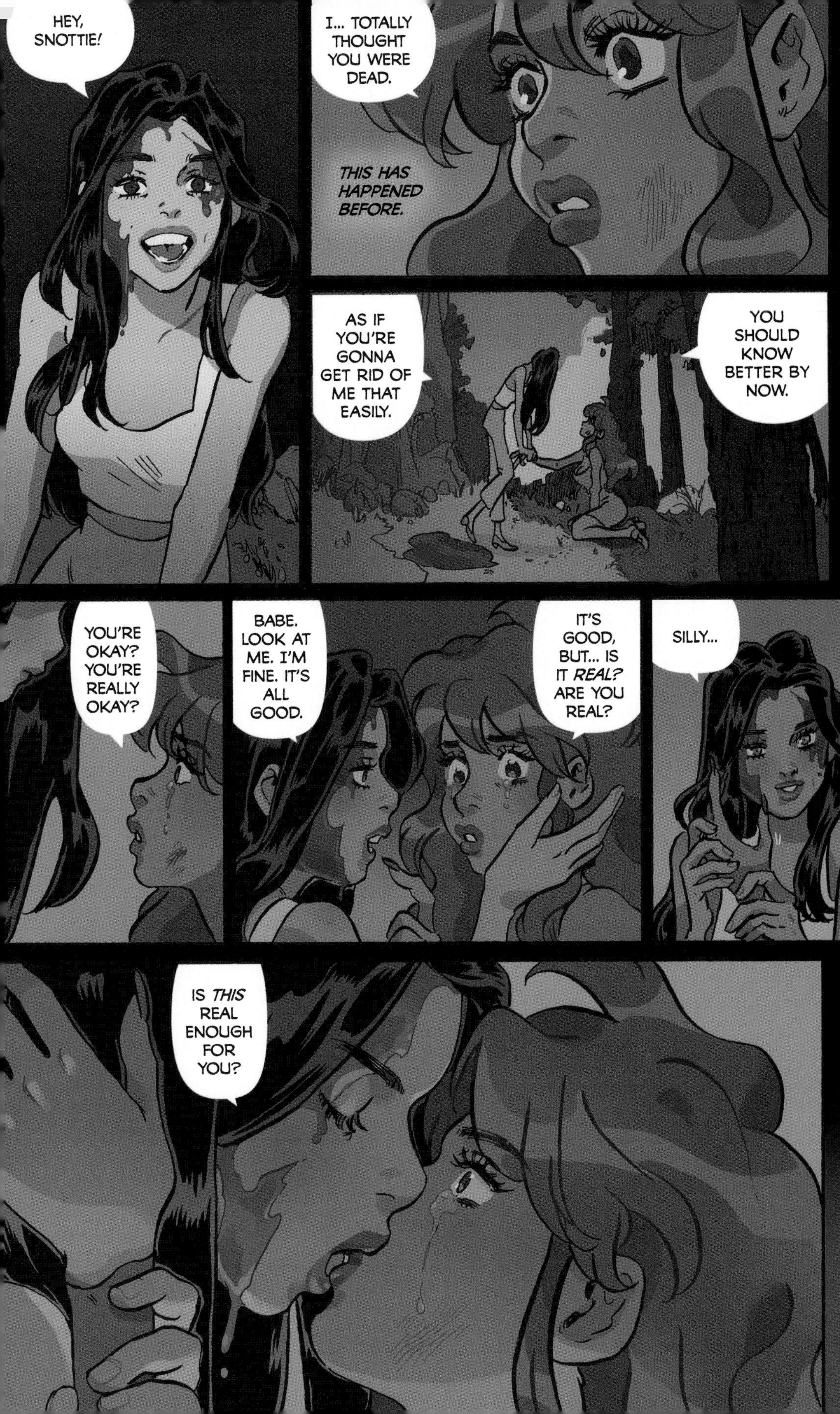
HEY, SNOTTIE!
I... TOTALLY THOUGHT YOU WERE DEAD.
THIS HAS HAPPENED BEFORE.
AS IF YOU'RE GONNA GET RID OF ME THAT EASILY.
YOU SHOULD KNOW BETTER BY NOW.
YOU'RE OKAY? YOU'RE REALLY OKAY?
BABE. LOOK AT ME. I'M FINE. IT'S ALL GOOD.
IT'S GOOD, BUT... IS IT *REAL?* ARE YOU REAL?
SILLY...
IS *THIS* REAL ENOUGH FOR YOU?

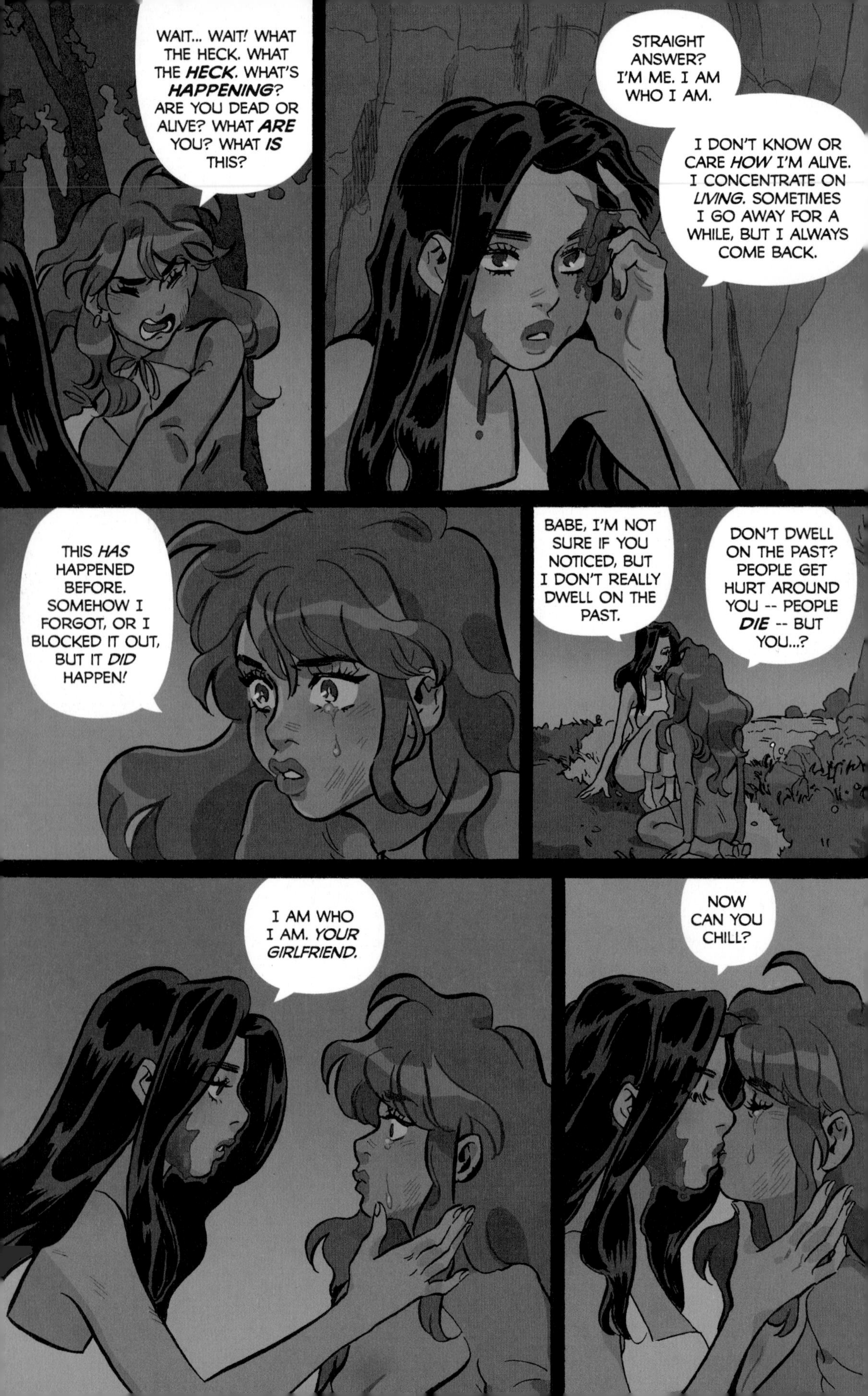
WAIT... WAIT! WHAT THE HECK. WHAT THE *HECK*. WHAT'S *HAPPENING*? ARE YOU DEAD OR ALIVE? WHAT *ARE* YOU? WHAT *IS* THIS?
STRAIGHT ANSWER? I'M ME. I AM WHO I AM.
I DON'T KNOW OR CARE *HOW* I'M ALIVE. I CONCENTRATE ON *LIVING*. SOMETIMES I GO AWAY FOR A WHILE, BUT I ALWAYS COME BACK.
THIS *HAS* HAPPENED BEFORE. SOMEHOW I FORGOT, OR I BLOCKED IT OUT, BUT IT *DID* HAPPEN!
BABE, I'M NOT SURE IF YOU NOTICED, BUT I DON'T REALLY DWELL ON THE PAST.
DON'T DWELL ON THE PAST? PEOPLE GET HURT AROUND YOU -- PEOPLE *DIE* -- BUT YOU...?
I AM WHO I AM. *YOUR GIRLFRIEND.*
NOW CAN YOU CHILL?

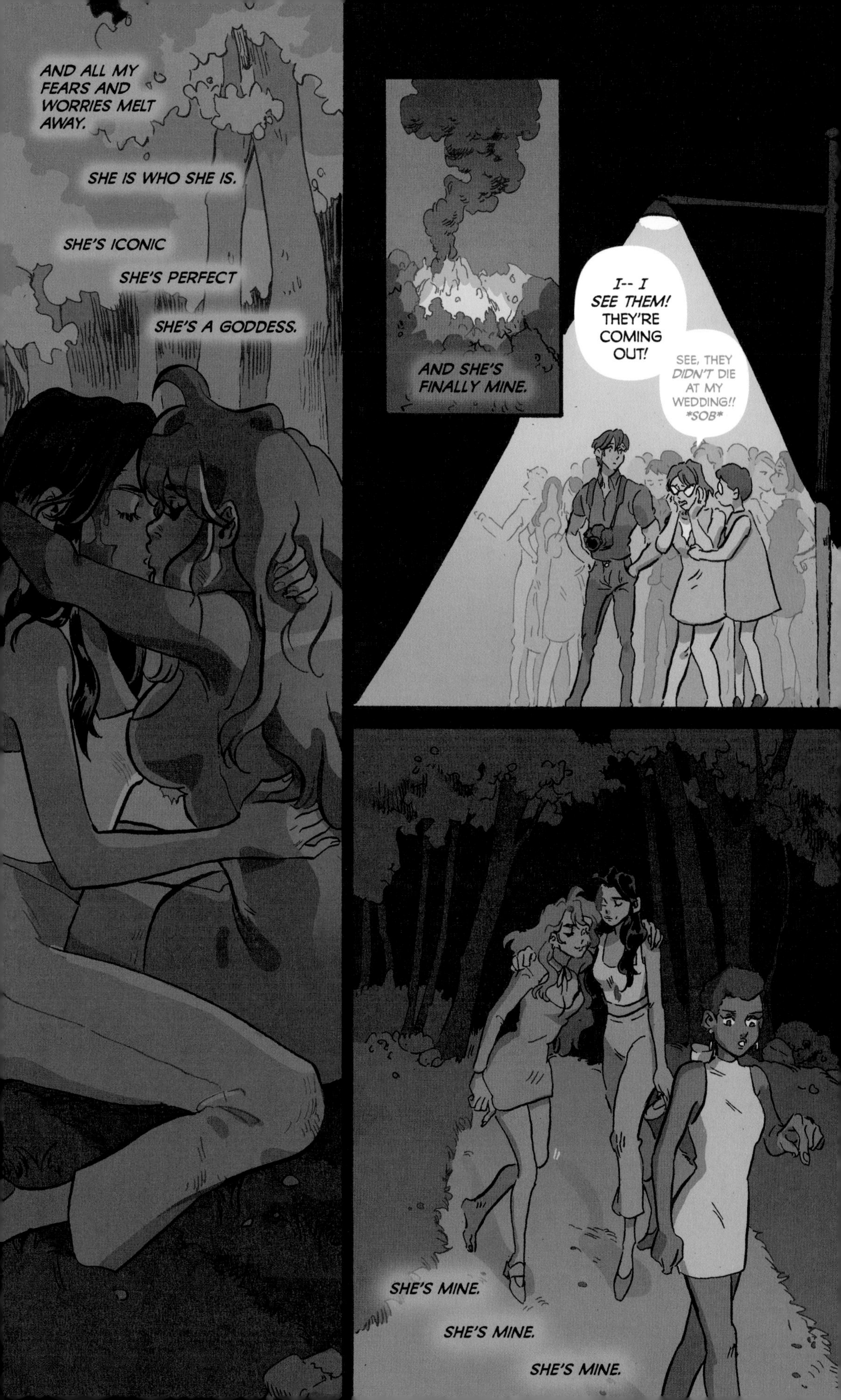
AND ALL MY FEARS AND WORRIES MELT AWAY.
SHE IS WHO SHE IS.
SHE'S ICONIC
SHE'S PERFECT
SHE'S A GODDESS.
AND SHE'S FINALLY MINE.
I-- I SEE THEM! THEY'RE COMING OUT!
SEE, THEY DIDN'T DIE AT MY WEDDING!! *SOB*
SHE'S MINE.
SHE'S MINE.
SHE'S MINE.

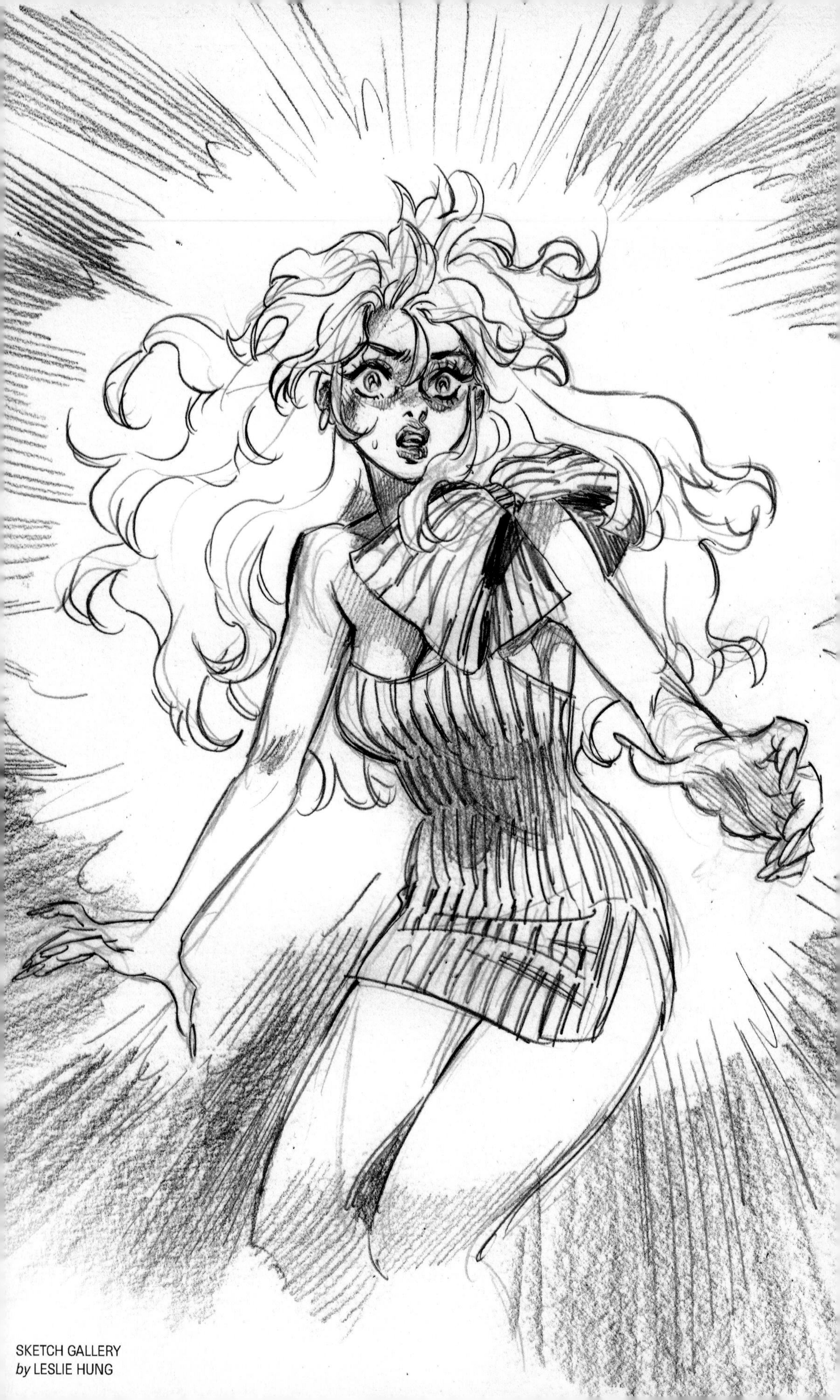

SKETCH GALLERY
by LESLIE HUNG

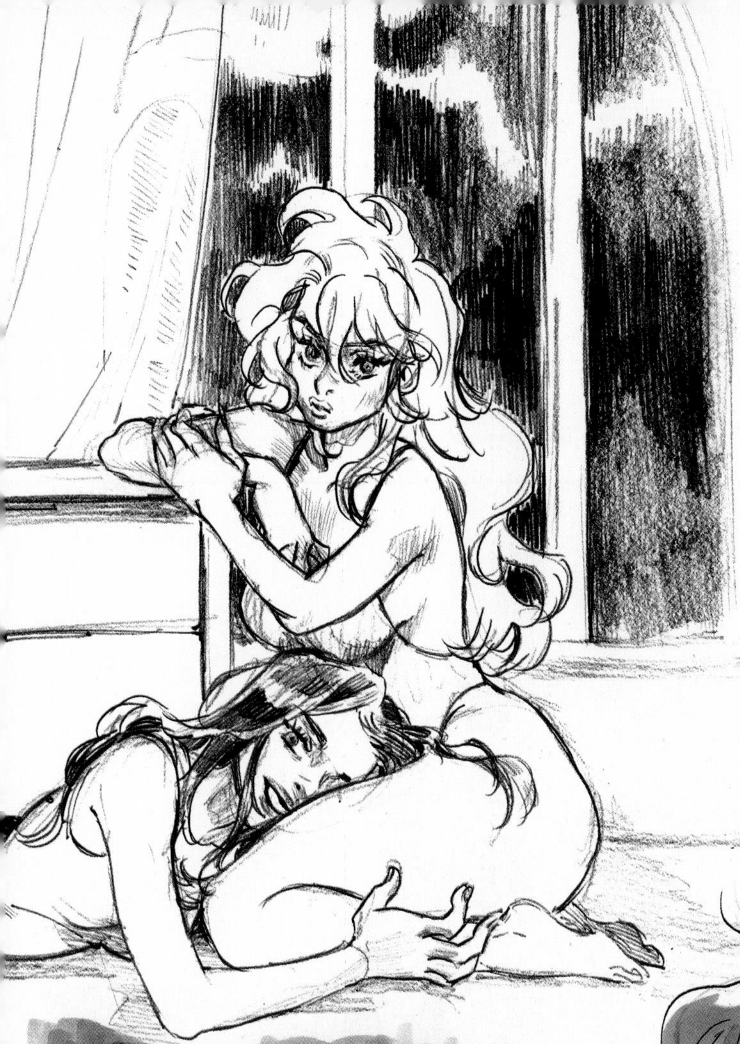

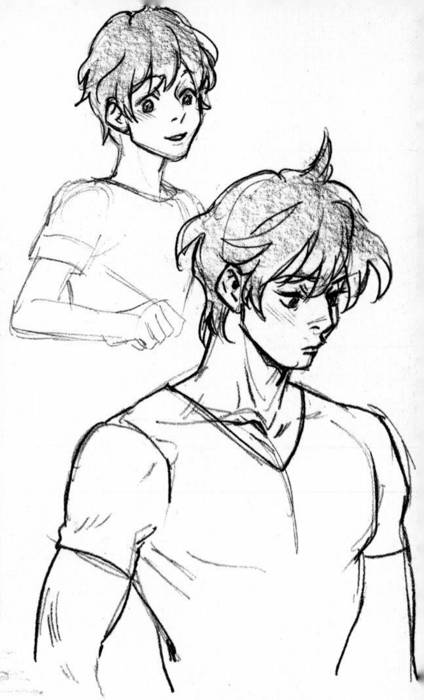

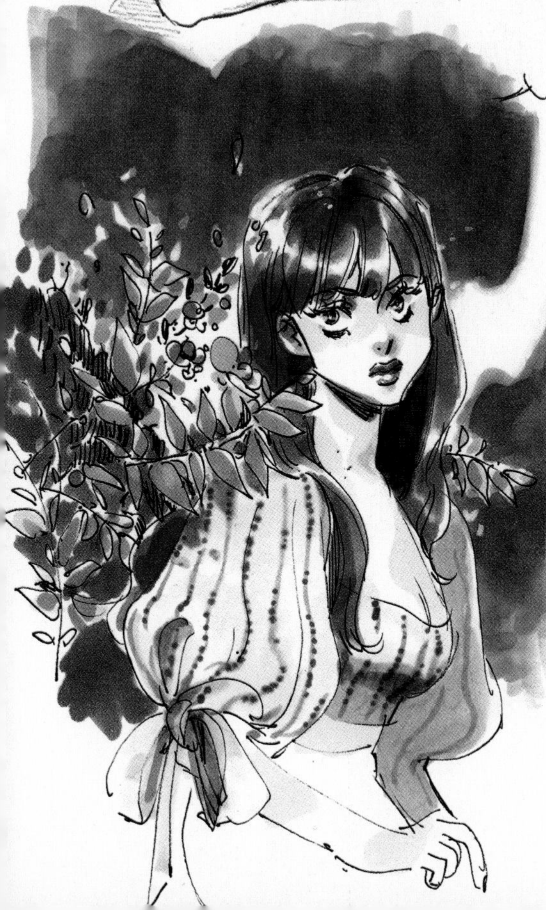

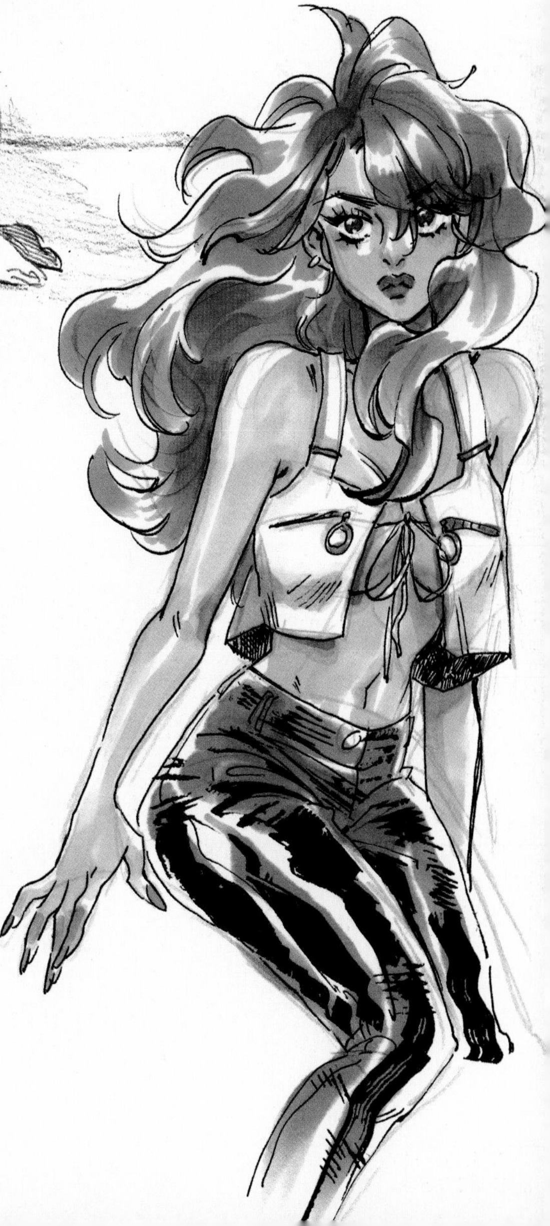

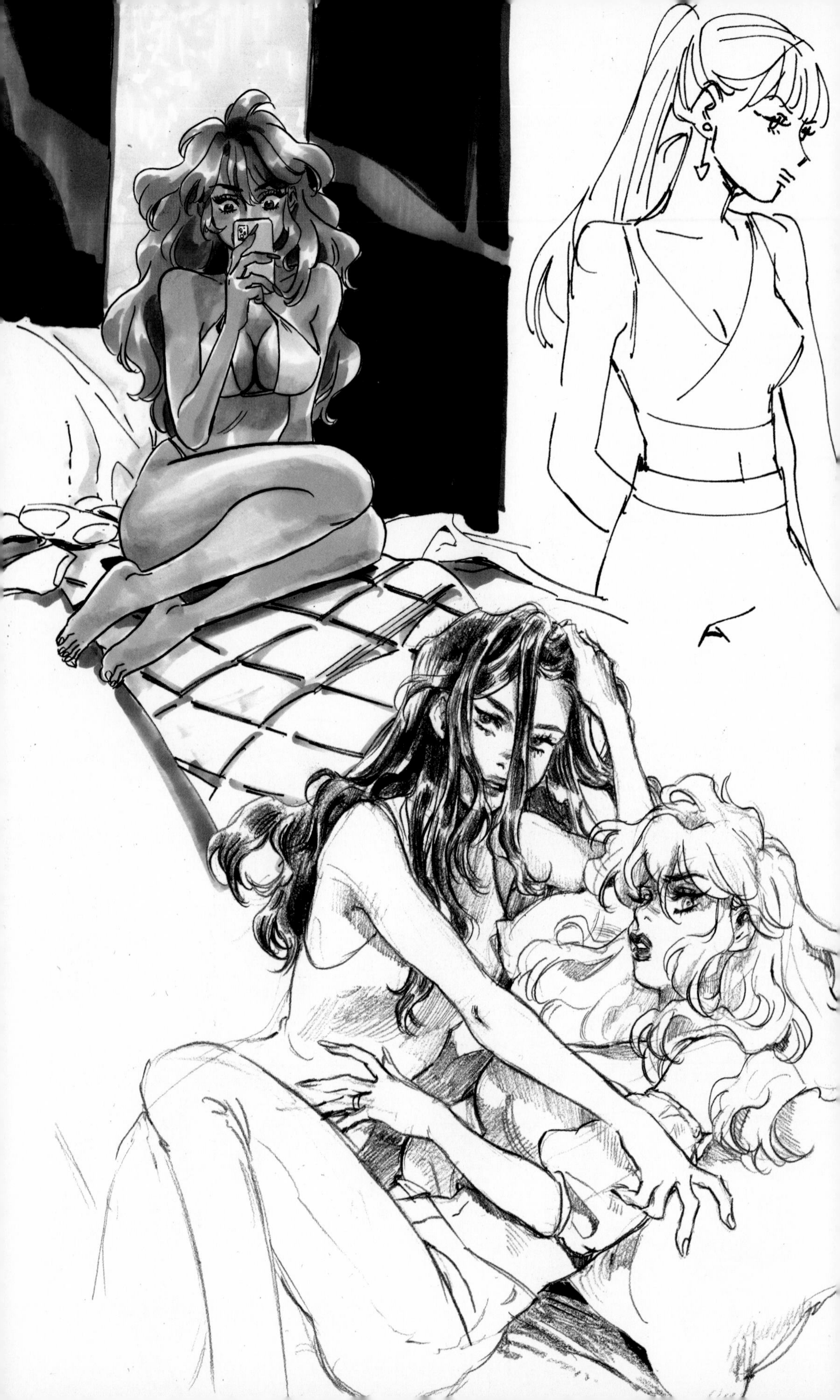

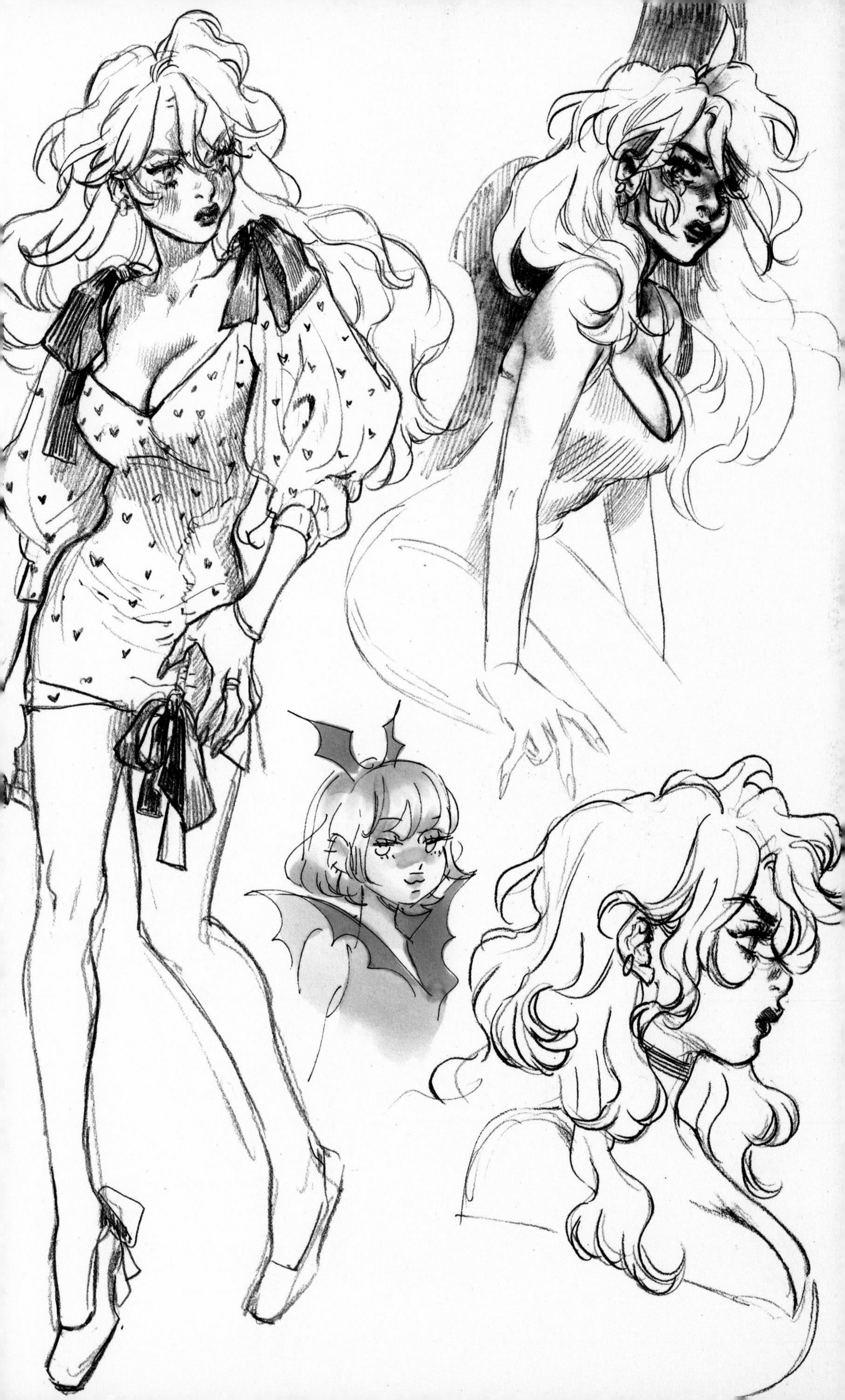

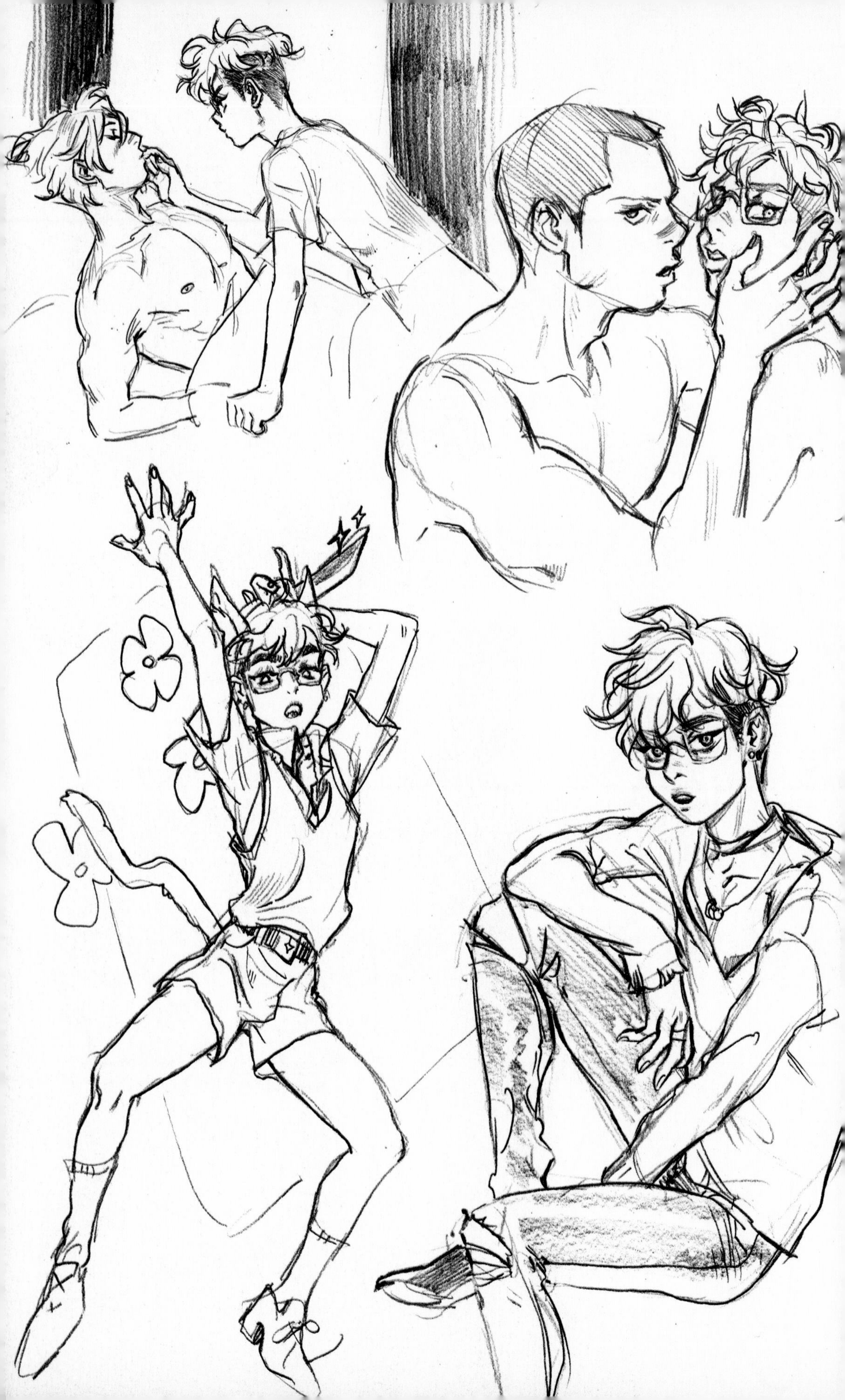

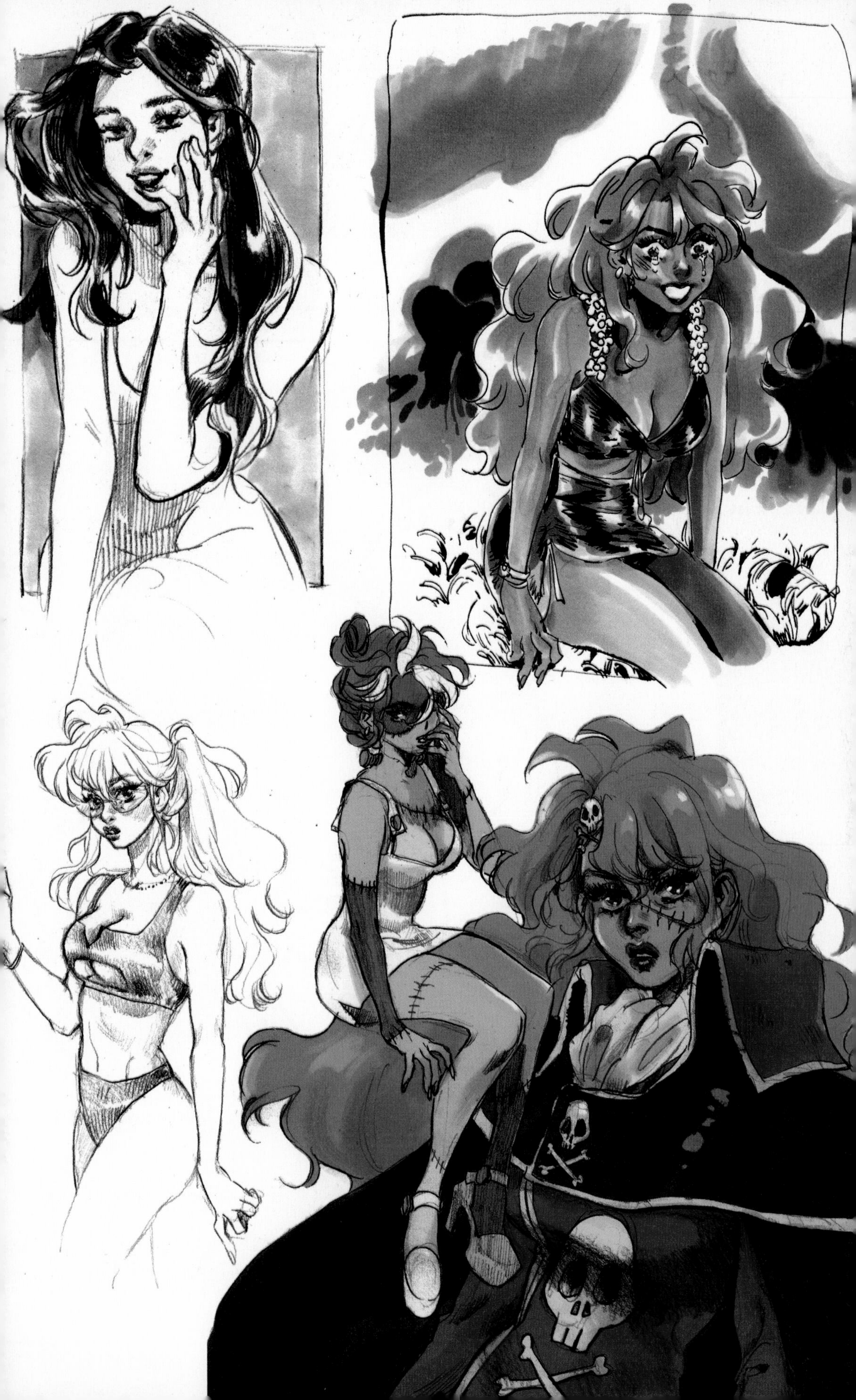

COVER GALLERY
ISSUE 11
LESLIE HUNG &
RACHAEL COHEN

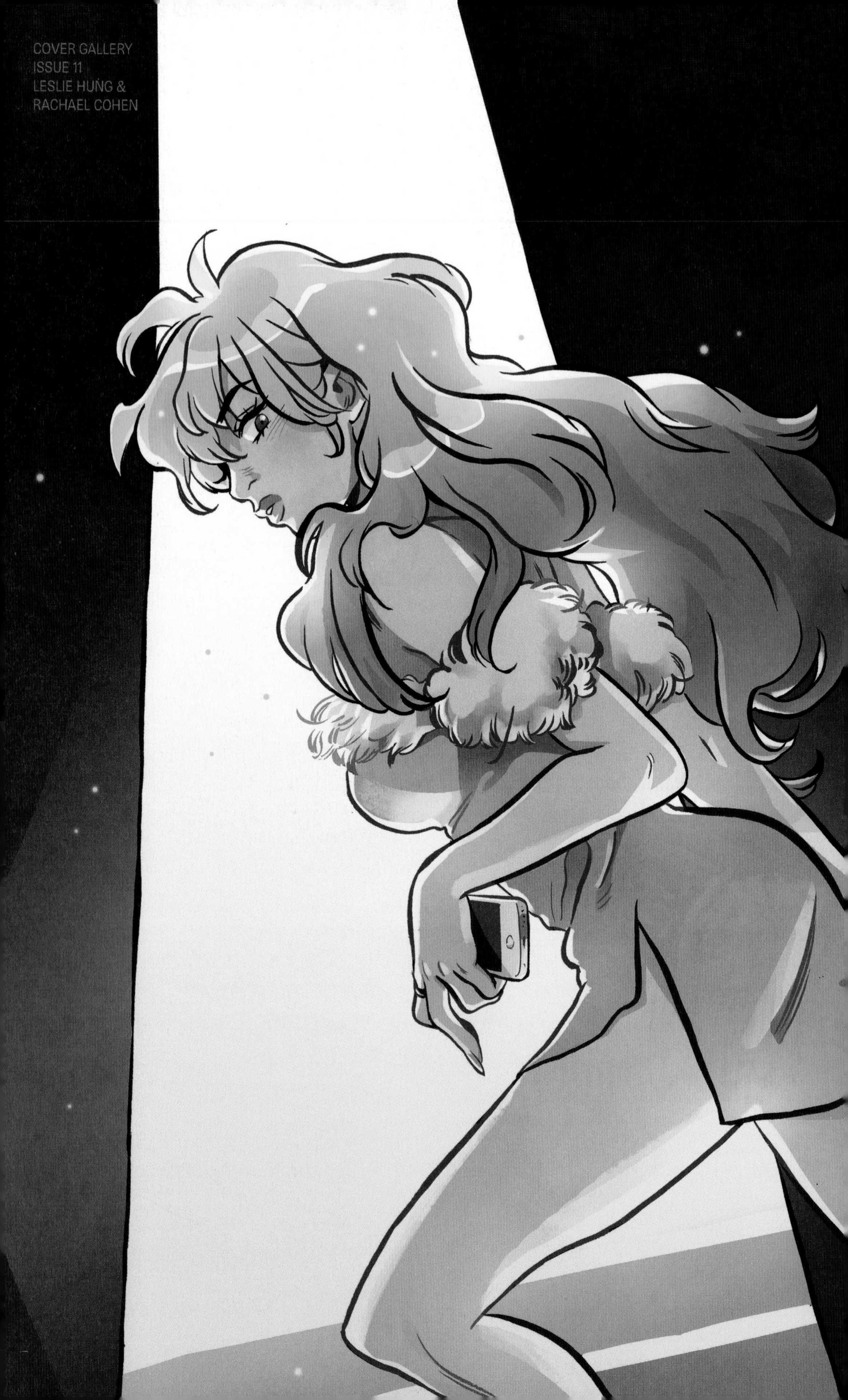

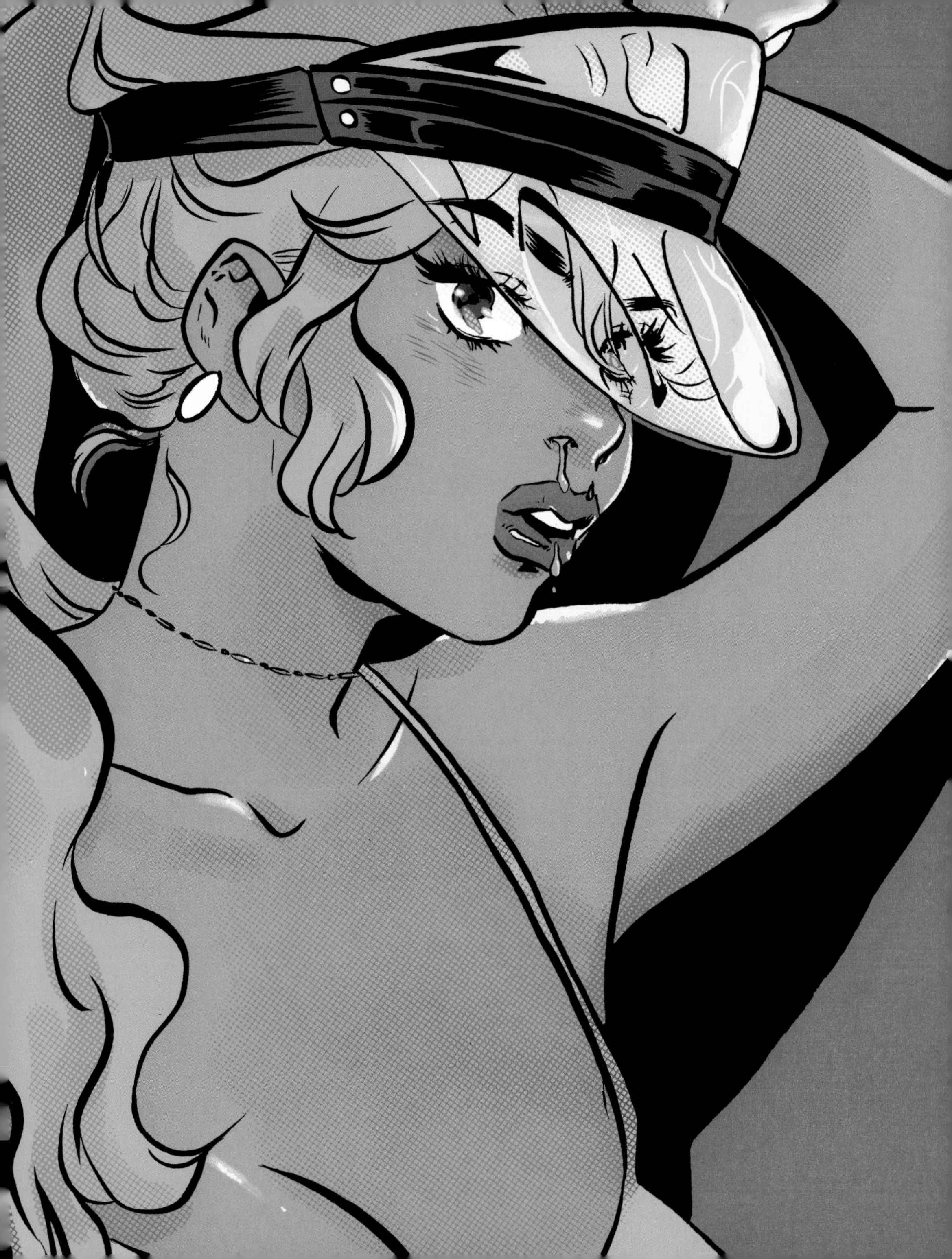

COVER GALLERY
ISSUE 13
LESLIE HUNG & RACHAEL COHEN

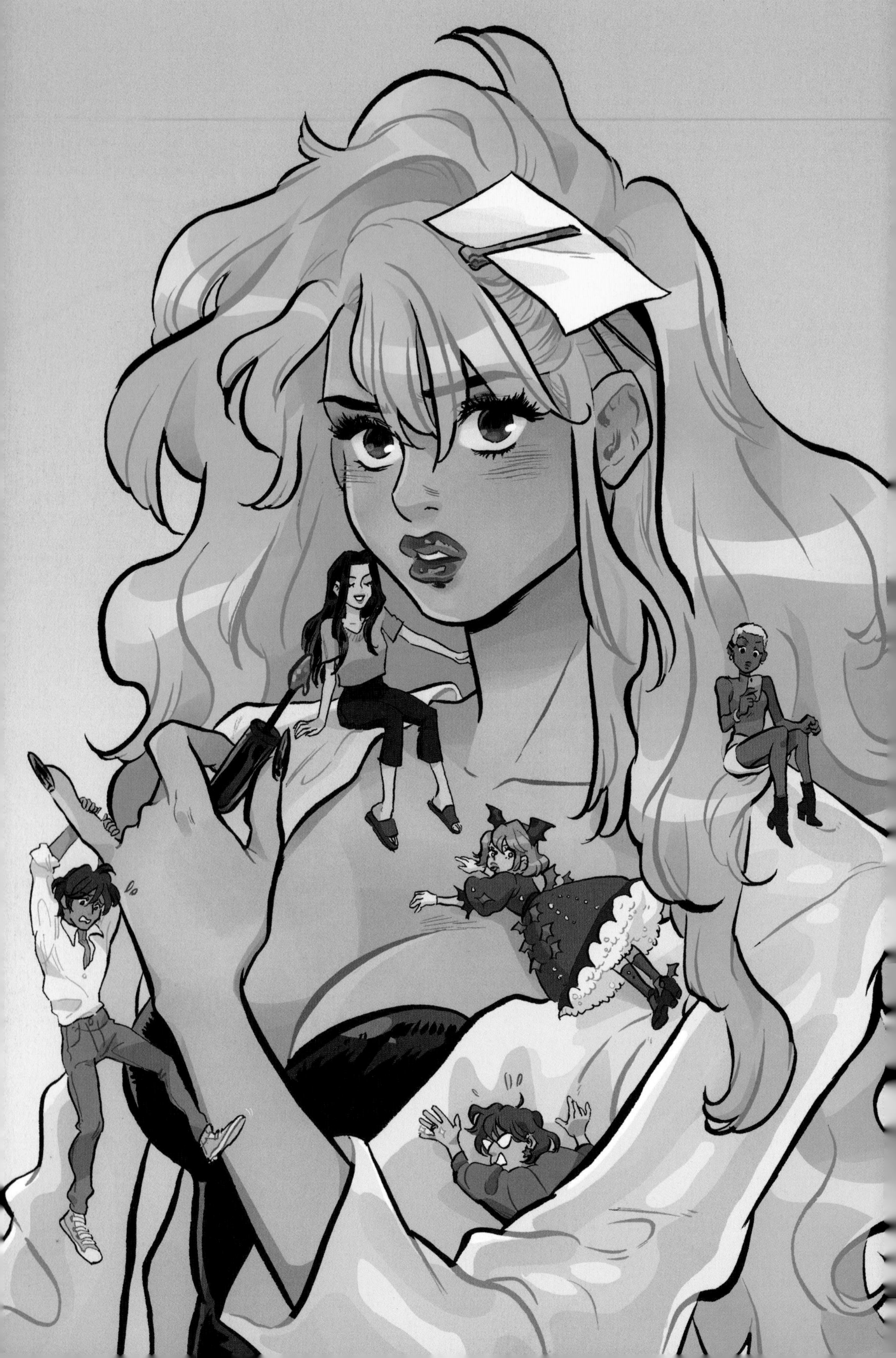

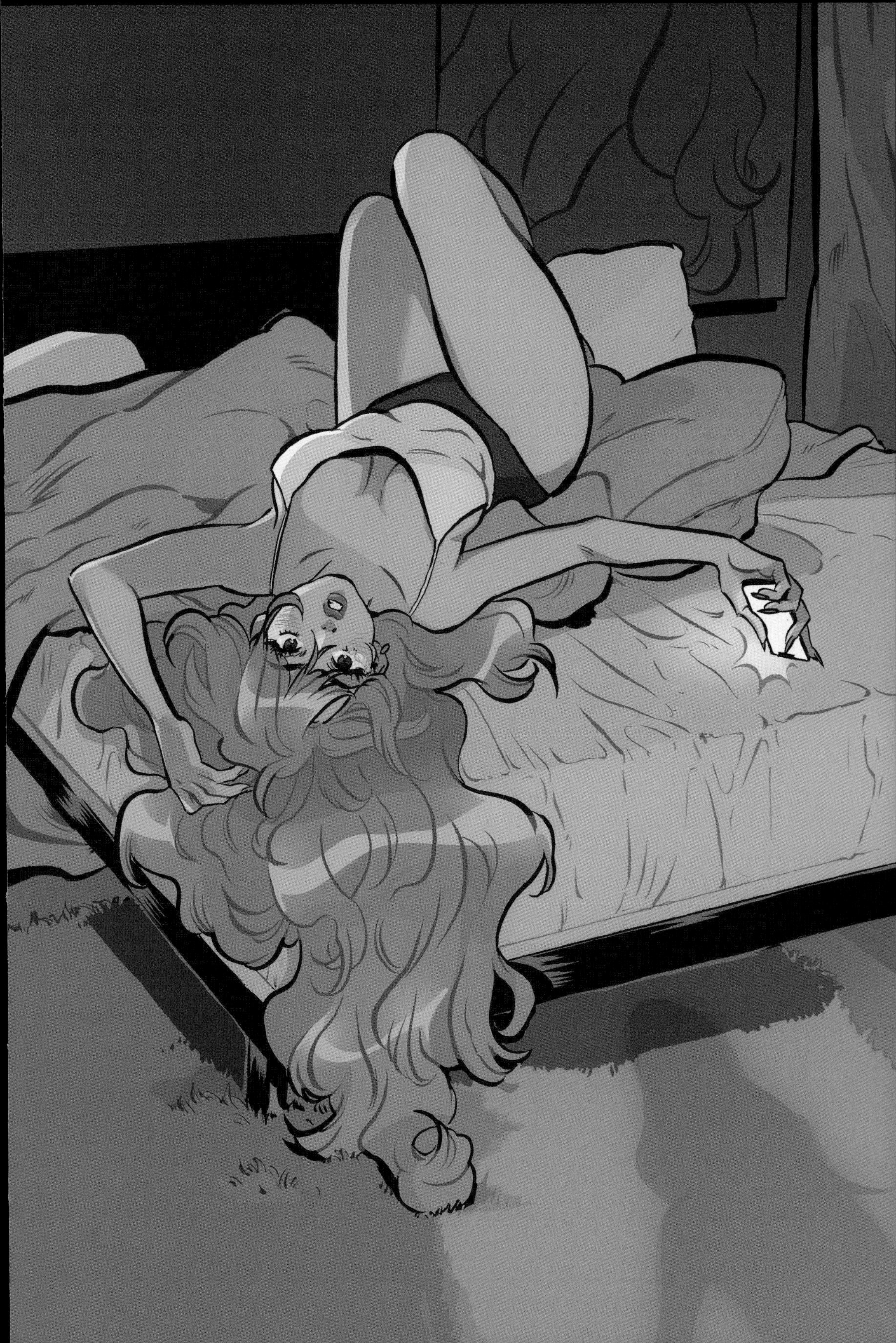

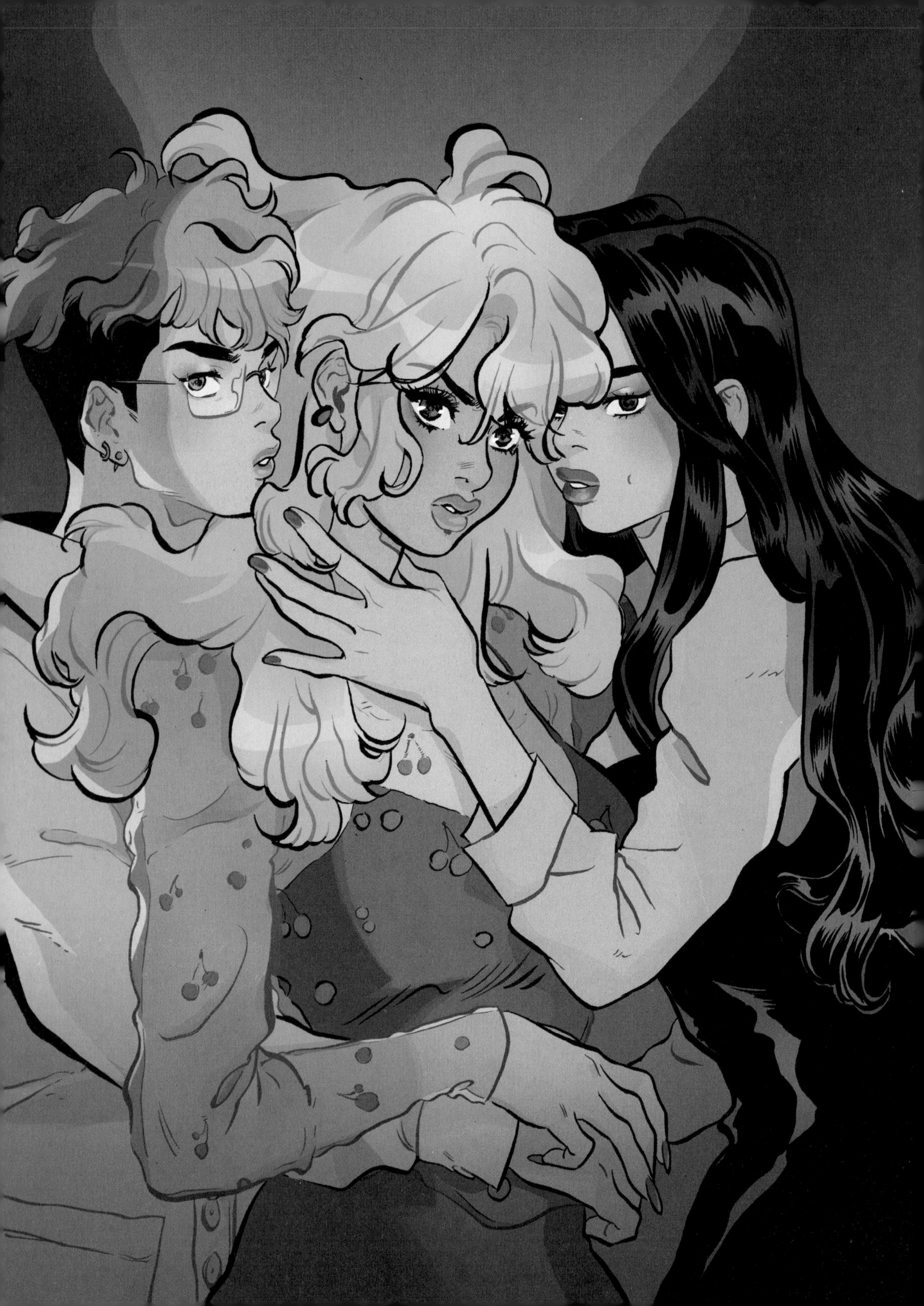

VARIANT COVER GALLERY
ISSUE 11
BRYAN LEE O'MALLEY

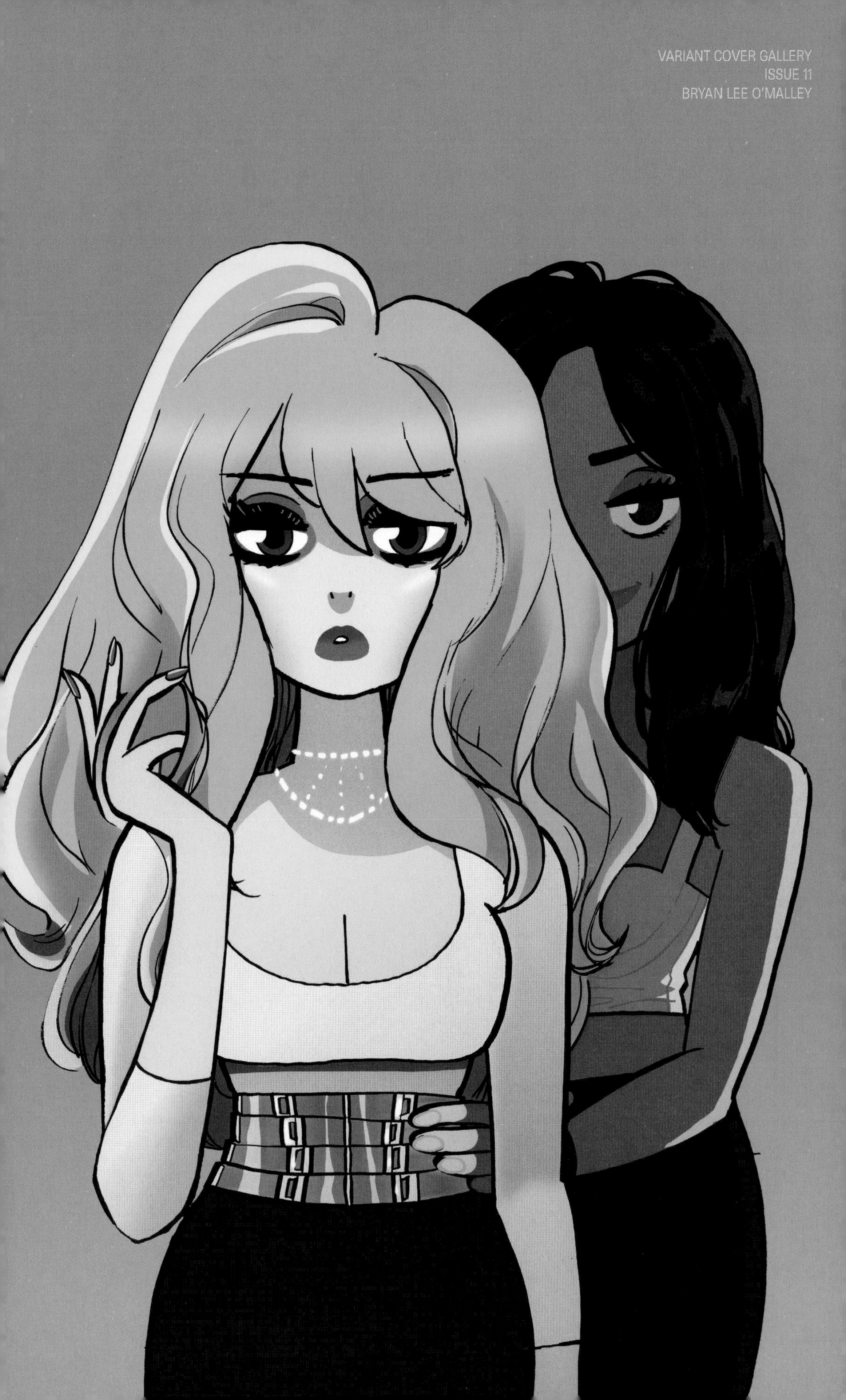

VARIANT COVER GALLERY
ISSUE 12
BRYAN LEE O'MALLEY

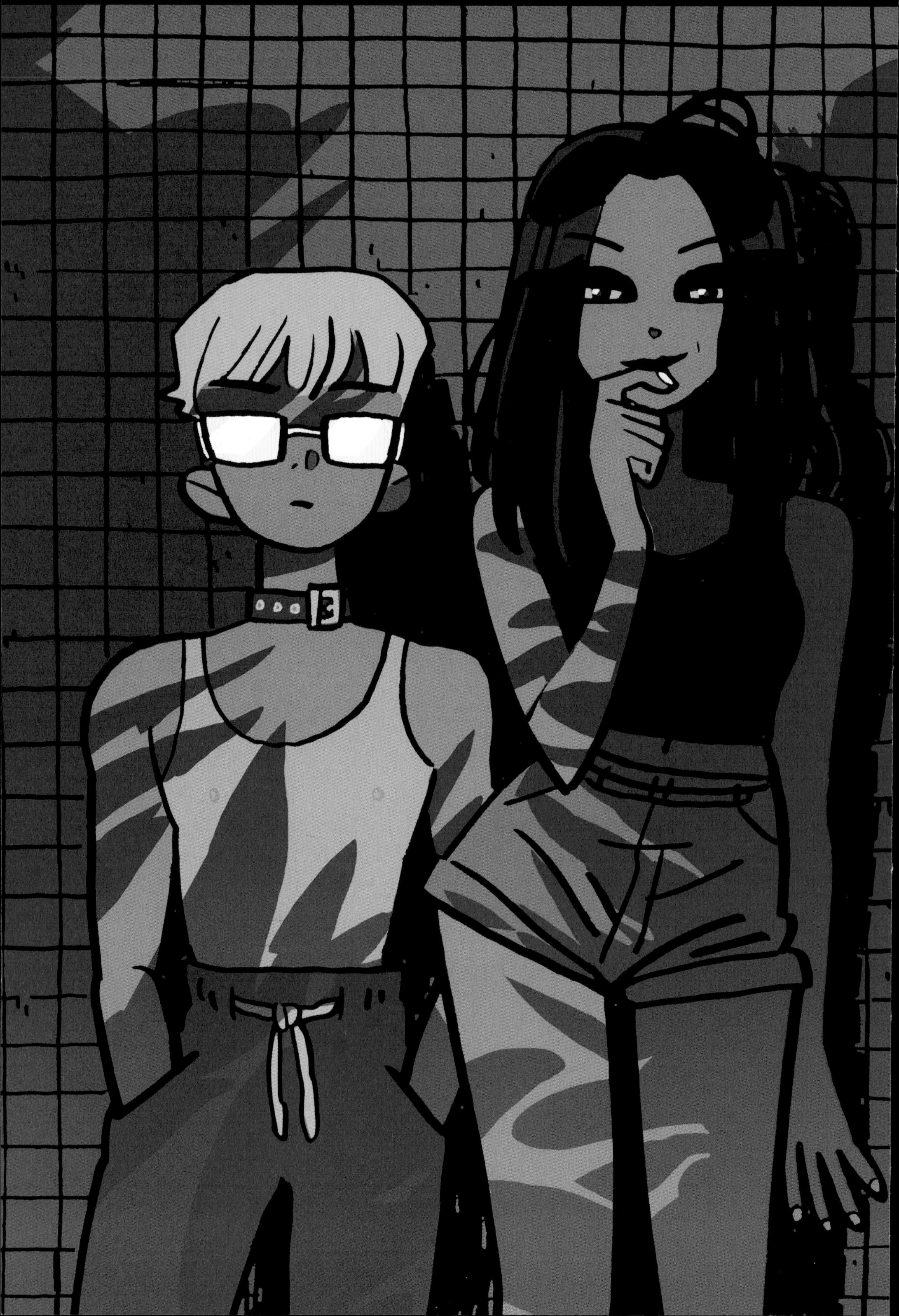

VARIANT COVER GALLERY
ISSUE 13
BRYAN LEE O'MALLEY & RACHAEL COHEN

VARIANT COVER GALLERY
ISSUE 14
BRYAN LEE O'MALLEY

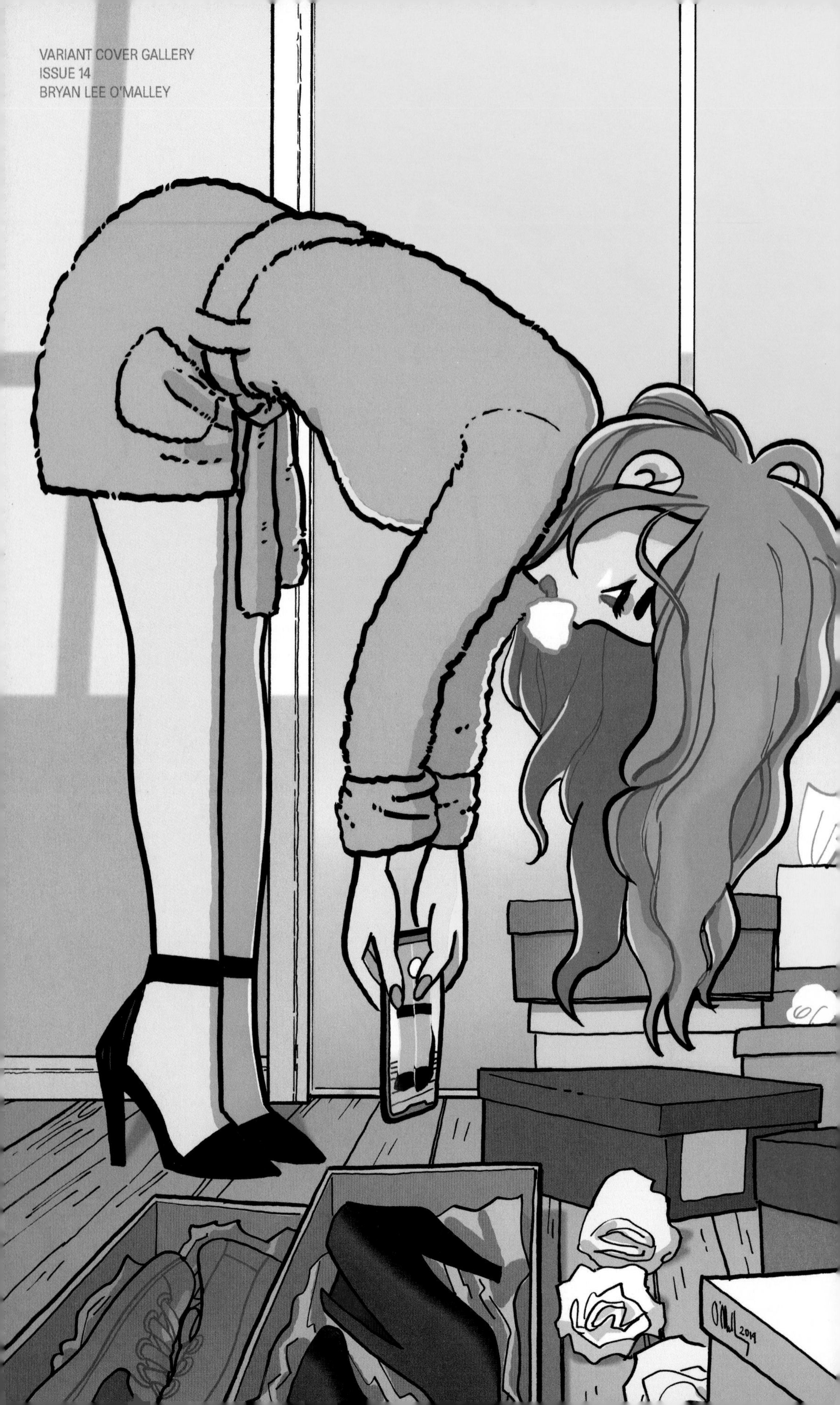

VARIANT COVER GALLERY
ISSUE 15
BRYAN LEE O'MALLEY & RACHAEL COHEN

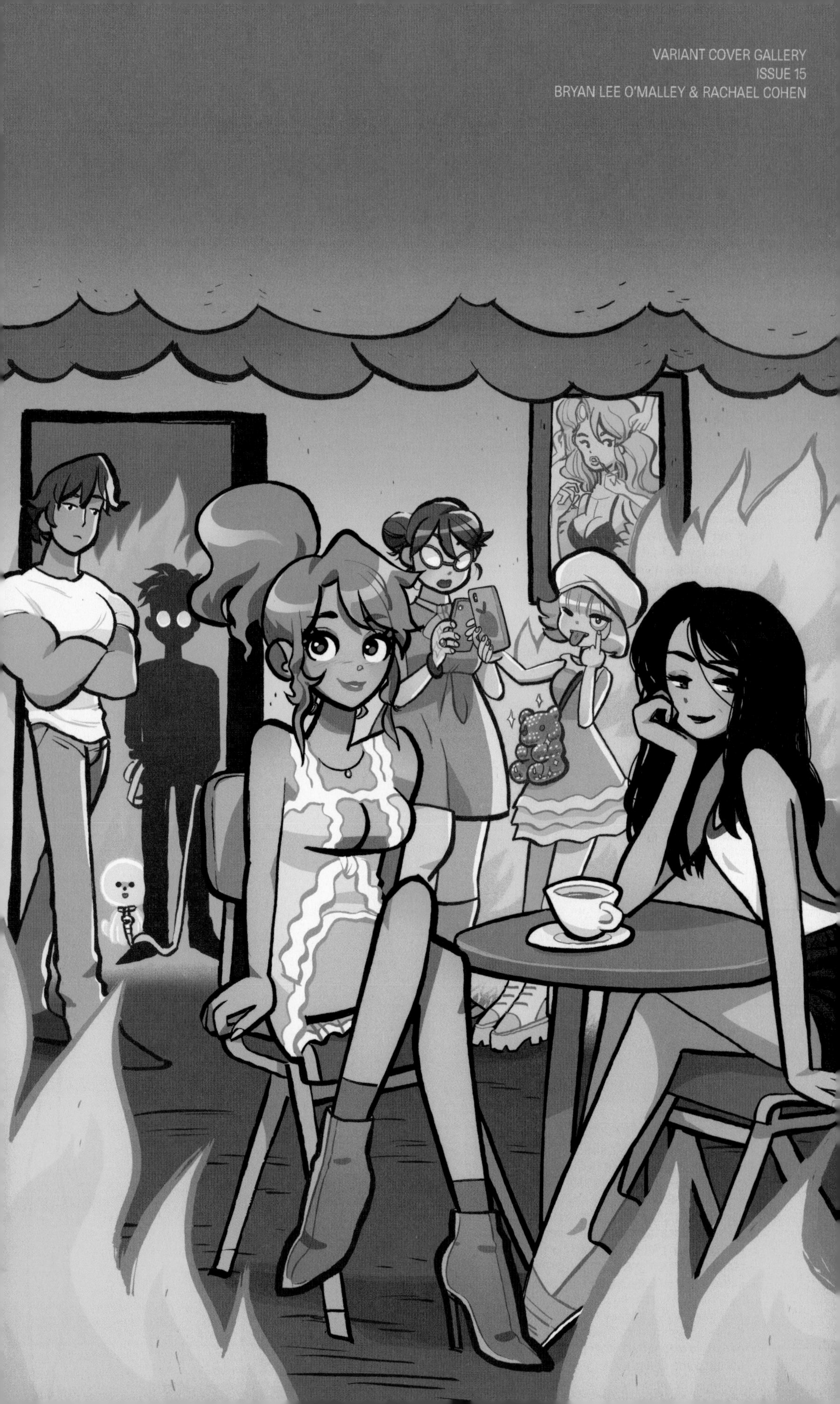

Leslie's Comment

by Leslie Hung

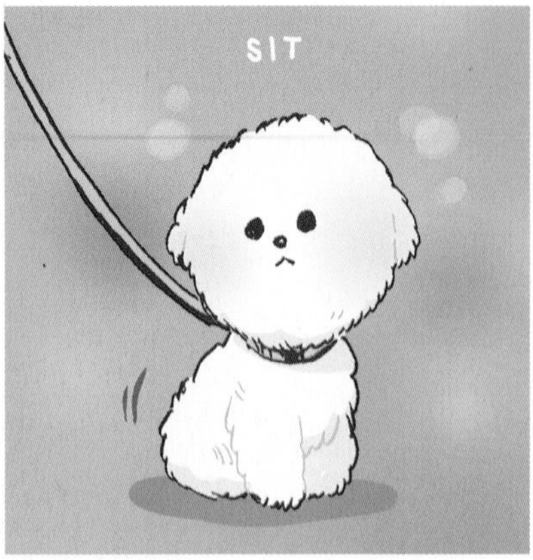

SIT

REGGIE AKA ROSCOE

Reggie was introduced to me as a dog that was "too cute for Meg" in the scripts, and we kind of ran with him from there. It's pretty obvious from early on that Meg is in over her head being a single mom, so he was conceived from the get-go to be a supplement to Cutegirl's character and brand. Many of her nearly wordless appearances throughout the volume have been some of the most fun and nonsensical pages to draw. His appearance is based off of the Bichon Frise dogs that a lot of Korean instagram accounts groom to look like perfect spheres.

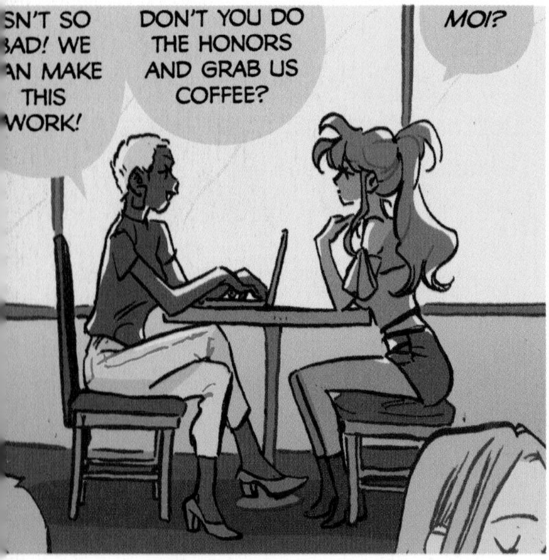

SN'T SO BAD! WE AN MAKE THIS WORK!
DON'T YOU DO THE HONORS AND GRAB US COFFEE?
MOI?

ESTHER (CONT'D)

Esther has always been the voice of reason for Snottie, but I hoped that her leaving and coming back to renegotiate would kind of put Snottie in her place. I definitely think she's becoming more appreciative of Esther's efforts—she's just overall pretty flippant towards a lot of people in her life. Esther doesn't let Snottie into her personal life, but I feel like we got more of a glimpse of Esther's personality beyond her being considerate to her childish partner. I think she's really conflicted and a bit mad at Snottie's dogged determination to date Caroline, but is the type of person to stay out of other people's business, because she doesn't want people in hers.

ROSIE AKA FUMICHAN

I think that the existence of Snottie's sisters had only been hinted at a little bit in the previous volumes. I actually wasn't sure we'd even get to introduce them in a fun way, especially since Rosie in her earliest concepts (med school student, better than Snottie but also jealous of her—reasons not expressed) didn't really fit in any meaningful way with Snottie's story. When we were brainstorming this arc, we were deep in our **Terrace House*** obsession, so it kind of seemed perfect for Rosie to have benefited from a different corner of the internet worshipping her for her not-so-great, yet still iconic personality.

I saw Rosie as a character who was outwardly confident and effortless, inwardly deeply flawed just like everyone else, but uncaring and brash about everyone else's struggles. Snottie and Rosie have been blessed with beauty and charm, but are also victims of their own insecurity and ego.

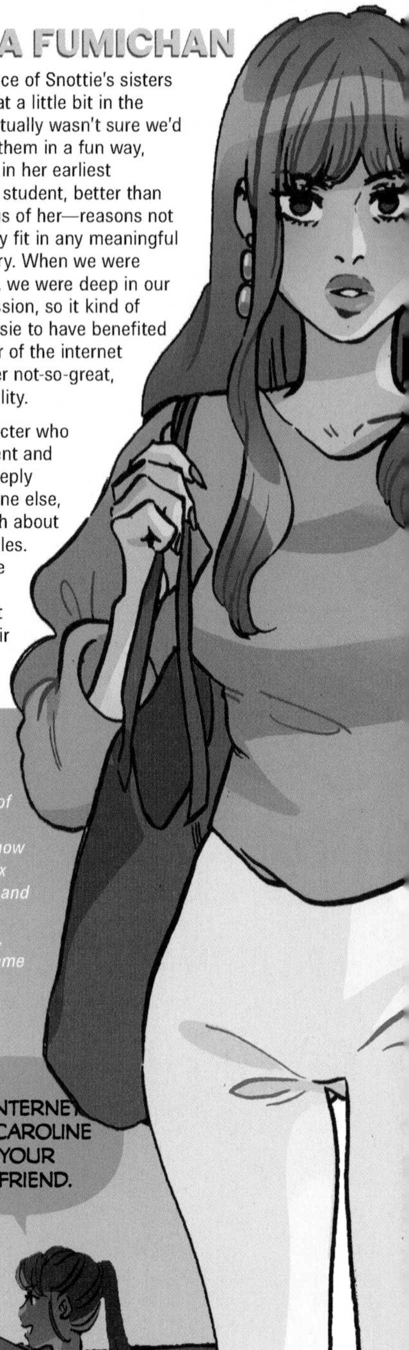

**Terrace House* is a Japanese reality television show franchise consisting of five series and one theatrical film. The show follows the lives of six strangers, three men and three women from different walks of life, who live under the same roof while getting to know and date each other. (Wikipedia)*

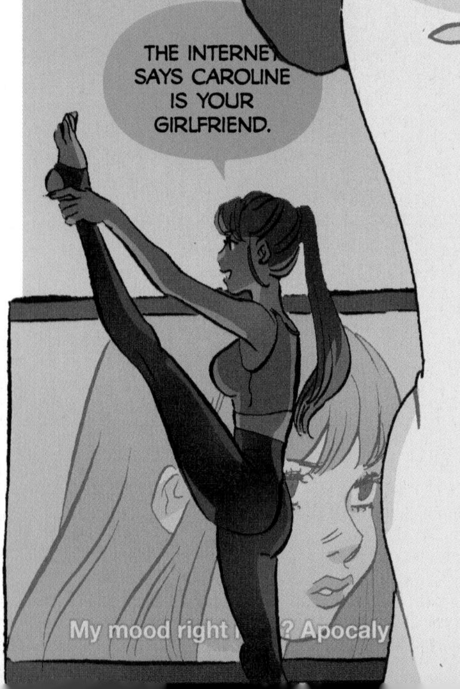

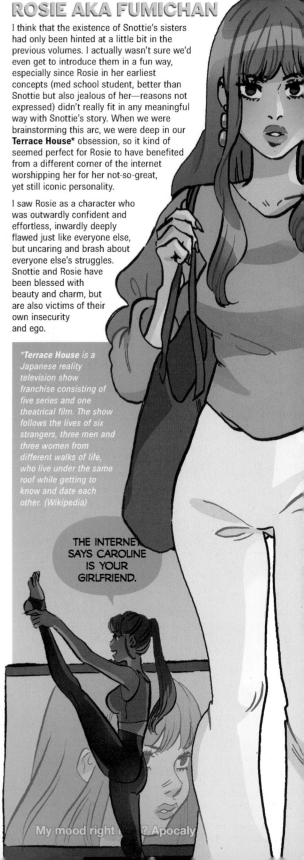

THE INTERNE SAYS CAROLINE IS YOUR GIRLFRIEND.
My mood right
? Apocaly

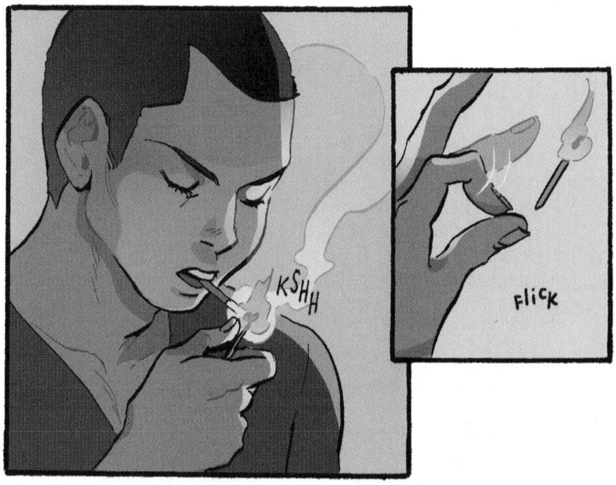
KSHH
FLICK

BIG BROTHER

I had the most difficulty figuring out what I wanted Caroline and Virgil's mysterious brother to look like. He was always meant to be foreboding and very strong, serious, and ominous. I made many sketches over the years, trying different types of hair styles on different types of faces, but what ended up sticking was, in my opinion, pretty understated. My idea is that I want him to look sharp, like a razor's edge, cutting to the quick. Not a lot is revealed about him in this volume, despite his appearing twice.

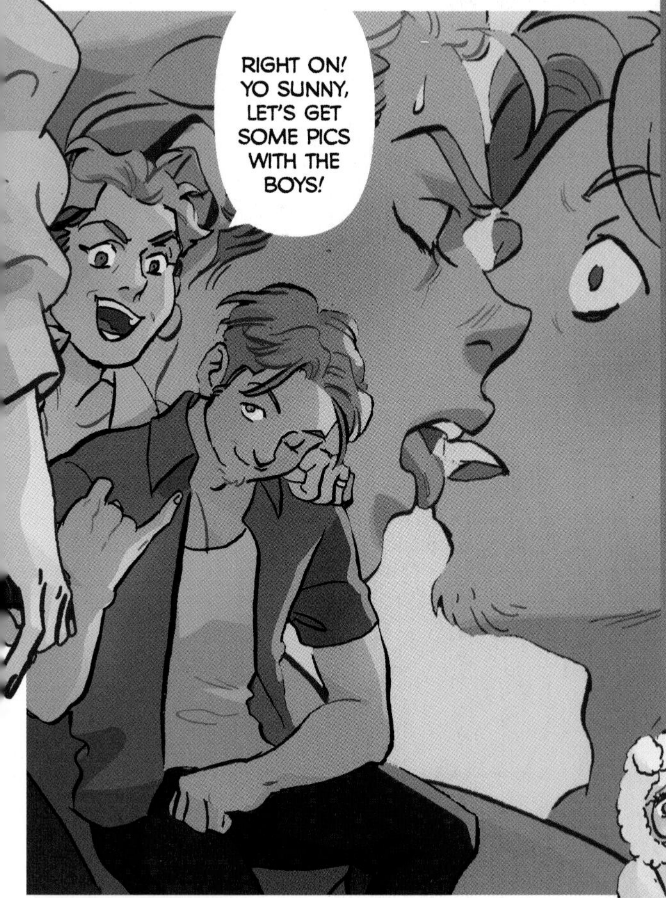
RIGHT ON! YO SUNNY, LET'S GET SOME PICS WITH THE BOYS!

BEST MAN

Ashley's unnamed best friend was conceived as a "normal" bro type. The initial roughs/thumbnails for this issue were pretty loose, because it was a hard one for me to pin down in the planning stage. I had to do some research on the different elements of the bachelor party, so best bro's character design is kind of an amalgamation of a lot of different, random men. His design was pretty unappealing to me at first, but after drawing it a bunch of times, I felt for him, which is kind of a thing that ends up happening a lot.

Cutegirl's Corner

Cutegirl isn't in this volume very much, but I wanted to make up for that with her outfits, which only get more elaborate as she bonds with Reggie/Roscoe.

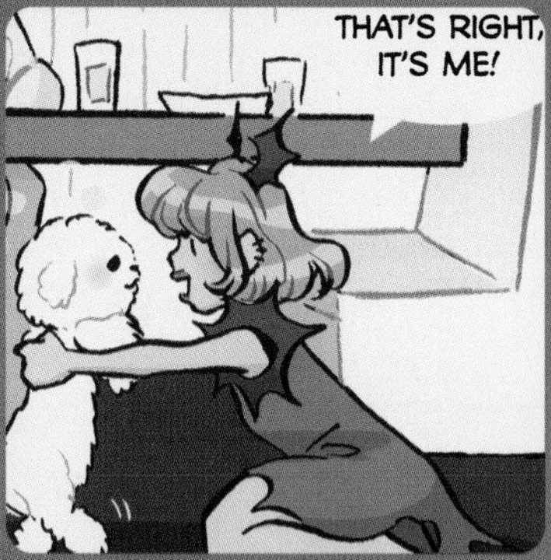
THAT'S RIGHT, IT'S ME!

THE BAT In the flashback in issue 1, Misty is already kind of wearing an outfit like this for Halloween, but she's the type of person to dress in a really over-the-top manner in everyday life. It's simple, but so themed that it's nonsensical.

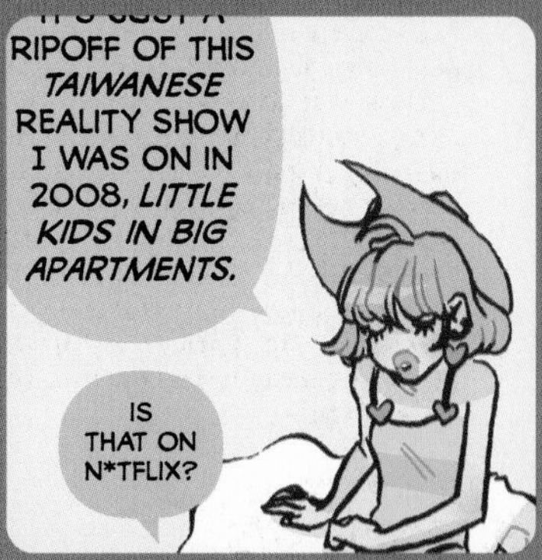
RIPOFF OF THIS *TAIWANESE* REALITY SHOW I WAS ON IN 2008, *LITTLE KIDS IN BIG APARTMENTS.*
IS THAT ON N*TFLIX?

COWGIRL Another limited appearance. The character Mimi from the first Digimon series wore a fringed dress with a cowboy hat, and it had a huge impact on me as a kid. I've always wanted to incorporate that into a drawing, so it kind of worked here. Cutegirl is also very into skincare, so on a hot and sunny day, having a hat on top of using SPF is vital.

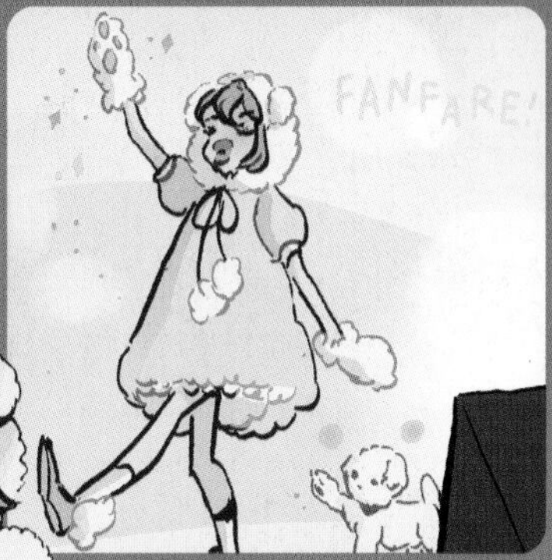
FANFARE!

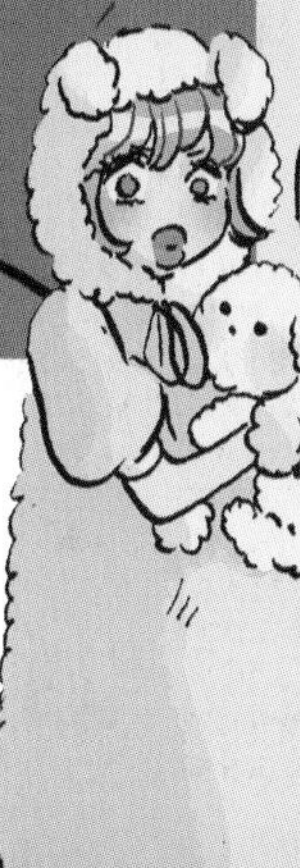

PUPPIES *This brief sequence ended up being one of my favorites. I wasn't sure how to make it work until, in the thumbnailing stage, I could hear the lights blinding Sunny and Virgil, and I could suddenly see Cutegirl's entrance. I feel totally free to just go crazy with the improbability and over-the-top nature of Cutegirl's outfits.*

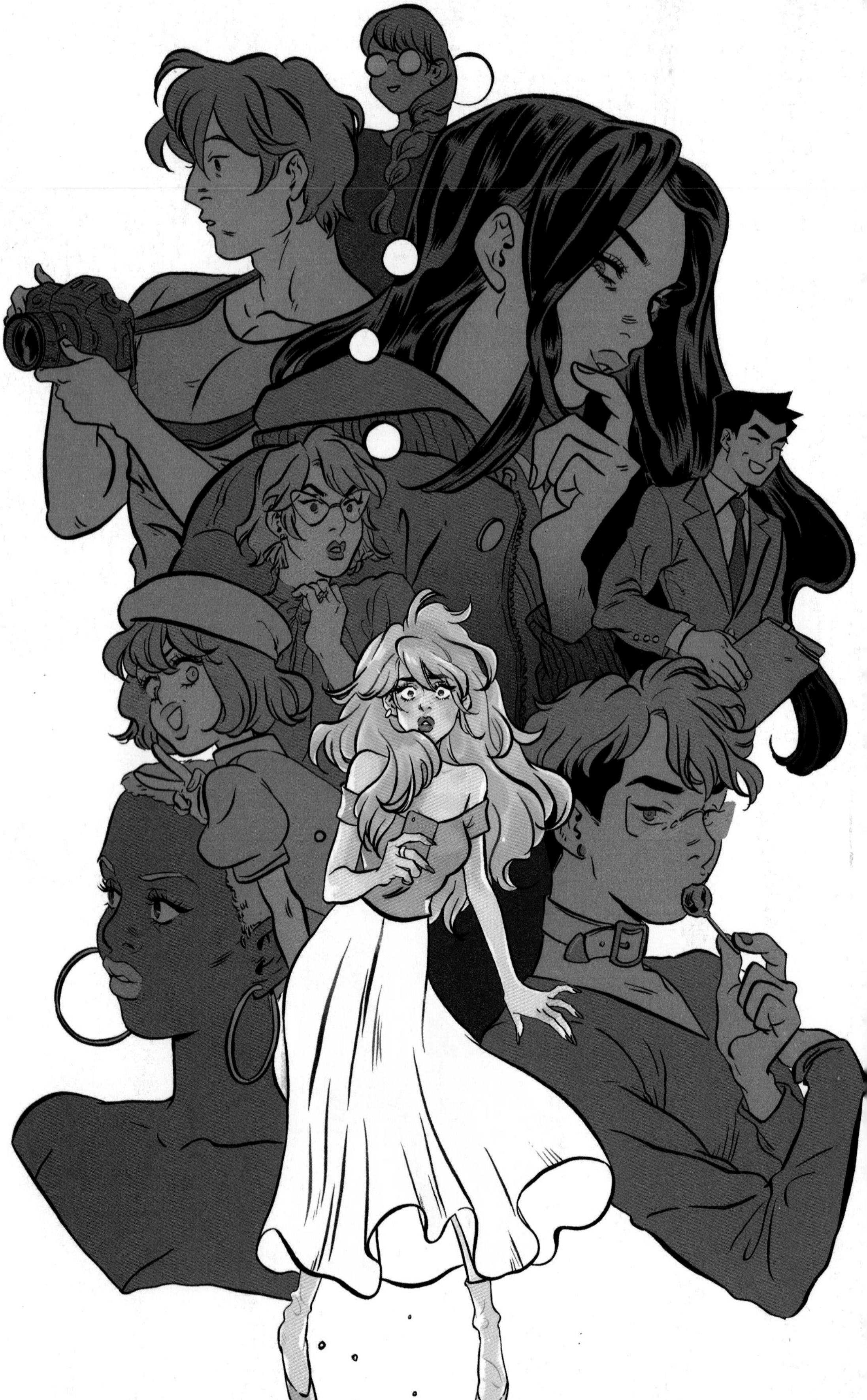

POSTER *by* LESLIE HUNG
(Alternate colorway for BEA 2018)